Rebecca Makkai is the author of three novels and a collection of short stories. Her work has appeared in *The Best American Short Stories*, *Harper's* and *Tin House*, among others. She lives outside Chicago with her husband and two daughters.

www.rebeccamakkai.com

'Stirring, spellbinding and full of life' Téa Obreht, *New York Times*-bestselling author of *The Tiger's Wife*

'This expansive, huge-hearted novel conveys the scale of the trauma that was the early AIDS crisis, and conveys, too, the scale of the anger and love that rose up to meet it. Makkai shows us characters who are devastated but not defeated, who remain devoted, in the face of death, to friendship and desire and joyful, irrepressible life. I loved this book' Garth Greenwell, author of *What Belongs to You*

'*The Great Believers* is by turns funny, harrowing, tender, devastating, and always hugely suspenseful. It reminds us, poignantly, of how many people, mostly young, often brilliant, were lost to the AIDS epidemic, and of how those who survived were marked by that struggle. This is Rebecca Makkai at the height of her powers' Margot Livesey, *New York Times*-bestselling author of *Mercury*

'Well-imagined, intricately plotted, and deeply felt, both humane and human' Rabih Alameddine, author of *The Angel of History* and *An Unnecessary Woman*

'Makkai has created a moving story about Chicago and Paris, the past and present, the young men lost to AIDS and the ones who survived. And just as her novel evokes art's power to commemorate the departed, *The Great Believers* is itself a poignant work of memoir' Viet Thanh Nguyen, Pulitzer Prize-winning author of *The Sympathizer*

'Time is a healer and a heartbreaker in Makkai's brilliant and beautiful novel. *The Great Believers* kept me hoping and guessing, heart in hand, until the very last page' Carol Rifka Brunt, author of *Tell the Wolves I'm Home*

'Sure to become a classic Chicago novel ... a deft, harrowing novel that's as beautiful as its cover' *Chicago Review of Books*

'An antidote to our general urge to forget what we'd rather not remember, but it's also – which is more important – an absorbing and emotionally riveting story about what it's like to live during times of crisis' Michael Cunningham, *New York Times*

'*The Great Believers* is beautiful and compelling' Running in Heels

'Magnificent ... it doesn't set a foot wrong ... Makkai has full command of her multi-generational perspective, and by its end, *The Great Believers* offers a grand fusion of the past and the present, the public and the personal. It's remarkably alive' *Chicago Tribune*

'Spookily relevant in the age of Trump. Makkai has created a gorgeous and compassionate narrative, one which asks how we can move forward from disaster' Rumpus

The Great Believers

Rebecca Makkai

FLEET

2019

FLEET

First published in the United States in 2018 by Viking
First published in Great Britain in 2018 by Fleet
This paperback edition published in 2019 by Fleet

7 9 10 8

A CIP catalogue record for this book
is available from the British Library.

ISBN 978-0-7088-9912-0

Typeset in Garamond by M Rules
Printed and bound in Great Britain by
Clays Ltd, Elcograf S.p.A.

Papers used by Fleet are from well-managed forests
and other responsible sources.

Fleet
An imprint of
Little, Brown Book Group
Carmelite House
50 Victoria Embankment
London EC4Y 0DZ

An Hachette UK Company
www.hachette.co.uk

www.littlebrown.co.uk

"We were the great believers.

I have never cared for any men as much as for these who felt the first springs when I did, and saw death ahead, and were reprieved—and who now walk the long stormy summer."

—F. Scott Fitzgerald, "My Generation"

"the world is a wonder, but the portions are small"

—Rebecca Hazelton, "Slash Fiction"

1985

Twenty miles from here, twenty miles north, the funeral mass was starting. Yale checked his watch as they walked up Belden. He said to Charlie, "How empty do you think that church is?"

Charlie said, "Let's not care."

The closer they got to Richard's house, the more friends they spotted heading the same way. Some were dressed nicely, as if this were the funeral itself; others wore jeans, leather jackets.

It must only be relatives up at the church, the parents' friends, the priest. If there were sandwiches laid out in some reception room, most were going to waste.

Yale found the bulletin from last night's vigil in his pocket and folded it into something resembling the cootie catchers his childhood friends used to make on buses—the ones that told your fortune ("*Famous!*" or "*Murdered!*") *when you opened a flap.* This one had no flaps, but each quadrant bore words, some upside down, all truncated by the folds: "*Father George H. Whitb*"; "*beloved son, brother, rest in*"; "*All things bright and*"; "*lieu of flowers, donatio.*" All of which, Yale supposed, did tell Nico's fortune. Nico had been bright and beautiful. Flowers would do no good.

The houses on this street were tall, ornate. Pumpkins still out on every stoop but few carved faces—artful arrangements, rather, of gourds and Indian corn. Wrought iron fences, swinging gates. When they turned onto the walkway to Richard's (a noble brownstone sharing walls with noble neighbors), Charlie whispered: "His wife decorated the place. When he was *married*. In '72." Yale laughed at the worst possible moment, just as they passed a gravely smiling Richard holding open his own door. It was the idea of Richard living a hetero life in Lincoln Park with some decoratively inclined woman. Yale's image of it was slapstick: Richard stuffing a man into the closet when his wife dashed back for her Chanel clutch.

Yale pulled himself together and turned back to Richard. He said, "You have a beautiful place." A wave of people came up behind them, pushing Yale and Charlie into the living room.

Inside, the decor didn't scream 1972 so much as 1872: chintz sofas, velvety chairs with carved arms, oriental rugs. Yale felt Charlie squeeze his hand as they dove into the crowd.

Nico had made it clear there was to be a party. "If I get to hang out as a ghost, you think I wanna see sobbing? I'll haunt you. You sit there crying, I'll throw a lamp across the room, okay? I'll shove a poker up your ass, and not in a good way." If he'd died just two days ago, they wouldn't have had it in them to follow through. But Nico died three weeks back, and the family delayed the vigil and funeral until his grandfather, the one no one had seen in twenty years, could fly in from Havana. Nico's mother was the product of a brief, pre-Castro marriage between a diplomat's daughter and a Cuban musician—and now this ancient Cuban man was crucial to the funeral planning, while Nico's lover of three years wasn't even welcome at the church tonight. Yale couldn't think about it or he'd fume, which wasn't what Nico wanted.

In any case, they'd spent three weeks mourning and now Richard's house brimmed with forced festivity. There were Julian and Teddy, for instance, waving down from the second-story railing that encircled the room. Another floor rose above that, and an elaborate round skylight presided over the whole space. It was more of a cathedral than the church had been. Someone shrieked with laughter far too close to Yale's ear.

Charlie said, "I believe we're meant to have a good time." Charlie's British accent, Yale was convinced, emerged more in sarcasm.

Yale said, "I'm waiting on the go-go dancers."

Richard had a piano, and someone was playing "Fly Me to the Moon."

What the hell were they all doing?

A skinny man Yale had never seen before bear-hugged Charlie. An out-of-towner, he guessed, someone who'd lived here but moved away before Yale came on the scene. Charlie said, "How in hell did you get younger?" Yale waited to be introduced, but the man was telling an urgent story now about someone else Yale didn't know. Charlie was the hub of a lot of wheels.

A voice in Yale's ear: "We're drinking Cuba libres." It was Fiona, Nico's little sister, and Yale turned to hug her, to smell her lemony hair. "Isn't it ridiculous?" Nico had been proud of the Cuban thing, but if he knew the chaos his grandfather's arrival would cause, he'd have vetoed the beverage choice.

Fiona had told them all, last night, that she wasn't going to the funeral—that she'd be here instead—but still it was jarring to see her, to know she'd followed through. But then she'd written off her family as thoroughly as they'd written Nico off in the years before his illness. (Until, in his last days, they'd claimed him, insisting he die in the suburbs in an ill-equipped hospital with nice wallpaper.) Her mascara was smudged. She had discarded her shoes, but wobbled as if she still wore heels.

Fiona handed her own drink to Yale—half full, an arc of pink

3

on the rim. She touched a finger to the cleft of his upper lip. "I still can't believe you shaved it off. I mean, it looks good. You look sort of—"

"Straighter."

She laughed, and then she said, "Oh. *Oh!* They're not making you, are they? At Northwestern?" Fiona had one of the best faces for concern Yale had ever seen—her eyebrows hurried together, her lips vanished straight into her mouth—but he wondered how she had any emotion left to spare.

He said, "No. It's—I mean, I'm the development guy. I'm talking to a lot of older alumni."

"To get money?"

"Money and art. It's a strange dance." Yale had taken the job at Northwestern's new Brigg Gallery in August, the same week Nico got sick, and he still wasn't sure where his responsibilities started and ended. "I mean, they know about Charlie. My colleagues do. It's fine. It's a gallery, not a bank." He tasted the Cuba libre. Inappropriate for the third of November, but then the afternoon was unseasonably warm, and this was exactly what he needed. The soda might even wake him up.

"You had a real Tom Selleck thing going. I hate when blond men grow a mustache; it's peach fuzz. Dark-haired guys, though, that's my favorite. You should've kept it! But it's okay, because now you look like Luke Duke. In a good way. No, like Patrick Duffy!" Yale couldn't laugh, and Fiona tilted her head to look at him seriously.

He felt like sobbing into her hair, but he didn't. He'd been cultivating numbness all day, hanging onto it like a rope. If this were three weeks ago, they could have simply cried together. But everything had scabbed over, and now there was this idea of *party* on top of everything else, this imperative to be, somehow, okay. Merry.

4

And what had Nico been to Yale? Just a good friend. Not family, not a lover. Nico was, in fact, the first real friend Yale had made when he moved here, the first he'd sat down with just to *talk*, and not at a bar, not shouting over music. Yale had adored Nico's drawings, would take him out for pancakes and help him study for his GED and tell him he was talented. Charlie wasn't interested in art and neither was Nico's lover, Terrence, and so Yale would take Nico to gallery shows and art talks, introduce him to artists. Still: If Nico's little sister was holding it together this well, wasn't Yale obliged to be in better shape?

Fiona said, "It's hard for *everyone*."

Their parents had cut Nico off at fifteen, but Fiona would sneak food and money and allergy medicine to the place he shared with four other guys on Broadway, taking the Metra and then the El there by herself from Highland Park. At the age of eleven. When Nico introduced Fiona, he always said, "This is the lady that raised me."

Nothing Yale could find words for was worth saying.

Fiona told him to check out the upstairs when he got a chance. "It's Versailles up there."

Yale couldn't find Charlie in the crowd. Despite exuding tremendous height, Charlie was only a bit taller than average—and Yale was always surprised in situations like this not to spot his crew-cut head, his neat beard, his droopy eyes, above everyone else.

But Julian Ames was beside him now, down from upstairs. He said, "We've been going since lunch! I'm sloshed!" It was five o'clock, the sky already inking itself out. He leaned against Yale and giggled. "We ransacked the bathrooms. He has *nothing*, or else he's hiding it. Well, someone found some old poppers in the back of the fridge. But is there any point to poppers if you aren't getting laid?"

"No. Jesus. *Poppers*?"

"I'm asking seriously!" Julian pulled himself straight. He had a lock of dark hair in front that Charlie maintained made him look like Superman. ("Or a unicorn," Yale would add.) He brushed it out of his eyes and pouted. Julian was too perfect, if anything. He'd had a nose job when he left Atlanta—better for his acting career—and Yale wished he hadn't. He'd have preferred an imperfect Julian.

"I'm answering seriously. There's absolutely no point to doing poppers at a memorial."

"But this isn't a funeral, it's a *party*. And it's like—" Julian was close again, conspiratorial in his ear. "It's like that Poe story, the Red Death one. There's death out there, but we're gonna have a fabulous time in here."

"Julian." Yale drained the Cuba libre and spat an ice chip back into the glass. "That is not the point. That's not how the story ends."

"I was never one to finish my homework."

Julian put his chin on Yale's shoulder—a thing he was prone to do, one that always made Yale worry Charlie would glance over right then. Yale had spent the past four years reassuring Charlie he wouldn't run off with someone like Julian, or like Teddy Naples, who was now leaning out precariously over the railing, his feet off the ground, calling to a friend below. (Teddy was so small that someone could probably catch him if he fell, but still, Yale cringed, looked away.) There was no reason for Charlie's insecurity, beyond both men's looks and flirtatiousness. Beyond the fact that Charlie would never feel secure. Yale had been the one to propose monogamy to begin with, but Charlie was the one who dwelt on its possible unraveling. And he'd picked the two most beautiful men in Chicago to affix his anxieties to. Yale shrugged Julian off his shoulder, and Julian smiled dopily and wandered away.

6

The room had loudened, the sound bouncing off the stories above, more people flooding in. Two very pretty, very young men circulated with trays of little quiches and stuffed mushrooms and deviled eggs. Yale wondered why the food wasn't Cuban, too, to match the drinks, but Richard probably had just one plan for every party: Open the doors, open the bar, boys with quiche.

In any case, this was infinitely better than that strange and dishonest vigil last night. The church had smelled nicely of incense, but otherwise there was little about it Nico would have liked. "He wouldn't be caught dead here," Charlie had said, and then he'd heard himself and tried to laugh. The parents had carefully invited Nico's lover to the vigil, saying it was "an appropriate time for friends to pay respect." Meaning, don't come today to the actual mass. Meaning, don't really even show up for the vigil, but aren't we generous? But Terrence *had* gone last night, and so had eight friends. Mostly to surround Terrence, and to support Fiona, who, it turned out, had convinced her parents to issue the invitation; she'd told them that if Nico's friends weren't invited, she'd stand up during the service and say so. Still, plenty of friends had bowed out. Asher Glass had claimed his body would revolt at setting foot in a Catholic church. ("I'd start yelling about rubbers. Swear to God.")

The eight of them sat shoulder to shoulder in the back, a phalanx of suits around Terrence. It would have been nice if Terrence could have blended in anonymously, but they weren't even seated yet when Yale heard an older woman pointing him out to her husband: "That one. The black gentleman with the glasses." As if there were another black guy in this church, one with perfect vision. That woman wasn't the only one who kept glancing back throughout the service to observe, anthropologically, when and if this gay black specimen might start weeping.

Yale held Charlie's hand low down—not as a statement, but

because Charlie was so allergic to churches. "I see kneelers and hymnals," he said, "and five tons of Anglican guilt lands on my neck." So, far below anyone else's sightline, Yale had rubbed his wide thumb over Charlie's bony one.

Family members told stories only about Nico as a child, as if he'd died in adolescence. There was one good one, told by Nico's stoic and ashen father: Fiona, when she was seven, had wanted twenty cents to buy a handful of Swedish Fish candy from the bin on the counter of the convenience store. Their father pointed out that she'd already spent her allowance. Fiona had started to cry. And Nico, who was eleven, sat down in the middle of the aisle and, for five minutes, twisted and yanked at his barely loose molar until it came out. It bled—and their father, an orthodontist, was alarmed at the jagged root still attached. But Nico pocketed the tooth and said, "The Tooth Fairy's bringing a quarter tonight, right?" In front of Fiona, Dr. Marcus couldn't say no. "So can you give me a loan?"

The crowd laughed at this, and Dr. Marcus barely needed to explain that Nico gave the money straight to his sister, that it was another year before the permanent tooth grew in.

Yale looked now for Terrence. It took a minute, but there he was, sitting halfway up the stairs, too surrounded for Yale to chat with him yet. Instead, Yale took one of the mini quiches off a passing tray and slipped it to him through the balusters. "You look stuck!" Yale said, and Terrence put the quiche in his mouth, held his hand out again, said, "Keep 'em coming!"

Fiona had wanted to trick her parents, to exchange Nico's ashes with fireplace ones and give the real ones to Terrence. It was hard to tell if she was serious. But Terrence wasn't getting any ashes, and he wasn't getting anything else either, besides Nico's cat, which he'd taken when Nico first went into the hospital. The family had made it clear that when they began dismantling Nico's apartment tomorrow, Terrence would be excluded. Nico had left no will. His illness had been sudden, immediately debilitating—first a few days of what had seemed like just shingles, but then, a month later, moon-high fevers and dementia.

Terrence had been an eighth-grade math teacher until this summer, when Nico needed him around the clock and Terrence learned he was infected himself. And how would Terrence get through the fall, the winter, with no Nico, no job? It wasn't just a financial question. He loved teaching, loved those kids.

Terrence had some of the vague early symptoms, some weight loss, but nothing serious yet, not enough to go on disability. He'd taken the test after Nico got sick—whether out of solidarity or just to *know*, Yale wasn't sure. It wasn't as if there were some magic pill. Yale and Charlie had, just on principle, been among the first to get tested that spring. Charlie's paper had been advocating for testing, education, safe sex, and Charlie felt he had to put his money where his mouth was. But on top of that, Yale had just wanted to get it over with. Not knowing, he figured, was bad for his health in and of itself. The clinics weren't giving the test yet, but Dr. Vincent was. Yale and Charlie opened a bottle of champagne when they got the good results. It was a somber toast; they didn't even finish the bottle.

Julian was back at Yale's ear, saying, "Get yourself a refill before the slide show starts."

"There's a slide show?"

"It's *Richard*."

At the bar Yale found Fiona talking to someone he didn't know, a straight-looking guy with a jaw. Twisting her blonde curls around her finger. She was drinking too fast, because that was an empty glass in her hand. And she'd gotten it since she gave Yale her half-drink, and Fiona weighed maybe a hundred pounds. He touched her arm. He said, "You remember to eat?"

Fiona laughed, looked at the guy, laughed again. She said, "*Yale*." And she kissed his cheek, a firm kiss that probably left lipstick. To the guy she said, "I have two hundred big brothers." She might fall over any second. "But as you can *see*, he's the *preppiest*. And look at Yale's hands. Look at them."

Yale examined his palm; there was nothing wrong with it.

"No," she said, "The back! Don't they look like paws? They're furry!" She ran her finger through the dark hairs clustered thickly on the pinky side of his hand. She whispered loudly to the man: "It's on his feet too!" Then, to Yale, "Hey, did you talk to my aunt?"

Yale scanned the room. There were only a few women here, none much over thirty.

He said, "At the vigil?"

"*No*, she can't drive. But you must have talked, because I *told* her. I told her, like, *months* ago. And she said she had."

He said, "Your aunt?"

"No, my *father's* aunt. She loved Nico. Yale, you have to know that. She *loved* him."

Yale said to the guy, "Get her some food," and the guy nodded. Fiona patted Yale's chest and turned away, as if he were the one whose logic couldn't be followed.

He got his refill, almost straight rum, and looked for Charlie. Was that his bearded chin, his blue tie? But the curtain of people closed again, and Yale wasn't tall enough to see over a crowd. And now Richard dimmed the lights and pulled up a projector screen, and Yale couldn't see anything but the shoulders and backs boxing him in.

Richard Campo, if he had any job at all, was a photographer. Yale had no idea where Richard's money came from, but it let him buy a lot of nice cameras and gave him time to roam the city shooting candid photos in addition to the occasional wedding. Not long after Yale moved to Chicago, he was sunbathing on the

Belmont Rocks with Charlie and Charlie's friends, though this was before Yale and Charlie were an item. It was heaven, even if Yale had forgotten a towel, even if he always burned. Guys making out in broad daylight! A gay space hidden from the city but wide open to the vast expanse of Lake Michigan. One of Charlie's friends, a man with wavy, prematurely silver hair and a lime-green Speedo, had sat there clicking away on his Nikon, changing film, clicking again at all of them. Yale asked, "Who's the perv?" and Charlie said, "He might be a genius." That was Richard. Of course Charlie saw genius in everyone, prodded them till he discovered their passions and then encouraged those, but Richard really was talented. Yale and Richard were never close—he'd never set foot in the guy's house till today—but Yale had grown used to him. Richard was always on the periphery, watching and shooting. A good fifteen years older than everyone else in their circle: paternal, doting, eager to buy a round. He'd bankrolled Charlie's newspaper in the early days. And what had started as a strange quirk had become, in the past few months, something essential. Yale would hear the camera's click and think, "He got *that*, at least." Meaning: Whatever happens—in three years, in twenty—that moment will remain.

Someone messed with the record player, and as the first slide displayed (Nico and Terrence toasting last year at Fiona's twentieth birthday) the music started: the acoustic intro to "America," the version from Simon and Garfunkel's Central Park concert. Nico's favorite song, one he saw as a defiant anthem, not just a ditty about a road trip. The night Reagan won reelection last year, Nico, furious, played it on the jukebox at Little Jim's again and again until the whole bar was drunkenly singing about being lost and counting cars and looking for America. Just as everyone was singing now.

Yale couldn't bear to join, and although he wouldn't be the only one crying, he didn't think he could stay here. He backed out of the crowd and took a few steps up Richard's stairs, watching the heads from above. Everyone stared at the slides, riveted. Except that someone else was leaving too. Teddy Naples was at Richard's heavy front door, slipping his suit jacket back on, turning the knob slowly. Usually Teddy was a little ball of kinetic energy, bouncing on his toes, keeping time with his fingers to music no one else could hear. But right now he moved like a ghost. Maybe he had the right idea. If he weren't trapped on this side of the crowd, Yale might have done the same. Not *left*, but stepped outside for fresh air.

The slides: Nico in running shorts, a number pinned to his chest. Nico and Terrence leaning against a tree, both giving the finger. Nico in profile with his orange scarf and black coat, a cigarette between his lips. Suddenly, there was Yale himself, tucked in the crook of Charlie's arm, Nico on the other side: the year-end party last December for Charlie's paper. Nico had been the graphic designer for *Out Loud Chicago*, and he had a regular comic strip there, and he'd just started designing theater sets too. Self-taught, entirely. This was supposed to have been the prologue of his life. A new slide: Nico laughing at Julian and Teddy, the Halloween they had dressed as Sonny and Cher. Nico opening a present. Nico holding a bowl of chocolate ice cream. Nico up close, teeth shining. The last time Yale saw Nico, he'd been unconscious, with foam—some kind of awful white foam—oozing suddenly from his mouth and nostrils. Terrence had screamed into the hallway for the nurses, had run into a cleaning cart and hurt his knee, and the fucking nurses were more concerned about whether or not Terrence had shed blood than about what was happening to Nico. And here on the slide was Nico's full, beautiful face, and it was too much. Yale dashed up the rest of the stairs.

He worried the bedrooms would be full of guys who'd been taking poppers, but the first one, at least, was empty. He closed the door and sat on the bed. It was dark out now, the sparse streetlights of Belden just barely illuminating the walls and floor. Richard must have redone at least this one room after the mysterious wife moved out. Two black leather chairs flanked the wide bed. There was a small shelf of art books. Yale put his glass on the floor and lay back to stare at the ceiling and do the slow-breathing trick Charlie had taught him.

All fall, he'd been memorizing the list of the gallery's regular donors. Tuning out the downstairs noise, he did what he often did at home when he couldn't sleep: He named donors starting with *A*, then ones starting with *B*. A fair number overlapped with the Art Institute donors he'd worked with for the past three years, but there were hundreds of new names—Northwestern alumni, North Shore types—that he needed to recognize on the spot.

Recently he'd found the list disconcerting—had felt a dull gray uneasiness around it. He remembered being eight and asking his father who else in the neighborhood was Jewish ("Are the Rothmans Jewish? Are the Andersens?") and his father rubbing his chin, saying, "Let's not do that, buddy. Historically, bad things happen when we make lists of Jews." It wasn't till years later that Yale realized this was a hang-up unique to his father, to his brand of self-hatred. But Yale had been young and impressionable, and maybe that's why the reciting of names chafed.

Or no, maybe it was this: Lately he'd had two parallel mental lists going—the donor list and the sick list. The people who might donate art or money, and the friends who might get sick; the big donors, the ones whose names you'd never forget, and the friends he'd already lost. But they weren't close friends, the lost ones, until tonight. They'd been acquaintances, friends of friends like Nico's old roommate Jonathan, a couple of gallery owners, one bartender, the bookstore guy. There were, what, six? Six people he *knew* of, people he'd say hi to at a bar, people whose middle names he couldn't tell you, and maybe not even their last names. He'd been to three memorials. But now, a new list: one close friend.

Yale and Charlie had gone to an informational meeting last year with a speaker from San Francisco. He'd said, "I know guys who've lost no one. Groups that haven't been touched. But I also know people who've lost twenty friends. Entire apartment buildings devastated." And Yale, stupidly, desperately, had thought maybe he'd fall into that first category. It didn't help that, through Charlie, he knew practically everyone in Boystown. It didn't help that his friends were all overachievers—and that they seemed to be overachieving in this terrible new way as well.

It was Yale's saving grace, and Charlie's, that they'd met when they had, fallen in love so quickly. They'd been together since February of '81 and—to the bemusement of nearly everyone— exclusive since fall of the same year. Nineteen eighty-one wasn't too soon to get infected, not by a long shot, but then this wasn't San Francisco, it wasn't New York. Things, thank God, moved slower here.

How had Yale forgotten he hated rum? It always made him moody, dehydrated, hot. His stomach a mess.

He found a closet-size bathroom off this room and sat on the cool toilet, head between his knees.

On his list of people who might get sick, who weren't careful enough, who might even already be sick: Well, Julian, for sure. Richard. Asher Glass. Teddy—for Christ's sake, Teddy Naples, who claimed that once he managed to avoid checking out of the Man's World bathhouse for fifty-two hours, just napped (through the sounds of sex and pumping music) in the private rooms various older men had rented for their liaisons, subsisting on Snickers bars from the vending machine.

Teddy opposed the test, worried names could get matched with test results and used by the government, used like those lists of Jews. At least this was what he said. Maybe he was just terrified, like everyone. Teddy was earning his PhD in philosophy at Loyola, and he tended to come up with elaborate philosophical covers for terribly average feelings. Teddy and Julian would occasionally have a "thing" on, but mostly Teddy just floated between Kierkegaard and bars and clubs. Yale always suspected that Teddy had at least seven distinct groups of friends and didn't rank this one very highly. Witness his leaving the party. Maybe the slides were too much for him, as they'd been for Yale; maybe he'd stepped out to walk around the block, but Yale doubted it. Teddy had other places to be, better parties to attend.

And then there was the list of acquaintances already sick, hiding the lesions on their arms but not their faces, coughing horribly, growing thin, waiting to get worse—or lying in the hospital, or flown home to die near their parents, to be written up in their local papers as having died of pneumonia. Just a few right now, but there was room on that list. Far too much room.

When Yale finally moved again, it was to cup water from the sink, splash it over his face. He looked frightful in the mirror: rings under his eyes, skin gone pale olive. His heart felt funny, but then his heart always felt funny.

The slide show must be over, and if he could look down on the crowd he'd be able to spot Charlie. They could make their escape. They could get a cab, even, and he could lean on the window. When they got home, Charlie would rub his neck, insist on making him tea. He'd feel fine.

He opened the door to the hall and heard a collective silence, as if they were all holding their breath, listening to someone make a speech. Only he couldn't quite hear the speech. He looked down, but there was no one in the living room. They'd moved somewhere.

He came downstairs slowly, not wanting to be startled. A sudden noise would make him vomit.

But down in the living room was just the whir of the record, spinning past the last song, the needle arm retired to the side. Beer bottles and Cuba libre glasses, still half full, covered the tables and couch arms. The trays of canapés had been left on the dining table. Yale thought of a raid, some kind of police raid, but this was a private residence, and they were all adults, and nothing much illegal had happened. Probably someone had some pot, but come on.

How long had he been upstairs? Maybe twenty minutes. *Maybe* thirty. He wondered if he could've fallen asleep on the bed, if it was 2 a.m. now. But no, not unless his watch had stopped. It was only 5:45.

He was being ridiculous, and they were out in the backyard. Places like this had backyards. He walked through the empty kitchen, through a book-lined den. There was the door, but it was dead-bolted. He cupped his hand to the glass: a striped canopy, a heap of dead leaves, the moon. No people.

Yale turned and started shouting: "Hello! Richard! Guys! Hello!"

He went to the front door—also, bizarrely, dead-bolted—and fumbled till it opened. There was no one on the dark street.

The foggy, ridiculous idea came to him that the world had ended, that some apocalypse had swept through and forgotten only him. He laughed at himself, but at the same time: He saw no bobbing heads in neighbors' windows. There were lights in the houses opposite, but then the lights were on here too. At the end of the block, the traffic signal turned from green to yellow to red. He heard the vague rush of cars far away, but that could have been wind, couldn't it? Or even the lake. Yale hoped for a siren, a horn, a dog, an airplane across the night sky. Nothing.

He went back inside and closed the door. He yelled again: "You

16

guys!" And he felt now that a trick was being played, that they might jump out and laugh. But this was a memorial, wasn't it? It wasn't the tenth grade. People weren't always looking for ways to hurt him.

He found his own reflection in Richard's TV. He was still here, still visible.

On the back of a chair was a blue windbreaker he recognized as Asher Glass's. The pockets were empty.

He should leave. But where would he even go?

Cigarette butts filled the ashtrays. None were half smoked, none smashed out in haste. Copies of some of Nico's comics had been laid out on the end tables, the bar, but now they were scattered—probably more a product of the party than its end—and Yale plucked one off the floor. A drag queen named Martina Luther Kink. A silly punch line about having a dream.

He walked through every room on the ground floor, opening every door—pantry, coat closet, vacuum closet—until he was greeted with a wall of cold air and descending cement steps. He found the light switch and made his way down. Laundry machines, boxes, two rusty bikes.

He climbed back up and then all the way to the third floor—a study, a little weight room, some storage—and then down to the second again and opened everything. Ornate mahogany bureaus, canopy beds. A master bedroom, all white and green. If this had been the wife's work, it wasn't so bad. A Diane Arbus print on the wall, the one of the boy with the hand grenade.

A telephone sat next to Richard's bed, and Yale grabbed it with relief. He listened to the tone—reassuring—and slowly dialed his own number. No answer.

He needed to hear a voice, any human voice, and so he got the dial tone back and called Information.

"Name and city please," the woman said.

"Hello?" He wanted to make sure she wasn't a recording.

"This is Information. Do you know the name of the person you wish to call?"

"Yes, it's—Marcus. Nico Marcus, on North Clark in Chicago." He spelled the names.

"I have an N. Marcus on North Clark. Would you like me to connect you?"

"No—no thank you."

"Stay on the line for the number."

Yale hung up.

He circled the house one more time and went, finally, to the front door. He called to no one: "I'm leaving! I'm going!"

And stepped out into the dark.

2015

When they started across the Atlantic, the guy in the window seat jerked awake. He'd been asleep since O'Hare, and Fiona had tried to distract herself by lusting after him. The inflight magazine had been open on her lap for an hour, and all she'd done was tightly roll the corner of the crossword page again and again. The guy had the body of a rock climber, and the clothes and hair and beard (messy, all three, the hair chin-length and curly, the shorts stained with blue ink) to match. He'd slept with his forehead against the seat in front, and when he sat up and looked around, dazed, Fiona realized she hadn't seen his face earlier. She'd invented a face for him, so that this one—while handsome and weathered—seemed wrong. She'd already known from the muscles of his bare legs, the meat of his arms, that he was too young for her. Early thirties.

He pulled his backpack from under his feet and went through the contents. He had the window seat, Fiona the aisle. He felt his pockets, felt the seat around him. He went through the backpack again, removing things: rolled-up socks, plastic bag with toothpaste and Scope, a small journal. He turned to Fiona and said, "Hey, I buy a drink?" She wasn't sure she'd heard right. He might have been offering to buy her a cocktail, but this was an urgent question, not a flirtatious one.

She said, "I'm sorry?"

"Did I buy any drinks? On this flight?" His speech was slightly slurred.

"Oh. You've been asleep."

"Fuck," he said, and leaned his head back so far his Adam's apple pointed at the ceiling.

"Something wrong?"

"I left my wallet at the bar." He whispered it, as if saying it aloud would make it true. "At O'Hare."

"Your whole wallet?"

"Big, leather thing. You haven't seen it, have you?" He peered, suddenly inspired, into his magazine pouch, and then into Fiona's. "Fuck. I got my passport at least, but fuck."

She was horrified for him. This was the kind of thing she would have done herself in her wild days. Left her purse at some club, found herself on the wrong side of the city with no way home.

"Should we call the flight attendant?"

"Nothing she can do." He shook his head, bewildered, his curls hitting his beard. He let out a short, bitter laugh. "Fucking alcoholism, man. Fuck me. Fuck."

She couldn't tell if he was joking. What alcoholic spoke about it so openly? But at the same time, would you say it if it weren't true?

She said, "Do you have friends in Paris who can help?"

"There's someone I'm supposed to stay with for the weekend. I don't think she's gonna put me up longer than that."

And suddenly it hit Fiona: This was a scam. This was his sob story. She was supposed to look at him with maternal concern, to hand him a hundred bucks and say, "Perhaps this will help." If she were his age, he'd have tried to seduce her on top of it.

She said, "What a nightmare." She made her face empathic, and then she turned her magazine page. She could've said, *I've got bigger problems than you, buddy.* She could've said, *There are worse things to lose.*

When the cabin lights turned off, Fiona curled her body toward the aisle, settled into her thin pillow.

She'd never sleep, but it was nice to go through the motions. She had a million decisions to make in Paris, and the past week had been a frenzy of panicked planning, but for these eight hours, she was mercifully unable to do a thing. Being on an airplane, even in coach, was the closest an adult could come to the splendid helplessness of infancy. She'd always been irrationally jealous when Claire got sick. Fiona would bring her books and tissues and warm Jell-O water and tell her stories, wishing to trade places. Partly to spare her daughter the pain of illness, but also to feel mothered. These were the only times Claire would accept Fiona's doting, the only times she'd curl up in Fiona's lap to sleep—her body emanating fever-heat, the soft hair around her forehead and neck curling and sticking to her sweat. Fiona would stroke her hot little ear, her burning calf. When Claire got older, it wasn't the same—she wanted to be alone with her book or her laptop—but she'd still let Fiona bring her soup, let her perch on the edge of the mattress for a minute. And that was something.

She must have slept a bit, but with the time change and the cabin lights and their flying against the sun, she wasn't sure if half an hour had passed or five. Her seatmate snored, cheek to shoulder.

The plane lurched, and a flight attendant came through to touch all the overhead bins with two fingertips. Everything secured. Fiona wanted to live on the plane forever.

Her neighbor didn't wake till breakfast was served. He ordered a coffee, miserably. "What I want," he said to Fiona, "is a whiskey." She didn't offer to buy him one. He pulled up the window shade. Still dark. He said, "I don't like these planes. The 767s."

She bit. "Why not?"

"Yeah, in another life, I used to fly these. One of my many previous lives. I don't like the angle of the landing gear."

Was this another part of the scam? The beginning of his bad-luck tale, how he lost his job and maybe his wife too? He didn't look old enough to have had previous lives, or a previous life long enough to fly a plane this big. Didn't you need years of experience?

She said, "It's not safe?"

"You know, it's all completely safe, and it's all completely unsafe. You're hurtling through the air, right? What do you expect?"

He seemed sober enough not to vomit in her lap, or put his hand there. Just a little loud. Against her judgment, she kept talking to him. It was something to do. And she was curious what he'd say next, how the scam would unfold.

He told her how he used to name every plane he flew, and she told him her daughter used to name *everything*—toothbrushes, Lego people, the individual icicles outside her bedroom window.

"That's wild," he said, which seemed an overstatement.

On the runway he asked if she'd been to Paris before. "Just once," she said, "in high school."

He laughed. "So this'll be different, right?"

She couldn't remember much of that trip, beyond the other members of the French Club and the boy she'd hoped to kiss, who instead wound up getting caught in bed with Susanna Marx. She remembered smoking pot and eating nothing but croissants. Sending Nico postcards that wouldn't reach him till she was home. Waiting in lines at the Louvre and the Eiffel Tower, feeling she should have a more profound reaction. She'd only taken French to rebel against her mother, who believed she ought to know Spanish.

Fiona asked if he'd been there himself, and then she said, "I guess if you were a pilot—" She'd forgotten because she didn't believe him.

He said, "Second best city in the world."

"What's the first?"

"Chicago," he said, as if it were obvious. "No Cubs in Paris. You staying Left Bank or Right?"

"Oh. Between them, I guess? My friend has a place on Île Saint-Louis." She liked how it made the trip sound glamorous rather than desperate.

The man whistled. "Nice friend."

Maybe she shouldn't have said it, shouldn't have made herself sound moneyed and scammable. But because it felt so lovely and warm inside this version of the story, she went on. "He's actually— have you heard of the photographer Richard Campo?"

"Yeah, of course." He looked at her, waited for the rest. "What, *that's* your friend?"

She nodded. "We go way back."

"*Holy*," the man said. "You serious? I'm a big art freak. I get him mixed up with Richard Avedon. But Campo did those deathbed shots?"

"He's the one. Grittier than Avedon."

"I didn't know he was still alive. Wow. Wow."

"I won't tell him you said that." Really, she had no idea what shape Richard was in. He was still working at eighty, and when he passed through Chicago a few years ago for his show at the MCA, he was stooped but energetic, gushing about the twenty-nine-year-old French publicist who was apparently the love of his life.

They waited a long time to approach the gate. He asked if she planned to hit the museums with Richard Campo, and Fiona told him she was really there to visit her daughter. It was true, in the most optimistic sense. "And her daughter too," she said. "My granddaughter."

He laughed and then realized she was serious. "You don't look—"

"Thanks," she said.

To her relief, the seatbelt light dinged off. No time for the guy to ask questions she didn't have answers to. (What arrondissement? How old is the grandkid? What's her name?)

She waited for room to stand. "Your wallet couldn't be in your suitcase, could it?" She gestured at the overhead bins.

"Checked my bag at O'Hare."

She believed him more now, but not enough to offer money. She said, "I'll share my cab, if that would help."

He grinned, and his teeth were nice. Square and white. "A ride's the one thing I got."

There was space for her finally, and she stood, knees popping. She said, "Good luck." And although he couldn't have known how much she needed it, he said, "Same to you."

She hefted down her carry-on. Out the pill-shaped windows, a pink sun was rising.

1985

Yale watched, relieved, as a car rumbled down Belden. Someone unlocked the door of the house across the street.

If he moved faster, it would only take half an hour to get home—but he went as slowly as he could. He didn't want to walk into an empty apartment, or—worse—find Charlie there, ready to tell him whatever horrible thing had sent everyone out of the house. An emergency call, another death. They might have turned on the TV, seen news from Russia, something so alarming they'd had to run home, make preparations.

He turned onto Halsted: a long, straight path to his own bed. He looked into shop windows, stood at "Don't Walk" lights even when he could have crossed. He let people pass. Maybe he expected the whole party to come up behind him, to say they'd gone barhopping and wondered where he'd been.

He walked much farther than he needed to, beyond his own corner. He looked into each bar he passed—opening the door when the windows were mirrored or painted black—scanning for Charlie, for Fiona, for any of them.

In one dank entryway, a man leaned on a cigarette machine, his hand down the fly of his jeans. "Hey," the guy said. He was wasted, his voice full of slobber. "Hey, *gorgeous*. I got a job for you."

At the next bar, a nearly empty one, a TV on the wall was for some reason showing *60 Minutes* instead of porn or music videos. The giant stopwatch, ticking down. No nuclear war, at least. No breaking news.

Yale's legs were tired, and it was late. At the police station he stopped and walked back down the other side of the street, all the way back to the corner of Briar. He turned down it and looked for lights on the top floor of the three-flat. There were none.

He didn't go in. He walked, slowly, a block and a half east to the small blue house with black shutters, the shiny black door. Most of the houses on this street were as large as the structurally unsound one-time mansion that contained Yale and Charlie's apartment, but Yale had always loved this little one that stood sandwiched between stone giants. Compact and tidy and not too glamorous, which was why, ever since he'd noticed the "For Sale" sign out front, he'd been entertaining the wild question of whether he and Charlie might be able to afford it. Who on earth ever bought a house? But maybe they could. To own a piece of the city, to have something that was theirs, that no one could kick them out of on any pretext—that would be something. It might start a trend! If Charlie did it, other guys who could afford to would follow.

He looked back up the block. No Charlie, no crowd of drunken revelers. This was as good a place as any to wait. Better than the empty apartment. He stepped closer to the sign, so he wouldn't look like a creep.

They could have parties where people gathered on the porch to smoke and talk, where they'd grab more beer from the kitchen and bring it out and sit right there on a big wooden swing.

He wanted, suddenly, to scream for Charlie, to call into the city so loudly they'd all hear. He pushed his foot hard against the sidewalk and breathed through his nose. He looked at the beautiful house.

Yale could memorize the real estate agent's number—the last

26

three digits were all twos—and call this week. And then this wouldn't just be the night they didn't go to Nico's funeral, the night Yale felt so horrifically alone; it would be the night he found their house.

He was getting cold. He walked back up Briar and up to the apartment. Everything was dark and still, but he checked the bed. Empty, the blue comforter still bunched on Charlie's side. He wrote down the agent's number before it fled his mind.

It was seven o'clock, which explained his growling stomach. He should have filled up on abandoned hors d'oeuvres before he left.

And suddenly he had a new theory: food poisoning. He'd been a little sick, hadn't he? It could have hit everyone else harder, sent them carpooling to the hospital. It was the first reasonable story he'd come up with. He congratulated himself for not taking a deviled egg when they came by.

He made a double cheese sandwich—three slices of provolone and three of cheddar, brown mustard, lettuce, onion, tomato, rye bread—and sat on the couch and bit in. This was a better version of what he'd lived on at Michigan, at the campus snack bar where burger toppings—including cheese—had been free. He'd stick two slices of bread in his backpack in the morning, then load them up at noon.

He dialed Charlie's mother. Teresa was from London—Charlie's slightly faded accent magnified, in her, into something glorious—but she lived in San Diego now, drinking chardonnay and dating aging surfers.

She said, "How *are* you!" And he knew from her lightness, her surprise, that Charlie hadn't called her from a hospital or prison cell tonight.

"Good, good. The new job is perfect." It wasn't unusual for Yale to call Teresa independent of Charlie. She was, as she knew, his only mother in any real sense of the word. Yale's own mother was a former child actress who'd tried to settle down in small-town Michigan, then ran off when Yale was three to act again. He grew up watching her on the sly, first on *The Guiding Light* and then on *The Young and the Restless*, on which she still made rare appearances. Her character, it seemed, was too old for regular storylines now, but her character's son, who actually looked a bit like Yale, was still central; so she'd come back to weep whenever the son was kidnapped or had cancer.

Yale had seen his mother exactly five times after the day she left, always when she swept through town with belated presents for the holidays she'd missed. She was a lot like her soap characters: aloof, mannered. Her last visit was Yale's fourteenth birthday. She took him out for lunch and insisted he have a milkshake for dessert. Yale was full, but she was so vehement that he gave in and then spent weeks wondering if she thought he was too thin, or if it really meant something to her, giving her son something sweet, something that ought to make him happy. It hadn't made him happy, and Yale still couldn't see a milkshake without also seeing his mother's red fingernails tapping anxiously on the table, the only part of her body that wasn't completely controlled. "It's going to be so *interesting*," she'd said to him that day, "to see what you become." When he turned twenty, she sent him a check for three thousand dollars. Nothing when he turned thirty. Teresa, on the other hand, had flown into town and taken him to Le Francais, which she couldn't afford. Teresa would send him clippings from magazines, articles about art or swimming or asthma or the Cubs or anything else that made her think of Yale.

"Tell me all about it," Teresa said. "You're wooing the rich folks, is it?"

"Partly. We're trying to build the collection."

"You know you have a gift for charm. Mind, I'm not calling you slick. You're charming like a puppy."

"Huh," he said and laughed.

"Oh Yale, learn to take a compliment."

He managed to keep her on the phone for twenty minutes, telling her about the gallery space, the donors, the university. She told him the rabbits were into her lettuce, or *someone* was eating her lettuce, and didn't that sound like a thing the rabbits would do? Yale ran the dust cloth along the television, the picture frames, the antique shaving mirror he kept out here on the bookshelf, the wooden box that housed Charlie's childhood marble collection.

She said, "This must be costing a fortune. Is Charlie there?"

"He's out," Yale said, as cheerfully as he could.

"Well. Tell him his old mum had two sons last she checked, and it's been weeks since she's heard from the one she carried."

He said, "We love you, Teresa."

It was the absolute middle of the night, Yale could tell without rolling toward the clock, when he heard the door and then the refrigerator, when he saw the hall light through his eyelids. He said, "Charlie?"

There was no answer, so he sat up, swung his feet off the bed. And there was Charlie's silhouette, leaning against the doorframe. Drunk.

Yale would have shouted if he were more awake, but he could just barely manage to speak. "What the fuck happened?"

"I could ask the same."

"No, you couldn't. No, you could not. I go—I go upstairs for five minutes. What the hell time is it?" He grabbed his alarm clock, turned the red numbers toward himself: 3:52 a.m. "What *happened* to you?"

"I went out after."

"After *what*?"

"The raid."

29

"There—the cops came?" It was the first thing he'd considered, but he'd dismissed it so quickly.

"What? No. After we went to Nico's."

Yale looked around the room, made sure he was awake.

Charlie said, "Look, I don't know when you vanished, but by the time we went to Nico's, you were missing. I hope you had a brilliant time. I hope it was splendid."

Yale said, idiotically, "You went to Nico's."

"We raided his apartment."

"Oh."

"We went— You know how his parents weren't going to let Terrence back in. But Terrence had a key, and he was—were you gone by then?" Charlie hadn't moved from the doorway. It seemed to take him great effort to assemble a sentence, even to form consonants. "He had the key and he showed it to Richard, and Richard said we should all go there straightaway. And we did. And Fiona's going to cover for us. And we got his stuff. Look." He started unwrapping something from his own neck. Backlit as Charlie was, Yale could only see the long untwisting of it.

"Is that Nico's scarf?" He was trying to piece it together. That everyone had abandoned their drinks en masse and walked to Clark to divvy up Nico's belongings. That they had pillaged, in the best possible way. And he hadn't been there.

Nico wore that stripy orange scarf everywhere. It was how you'd recognize him from across a winter street.

"What about the servers? The boys with the food?"

"I imagine they took off. We just moved the party. But you were already doing lord knows what."

"Charlie, I was *lying down*. For like five minutes, upstairs." Maybe it had been half an hour, but wasn't it basically the same?

"I know where you were. It was a great topic of conversation."

"And no one came to get me?"

30

"We didn't want to *interrupt* you." Charlie seemed furious—seething, barely holding something in.

"From lying down with an upset stomach?"

"Everyone saw you go up with Teddy."

"*Teddy?*" He wanted to laugh but stopped himself. It would sound defensive. "Teddy left. He walked out the front door when the slide show started."

Charlie was quiet. He might have been processing something, or he might have been about to vomit.

Yale said, "Even if he stayed, what the hell would I be doing with him? Listen. I went upstairs because I needed to be alone."

Charlie said, slowly, unsurely, "I saw him. I saw him during the slide show."

"Are you thinking of the *picture*? Teddy dressed up as Cher? Charlie, sit down." He didn't. "Listen: I felt woozy, and I came down maybe five, ten minutes later. Fifteen at most. And I thought—I don't even know what I thought. Everyone was gone, and I was the only one left. It was the weirdest fucking moment of my life. And I still don't understand why you're getting home ten hours later."

"I—we went out after." Charlie sounded, bizarrely, disappointed—as if he'd hung so much anger on Yale's having been with Teddy that he didn't know what to do with himself now. "Fiona said you were with Teddy."

"*Fiona* is the 'everyone' who saw this?"

"The main one."

"Fiona was wasted. And Christ, she's been a wreck."

"You were both gone. You both vanished at the same time."

"And she saw us do what? She saw him carry me up the stairs like a bride?"

"No, she just—I asked where you were, and she said you were upstairs. And I said, 'Why would he go upstairs?' and she said, 'I

31

think Teddy's up there too.'" And then he paused, as if he'd just heard how ridiculous he sounded.

"Okay then."

"But she kept saying it."

"Well, she was drunk."

"Go back to sleep," Charlie said. "I'll be there in a minute."

Yale hadn't expected to fall asleep, but the next time he rolled over it was 6 a.m. and Charlie was curled into a ball beside him. Two full water glasses and a bottle of aspirin sat on Charlie's nightstand next to his usual bottles of vitamin B and ginseng; he expected to wake up hung over. It was a scene Yale would rather miss any day, but especially now. At least Charlie's paper had been put to bed early this week, so they all could attend the party. The drivers would distribute the paper today while the staff slept in or hunched over toilet bowls.

He watched Charlie's ribs rise and fall through his pale skin. Blond freckles covered his shoulders, his face, his arms, but his chest was polished ivory. He was soft, as if his skin had never seen the weather, and when a bone—an elbow, a kneecap, a rib—showed through, it was like a foreign object poking at a piece of silk.

Yale showered and dressed as quietly as he could. He didn't want breakfast.

Nico's orange scarf lay on the floor with Charlie's clothes. And on the kitchen counter, in a shopping bag, were other things: a half-empty vodka bottle, Nico's blue Top-Siders, a blank postcard from Vancouver, pewter cuff links in a velvety box, *Leaves of Grass*. Yale wished he'd been there. Not to wind up with some keepsake necessarily but just to touch everything, to think about Nico, to learn things about him he'd never known. If you learned new details about someone who was gone, then he wasn't vanishing.

He was getting bigger, realer. The Top-Siders would never fit Charlie's enormous feet; they must have been for Yale. How typical of Charlie: Even when he was furious, even when he thought Yale might have been screwing around with someone else, he'd gotten him a present.

Yale slipped off his own loafers and slid the shoes on. They were snug, his toes pushing against the stitching and puckered leather, but he liked it that way, his feet being squeezed by Nico. They didn't look right with his khakis, but they didn't look wrong exactly either.

He took the El from Belmont up to Evanston, resting the back of his head against the window. What had once been the center of a cowlick was growing into a small bald spot—unfair! He was only 31!—mercifully hidden by the dark curls around it. If he found a good angle, the coolness of the window soaked into his scalp, chilled his whole body. Yesterday it had been too warm for coats; today you'd be miserable without one. Even so, the air felt good, bracing. And the cold walk from the station to the gallery was nice too. It was just after seven, only joggers out.

The Brigg occupied the ground floor of what used to be a small classroom building, with a modified hallway serving as the gallery itself. The heating was temperamental and voices traveled through the walls, but the place had character. They had room for only small shows right now, and the hope was to outgrow this space in the next few years, and (this was where Yale came in) to have the money to outgrow it. Part of which had to do with fundraising, and part of which had to do with sucking up to the president, the university board.

Yale's office was made smaller by dark bookshelves on all four walls, and he loved it that way. He'd been bringing books from home, one box at a time, but still most of the shelves remained empty. Or, rather, were filled with dust and old coffee mugs. He was supposed to get a student intern next quarter, and he imagined asking this industrious young person to fill the shelves with auction catalogs, to scour used bookstores for decent art books.

His side project for the week was to assemble his Rolodex, and he attempted this now: pink cards for colleagues, blue for previous donors, green for potential donors, yellow for collectors, white for other contacts. He fed each card carefully into the typewriter, copied out the addresses. But what he'd thought would be a mindless task proved frustratingly complex. The files he'd inherited were largely undated, so he sometimes couldn't tell which of two addresses was current. He typed four different phone numbers onto one card, then stopped and realized he should just try calling, introduce himself. But it was too early in the morning, and so he put the card aside.

At nine, he started hearing footsteps and smelling coffee. At 9:30, Bill Lindsey rapped on Yale's open door with one knuckle. Bill, the gallery director, had long ears and wet, darting eyes. An old-school academic, all bow tie and elbow patches. Yale was fairly sure he was closeted and would never come out.

Bill said, "Getting the worm!"

"I'm sorry?"

"You're early."

"Oh. I wanted the weekend to be over."

"Have you met—" Bill walked in and lowered his voice. "Have you met Cecily Pearce?"

"Several times."

It was a ridiculous question. Cecily was Director of Planned Giving for the university—a job at once parallel to and infinitely larger than Yale's.

"She called Friday after you left. I think she'll be dropping in. Now my advice with Cecily is, if you disagree, you don't tell her. You just ask a question. You go, 'Are you worried this could result in thus-and-such?' I'm saying this because I don't know why she's coming down here. She gets these grand ideas."

"Thanks for the heads-up."

Bill's eyes swam around the room. "I'd maybe—hmm. You don't have personal photos, do you?"

"What, of *Charlie*? Of course not." What on earth was Bill imagining, a Sears studio portrait? Yale attempted to smile neutrally.

"Good. Just—she's okay, I don't mean to imply otherwise. I never know what sets her off. She's a hard nut."

At noon, right as Yale intended to head out for lunch, Cecily Pearce appeared in the doorway with Bill. Cecily had a Princess Diana haircut, soft and voluminous. She was quite a bit older than Diana, certainly over forty—but with some pearls, a tiara, she'd be a convincing double. And yet there was, indeed, something terrifying about the woman. It might've had to do with the way she briskly looked you over, a headmistress examining you for dress code violations.

She said, "Mr. Tishman," and advanced to his desk, extending a dry hand. "I'm hoping you're free tomorrow." She spoke at a tremendous clip.

"I can be. What time?"

"All day. Possibly all night as well." No evident embarrassment. Either she didn't realize what she'd said, or she already had Yale completely figured out. Behind her, in the doorway, Bill cocked his head, bemused. "I'll supply the car," she said, "unless you have one. Do you have a car?"

"No, I—"

"But you drive?"

"I have a license."

"Let's leave around nine."

35

Yale wasn't sure if he was allowed to ask where they were going. He said, "How shall I dress?"

"Warm, I suppose. She's in Door County."

Yale knew about Door County, the bit of Wisconsin that spiked up into Lake Michigan. In his mind it was a place where vacationing families went to pick their own fruit.

He said, "We're visiting a donor?"

"It's a rush situation, or I wouldn't spring this on you." She pulled a folder from under her arm, handed it over. "I have no idea if the art is any good. She clearly has money, at least. But you're the one she wants to talk to. We can go over strategy tomorrow. It's a four-and-a-half-hour drive."

Yale opened the file after she left, after Bill Lindsey shot him a sympathetic look and walked her out of the building. On top was a Xerox of a handwritten letter from back in September, the cursive slanted and mannered. "*Dear Mr. Tishman*," it began. So Cecily had kept, for two months, a letter addressed personally to him. It was dated after he'd been hired but before he'd begun the job. Had Bill passed it to her? And now she was throwing this at him with a day's notice. Yale would tell Charlie about it when he got home. Righteous anger was a reliable way to break the chill. It continued:

> *My husband was Dr. David Lerner, Northwestern class of 1912. He passed in 1963, after military service, a medical degree from Johns Hopkins, and a career in oncology. He spoke fondly of his time as a Wildcat and wished to do something for the school, a fact I've kept in mind as I've planned my estate. My grandniece, Fiona Marcus, encouraged me to contact you, and I hope this letter finds you well. I understand the Brigg Gallery to be building a permanent collection.*

This was the aunt, then, that Fiona was talking about last night. The coincidence of it unsettled him. That she should mention it months after the letter was sent, and it would instantly land on his desk. Would Teddy Naples land on his desk now, too, conjured from Fiona's drunken mind?

I am in possession of a number of pieces of modern art, most dating from the early 1920s. The paintings, sketches, and line drawings include works by Modigliani, Soutine, Pascin, and Foujita. These have never been exhibited, nor have they been in any collection but my own; they were obtained directly from the artists. I'm afraid I have no paperwork on the pieces, but I can personally vouch for their authenticity. In all, I have around twenty pieces that might interest you, as well as some corresponding artifacts.

I am in poor health and cannot travel, but wish to meet with someone who can speak to how these pieces would be cared for. I am concerned that they find a home in which they'll be exhibited, appreciated, and preserved. I invite you to visit me here in Wisconsin, and hope we may correspond regarding a date for meeting.

With warmest regards,
Nora Marcus Lerner
(Mrs. David C. Lerner, Northwestern '12)

Yale squinted at the paper. "Obtained directly from the artists" was a little suspect. The men Nora Lerner had listed were not, for the most part, ones who hawked their own paintings on street corners to visiting Americans. And this could be a logistical nightmare. Proving authenticity on any one piece—with no paperwork, no catalog listings—might take years. This woman would need to get everything authenticated before it could be appraised for her taxes, and it would either turn out to be junk, or she'd realize how much she was giving away and change her mind. In Yale's last months at the Art Institute, a man was set to donate a Jasper Johns (numbers stacked in a glorious mess of primary colors), until he learned the current value of the piece and his daughter convinced him to will it to her instead. Yale was a development guy, not an art guy, or at least he wasn't *supposed* to be an art guy, but he had let himself fall in love with that painting. He knew better. Farmers shouldn't name their animals. But then, the whole reason he'd taken this job was the chance to build something on his own. He ought to be thrilled.

A small, cowardly part of him hoped he'd get up to Door County and find that the pieces were such obvious forgeries that Northwestern could refuse the gift. Better, in some ways, than finding a plausible van Gogh, an invitation to heartbreak. But no, it didn't make a difference, really, what he found. He'd have to bend over backward for this woman even if these pieces were traced out of an art book, just so he wouldn't offend an endowment case.

The rest of the file did little to clarify things. There were further letters, far more tedious, about meeting times, and someone in Cecily's office had assembled a dossier on the Lerners. David Lerner was decently successful, and had given unremarkable amounts to Northwestern when he was alive, but there was nothing to suggest they could afford millions of dollars of art. You never knew, though, where people got their money, or where they hid it. Yale had learned not to ask. And hadn't Fiona and Nico grown up on the North Shore? There was money up there, even if Nico and Fiona were always broke, even if he'd never heard them mention any millionaires.

On the bottom of one memo, a handwritten scrawl: "*Cecily,*" it said, "*are we involving the Brigg people yet?*" The memo was two weeks old. Yale should have been indignant, but he did see where Cecily was coming from. He was new, the gallery itself was relatively new, and this was, potentially, a major donor. She was involving him now, at least. Except part of him wished she weren't. Probably he was just tired, but all he felt was a sort of pre-dentist-visit dread.

He didn't know what condition he'd find Charlie in. He might be sweet and contrite, or he might still be angry about nothing. Or he might have taken off, buried himself in work to avoid the whole situation.

But before Yale opened the door, he heard voices. A relief: A crowd was good. Charlie and two of his staffers, Gloria and Rafael, sat around the coffee table poring over back issues. Charlie was in the habit of overworking his staff on the sly by inviting them over on Mondays to celebrate after the week's issue was out. He'd feed them and then get them working again, right in the living room. As publisher, Charlie might have been hands-off with the paper, but he'd stayed involved with every decision from alderman endorsements to ads. He owned a travel agency with an office on Belmont, and he'd funneled its proceeds into *Out Loud Chicago* since the paper's founding three years ago. Charlie wasn't even particularly interested in travel or in helping other people travel; he'd bought the agency in '78 from an older lover who was particularly charmed by him and ready to retire. Charlie only went in once a week these days to make sure the place hadn't burned down and to meet with the few clients who'd specifically requested his attention. He had no problem giving complete autonomy to his agents, but believed his editors and writers required his constant supervision. It drove them nuts.

Yale waved and got himself a beer and disappeared into the

bedroom to pack. It took him a few minutes to notice the bed: Charlie had spelled out "SORRY" down Yale's side in M&Ms. Tan for the *S*, yellow for the *O*, and so on. He grinned, ate three orange candies from the tail of the *Y*. Charlie's apologies were always tangible and elaborate. The most Yale ever managed was a feeble note.

Yale was debating sweaters when Gloria called him back to the living room. Gloria was a tiny lesbian with earrings all the way up both ears. She handed him an old issue, open to rows of beefcake photos, each advertising a bar or video or escort service. "Flip through," she said. "Tell me when you see a woman. Or anyone who isn't a young white guy, for that matter."

Yale had no luck in the ad section. In a photo of the Halloween party at Berlin, he found two drag queens. "I don't suppose this counts," he said.

"Look," Charlie said. He was worked up. "Ads will dominate the visuals no matter what, and we can't ask a bathhouse to show, what? The cleaning lady?"

Rafael said, "Yeah, but *Out and Out*—" and then he swallowed his words. *Out and Out* was new, founded by three staffers who'd quit Charlie's paper last year, in a huff that *Out Loud Chicago* still relegated lesbian-specific coverage to four color-coded pages in the back. Yale had to agree—it seemed regressive, and the headlines were *pink*—but Charlie's remaining lesbian staffers preferred the editorial control it gave them. The new paper was cheaply printed and didn't have great distribution, but even so, Charlie had stepped up his game in response. Same party shots but more activism, editorials, theater and film reviews.

Charlie said, "*Out and Out* doesn't have the same problem because they can't sell ads to save their life."

Yale grabbed pretzels from the bag on the table, and Rafael nodded meekly. He'd been appointed Editor in Chief after those three staffers left, but he hadn't learned to shout Charlie down yet, and he'd have to. Funny, because Rafael was hardly shy. He was known for coming right up and biting your face if he was drunk enough. He'd started out as the nightlife reviewer—he was young and cute, with spiked-up hair, and he'd worked as a dancer—but he turned out to be an excellent editor, and despite his deference to Charlie, despite the diminished staff, the paper was better than ever. Hipper too.

Yale said, his mouth full, "Gloria, I never see many photos from the dyke bars. Could you do more coverage there?"

"We don't like to pose as much as you guys!" she said, and when Charlie threw his hands up in exasperation, she laughed at herself.

Charlie said, "I tell you what. We'll do a new quarter-pager for my agency, and we'll have two women for the photo. Walking along sharing a suitcase, something like that."

Gloria nodded, appeased. To Yale she said, "He's hard to stay mad at, you know."

"Story of my life."

Yale managed to get back to the bedroom, finish packing. He laid out Nico's blue Top-Siders to wear for luck. He swept the M&Ms into his hand, put them in his blazer pocket for tomorrow.

He dialed Fiona from the phone by the bed. Mostly he wanted to check in, see if she was eating, if she'd made it home safely. He worried about her. She had no family left, not really. She was close to Terrence, but when Terrence died too—he could picture a million terrible endings to her story, drugs and alleys and botched abortions and violent men.

And he would ask about this great-aunt, thank her for making the connection. On a selfish level, he also wanted to lead the conversation around to last night—to why Fiona would have said that about him and Teddy. But he could imagine how it played out. She was drunk, confused, devastated. Not malicious. He forgave her. And if she'd answer the phone, he'd say so. But she never picked up.

He was doing a crossword in bed when Charlie came in, the living room empty at last. Charlie looked at the suitcase and didn't say anything. He went into the bathroom for a long time, and when he came out he said, flatly, "You're leaving me."

Yale sat up, put his pencil down.

"Good God, Charlie."

"What am I supposed to think?"

"That I'm gone for one night. For work. Why the hell would I leave you?"

Charlie rubbed his head, watched his own foot toe the suitcase. "Because of how awful I was."

Yale said, "Come to bed." Charlie did, unfolding himself on top of the covers. "You never used to freak out like this."

When they first got together, it was casual for a few months. Yale was still new to Chicago, and Charlie took perverse joy in shocking Yale with the options available to him in the city, the things he hadn't seen in Ann Arbor. He brought him to The Unicorn—the first time Yale had ever been in a bathhouse. He'd had fun laughing at Yale's squeamishness, the way he folded his arms over his stomach, his questions about whether this was legal. They just ended up making out with each other in a corner, in the dim red light, then leaving for the privacy of Charlie's place. Another time, Charlie took him to the Bistro and pointed out the men on the dance floor that Yale should, one day, be sure to "snog." Charlie used to overdo his Briticisms, knowing Yale loved it. "I feel like I'm part of some news report," Yale had said that night. "You know how every report on, like, *Who Are the Gays?* has that stock disco footage in the background? We've stepped into stock gay footage." And Charlie said, "Well, you're messing it up by standing still and looking frightened." Yale remembered "Funkytown" ending and Charlie saying, "Watch!" The glitter cannons at the corners of the dance floor shot off, and the shirtless men who'd already looked like fitness models suddenly shone with blue and pink and green glitter. It stuck to their sweat, defined their shoulders. "That one," Charlie said, pointing at a luminescent dancer. "Give that man your number *now*."

Even as Yale had wanted nothing right then but to be alone with Charlie, he'd taken huge delight in the idea of the Bistro. There had been one real gay bar in Ann Arbor, but nothing like this, not a gay *disco*, not a space where everyone was so happy. The place in Ann Arbor had been filthy, with a sad jukebox and windows full of dying geraniums meant to obstruct the view from the street. There'd always been a skulking vibe, a sense that any happiness was somehow stolen. Here the music blasted and there were three bars and a pair of neon lips and multiple mirror balls. The excess of the place felt exultant. There wasn't as much on Halsted, five years back—bars were just starting to pop up; people were just starting to move there; and Boystown (no one had even called it that yet) was just starting to coalesce—and so this place, way down by the river, was where Yale first fell in love with the city.

At the Bistro, Yale felt entitled to joy. Even if he was just watching from the wall, drink in hand. This, the Bistro announced, was a town where good things would happen. Chicago would unfurl its map to him one promising street, one intoxicating space, at a time. It would weave him into its grid, pour beer in his mouth and music in his ears. It would keep him.

The relationship grew serious that fall—drunk, Yale whispered into Charlie's ear that he was in love, and Charlie whispered back, "I need you to mean that," and things progressed from there—and for about a year, Charlie worried aloud that Yale hadn't experienced the city's freedoms, hadn't been with enough men, and that one day he'd wake up and decide he needed to live some more. Charlie would say, "You're going to look back on this and wonder why you wasted your youth." Yale was twenty-six then, and Charlie somehow imagined their age gap to be practically generational even though he only had five years on Yale. But Charlie had started alarmingly young, in London. Yale was still figuring himself out sophomore year at Michigan.

Eventually things settled. Yale was suited to relationships, to the point that Teddy thought it was great fun to call him a lesbian, to ask how life on the commune was going. He'd stayed with each of his first two lovers for a year. He hated drama—hated not only the endings of things but the bumpy beginnings as well, the self-doubt, the nervousness. He was tired of meeting guys in bars, would rather lick a sidewalk than look for action in some parking lot by the beach. He enjoyed having standing plans with someone. He liked going to the movies and actually watching the movie. He liked grocery shopping. For two years, things were easy.

And then, after the virus hit Chicago—slow-motion tsunamis from both coasts—Charlie suddenly, inexplicably, worried all the time, not about AIDS itself but about Yale leaving him for someone else. Last May, before he realized how deep the insecurity had grown, Yale had said yes to a weekend pilgrimage with Julian and Teddy up to the Hotel Madison—a trip Charlie couldn't join because he wouldn't leave the paper, even for three days. They explored the city and danced in the hotel's bars and Yale spent most of Saturday night listening to the Cubs on the radio, but when they got back, Charlie questioned him for an hour about where everyone had slept and how much they'd drunk, about every single thing Julian had done—and then he barely spoke to Yale for a week. He claimed to understand now that nothing happened up there, but the idea of Yale with Julian or Teddy or both of them had taken his imagination hostage. It was more often Julian that

Charlie worried about, in fact. Julian was the flirt, the one who'd offer you a bite of cake off his own fork. The Teddy thing was odd, specific to last night.

Yale rolled toward Charlie and decided to apply Bill Lindsey's advice on talking to Cecily Pearce. He phrased it as a question: "Do you think it's possible that all the sickness and funerals and everything—they've made us feel less secure? Because this is new for you. And I've never given you reason to worry."

Charlie spoke to the window. "I'm going to say something terrible, Yale. And I don't want you to judge me." And then he didn't say anything at all.

"Okay."

"The thing is, the most selfish part of me is *happy* about this disease. Because I know until they cure it, you won't leave me."

"That's fucked up, Charlie."

"I know."

"No, that's *really* fucked up, Charlie. I can't believe you said that out loud." He could feel a vein pulse in his throat. He might get in Charlie's face and scream.

But Charlie was shaking.

"I know."

"Come here." He rolled Charlie toward him like a log. "I don't know what's going on with you, but I'm not looking for anyone else." Yale kissed his forehead, and he kissed his eyes and chin. "We're all under a lot of stress."

"That's generous."

"You get afraid of one thing, and suddenly you're afraid of everything."

2015

Fiona realized, as her cab approached the center of the city, that it was too early. She'd imagined delays and traffic, but here they were at 7:22 a.m., and she'd told Richard nine o'clock. She had the cabbie pull over and show her, on her fold-out map, where she was—she didn't want to wear out her phone battery till she was sure her charger would work with the converter she'd bought at O'Hare—and then she got out and started walking definitively down the broad sidewalk, even though she wasn't sure it was the right way at all.

At the corner, she checked the map again (her face buried in it, suitcase next to her, like the world's most muggable tourist), and it looked like three miles. Walking, she could keep her eyes peeled in a way she couldn't from a cab. Better use of her time than sitting on her ass at Richard's, waiting for business hours so she could call the private investigator back. (A private investigator! How was this her life?) She had booked the first flight she could afford, and the urgency of the packing and dog-sitting arrangements made the whole thing feel like a race, but what was one more hour? The video was two years old. Still, walking felt like a delay. She should be getting there and *doing* something.

If she saw the Seine, she'd feel better. She just needed to follow it west. Fiona remembered both islands from her high school trip;

they'd stopped at Notre Dame, on the bigger island, where some classmate had read grisly suicide statistics out of a guidebook.

She passed a father carrying a little boy on his shoulders. The boy held a Buzz Lightyear, zoomed it in front of his father's glasses.

It was a stroke of fate that she'd be staying right in the middle of the river, because hadn't the video shown Claire on a bridge? It had been impossible to tell which one—the video was grainy and didn't reveal much background—but after looking at photos online, Fiona had eliminated a few. It was one with padlocks all over the chain link, but apparently most bridges had that now.

She passed bouquinistes opening up their green stands of paperbacks and antique pornography. She stopped at each bridge to see if it looked like Claire's bridge, to see if Claire had been magically frozen to the spot. It was a gorgeous day, she'd failed to notice. And my God, she was in Paris. *Paris!* But she couldn't summon much awe. Her daughter may or may not have still been involved with the Hosanna Collective, and was probably still under Kurt Pearce's thumb. Her daughter may or may not have been the mother of the little girl in the video, the girl with blonde curls like Fiona's. All of those things felt more foreign to her than the simple fact of Paris. Paris was just a city. Anyone's path might lead here. But who ever thought their baby would get mixed up in a cult? Who imagined this was how they'd experience Paris—searching it for someone who didn't want to be found?

It was quite possibly a hopeless quest. When had her attempts to reach Claire not backfired?

She'd been thinking lately about a time when Claire was seven, when they'd all been in Florida at the beach—she and Damian still married, just barely—and Fiona had announced that it was time to go, that Claire had already been given extra time to finish her sandcastle. Claire had started to cry, and instead of leaving her alone, instead of letting her have her way, Fiona decided to hug her.

Claire pushed her away and ran to the water, throwing herself into the surf with her sundress on. "Let her cry it out," Damian had said, but twenty yards down the sand Claire had picked herself up and walked into the ocean, thigh deep, waist deep. "She's not going to stop," Fiona said, and Damian laughed and said, "She's Virginia Woolfing herself." But she really was, and Fiona was up and running, knowing better than to call to Claire, knowing that at the sound of her voice Claire might throw herself under the waves. By the time she reached her, grabbed Claire from behind, the water was up to her own chest; Claire's feet hadn't touched sand in a long time. That was just one day. Claire had done similar and worse on a thousand others. But the incident had taken on greater meaning lately: the first time Claire had flung herself off the continent.

Fiona crossed to Île Saint-Louis and passed an ice-cream shop, the smell of the waffle cones reminding her that she was starving, and she passed shops selling bright leather purses and wine and Venetian masks. Here, finally, was Richard's building, three stone stories above a shoe shop. "Campo/Thibault," it said beside one of the five black buzzers. It was 8:45 now—close enough, good enough. She rang, and a minute later it wasn't Richard who came down but a thin young man in a motorcycle jacket. He said, "You've arrived! I'm Serge, partner of Richard." Ree-*sharr*. "I take you up, okay? You get settled. Richard is having a shower, then he joins us."

Serge plucked up her suitcase as if it were empty, and she followed him up the dark stairs.

The apartment was chic and sparse, but the light fixtures and windows and the wrought iron railings outside the glass doors looked wonderfully ancient, and the details on the walls—the relief pattern of vines, and even the light switch panels—had been softened by endless layers of paint. Fiona remembered Richard's place in Lincoln Park, the treacly peaches and pinks. This was its opposite:

48

bright monochromatic paintings over gray furniture straight out of an architecture magazine. Serge showed her where she'd be staying—a book-lined room with a white bed and a single plant—and then brought her to the kitchen and poured her an orange juice. She heard Richard's shower end, and Serge called that Fiona was here. Richard called back something she couldn't understand, and it took her a moment to realize he'd answered in French.

A minute later, there he was, interrupting Serge's tour of the view. He'd combed what remained of his hair wetly to his scalp, and he wore a pressed shirt that was too large, as if he'd recently shrunk. He cried, "Fiona Marcus in the flesh!" and grabbed her arms to air-kiss both cheeks, and although she hadn't used that surname in decades, she didn't correct him. It was a gift, this name of her youth handed back to her by someone she associated with a time when she'd been optimistic and unencumbered. Granted, she associated him with the next years, too, the ones with Nico gone, with Nico's friends, who'd become her only friends, dying one by one and two by two and, if you looked away for a second, in great horrible clumps. But still, still, it was a time she missed, a place she'd fly back to in a heartbeat.

"Now the trick, my dear, is to keep you awake the rest of the day. No sleep whatsoever. Caffeine, but only if you drink it regularly. And no wine, not a drop, till you're rehydrated."

"He's an expert," Serge said. "Before I met Richard I hadn't crossed the Atlantic."

"And now how many times?" Richard asked. "Twenty?"

"*Alors, beaucoup de temps,*" Fiona said, speaking French for no reason at all, and then became certain that she'd just said "a lot of weather." She felt dizzy and stupid and like she really should lie down, against Richard's advice. She said, "You mentioned coffee."

And soon they were sprawled across Richard's gray furniture. She wanted to pry open the clamshell packaging on her converter and charge her phone, call the detective even if it was still seven minutes too soon, but she forced herself to sit still and tell them how grateful she was for the place to stay, the warm welcome. It felt good, in fact, to rest for a moment, to be Fiona Marcus again, twenty years old again, doted on by Richard Campo again. It filled her up.

Serge had made her a latte, right there in the kitchen with a machine that belonged in a cockpit, and now she sipped at the thick foam. He said, "You tell me everything about this guy when he was young, yeah? I need some scandals!"

At that, Richard went to a low shelf by the windows and pulled out a photo album he'd apparently lugged all the way to Paris and into the new century. He sat between Fiona and Serge on the long couch, started flipping through. How strange to see Richard Campo's work in snapshot form, yellowed Polaroids and Kodak prints. He'd been doing more serious work back then, too, but those photos weren't the ones preserved in cheap cellophane slots.

Richard said, "Nico's here somewhere," and then he must have found a picture, because he handed the album to Serge, tapping a page. "*Oh*, was I in love with him."

"You were in love with everyone," Fiona said.

"I was. All those boys. They were younger, and so *open*, not like my generation. I envied them. They came out at eighteen, twenty. They hadn't wasted their lives."

"You've hardly wasted yours," Fiona said.

He handed her the open album. "I was always making up for lost time."

There was Nico, curly brown hair and long teeth, his face tan and freckled, looking just past the camera and laughing. Some joke, crystallized forever. She had a copy of this photo, but an enlarged and cropped one. This version bore an orange date stamp: 6/6/82. It would be three years until he got sick. And this version showed not just Nico but the two men on either side of him. One was Julian Ames. Beautiful Julian Ames. The other she didn't know or remember, but as she studied his face she saw above the man's left eyebrow a small, oblong purple spot. "Christ," she said, but Richard was busy explaining to Serge the way Chicago had been in the early eighties, the smallness of Boystown and the way it still hovered then, somewhere between gay ghetto and gay mecca. How there was no place like it, not in San Francisco, not in New York. She tried to wipe the spot away, in case it was on the cellophane, but it didn't move. She stared at these sick men who didn't know they were sick, the spot that was still, that summer, only a rash. She handed the album back and Richard continued his narration. Fiona pretended to peer into his lap as he turned the pages, but really she let the jet lag overtake her vision, let the pictures blur. It was too much.

"This was Asher Glass," Richard said. "Big activist, a dynamo. The most beautiful *voice*, a big loud lawyer voice. The shoulders on him! Built like a brick shithouse, is what we used to say. I don't think you can translate that into French. I have no idea who this one is. Cute, though. This one's Hiram something, who owned a record store on Belmont. Belmont would be, like, I don't know. What's the equivalent?"

Serge laughed. "All of Paris?"

"*No*, dear, like some street in Le Marais. We weren't that provincial. This was Dustin Gianopoulos. Teddy Naples. A pocket twink, as you can see. Never stopped moving. This one, I don't remember either. He looks like a manatee."

"I don't know this word," Serge said.

"A lumpy walrus," Fiona offered, without looking at the picture.

"This was Terrence, Nico's boyfriend. Yale Tishman and Charlie Keene. That's a saga *there*. Look how sweet they are. This one's Rafael Peña. Remember him?" This was directed at Fiona, obviously, and she roused herself to nod.

She said, ostensibly to Serge but really to Richard, in a harsh voice she didn't expect, "They're all dead."

"That's not true!" Richard said. "Not all of them. Maybe half. Exaggeration never did any good."

"This is the American habit," Serge said to Richard. "You exaggerate."

"Don't listen to her. They're not all dead."

Fiona said, "I need a sharp knife." Her poor timing didn't register until both men started laughing, and she realized she hadn't said anything yet about the converter, the clamshell packaging. She explained, and Serge left the room to return with a massive pair of shears. He made quick work of the plastic, and soon her phone was charging happily.

Richard said, "Two things I haven't told you. One's just a minor nuisance, and one is nothing at all."

"*Not* nothing at all," Serge said. "A very big deal."

"But it shouldn't affect you. I didn't mention, when you wrote, that the next few weeks are a bit of a circus for me. I have a show going up."

"At the Centre Pompidou," Serge added. "A big fucking deal."

"But it's all done, all my work, until, you know, the day before. I have a number of interviews, though, and some of them will be kind enough to meet me here. So just *ignore, ignore, ignore.*"

"But you come to the *vernissage*! If you're still here," Serge said.

"The preview," Richard explained. "For the press and the VIPs. They wanted to do two nights, but I told them I'm *old.*"

"The sixteenth," Serge said. More than a week from now. Fiona hadn't thought that far ahead. "And a big party in two nights!"

"I'll—sure," she said, in what she hoped was a vague way.

"The other thing is the nuisance. They're shooting some kind of film on this street. An American one, romantic comedy I believe. Or at least they promised no explosions, no car chases. It's this block and the next two down. I don't even know when they start, but it's soon. I'm afraid you've walked into a zoo."

"It could be interesting," Fiona said. She was thinking about how Claire used to want to be a director, the way she'd recite entire scenes of *Annie Hall* or *Clue* from memory. Maybe things had changed, but the old Claire would have wanted to scope out the filming, to stand behind the barricades and watch the action.

Serge said, "This connects to the third thing."

"There's a third thing?"

"Oh, that's a surprise, shush! Trust me," Richard said, although Fiona didn't think her skepticism had manifested on her face, "it's a good one. A very good surprise. Listen, honey, I'm glad you're here. I know the circumstances aren't ideal, but it's damn good to see you."

"It's good to see you too." Really she'd never seen this version of Richard before, this markedly *old* version. Everyone seemed to hit old at a different point, but sometime since she'd seen him last, Richard had hit it.

It was 9:07. She sat on the floor next to where the phone was still plugged in and dialed the PI's number. A woman picked up, speaking rapid-fire French, and Fiona panicked. "Hello?" she said, and the woman repeated herself, even faster. Fiona handed Serge the phone, a hot potato. "*Allô?*" Serge said, and explained that he was calling on behalf of Fiona Marcus ("Blanchard," she corrected) and that she was here now and ready to meet. At least this was what Fiona assumed he was saying. "*Bien,*" he said, and then covered the mouthpiece and whispered, "What time?" Fiona shrugged helplessly, and Serge said things she didn't understand and hung up. "Half an hour, Café Bonaparte."

"Oh." This was good news, great news, but Fiona didn't feel prepared, hadn't changed or looked in a mirror, hadn't expected to meet the guy till the afternoon, had no idea where this café was.

"No worries. I take you on my motorbike."

1985

Cecily and her gold Mazda were already outside the gallery when Yale arrived out of breath. It was drizzling, and he hadn't managed an umbrella.

She said, "I brought coffee."

So he sat there, wet, in the passenger seat, holding the hot McDonald's cup, trying to warm himself palms-first as she drove north.

"The first thing you need to know," Cecily said, "is that Nora's granddaughter wants to be involved, as well as her lawyer. But there are no financial planners, which is either a gift from above or a very bad sign."

Yale wondered how Fiona fit into it all. Presumably, the grand-daughter was her cousin. No, her second cousin. Was that right?

"I've got music in the console."

Yale found some classical tapes and mix tapes and both volumes of Billy Joel's *Greatest Hits*, the first of which he opted for. It started in the middle of "She's Always a Woman."

He said, "So this could all be for nothing."

"Well. It could *always* all be for nothing. There are people we spend years on, we spend a lot of *money* on, frankly, and in the end they give everything to some cat-spaying charity."

"Okay, then I'll say—the artists she mentioned, in that letter?

They're just very unlikely. Especially Modigliani. He's kind of a red flag artist. Everyone thinks they have a Modigliani, and no one does."

"Hmm." She took a hand off the steering wheel to twist her earring.

"But good forgeries cost a lot of money. Forgers go after people with cash to throw away." He didn't want Cecily stewing for the whole trip. And, he realized, he didn't want her to turn the car around. The make-up sex with Charlie had been good, if not worth the fighting, but he didn't want to be home right now. He wanted to come home tomorrow afternoon, exhausted, with stories, and he wanted Charlie to be exhausted too, and he wanted Charlie to say, "Let's get takeout," and then Yale would say, "You read my mind," and they'd sit on the couch eating Chinese with disposable chopsticks and watching prime time. If he came home tonight, that wouldn't happen.

They crossed the Wisconsin border, and they passed the Mars Cheese Castle and then the brown sign for the wooded Bong Recreation Area. Yale said, "I bet frat boys steal that sign constantly."

"What do you mean?" She'd had enough time to read it; she was looking straight at it.

"I mean, to hang in the basement. They steal stop signs. I'd think they'd want a bong sign."

"I don't follow."

"Oh. It's just a funny word."

"Hmm."

They bought Yoplaits and Pringles at a gas station, and Yale took over driving. He hadn't driven much since he'd moved to the city, but he'd learned in high school, had even spent two summers delivering pizza in his father's car—and once he figured out the clutch, everything was muscle memory. Cecily opened a folder across her lap and said, "What we're hoping for is a flat-out bequest. She hasn't given to the annual fund since 1970, and those were small gifts. Which, optimistically, might just mean she's a bit of a miser. Sometimes those wind up being the largest bequests, for obvious reasons. If she's not on top of her finances, we might aim for a percentage rather than a cash amount. People like that tend to underestimate how much they have. She thinks she has five million, leaves us one million, when actually she has seven point five, and twenty percent is a lot more."

"But she was only—" Yale stopped, remembered to ask a question. "Why do you suppose the letter was only about the artwork?"

"It might just be what's on her mind. Maybe she's promised the money to her family, but doesn't want to disperse the collection."

She seemed to see this as only a minor inconvenience. Cecily must have been well practiced at cutting down the heirs' chunk of an estate. It hit him that perhaps Fiona was in this old woman's will. Hadn't Fiona said that Nora had especially loved Nico? And wouldn't it follow that she was fond of Fiona too?

Yale learned, as they drove, that Cecily had an eleven-year-old son and an ex-husband, a small apartment on Davis Street, and a degree from Skidmore. She didn't ask a single thing about him in return.

When they reached Sturgeon Bay, at the bottom of the Door County spike, Cecily unfolded a giant Wisconsin map and pointed with a clear-polished nail to the two routes that climbed either side of the peninsula. "It looks like they meet again in Sister Bay, which is where we're headed anyway."

"What have they got up here?" Yale said. "What's the big attraction?"

"Lighthouses, I think. Honeymooners."

"It *is* beautiful."

She snapped her head up and looked across Yale, out his window, as if she'd just realized where she was. "Yes. Very."

"So, you'll run the show?"

"If you don't mind."

Yale did mind, in principle. The letter was intended for him. But this was an issue of rank. And he'd wind up glad it wasn't all about the art if the art proved forged.

He had chosen the western route, and Cecily directed him to County Road ZZ. "I wonder if they say Double Z," she said. "Or just Z."

"Or Zee-Zee," Yale said. "Like ZZ Top."

Cecily actually laughed, a small miracle. But then, as she watched out her window, he saw her shoulders tense, her face fall. These were not mansions. They'd driven past some large estates on the way, but now they passed modest farmhouses, small places set in big fields. Stunning, in fact, but not millionaire land.

They pulled up in front of a white house with a screened porch out front and a single gabled window upstairs. Hanging baskets of flowers, neat cement steps to the porch door. Two old Volkswagens sat outside a freestanding one-car garage in disrepair.

Cecily checked her hair in the rearview. She said, "We're screwed."

"Maybe she's senile," Yale said. "Could she be delusional?"

Before they reached the door, a young woman came out on the steps. She waved, not happily.

Cecily and the woman shook hands. This was Debra, the granddaughter, and she apologized that, although Nora was dressed and ready, the lawyer wasn't here yet. She bore no resemblance to Fiona or Nico. Black hair, dark circles under her eyes, skin that was somehow both tanned and pasty. Maybe it was makeup, the wrong shade of powder.

They followed her through the screened porch and into a living room that reminded Yale of the house where he took piano lessons as a kid. Like his piano teacher, Nora had covered every inch of shelf and windowsill with carefully chosen *objets*—glass figurines and seashells and plants and framed photographs. The books looked read, and a stuffed record case abutted the fireplace. The couch back was frayed. This might have been the home of a college professor or a retired therapist, someone of relative means who didn't put stock in pretentious furnishings. But it was not, no, the home of a major art collector.

Nora—it had to be her, though while the dossier said she was ninety, this woman's face looked no older than seventy-five—appeared in the opposite doorway, aided by a walker. She took a long while to start speaking, her lips moving silently before the sound came out. "I'm so glad you could make it up." Her voice, surprisingly, was assured, quick, and as she kept talking Yale realized it wasn't her mind or her mouth that had tripped her up, but something else. "Now Debra's going to bring us some tea," she said, "and Stanley, that's my lawyer, Stanley will be here in a minute. And we can get acquainted!" She lowered herself, with Debra's help, into a chair that was still brown at the creases but putty-colored where the sun hit. She stared intensely at Yale, and only Yale, the entire time, and he began to wonder if *he* was why she'd paused in the door, why she'd hesitated. Perhaps Fiona had filled her in, explained how Yale fit into Nico's world. Yale was suddenly conscious of his shoes, worried she'd recognize them.

Yale and Cecily sat on a low blue couch whose gravity pulled them both toward the middle. Yale had to fight sliding in that direction and colliding with Cecily, who had anchored herself by holding onto the couch arm. She'd been silent since they walked in, and he could feel her seething beside him.

Debra said, "I'm happy to get the tea, but would you refrain from discussing things while I'm gone?"

Yale assured her, and Nora, behind her granddaughter's back, mugged—a child-behind-the-substitute-teacher roll of the eyes.

Nora wore a pink tracksuit, velour, and moccasins with ripping seams. Yale wondered if it was her haircut that made her look younger than her age. Instead of short curls, the classic old lady cut, her white hair fell in a straight, smooth bob. She was built like Fiona, small and slender. There were older people you couldn't imagine young, and there were those whose faces still held on to what they'd looked like at twenty-five. Nora was of another breed, the ones who had apparently reverted to their own childhood faces. Yale looked at Nora and saw the five-year-old she'd been, impish and precocious and blue-eyed. Maybe it had something to do with her smile, too, the way she touched all her fingers to her cheeks.

Cecily was just sitting there, so Yale filled the silence. "You're Fiona's great-aunt," he said.

Nora beamed. "Don't you just love her? My brother Hugh, that was her grandfather. Hers and Nico's," she said. "Nico and I were the artists in the family. Everyone else is so literal-minded, every one of them. Well, we're still waiting on Fiona. We'll see about her. Don't you worry a bit? But Nico was a true artist."

Yale said, "We were close friends." He didn't want to get emotional now. What would Cecily think if he broke down here on the couch? This old woman didn't look much like Nico, but she was beautiful, and Nico had been beautiful, and wasn't that enough?

Nora rescued him. "Tell me about the gallery." She coughed into the balled-up Kleenex she'd held, this whole time, in her hand.

Yale turned to Cecily, who shrugged. And though Yale had no serious illusions left about the woman's art collection—the only framed things in the room were snapshots and studio family portraits—he began talking. "We started five years ago. Right now we only do rotating exhibitions, both our own and from peer institutions, but we're starting to build a permanent collection. That's my job."

"Oh!" Nora looked agitated, impatient. She shook her head quickly. "I hadn't realized you were a *Kunsthalle*."

Yale was surprised by the word, and Cecily looked confused, irritated. "It just means a rotating gallery," he said to Cecily, but perhaps it was the wrong thing to do, making her seem uninformed. To Nora he said, "But we're *building* a permanent collection. We have the power of a world-class university behind us, plus the donor potential of a successful alumni base and one of the world's major art cities." He was talking like a fundraising robot, not like someone who'd slow danced with this woman's grandnephew last New Year's Eve, someone who'd stood over Nico's hospital bed and said that no matter what happened, he and Charlie would take care of Fiona. Nora blinked, expecting more. He said, "We're already strong in prints and drawings. I understand some of your works are sketches."

He stopped, because here was Debra with a tray and a real old-fashioned tea service: thin, chipped cups with little flowers, a steaming teapot.

Nora looked at Cecily and said, "And you're his assistant?"

Yale was so offended for Cecily that he almost answered the question himself—but that would only make things worse. So he poured everyone tea while Cecily explained her role and said, "I thought I could offer perspective on the broader picture of planned giving."

Nora said, "Debra, would you be a dear and stand out front to flag down Stanley? He always drives too far and has to turn around."

Debra threw a coat over her baggy sweater. She was almost chic, in a careless way, and too young to look as tired as she did. She was probably Yale's age, early thirties, but with all the charm of a sullen adolescent.

Once Debra was out the door, Nora leaned in. "My granddaughter doesn't like this, I have to tell you. She has the notion that if we sold the art instead, she'd never have to work. I don't know when on earth she got so spoiled. Now, my son—her father—he has a new wife, younger than Debra, and they already have two little children, just as spoiled as anything. I hate to say my son is the problem, but he's the common factor, isn't he?" There was a wheeze to her voice, as if she were squeezing her words down a narrow hallway.

Yale had a million questions—about family, finances, the art, provenance, Nora's sanity—but he wasn't here to grill her. He said, "I've brought some brochures from the gallery." He unfolded one on the coffee table.

"Oh, honey," Nora said, "I don't have my reading glasses, do I. Why don't you tell me about it. Do the students go there? Is it a regular spot for them?"

Yale said, "Not only that, but our graduate students and art majors have opportunities for—"

But there were already voices on the porch. Yale and Cecily stood to greet the lawyer. Stanley was a tall, gray-haired man with a newscaster face and wildly untamed eyebrows. "My favorite lady!" he said to Nora. The booming voice matched the man. He would've done a fine job informing people that stocks were down, that fifteen people died on the Sinai Peninsula today.

Yale could see it coming as they were introduced, and he was right. Stanley slapped his back and said, "No kidding! You go there? That'd be something: Yale at Yale. Or were you a Harvard man? Yale goes to Harvard!"

"University of Michigan," Yale said.

"Must've disappointed your parents!"

"It's a family name."

Yale had, in fact, been named for his Aunt Yael, a detail he'd learned, around age six, never to share.

Stanley turned to Cecily then and made a great show of looking her up and down, and Cecily jumped in firmly before he had the chance to compliment her. "Cecily Pearce, Director of Planned Giving for Northwestern. We're glad you could make it."

Stanley, they learned, lived down in Sturgeon Bay and had been a friend for years. He picked up a teacup, a thimble in his large hand. He was an estate lawyer, Cecily seemed aggrieved to hear. Yale knew that whatever small part of her still held out hope had been wishing for a divorce attorney or ambulance chaser.

And then, as they all sat back down, Stanley put the nail in Cecily's coffin, if not necessarily in Yale's. He said, "Miss Nora here puts the *bono* in *pro bono*."

"Stanley!" Nora blushed, flattered.

Yale felt the couch shift as Cecily loosened her grip on the arm, gave up.

So Yale said, "I'd love to talk about the art."

Debra preempted her grandmother. "None of it's here, first of all," she said. "It's in the safe deposit at the bank."

"That's good. Very smart."

"And she refuses to get it appraised." She sounded furious. Well, sure. A grandmother accepting *pro bono* legal work would not have much to pass down except the tchotchkes around them, and maybe the little house itself. And, ostensibly, a fortune in art that Debra wouldn't get.

"Okay. And they haven't been authenticated, either?"

Nora said, "I don't need them authenticated! I got these directly from the artists. I lived in Paris twice, I don't know if my letter said, from 1912 to 1914—I was just a teenager—and then again after the war until 1925. I sat out the fighting." She gave a small laugh. "And, if you can believe it, I was an art student, and I was pretty, and it just wasn't too terribly hard to meet these artists. I began to model for them after the war, which—my parents would have been *scandalized*, it was looked at like prostitution—and most of these pieces were my payment for modeling. Now there are a few others I didn't mention in the letter, some works that might not be worth a dime. Plus a lot that I gave away over the years. Someone would die and I'd send the sketch off to his widow, that sort of thing." She stopped and caught her breath. "They weren't *all* geniuses, and I wasn't going about picking and choosing. But some were big names even then. Oh, was I starstruck. Now they're signed, almost all of them. That was my condition. And they didn't always want to sign, especially not with a quick sketch. But it was my price."

Yale was, if nothing else, intrigued. Nora might be a front for a clever forgery ring (stranger things had happened) or be outright delusional, but she herself hadn't been the victim of forgers. And in so many of these cases, that was what happened—you had to sit by while some millionaire learned the de Chirico he'd been showing off for years was an utter fake.

"They're insured?" he asked.

Debra cut in: "For not nearly enough." She sat with her teacup, not drinking, her glare leveled at the coffee table.

Nora said, "But can't you authenticate them yourself? At the museum?" And then she said, "Good heavens, look at that!" because outside it had started raining in sheets.

Yale spoke gently. "If museums were allowed to authenticate their own works, everyone would have a hundred Picassos. But listen, if we have reason to believe the pieces are what you say, we might be able to help *financially* with authentication. We can't pay for it directly, but maybe we could find another donor who could." He wasn't sure this was tenable, but it was worth saying for now.

Nora looked at him strangely. *"If they are what I say!"*

"I don't doubt you." He checked Debra's and Stanley's faces. They looked serious, not like they were just humoring this woman.

He said, "I'm trying to curb my excitement because this would be such an amazing boon, not just to the university but to the art world—and I don't want to get my heart broken here." It was the truth.

Cecily said something then, but Yale was busy wondering if this was the governing factor of his life: the fear of getting his heart broken. Or rather, the need to protect the remaining scraps of his heart, the ones torn smaller by every breakup, every failure, every funeral, every day on earth. Was this why a shrink would say he was with Charlie, out of all the men in Chicago? Yale might break Charlie's heart—he did it almost every day—but Charlie, for all his possessiveness, would never break Yale's.

The rain was trying to tear the whole house apart.

Stanley said, "Let's assume everything checks out. Can you guarantee these pieces will be displayed prominently? You wouldn't turn around and sell them?"

Yale assured him the works would be in regular rotation. That if the space expanded, they could be on permanent display.

"Now," Nora said, and she leaned in to look straight at Yale as if what she had to say next was the most important thing. "I wouldn't want you to play favorites. I want the whole collection displayed."

"That's not really up—"

"There are a couple of unknowns in there, and one in particular, Ranko Novak, I've hung onto his work for sentimental reasons. It's *good*, don't think it's some dreadful thing, but he's not a *name*. I don't want you displaying the Soutine and consigning Ranko to a closet." She pointed a finger at him. "Do you know Foujita?"

Yale was able to nod honestly. He did know a lot more about art than the average money guy, a huge asset. He had a joke now, a practiced line, about how he could have told his dad either that he was gay or that he was majoring in art, and he'd picked gay because it seemed like less trouble. In reality, during the whole ride home for sophomore winter break, Yale had silently rehearsed the news that he was switching from finance to art history—and then that night, his boyfriend had called and mistaken Yale's father's voice for Yale's ("I miss you, baby," he'd said, and Yale's father had said, "*How's* that?" and Marc, as was his wont, had elaborated), and so the rest of vacation had been devoted to that bombshell, to their mutual avoidance, their silent eating of leftover spaghetti. Yale had planned to tell his father about the professor he could do an independent study with next fall—about how he wasn't in love the same way with finance, about how with this degree, he could teach or write books or restore paintings or even work at an auction house. He'd planned to explain that it was Caravaggio's *Saint Jerome* that had sent vibrations down his arms, made the rest of the world fall away—Caravaggio's light, oddly, and not his famous shadows. But Marc's call ruined it; Yale would have been too humiliated to say that all now. Not just gay, but a gay art major. He went back to school in January and lied to his adviser, told her he'd had a change of heart. But between finance classes, he audited course after course, sitting in the backs of lecture halls illuminated only by slides of Manet or Goya or Joaquin Sorolla.

Nora said, "I'm *thrilled* you know him, because Stanley and Debra haven't the slightest clue. The instant Fiona mentioned you, I knew this was meant to be. I used to go visit Nico, you know. I saw that neighborhood, and those boys, and I can't tell you how much it reminded me—all my friends in Paris, we were foreigners. Flotsam and jetsam."

Yale wondered if Cecily had understood. He kept his hands still, didn't look her way.

"I'm not calling Nico's neighborhood Paris, don't get me wrong, but all those boys landing there from every direction, it was the same! We never knew it was a *movement* when I was young, but now they speak of it as the *École de Paris*, and what they really mean is all the riffraff that washed up there at the same time. Everyone born in some godforsaken shtetl, and then there they were in heaven."

Yale took the end of her sentence as a chance to change the subject. "I'd love to see the pieces," he said.

"Oh—" Here Nora gave a theatrical sigh. "Now, this is Debra's fault, isn't it? We were planning to go to the bank with her Polaroid, but it was missing something."

Debra said, "This is what happens when the gift shops all close for winter. I had film but no flash bar."

"I could find you one in Sturgeon Bay," Stanley said, and Debra didn't look pleased.

"Here's what we'll do," Nora said. "I'll send you some Polaroid shots in the mail. I know you can't tell much from a photo, but you'll have an idea."

Because the possibility of their all heading to the bank in the rain hadn't been raised, Yale didn't mention it himself. He didn't want Debra and Stanley to feel he was being too aggressive, didn't want them counseling Nora against him. His job was to win her trust, not finger the art. Yale said, "I'll send you photos of the gallery in exchange. And let me give you my address again, so the package will come straight to me." He glanced at Cecily, but she'd long since checked out. He handed a card to Nora and one to Stanley. "My private line is on there."

They left Stanley with the sheets of sample language for in-kind donations and general bequests and headed out the door umbrella-less. Cecily held her file folder over her head as they ran for the car; she didn't seem to care if it got soaked. Debra, who had seen them out, watched without waving.

"She was certainly enamored of *you*," Cecily said. She was trying to figure out the windshield wipers.

"We can work with that." He didn't want to explain about Nico, explain that the way Nora had taken to him had nothing to do with the gallery.

"What a disaster." The wipers blasted on, sending cascades of water down each side of the windshield.

"It was?"

"Tell me you were just humoring her."

"I'm not sure."

"Something about that woman and that house made you think her Modigliani is real?"

"I mean—actually, yes. I've come around. I think there's a decent chance."

"Well. Good luck to you. If you can get past that granddaughter. And the son, for that matter. When they make their wills this late, it's always contested. 'Oh, she was senile! The lawyer took advantage!' But good luck to you."

Cecily, he realized as she peeled out onto County Road ZZ, was a sore loser. It was probably what made her so good at her job—she was consumed by ambition the same way Charlie was. And he admired that in a person. Nico was the one who'd first introduced him to Charlie, and when Charlie had turned his back to greet someone who'd just arrived at the bar, Nico had whispered, "He's gonna be the first gay mayor. Twenty years." And the reason Charlie was so good at organizing people, lighting fires under them, getting his paper read, was that he took loss extremely hard. He absorbed failure by staying up till five in the morning, calling people and scribbling in notebooks until he had a new plan of action. It was hard to live with, but Yale couldn't imagine his own life anymore without the whirring clock of Charlie at its center.

Cecily said, "I wanted to take a pair of scissors and trim that man's eyebrows. The lawyer."

She was driving too fast for the rain. Instead of asking her to slow down, Yale said, "I'm famished." It was true; it was 3 p.m., and they hadn't eaten beyond their gas station snack.

They stopped at a restaurant that advertised a Friday fish fry and rooms upstairs. Inside they found mismatched tablecloths and a long wooden bar.

Cecily said, "Are we getting back on the road after this, or are we drinking our troubles away?"

Yale didn't even have to think about it. "I'm sure they have space." Tomorrow they could drive home in sunshine.

Cecily sat at the bar and ordered a martini; Yale asked for a beer and said he'd be right back. There was no pay phone in the lobby, but the innkeeper let him use the house phone.

Charlie picked up after ten rings.

Yale said, "We're definitely staying overnight," and Charlie said, "Where are you again?"

"Wisconsin. The spiky part."

"Who are you with?"

"Jesus, Charlie. A woman who looks like Princess Diana's older sister."

Charlie said, "Okay. I miss you. You've done too much vanishing lately."

"That's deeply ironic."

"Listen, I'm going out to Niles tonight." Yale had lost track of Charlie's protests, but he believed this one was about a bar the police kept targeting. Yale had let him know, when they first got together, that he'd never be joining in; his nervous system was fragile enough without the threat of billy clubs and tear gas thrown in.

He said, "Be safe."

"I'd look great with a broken nose. Admit it."

Back in the dining room, the bartender was telling Cecily how Al Capone used to stay here, how the gangster's men would drive carloads of liquor across the frozen lake. Cecily gulped down the last of her martini, and the bartender chuckled. "I make 'em good," he said. "Now I do a cherry one, too, call it the Door County Special. You care to give that a try?" Yes, she did.

They sat there long enough that the room slowly filled. Families and farmers and lingering vacationers. Cecily was drunk, and she picked at the potpie she'd ordered, said it was too greasy. Yale offered her some of his fish and chips, but she declined. When she ordered herself a third martini, Yale pointedly asked for more bread.

She said, "I don't need *bread*. What I need is an avocado with some cottage cheese. That's the *diet* food. Have you ever had avocado?"

"Yes."

"Of course you have. I mean, not to imply."

"I'm not sure what that could possibly imply." He glanced around, but no one was listening.

"*You* know. You guys are more urbane. Wait, urban, or urbane? Urbane. But listen." She rested two fingers on his thigh, close to the fold his khakis made near his crotch. "What I want to know is, don't you ever have fun anymore?"

Yale was baffled. The bartender, passing, winked. He supposed they made a believable couple, even if she was several years older than him. Waspy career woman and her young Jewish boyfriend. He whispered, hoping she'd follow suit. "Are you talking about me personally, or all gay men?"

"*See?* You *are* gay!" Not too loudly, thank God. She didn't move her hand; maybe it wasn't a sexual move after all.

"Yes."

"But what I was saying was, I was saying how gay men—I mean, I'm sorry for assuming, but I assumed, and I was *right*— how gay men used to have more fun than anyone. You used to make me jealous. And now you're all getting so serious and staying home because of this stupid *disease*. Someone took me to the Baton Show once. The Baton Club? *You* know. And it was amazing."

There was still no one listening. A toddler pitched a fit over by the window, throwing her grilled cheese on the floor. Yale said, "I'd say there was a good ten years where we had a lot of fun. Look, if you know people who are toning things down, I'm glad. Not everyone is."

Cecily pressed with her fingers, leaned in. He worried she'd fall off her stool. "But don't you *miss* having fun?"

He carefully removed her hand and set it on her own lap. "I think we have different ideas of fun."

She looked hurt, but recovered quickly. She whispered. "What I'm saying is, I have some C-O-K-E in my purse." She pointed to the pale yellow bag under her barstool.

"You have what?" He couldn't have heard right. She hadn't even gotten the bong joke.

"C-O-C-A-I-N-E. When we go upstairs, we could have a party."

Yale had quite a few simultaneous thoughts, chief among them the fact that Cecily would be horrified in the morning by how she'd acted. He was so embarrassed for her that he wanted to say yes, to snort coke right here off the bar. But lately his heart couldn't handle more than one coffee a day. He hadn't so much as smoked pot in a year.

He looked at her as kindly as he could and said, "We're going to get you a big glass of water, and you're going to eat some bread. You can sleep as late as you want, and when you feel ready I'll drive the whole way back."

"Oh, you think I'm *drunk*."

"Yes."

"I'm actually fine."

He slid the bread toward her, and the water.

Cecily might take it out on him, try to screw him over on future Brigg bequests—but really, no, he had dirt on her now. He wouldn't blackmail her, nothing like that, but this might put them on a more equal footing.

He said, "When you wake up, don't worry about this. It's been a good trip, right?"

"Sure," she said. "For you."

In the morning, Yale ordered pancakes and coffee. He'd written Cecily a note last night, in case she couldn't remember the plan, and propped it on her dresser when he saw her to her room: *I'll be downstairs whenever you're ready.*

He read the *Door County Advocate* and the *Tribune*, and in the latter he found two articles to mention to Charlie: one on the proposed anti-Happy Hour legislation, the other an editorial on Congress's paltry AIDS spending. A minor miracle that people were still talking about it, that the *Trib* was giving it space. Charlie had been right; he'd said what they needed was one big celebrity death. And *poof*, there went Rock Hudson, without the courage to leave the closet even on his deathbed, and finally, four years into the crisis, there was a glimmer of something out there. Not enough, though. Charlie had once sworn that if Reagan ever deigned to give a speech about AIDS, he'd donate five dollars to the Republicans. ("And in the memo line," Charlie said, "I'm gonna write *I licked the envelope with my big gay tongue.*") But at least now Yale was overhearing the word on the El. He'd heard two teenagers joking about it in a hotel lobby where he went to pick up a donor. ("How do you turn a fruit into a vegetable?") He'd heard a woman ask another woman if she should keep going to her gay hairdresser. Ridiculous, but better than feeling like you lived in some alternate universe where no one could hear you calling for help. Now it was like people could hear and just didn't care. But wasn't that progress?

Cecily finally showed up at 10:30, crisply dressed in slacks and a sweater, makeup and hair done. She said, "It's much nicer out!"

"You feel okay?"

"I'm fabulous! I have to tell you, I'm not even hung over. I really wasn't drunk. It was sweet of you to worry."

He drove, Cecily leaning her head against the passenger window. He tried to avoid bumps, to take the curves softly. They didn't talk much, except to discuss strategy if the art turned out to be real. Yale would deal with Nora and her family until the time came for the actual bequest, when Cecily would step back in if needed.

Yale glanced at the yellow purse at Cecily's feet, which he now knew contained a baggie of cocaine—unless she'd used it up this morning, which it didn't appear she had. If they got pulled over, if a cop searched the car, they'd both be arrested. He drove even slower.

He reached into his blazer pocket and pulled out the M&Ms. He offered them to Cecily, and she took just one.

Cecily said, "You knew her nephew."

"Her grandnephew. He was my first real friend in the city."

She said, "I hope that doesn't cloud your judgment."

2015

Fiona wasn't aware that she had any preconceptions about the detective until they were face to face with him, she and Serge, across a round table at Café Bonaparte. What she'd pictured, she realized, looking at this small, quiet man, was a bumbling person in a trench coat, a sweaty former gendarme who'd turned out to be a genius. But Arnaud ("You can call me Arnold," he offered in perfect British English, as if she couldn't handle a simple *O* sound) was like a freshly sharpened pencil, a pointed nose the primary feature of his small, dark face. Not that she needed a movie detective. This wasn't a movie case. If Claire was really in Paris, she shouldn't be hard to find. Convincing her to meet was another matter.

Arnaud accepted the check she handed him, folded it into his breast pocket. He hunched over his fruit salad, ate, asked his questions quickly.

"How is her French? Your daughter's?"

Fiona looked at her cheese omelet; she'd been so hungry earlier, but now she couldn't bring herself to take the first bite. "She studied it in high school."

"Lycée," Serge clarified. Serge, having driven Fiona there (she'd clung to his waist with her eyes closed), had stuck around and ordered an espresso and now seemed to feel the need to justify his presence.

When Claire was in sixth grade, Fiona had tried the same tack her mother had taken years before: "You're part Cuban, you know. Don't you think Spanish—" and Claire had said, "I'm French too. And I share ninety-nine percent of my DNA with a mouse. Do I need to learn to *squeak*?"

Fiona continued now: "But I don't know how long she's been here. Three years, possibly."

"Three years is when she left the cult?"

"Yes," Fiona said, "but—" and she didn't know how to finish. Something about how you never really leave a cult. How there was the cult *itself*, and then there was Claire's own private cult, her devotion to Kurt Pearce. One leader and one follower.

"And now you believe she's in Paris."

"Well—" And suddenly she couldn't remember why she'd been so convinced the video showed Paris. Was the Eiffel Tower in the background? No, but—it was a video *about* Paris. She was so tired. When she turned her head, it took her vision a second to catch up. She said, "You saw the video?" She'd sent him the link when they first communicated earlier this week.

He nodded, pulled a slim laptop from the bag at his feet and, in one fluid motion, opened it and clicked to start the video. That a French café would have Wi-Fi seemed wrong. In her mind, Paris was always 1920. It was always Aunt Nora's Paris, all tragic love and tubercular artists.

"The three-minute mark," she said. It was ten days ago that Claire's college roommate Lina had emailed a YouTube link and a cautious note: "*Someone sent me this,*" she wrote, "*wondering if that could be Claire, three minutes in. I can't tell—do you suppose?*" And Fiona's stupid computer hadn't been able to speed forward, so she'd sat through seven minutes of "family friendly travel tips" for the upper middle class tourist looking to drag children to France. Carousels, hot chocolate at Angelina, little boats on the pond in the Jardin du Luxembourg. And then the pixie-cut host began walking backward on a bridge, talking about the artists "capturing the scene for you to bring home." And there, behind her—and here, again, on Arnaud's screen—was a woman on a folding stool, squinting at a small canvas, daubing a paintbrush as if she'd been directed to. Did it look like Claire? Yes. But a bit heavier, a stylish scarf knotted around her hair. "Who knows?" the host chirped. "They might even have their own *enfants* in tow!" This was in reference to the little girl, a toddler really, playing with some small red toy by the woman's feet.

"This is her?" Arnaud said, and tapped Claire's face on the screen.

"Yes." It did no good to say that she was *almost* sure, that her nightmares had been full of women on bridges who turned to show rotted faces, animal faces, faces that just weren't Claire's. If he was going to look for her, Fiona wanted him to believe he'd find her.

"The scarf doesn't look religious."

"No, but the cult didn't do that anyway."

He said, "I know this bridge."

"Is it the Pont des Arts?"

"What? No, no. Pont de l'Archevêché. Right by Notre Dame. You see the cars passing? No cars on Pont des Arts."

It must have been obvious that she wanted to jump up, to steal Serge's motorbike and drive there recklessly.

"It's unusual for an artist to set up on this bridge. I suspect"— he looked at Serge as if for confirmation—"she was put there for the film."

Fiona said, "But she might be in that neighborhood. Or the filmmakers might know her!"

Arnaud nodded gravely. "Small American production company, based in Seattle. Could she be living there? She could be

75

part of the film crew and they asked her to pose on the bridge."

And although this was a possibility—Claire *did* love film-making—it was one Fiona could deal with later. So she said, "It's much more likely that she's painting than working on films. Her cult—they were antitechnology. I don't know."

"But she left the cult." Arnaud closed his laptop and picked up his fork, so Fiona figured she was meant to give the full story now, the one she'd only roughly sketched in her emails.

"I actually introduced her to this guy," she said. "Kurt. He's older, sort of a family friend. He'd be forty-one now."

"I have the photos," Arnaud said, strawberry at his lips.

"I didn't mean for them to get involved, it's just that she was spending the summer in Colorado to wait tables and explore, and he was living there. This was 2011, right after her freshman year of college. And before I know it, she's in *love*, and then she isn't going back to school in the fall, she's going to stay in Boulder and work on some kind of ranch. And then I don't hear from her, and I don't hear from her, there's no phone there, no Internet, just mail, and finally I write and tell her I'm coming to visit, and she says I can't. Which is when I panic."

Not that it was the first time Claire had shut her out. For an entire semester of high school, she wouldn't speak to either parent. And one day, back when Fiona and Damian first split—Claire was nine—she ran away to the church down the street. Claire hadn't set foot in a church at that point outside of one wedding, but Fiona had always told her that if she ever needed help in an emergency, she could go to a church and ask. By the time Claire went missing, though, Fiona had forgotten she'd said it.

When the secretary at the Episcopal church finally called, Claire had been missing for five hours, and Fiona and Damian had been combing the streets with a police officer. It was a week after 9/11, and people still watched police cruisers from the sidewalks with concern. Oddly, it was a comfort—that her crisis was part of the general trauma. They found Claire in the church office, drinking chocolate milk and sitting with two women who positively glared at Fiona and Damian. What Claire had told these women about them, about the divorce, Fiona never knew. She handed the women a twenty and grabbed Claire's arm and marched her out while the officer and Damian stayed behind to ask questions.

It was only when Claire was in bed that night that Fiona looked at Damian, sitting there on the sofa that used to be his, too, and said, "Why do you suppose she ran away?" She kept her voice pleasant, but really she already had an answer.

He laughed and said, "Maybe it's genetic. I mean, why did you and your brother run away?"

"I *left home*," she said, "when I was eighteen. And Nico was kicked out, and you don't ever get to mention him again."

Damian raised his hands in surrender, if not apology.

"And my parents," she said, "my mom showed my brother's sketchbook to the *priest*. It was—Okay, I'm not talking about this to you. *Do you think it's possible*, Damian, that she overheard what you said?"

And Damian looked at the carpet instead of at her, because of course that's what had happened. The night before, after he'd dropped Claire off, he'd stayed to talk—to fight, really—and Claire hadn't been asleep yet when he shouted at Fiona, something he hardly ever did. It had been about the divorced man Fiona had been sleeping with, or, more specifically, about the fact that this man had two children, that Fiona had spent a weekend with them in Michigan that summer. About how it was bad enough that she'd cheated on *him*, but was she trying to replace their whole family?

"I'll talk to her," Damian said. And, stupidly, she'd let him be the one to go into Claire's bedroom. Maybe because he was the only one who could take it back, being the one who'd said it. She should have gone in herself. Why hadn't she?

Fiona didn't relay this all to Arnaud, but she told him about her trip to Boulder in 2011. It was winter, long enough after Claire hadn't returned to school that, in retrospect, her own delay was inexcusable. At the time it had seemed right, though—giving Claire her space. Damian was living in Portland by then, and she only spoke to him when they were in crisis mode over Claire. They finally talked in early January about how neither of them ever heard a word, how Claire had cashed the check Damian and his new wife had sent for Christmas, but never wrote to thank him. Worrying alone, Fiona had been able to tell herself this was just how Claire was, that she needed time, needed to realize on her own that she missed school. But listening to Damian, who never panicked, say that he didn't like this, that something felt wrong, it suddenly became clear it *was* wrong. Fiona flew out the next week. She rented a car in Denver and drove past Boulder, following her GPS.

It clearly wasn't the right address. This wasn't a ranch. A narrow, uneven road wound through woods to some sort of discount campground—trailers and cottages around a rundown yellow house, no lake or other natural attraction to explain their convergence.

Fiona wanted to leave, look things up on a proper map, figure out where the ranch really was, but she couldn't take off without knocking, without checking that her daughter wasn't being held captive inside. She called Damian just so there would be a witness if something horrible happened, and—with him on the line, the phone clutched to her chest—she approached the door.

"The man who answered," she told Arnaud now, "he was dressed like they do. I didn't understand at the time. Beard, long hair, clogs. They look a lot like hippies, especially the men." The men came off better than the poor women, who wore long sleeves, long dresses, no makeup.

"So even when it turned out Claire was there, when they called her to the door, that's what I thought it was—a hippie commune. I guess they don't really have those anymore."

She told him how Claire first backed up when she saw her, then hugged her like you might hug an ex you'd run into when you were both on dates with other people. Damian was still on the line, but Fiona couldn't stop to tell him everything that was happening. Claire grabbed a coat and came out to talk on the driveway, and soon Kurt joined, stood beside her like a bodyguard.

"He seemed so possessive," she said, "his hand on her back." How had Fiona forgotten his height? She'd been struck by it the first time she'd seen him grown, towering above his own mother. He must have been six foot five, and now he was paunchy too. His face was leathery from the sun and wind, and his blond hair brushed his shoulders.

"They didn't lie about what the place was, exactly. They said it was a planned community, and they gave me the name Hosanna Collective, which—well, you can tell right away it's not just an organic farm, right?"

Fiona didn't remember the details of the conversation. It was confusing and she was upset, and although she asked them about these people they were living with, she was more concerned with Claire's demeanor, her dull eyes and twitching foot, than with the answers. She remembered saying, lamely, "There are churches you can explore in Chicago too," and Kurt shaking his head at her. "The modern Christian church is the Whore of Babylon," he said.

Claire wouldn't leave, wouldn't even get in the car with her to have dinner in town, wouldn't take the phone to speak to her father, wouldn't step away from Kurt Pearce.

Kurt said, "This really is an intrusion." Calmly, as if he were the voice of reason here.

And Claire said, "Mom, we're fine. You didn't worry about me at college, and I was *miserable* at college. I'm much happier here."

"I did worry about you at college. But at least I knew what was going on there."

"No, you didn't." Fiona wasn't sure which fact Claire was refuting. Three adults and a child looked down at them from the porch of the big house, waiting.

Fiona knew better than to force the issue, to elbow her way in the door. She said, "I'll come back in the morning. I'll bring doughnuts."

"Please don't."

When Fiona returned the next day, a wooden barricade blocked the end of the long driveway. A man with a waist-length ponytail leaned against it, and as Fiona drove up, he made a "turn around" sign with one finger in the air. And she did, because Damian was already on a plane, and it was better to come back here with him, anyway.

Over the next insomniac week, asking around Boulder and scouring the Internet, the two of them discovered the things Fiona was now telling Arnaud: The Hosanna Collective was the small and restrictive offshoot of an already restrictive parent cult from Denver. It was ostensibly Judeo-Christian, but also astrological, vegetarian, antitechnology, male-dominated. They believed that the church needed to return to a pure state described in certain chapters of the book of Acts, that everything since Paul had been corruption. They called Jesus "Yeshua" and celebrated no holidays but Easter. No money of their own, the communal life made possible by the near-constant labor of the women and children. The men sold honey and salad dressing at farmers' markets, and did occasional construction work in town, contributing all their wages to the group.

Fiona and Damian went to the police, but there was nothing illegal going on. Damian reminded her of what she already knew: The more they chased Claire, the more she would shut them out. They tried once more in person, this time approaching the compound in the squad car of a sympathetic police officer—Fiona was so sure that Damian, too, was remembering their desperate ride around Chicago nine years back that she didn't need to mention it—but the same man who'd been at the barricade came out and unleashed an impressive string of legal language at the cop. And no, there was no warrant.

Fiona and Damian sat at a bar in the Denver airport with bags under their eyes, both of them crying, then stopping, then crying. They must have looked, to other travelers, like lovers parting for the last time. He with a wedding ring, she without. Fiona said, "We should stay." But there were more productive ways to spend their time and money. Damian would talk to lawyers. Fiona would contact Claire's high school and college friends, even offer to fly them out. She'd track down Cecily Pearce and see if she might talk some sense into her son.

Arnaud nodded along to all this but didn't write it down. Fiona worried he was going to ask why she hadn't refused to leave Boulder, why she hadn't battered down the door. It was because she didn't believe Claire could really stay long with those people. And because on some level, she wanted her daughter to learn something the hard way, and from someone other than her. For once, she wanted Claire to crawl home hurt, not run *away* from Fiona claiming she'd been gravely wounded. At least, this was what Fiona had worked out since then with her therapist. But maybe it was more complicated. Something about being done with unwinnable battles. After the bloodbath of her twenties, after everyone she loved had died or left her. After her love itself became poison.

Fiona wrote letters almost every day, saying Claire could always come home, that there would be no judgment. After a few weeks, the letters started returning, unopened.

And then when nearly a year had passed—a year of talking to cops and lawyers and some people from postcult support groups— they went back together, Damian and Fiona. They brought along a bodyguard they'd hired in Boulder. No squad car, no police. They weren't planning to kidnap her, just insist on a conversation. But Claire and Kurt, they were informed by the eczema-covered woman who answered the door, had left a month ago. No, she had no clue where; no one did.

Damian went to the Boulder Farmers Market, where some of the Hosanna men had a stand, and told them, casually, that he'd worked out a trade last time with a guy named Kurt. Was Kurt here today, by any chance? "Brother Kurt's not around anymore," one of them said. Another rolled his eyes.

And Fiona thought, *Well, at least they got out. Even if she's still with him.* She thought maybe she'd hear from Claire soon. She didn't. They hired a PI in Chicago, and he gladly took their money but turned up nothing. They looked into a missing persons report, but an adult who simply didn't want to be in touch with you was not missing.

Instead of asking why Fiona hadn't done more, Arnaud asked, "Was this typical of your daughter? To latch onto different religions?"

"No," Fiona said. "That was the oddest part. She was always a rebel. She quit Girl Scouts, she quit orchestra, she wouldn't date anyone longer than a month or two. Until Kurt."

"Does she have a reason to avoid you?"

Fiona stuck her fork into her omelet and pulled it out, watched the cheese ooze from the four holes. "We've had our issues, but there was no big fight." She could have gone into more detail about their head-butting, about how Claire was always closer to her father but then, after the divorce, was close to no one, about the guilt and second-guessing Fiona lived with every day—but it would only distract from the main point. She said, "Some people are just born difficult. That's a hard thing to say."

She didn't feel great. She was thirsty, but the water they'd given her was sparkling, which she hated. She took a tiny sip and it was worse than the thirst.

"Does the boyfriend hit?" This was from Serge, and although it was a legitimate question, Fiona resented the intrusion into Arnaud's line of reasoning.

"I don't think so. Some of the stories we found online, about the Hosanna—it sounded like they hit their *children*. For discipline. And I'm sure it went beyond that. But I've known Kurt a long time. Since he was a kid. He's good with animals, you know? I don't think you can hit women and be good with animals. Animals would sense it."

Arnaud nodded slowly. "Let's assume she left the cult when she discovered she was pregnant."

Fiona was impressed. She and Damian had come to a similar conclusion, but only days after she'd found the video, after they'd stayed up past midnight drinking wine in two different cities, planning and theorizing over the phone. The best they'd gotten along in fifteen years, but who cared about that now? Occasionally she'd hear Damian's wife in the background, and then he'd say, *Karen thinks we should do X*, but it was never anything helpful.

Karen had just been diagnosed with breast cancer, a treatable kind, and was starting radiation next week—which, along with his class schedule, was the reason Damian wasn't here too.

Arnaud said, "And the boyfriend's family? Have they heard from him?"

She said, "I only know his mother. She doesn't really—she doesn't want anything to do with him."

Her chest was tight, and her head was filling with gray noise. She felt Serge's hand on her arm and realized she was closer to her omelet than she should have been. She had fallen forward.

"She flew just this morning," Serge was saying.

Arnaud said, "She hasn't eaten her food."

"I'll take her home."

"I can hear you," she said. "I'm right here."

"I bring my motorbike around."

"No!" she said. "We're not done!"

Arnaud folded his napkin into a neat triangle, tucked it under the rim of his plate. "But we are. Now what I do is look."

1985

No one wanted to do much in the weeks after Nico's memorial. Whoever you called was busy taking food to Terrence's place, or you yourself were taking food to Terrence. Or people were sick, just regular sick, with coughs brought on by the drop in temperature. Guys with families flew home for Thanksgiving to play straight for nieces and nephews, to assure their grandparents they were dating, no one special, a few nice girls. To assure their fathers, who had cornered them in various garages and hallways, that no, they weren't going to catch this new disease. Charlie and his mother, being British, had no investment in the holiday, despite Yale's protests that it was a day for immigrants. British immigrants, in particular! Yale wound up cooking Cornish game hens for himself and Charlie, plus Asher Glass and Terrence and Fiona. Teddy and Julian would drop by for dessert.

Asher arrived first, and after he handed over the loaf of bread he'd baked (still warm, wrapped in a towel), he shoved a manila envelope at Yale. "Don't let me force this on them till the end of the night," he said. "Keep it from me. Not till there's coffee in my hand, okay?" Yale didn't understand, but he stuck the envelope on top of the refrigerator, found a serrated knife for the bread. Asher had a New York accent, and the way he pronounced certain words—*coffee*, for instance—made Yale want to mouth them in his wake.

Charlie poured a gin and tonic for Asher without asking. "You really pulled the plug," he said. "No going back?" The Howard Brown clinic, where they both were on the board, had finally, after much debate, decided that next month it would start offering the HTLV-III test, the one doctors had been giving since the spring. Asher had quit, vocally. According to Charlie, he'd stabbed a ballpoint pen into the table as he made a point, and the thing had burst, so that when Asher finally stormed out of the board meeting it was with blue hands.

Yale had harbored a crush, an occasionally overwhelming one, on Asher for years. It was quite specific: It would flare up mostly when Asher was angry about something, when his voice grew stentorian. (The most ridiculous of Yale's first loves was Clarence Darrow, as portrayed in *Inherit the Wind*, which he'd read in tenth grade. He'd avoided speaking in class for two whole weeks, terrified his cheeks would redden if he tried to discuss the play.) Funny, because when Charlie got similarly agitated, Yale wanted to stuff his own ears with cotton. And his attraction would flare up when Asher's dark hair got shaggy, which it was right now, making him look like a young, unkempt Marlon Brando. Stockier and clumsier, but still.

Asher ran his law practice out of his own apartment on Aldine, and what had started out as housing equality work had quickly turned into wills and insurance battles. He was a daytime friend, not someone to hit the bars with at night. His love life, in fact, was a mystery, and Yale could never figure out if Asher would approach sex with the same intensity with which he approached his work, or if, having spent all his passion on the day's battles, he'd rather just call an escort once a week. He'd been talking a lot lately about the difference between activism and advocacy, and Yale couldn't remember which Asher was in favor of, or if he wanted everyone to do both. He had shoulders like barrels, and his eyelashes were long and dark, and Yale required a valiant effort not to stare at his lips when he talked.

Asher's voice had already started to boom, loud enough that Yale worried Terrence might hear if someone had let him in downstairs and he was already out in the hallway. "Look. We all have a death sentence. Right? You and me, we don't know what that is. It's a day, it's fifty years. You wanna narrow the range? You wanna freak yourself out? That's all the test gives you. I mean, show me the line for the miracle cure and I'll take the damn test, I'll make everyone else take it too. Meanwhile, what? You want to end up in a government database?"

Charlie said, "You know where I stand."

"I do, and *listen*." Asher's hands were flying, gin spilling down the side of his glass. Yale leaned back against the sink, watched those hands like a fireworks show. "If your priority is safe sex, the test isn't helping. Half these guys get a false sense of security, the other half know they're dying. They're depressed, they get drunk, and what the hell do you think they do? They don't run out to the rubber store."

Charlie was still laughing over "rubber store," riffing about Helmet Hut and Trojans R Us, when Terrence and Fiona buzzed up. In the time it took them to get upstairs, Asher cleared his throat and deftly turned his ranting to the opinion that there was no decent Chinese food in Chicago. Yale argued that you just had to go to Chinatown and be willing to eat chicken feet.

Terrence and Fiona walked in, arm in arm.

Terrence handed Charlie a bottle of wine and said, in his whitest voice, "The wife and I got stuck in the *worst* traffic, driving in from Sheboygan. Thank God we're fixing up that infrastructure with the trickle-down and whatnot, God bless the USA."

They seemed to be doing well, both of Nico's bereaved, but what could you tell from the outside? Fiona's blonde curls always lent her a vibrancy, an alertness, that compensated for any fatigue. And Terrence—he looked thin, but you'd never know he was sick if it weren't for the test. And what good had the test done, really? Maybe he was drinking less. Maybe he was getting more sleep. Which was something.

"That envelope," Asher whispered to Yale. "Not till coffee."

Yale was antsy all night, unable to focus. It was partly that it was late November—he always grew agitated as the sun grayed its way into hibernation—and maybe it was partly Asher's presence, too, although usually that was a pleasant kind of agitation. Maybe it was the fact that Teddy would show up later, and this was the first time he'd seen Teddy since Nico's memorial, when his phantom self had vanished upstairs with Teddy's phantom self.

And beneath all that was the fact that he was still waiting for Nora's Polaroids to arrive, that as soon as he'd gotten excited about this project, it had stalled out. He'd written her a nice note, sent the lawyer a carbon copy. Then separately, as promised, he sent some photos of the gallery space. And heard nothing. He'd messed up; he'd assumed her number was in the file, and now Cecily said she'd never had it, that they'd communicated entirely by mail. Information didn't have it either. He wrote to Nora's lawyer, asking if he'd heard from her, suggesting that he'd love her number. Stanley wrote back that he'd learned better than to bother Nora, but she was sure to be in touch. No number. Yale called Stanley, whose phone was on his letterhead, but the secretary said that since he was semiretired, he only worked some days, and no, she couldn't predict which days, but she'd take a message. Yale called again, and she said she'd repeat the message. He was afraid of seeming pushy, of the lawyer telling Nora he had a bad feeling about those Northwestern folks.

And so, over the main course, while everyone else debated Live Aid, with which Asher had some arcane quibble, Yale brought Nora up with Fiona.

"Isn't she *incredible*?" Fiona said. "I want to be her when I grow up. She had affairs with so many artists! Seriously."

88

"You could run out and have sex with artists right now."

"Oh, you know what I *mean*. She had this *life*, you know? She was the only one in the whole family who didn't shut out Nico. She sent him a check for fifty dollars every month." Nico hadn't even needed to come out to her, Fiona said; Nora had known all along. But no, Fiona didn't have her number. She'd seen her at a family wedding up in Wisconsin in August, and as they sat there talking about art, about Paris, that's when Fiona had told her about Yale's position, told Nora she should write to him soon. Nora had called *her*, she said, to say how much she liked Yale. "And she must *love* you," she said, "because it's the only time she's *ever* called me." Maybe her father would have the number. She promised she'd try to get it. Yale knew better than to expect follow-through.

Down the table, Terrence was talking about his new meditation practice, his crystals, his stress-relief cassettes, and Asher was laughing, shaking his head. "Listen," Terrence said, "you keep figuring out how to save the world. I'm gonna work on buying myself a few extra months. If I have to *eat* the damn crystals, I'll do it."

Asher said, "I can tell you a couple other places you can put your crystals."

Fiona punched his arm, hard enough that Asher winced. She told him to behave.

Fiona was the one who helped Yale clear the dishes, or at least held open the swinging door that separated the tiny kitchen from the apartment's main room. The others migrated to the living room so Terrence could catch the second half of the Cowboys game.

Once the water was running, Yale lowered his voice. "Hey, did you tell Charlie I went upstairs with Teddy? After the memorial?"

"Oh! Oh God, Yale, I've been meaning to apologize." She backed up to the counter and launched herself up to sit there, her feet dangling. "You know how you get surer of things when you're drunk? I was drunk, and he couldn't find you, and I'd seen you

89

go upstairs, and someone else said they'd seen Teddy go upstairs, and I kept saying, 'Yale is upstairs with Teddy,' because I thought I was being helpful. I guess I wasn't."

"I thought so," Yale said. "That's what I thought. Teddy wasn't even there. He left when the slide show started."

"Oh Yale, I didn't mean to make a problem. I heard later that Charlie was—oh, God."

"It doesn't matter," he said. "It's the least important thing about that night."

Yale scraped the plates while Fiona joined everyone in the living room. If he didn't do it now, while Charlie was busy entertaining and pretending to understand American football, then Charlie would insist on doing every dish.

When Yale finally walked into the living room, the conversation abruptly stopped. "What?" he said.

Charlie said, "I'll tell you later."

"No, what?"

"Cowboys are winning," Terrence said.

Asher tried to drink from his glass, but his glass was empty.

"Just tell him," Fiona said.

Charlie patted the couch, bit his lip, stared at the TV. "I thought I saw your mum."

"Oh."

"I mean, I did see her. She was a nurse, in—it was a Tylenol advert. She said some stuff. Not much."

Asher said, "We didn't know your mom was a movie star."

He felt dizzy. "She's not."

This hadn't happened in a couple of years, this kind of ambush. There was a commercial for Folgers Crystals a while back, in which she was a waitress. She'd been a receptionist for an episode of *Simon & Simon*. He hated it—which Charlie must have told them, or why were they looking at him like that?—hated, on a

90

gut level, the humiliation of being afforded only the same two-second shots of his mother that the entire rest of the country was given. Hated that he needed to watch, that he couldn't look away in indifference. Hated that he'd missed seeing her just now, hated that they'd all seen her without him, hated that they were pitying him, hated that he hated it all so much.

When Yale was seven his father had taken him to see *Breakfast at Tiffany's*—and Yale, knowing his mother was an actress, and that actresses disguised themselves for their roles, became convinced that his mother was the one playing Holly Golightly. He wanted her to be the one singing "Moon River," which seemed like just the sort of song his mother might sing to him if she were still around. He soon outgrew the fantasy, but for years, when he had trouble sleeping, he'd imagine Audrey Hepburn singing to him.

He said, "It's nice to know she's alive."

He grabbed his legal pad from the shelf under the coffee table. He'd been drafting a letter for the Annual Fund that morning. He snatched up a pen and started circling things that didn't need circling.

Fiona said, "Are you okay?"

He nodded, and as the game came back on, Charlie twisted one of Yale's curls around his finger. Asher picked up the *TV Guide* and flipped through it as if they might change the channel at any moment.

And then the door buzzer sounded, thank God.

Teddy was alone. "Julian has as *emergency rehearsal*, whatever that means," he said. "He sends his regrets. Oh my god, it smells *amazing*." Teddy always talked like he'd just done a speedball, but it was just the way he was.

"So he's not coming at all?" Charlie said. "What did he say, exactly?"

Terrence said, "I hope this 'emergency rehearsal' is smoking hot."

Teddy acted normally, throwing his coat on the back of the couch, hugging everyone. Well, sure. He didn't know anything odd had happened the night of the memorial. It was like having a sex dream about someone, then seeing him the next day. You felt like he *had* to know; he'd been right there in the dream, so how could things ever be the same between you again? But they always were.

Teddy had golden waves cut close to his head. The fact that his skin was always golden-tan, even in the middle of winter, made him look like a bronze statue, or like some drawing of Hermes from a children's book of myths. There was a scar in the middle of his upper lip from a cleft palate in infancy, a faint line that might have marred his face but instead made him irresistible to just about anyone in the market for a twink. Which Yale never had been. Teddy was built like an adolescent, five foot four at most.

Charlie busied himself serving the trifle he'd made, avoided looking at either Teddy or Yale. He seemed distracted; he miscounted the bowls, and then he left the serving spoon in the kitchen. Yale wanted to stop him, massage his neck, but he didn't want to draw attention to Charlie's discomfort. He didn't even want to point it out to Charlie himself, who swore he understood now, one hundred percent, that nothing had happened at the memorial.

The trifle was one of Charlie's only recipes, and he prided himself on supersaturating the thing with sherry. Yale had learned to count each serving as a drink.

"Feef," Teddy said to Fiona when they'd dug in, "are you old enough for this stuff?"

She put on an affronted face. "I am fully twenty-one," she said. "As of September third."

"You didn't invite me to your party!"

"It was only for nice people."

92

Yale imagined she hadn't celebrated at all, in the throes of that wretched summer. Her twentieth had been a dance party at Nico's with strobe lights. This one she'd probably spent in a waiting room.

Teddy said, "I've only got ten minutes. I'm having a whole dinner at my thesis adviser's."

Asher said, "This is your *appetizer*?"

Teddy stuck the spoon in his mouth upside down, pulled it out dramatically by way of answer. He said, "It's my palate cleanser! I already ate at my mom's. So how's everyone feeling about the Howard Brown thing?" And then, when there was awkward silence, "They're doing testing."

"I'm sure they know," Terrence said.

"I mean, you know I'm still anti-test, but maybe these ones can really be anonymous. I mean, if I want *real* anonymity, I'm gonna get tested in Cleveland or something."

Fiona said, "Teddy, it's Thanksgiving. We shouldn't—"

Asher said, "Sure, they'll anonymously give everyone a false sense of security."

Terrence was looking down at his trifle, smoothing the whipped cream flat.

Charlie said, "Asher wants everyone to walk around dying of ulcers instead. Drinking themselves to death over stress." Yale kicked him under the table. But Charlie kept talking. "Does this mean you'll get tested now?"

"Hell no. I don't even think the tests *work*. How do we know they aren't all part of the same government conspiracy that cooked up the whole virus to begin with? I'm just saying that—"

"*Stop!*" Fiona slammed her glass onto the table.

Teddy opened his mouth, decided better.

Terrence said, "So. Hey, what do you call a black guy who studies rocks?"

Fiona was the only one who made any noise, a startled giggle. Then she said, "I don't know, what?"

"A geologist, you bunch of racists."

After the laughter, the conversation, thank God, split into three frivolous directions.

Yale got up to put a new record on.

Teddy made his excuses and grabbed his jacket and was gone.

"Is it time for coffee?" Yale asked. He directed it at Asher, because he was really asking about the envelope. Asher nodded and stood and fetched it off the refrigerator, but no one moved toward the coffeepot.

"Let's make this festive," Asher said. "Let's have a little ceremony." He pulled out the papers, asked Charlie for a pen.

Terrence said to Fiona, "Shall I get down on one knee?"

Yale looked at Charlie to see if he knew what was going on. Charlie mouthed, "Power of attorney."

It made sense. Nico's parents had botched his medical care horribly—moved him to a hospital that didn't even want him there—and then they'd claimed the funeral too. Terrence's family, Yale understood, wasn't one he'd want making his medical decisions. Terrence hadn't seen his mother in years, hadn't been back to his childhood home in Morgan Park, on the South Side, since he graduated high school. Still, it seemed a lot to put on Fiona. She was just a kid.

"We've got the limitations stuff filled in, but look that over. And you need to initial one of these three," Asher said, pointing. He took the cap off a pen and handed it to Terrence.

"I want the first one, right? *I do not want my life prolonged?*"

Asher cleared his throat. "That's what we'd talked about. But look them over."

Terrence took a long time reading the page.

94

"*Oh!*" Fiona said. And then it seemed she had to think of something to say, a thing to fill the silence. "I have to tell you the sweetest story!" She told them how one of the little girls in the family she nannied for, the three-year-old, could hear the lions and wolves from the Lincoln Park Zoo at night through her bedroom window and so had assumed, till recently, that the creatures roamed the city at night. Fiona had gotten the mother's permission to walk the girl over after bedtime, to see the animals secure in their enclosures.

"I used to cruise the zoo," Charlie said.

Terrence found this hilarious. He put his pen down.

"It's true! You remember Martin? That's where I met him. Well, *near* the zoo."

When Yale first met Charlie, he was seeing a huge, bearded guy named Martin who played the drums in a terrible New Wave band. How Charlie could go from someone like that to someone like Yale—small, cautious—Yale never could figure out. As Yale spent time with the two of them that summer, it became clear Martin was the one pursuing Charlie. He'd rest a hand on Charlie's shoulder when Yale showed up, keep it there as long as possible. By the time Charlie, in the locker room of the Hull House pool, first asked Yale out for a drink, Yale knew Charlie was available. Emotionally, if not logistically.

It was funny: Yale swam at Hull House specifically because there wasn't a scene there; the only friend he ever saw at the pool was Asher, who'd probably chosen it for similar reasons. The place was dank and completely unsexy. And then Charlie started showing up.

Yale and Charlie were both wet that day from swimming, and Yale was glad the flush coming over his body might be excused as post-workout blood flow. He learned later that Charlie hated to swim, had been choking down chlorine just so he could run into Yale on the pool deck. They were already friends, but there was something different—even in the most innocent ways—about the intimacy of the locker room. (Later, when people asked how they got together, they hated to admit it, to recite what might be the beginning of a porno flick.) They went from drinks back to Charlie's place, and Martin quickly became a distant memory, except for the few times he'd pop up to storm past Yale at bars. But Yale had always, because of Martin's size, felt smaller next to Charlie than he might have. Charlie had five inches on him—five inches and five years and five IQ points, was Yale's joke—but it might as well have been two feet.

Asher asked Terrence if he had any questions, and Terrence finally shook his head, initialed the papers. He signed on the last page with a tremendous flourish, elbow in the air.

Asher said to Fiona, "We need you to be sure."

"I am!"

"Anything that goes wrong," he said, "anyone who challenges this, I'll be there to set them straight. Okay? But listen, you have to consider what could happen if the family shows up."

"We'll deal with that if and when," she said.

"Right." Asher was being careful, speaking slowly. "But the 'we' might not include Terrence, if he's unconscious."

Yale refilled Terrence's wine glass. He wished Asher would stop talking. What Terrence feared most, Yale knew, was the variety of sickness that would make him a vegetable or—worse, to Terrence—make him walk around town in a fugue state. Everyone knew how Julian's friend Dustin Gianopoulos, near the end, had walked into Unabridged Books in the middle of the day with diarrhea running out of his shorts and down his legs, how he'd stood there buying a stack of magazines, manic and oblivious. And how, because it was the fall of '82 and no one had seen this yet, the story had gone around that he was coked out. Yale and Charlie, along with everyone else, had laughed about it until they heard, two weeks later, that Dustin had died of pneumonia.

Fiona said, "I'm an absolute veteran, Asher." She signed both copies of the document, then pulled the papers up near her mouth like she was going to kiss them, leave a lipstick mark.

"Don't," Asher said.

"*Kidding!* Yeesh." She laughed, tucked the pen behind her ear.

Asher asked if Yale and Charlie would sign as witnesses; yes, of course.

"Have you two thought about it?" he asked when they'd finished. He'd been badgering them about signing stuff for ages, but they hadn't yet pulled the trigger when the test came out and made it less urgent.

"We really should," Yale said. "Next time, okay?"

Terrence had fallen quiet. Fiona had opened another bottle of wine, and Yale had lost track of how many they'd already finished, but he was sure Fiona had drunk more than anyone. Her spoon slid from her fingers and crashed into her empty bowl. She laughed, and so did everyone but Yale.

He asked how she was getting home, and she pointed a finger at him, squinted.

She said, "Pixie dust."

By December, Charlie was busier than ever, and he was drinking more coffee than Yale thought was healthy. He'd gotten roped into the planning committee for the pre-Christmas fundraiser that would benefit the new AIDS hotline at Howard Brown, and he was doing all the publicity for the event. They were organizing a silent auction and a raffle upstairs at Ann Sather on Belmont, the restaurant a step up from the pass-the-bucket lectures in someone's apartment. Yale looked forward to it, really. He enjoyed Christmas, which he hadn't celebrated until he took up with Charlie, and he looked forward to seeing everyone.

One night Yale and Charlie were out at a Vietnamese place in

Uptown, huddled in sweaters in the back, and Yale said, "Why don't you have Richard do a photo essay on the party? For the paper? Like, artsy and journalistic, not just normal party shots. Someone's hand on a glass, that kind of thing."

Charlie set his chopsticks in his rice noodles and looked up at Yale. "Oh my God," he said. "Yes." Yale felt relieved, as if he'd just evened the score, made up for something. Charlie bit his lip, a code: *Wait till we get home.*

When they did get home, though, Charlie was tired and wanted to crash. He'd had a fever before Thanksgiving, one that hit him hard at first and seemed to be sticking around in milder form. A year ago they'd have both worried this spelled doom. The fact that a fever could just be a fever now, a cough could just be a cough, a rash could just be a rash—it was a gift the test had given them. This was where Asher was wrong; knowledge was, in some cases, bliss. Yale brought Charlie herbal tea in bed, told him he should take the next day off.

Charlie said, "God, no. If they ever do a whole issue without me, they'll get ideas."

Late the next afternoon, Cecily Pearce called to request that Yale meet her for coffee at Clarke's, a neon-laden place that always gave Yale a headache. There was something so agitated in her voice that, on his way there, Yale developed a paranoid theory: Cecily had blacked out some of that night in Door County nearly a month ago, and it had only this morning come back to her that she'd offered Yale cocaine, put her hand on his leg. Maybe she'd remembered that part but not the rest, not the confirmation of Yale's sexuality, the fact that he'd dropped her off at her room.

When he arrived, five minutes early, Cecily was already waiting, had already ordered him a to-go cup. She said, "I'm not in a sitting mood." Yale had been glad to get out of the cold, but she was buttoning her coat, heading out the door. He followed her onto the sidewalk and managed to steer them back toward campus before Cecily could turn toward the chill of the lake. She didn't complain. Her gloves matched her hat and scarf: all a soft cream that made her look fragile.

She said, "We have a bit of an issue. Have you heard more from our friend Nora?"

"Not a word."

"Okay. Just as well. I'm honestly hoping this whole thing disappears." She stopped and looked blankly through a store window at some headless mannequins. "There's a donor, a trustee actually, by the name of Chuck Donovan. Class of '52. This is someone who gives ten thousand a year to the annual fund, but there's a bequest in place for two million. Not our biggest donor of all time, but we need him. We can't throw people like this away."

"Of course." Yale sensed he was being reprimanded, but he couldn't imagine what for.

She said, "I have to set the stage for you here. This is a man who, and I'm not making this up, once donated a Steinway to the music school, and then when he had some beef with the dean over there, he came into the building himself and removed the little placard with his name on it. With a tiny screwdriver."

Yale started laughing—he couldn't help it—and Cecily joined. It surely hadn't been funny when it happened, when she'd had to deal with the guy's calls.

She started walking again, and Yale dodged students to keep up. "So. I got a call from Chuck Donovan yesterday, and he's been talking to Frank Lerner. Frank is Nora's son. He's the one who owns the house."

"Debra's father," Yale said.

"Right. They're both in medical supplies, and I imagine it's a golf-buddy situation."

Yale said, "So Frank is mad at us and told him so?" His coffee was way too hot, and it scalded the middle of his tongue. He wouldn't be able to taste his dinner.

"Ha. Yes. More than that. He had a little speech. He said, 'You can have that woman's art or you can have my bequest, but you can't have both.' Apparently he *promised* Frank—he said something about a 'gentleman's promise'—that he'd put an end to this. Maybe it's a moot point, if we don't hear back from her. And even if the art were real, there's no way it's worth two million, right?"

She meant it rhetorically, but Yale took in a long breath of frozen air. "I mean, it depends what she has. But with the Modiglianis, the Soutine—there's a good chance, if they're real, if there are full paintings in there, if everything's in good condition, that it would be more than two million."

Cecily was a foot ahead of him, so he couldn't see her face, but he heard the noise she made. "That's not what I want to hear," she said.

"I'm not going to lie to you."

"Here's the thing, Yale. This goes now from us just taking a chance on the work, maybe getting another donor involved in the authenticity thing, to our *paying* two million dollars for the art. We'd essentially be buying it for two million dollars. When it's not even a sure bet."

"Right," he said. "Right. He's serious, this Chuck guy? You don't think he's bluffing? I don't get it. He's got no personal investment in this, right? He just wants to look important?"

"His whole life is one big ego trip," she said. "He's the most difficult donor I've ever worked with."

Yale said, carefully, "Is it possible, though, that the reason he's so keen on helping Nora's son is that he knows the art is real? If these were fakes or quick scribbles, he's not going to throw his weight around to help his golf buddy."

"Chuck Donovan is no art expert," Cecily said. "I doubt Nora's son is either. And listen, it would be one thing if we were looking at a verified Rembrandt. But I have people to answer to. You understand."

"I do." The sun had fully set, and Yale wished he had a hat.

"If it *is* real," she said, "no offense, but why on earth would she want *us* to have it?"

"Good question." It was. Why not set her family up? Why not go to the Art Institute? He said, "But let's say we get a look at this art, and it's really promising. Something worth maybe a lot more than two million—and remember that the thing about art is, it often goes up in value—then it would be worth it, right?"

He wasn't making Cecily happy. She walked faster, watching her feet. She said, "Can't we just wait till it's all authenticated?"

"That could take *years*. We wait around, Nora dies, the son does lord knows what, and the whole thing falls apart."

"I'm not your boss, Yale. And technically I can't tell you what to do. But Chuck Donovan makes things difficult for a lot of people, and he might make them difficult for you."

A woman with a golden retriever darted between them, and the dog sniffed Yale's leg and managed to wipe its mouth there, leaving a streak of muddy drool on his khakis. The owner apologized, and Yale looked at his watch. He and Charlie had theater tickets, and now he'd have to change when he got home. It was already 5:05. He said, "I understand what you're saying. And maybe this is a conversation you should have with Bill as well."

"Oh, *Bill*," she said. "All Bill does is ask questions. I always feel I'm being *dealt with*. I'm talking to you because this is about money. And I want to ask that you don't screw me over. Okay? I have a kid to provide for, and my job is always on the line. This year more than most, for reasons I won't even go into."

Something had changed in her voice, and whether or not it was intentional, a careful manipulation, Yale felt that she was letting him in. That she was desperate, in fact.

He said, "Yeah. No. I get it. Ultimately, I do have a boss, and that's Bill. I'll apprise him of the situation. If we're lucky, the stuff is obviously fake. End of story. And if not—we'll talk again."

She said, "I'm going to leave you here and pick up some groceries." And instead of shaking his hand, she squeezed his bicep.

On the way back to the gallery, the wind was harsher and in his face. He tucked his head and walked like a charging bull. He wasn't sure what, if anything, he'd promised. Really, just a future conversation. How ridiculous to be scolded and warned over what was essentially a pipe dream. He felt for her, he did, but acid was burning his throat. The wind tore at his skin.

Yale and Charlie had long held tickets to see Julian in *Hamlet* at Victory Gardens. "Well," Julian had said when he invited them, "not so much *at* Victory Gardens as *in* it. Like, on off nights." The show was put on by the Wilde Rumpus Company, and this was how it operated—in other people's theaters, on nights when the house would otherwise be dark.

It was the last show Nico had set-designed. He'd just completed the sketches when he got sick, and the company had executed things as faithfully as it could. Julian was the one who'd introduced Nico to the theater world, who'd hooked him up with the company. But then Nico was the kind of guy who made you want to do things for him. He always smiled so earnestly, looked so pleasantly shocked that you'd be willing to do him some small favor.

Yale rushed home from Evanston and changed out of his mud-smeared slacks only to find that Charlie was suddenly uninterested in attending. He was lying on the bed, staring at the ceiling. "Did you see what they wrote in the *Reader*?" he said. "They called it 'unnerving.'"

"It's *Hamlet*," Yale said. "It's supposed to be unnerving."

"Do you know how long that play is? We'll be old before it's over."

Yale had taken off his loafers and was slipping his feet, again, into Nico's shoes. They'd stretched a bit, the leather holding the shape of his toes.

"Oh," Charlie said, "your dad called, I think."

Yale's father always phoned within the first few days of the month—regularly enough that Yale assumed it was something he scheduled, an item on his to-do list, like checking the batteries in the smoke detectors. It wasn't an insult; it was just the way his father's accountant brain worked. But if Charlie picked up, Leon Tishman wouldn't leave a message, would just stammer that he must have misdialed. Five years ago, when Yale was so newly in love with Charlie that he couldn't help shouting it from the rooftops, he'd tried telling his father he was in a relationship. His father said something like "*Bop bop bop bop bop*," a sound effect to cover Yale's voice, to stop his talking.

Yale said, "He was due for a call."

"Yeah, but he didn't say anything. Bit unusual. Just breathing."

"Could be your secret admirer," Yale said. "Was it *heavy* breathing?"

But Charlie didn't find it funny. He said, "Anyone else it might've been? Because it was odd."

Yale didn't like the direction this was headed. He could have gotten defensive, or he could have just reassured Charlie, but instead he said, "Nico *did* promise to haunt us."

Charlie rolled over, buried his face in the pillow. He said, muffled, "I really don't want to go tonight."

"Come on, get up. Let's just do the first half, so you can say you saw the set design."

"I do want to see the set. I just don't want to watch the play."

"What's this about? *Julian?* Because I don't get it. We can't suddenly not have friends just because you're going through this paranoid phase."

"Don't start that," Charlie said, and Yale was about to counter that he hadn't really started it, but Charlie was sitting up now, opening the dresser to change his socks.

It was an all-male production, Ophelia and Gertrude in drag, and not only were Guildenstern and Julian's Rosencrantz clearly meant to be a couple, so were Hamlet and Horatio. Yale found it all darkly hilarious, with lines like "What a piece of work is a man" suddenly taking on new meaning, but Charlie didn't laugh, kept folding his program.

Nico's set design was bleak and postapocalyptic. Hamlet didn't live in a castle, apparently, but an alleyway—all fire escapes and dumpsters. It was strangely beautiful, if slightly more suited to *West Side Story*. If Nico had been around to oversee things, Yale imagined he might have added more color, graffiti, light.

Julian looked, as always, made for the stage. His dark hair glowed like wet paint.

In high school, Yale had wished he'd had the acting bug. He didn't want the social fallout, but he wanted, desperately, something to talk about with the guys who got up there and, with no apparent self-consciousness, sang and even danced their way through *Guys and Dolls*, through *Camelot*. But the thought of going onstage was terrifying, beyond just the stigma. He could never have opened his mouth up there.

He'd mentioned it, offhand, to the shrink he'd seen at U of M, a guy who would occasionally suggest that Yale wasn't so much *homosexual* as lonely. "Could that desire be about your mother?" he'd said. "A desire to connect with your mother, through the theater?" And Yale had brushed it off, said that

104

wasn't it at all. But he'd wondered, in the years since, if it weren't even simpler than that—if he didn't possess some latent theater gene that would never emerge but that he could feel, now and then, tugging.

It wasn't till halfway through the first act that Yale spotted Asher Glass two rows ahead. The stage lights glowed through the backs of his ears, turned them translucent so Yale could see their threadlike veins.

At intermission, they found Asher in the lobby, looking at the racks of books and T-shirts the company had brought in for sale.

Yale said, "It's not bad, right?"

"Jesus, I don't know. I don't know why I'm here. I can't concentrate, can you?"

"I think it's okay to let your mind wander."

Asher looked back blankly. "No, I mean *Teddy*. I'm thinking about Teddy."

Charlie's voice turned thin. "Is he, what, is he sick?"

Asher let out a strange, short burst of laughter. "Someone broke his nose. Last night."

"What?"

"They banged his head into the sidewalk. He was on campus at Loyola. He teaches some undergrad class, right? And he was walking back afterward and someone just—" He pantomimed it on his own head, grabbing his hair and thrusting himself forward. "On the sidewalk. It wasn't a robbery even."

"Is he—"

"He's fine. He's got a bandage across, and two stitches, and a black eye. He's home, if you—but he's okay. It's more the *fact* of it. They have no idea who did this. One person, five. Students, punks, some asshole just strolling through campus."

"Have you seen him?" Charlie asked.

"Yeah. Yeah, I went to help him deal with the cops. You know

105

how they are. Even if someone's caught, they'll say it was gay panic, say you put your hand down their pants, whatever. You're covering this in the paper, right?"

"In general?" Charlie said. "Violence?"

"No, *this*. Will you write about Teddy?"

Charlie pulled at his lip. "It'd be up to Teddy. And my editor."

"You're gonna cover it. I'm following up tomorrow."

And then it was time to head back in.

Yale tried to pay attention, but he saw Teddy's face hitting the sidewalk again and again, and because there were so many different ways he could picture it, he was compelled to picture them all: undergrads following him out of class; teenagers on bikes, a sudden inspiration. Teddy was so small. He closed his eyes, squeezed the image out physically.

He glanced at Charlie a few times, tried to read his face. Charlie drummed his fingers on the armrest, but he'd done that through the first act too.

Afterward, Yale wanted to join the crowd waiting to congratulate Julian—Asher and those guys from the sandwich shop where Julian worked and the chubby accountant Julian used to see—but Charlie had to get to work. "You can hang back if you want," he said, but Yale wasn't an idiot.

That Friday was the day before Hanukkah began, and so when Yale walked in to work and Bill Lindsey grinned and said there was something waiting on his desk, Yale was terrified it was going to be a menorah. Bill was either overly interested in Judaism, or had been using a feigned interest in Judaism as a way to awkwardly flirt. But instead, Yale found a large envelope with a return address in Sturgeon Bay, Wisconsin. He felt adrenaline flood his thighs, as if the situation might require sprinting.

Bill hadn't followed him in, which he easily could have. He also could have opened the envelope. Yale had to give the man credit: He knew how to let people have their moments.

Yale hadn't told Bill yet about his conversation with Cecily. He'd been hoping to ignore the problem away. Bill did know the basic details of their trip north, and he knew that Yale was intrigued by the artwork. That was the word Yale had carefully chosen, *intrigued*, rather than *excited*. In part because it wasn't Yale's place to get worked up about art or to assess its value.

He tore into the package and spread the Polaroids—more than a dozen of them—across the surface. A blur of color and lines and reflective glare. There was a letter, too, but that could wait. He sat and closed his eyes and, blindly, plucked one photo to hold up in the window light. It was a Foujita, or it was *meant* to be a Foujita, he reminded himself, and at the very least it was instantly identifiable as such. And it was not a work he was familiar with, not a copy of something famous. A young woman in profile, a simple drawing done in ink, small bits—her hair, her green dress—filled in with watercolor. Charmingly incomplete, yet fully realized. Signed, in the corner, both in Japanese and in Roman letters.

"Okay," he said. "Okay." This was just going to be one of those times when he talked to himself. He would hand the photos over to Bill this afternoon, but for now they were his. He put his palms flat on the desk. He did not want a two-million-dollar repercussion, didn't want whatever legal battle might come from Nora's family, didn't want to make the phone call to Cecily, didn't want his job on the line over this, didn't want, even, to start hyperventilating right now with excitement. And yet, if these turned out to be real, this would be the find of his career. This was the *dream* version of his job. What Indiana Jones was to a regular archeology professor, Yale was right now to a regular development director of a modest gallery.

The Modigliani sketches struck him next. Well, *sketches* was the wrong word. They were simple drawings, perhaps studies for something else, perhaps—as Nora had suggested—pieces made in payment to a model. All appeared to be done in blue crayon. Three of the four were signed. All nudes. If these were real, if they could be authenticated, they'd be worth a lot more than the pencil sketches Yale had been imagining.

He examined three more Foujita line drawings—a woman in a robe, a woman holding a rose in front of bare breasts, a pile of fruit—plus a painting of an empty bedroom and a chicken-scratch pencil study of a man in a jacket, neither of which seemed to match any of the artists Nora had originally listed. It was when he picked up a wonderfully smudgy Soutine in one hand—God, this was a full painting, swirled and vertiginous and wild—that he stood straight up and then sat immediately down again, his knees not working properly. This piece showed, identifiably, the same woman as in the Foujitas: blonde, small ears, small breasts, impish tilt to her smile. Nora, presumably. If he tilted his head, it kind of even looked like Fiona. Was he nuts? It really did look like Fiona. The Modigilianis were too abstract to pin to Nora, all sinews and pointed ovals.

One of the photos showed not artwork but a shoebox full of papers, and so after he'd sorted and examined every other Polaroid, Yale looked at the letter, typewritten on law-firm letterhead, to see if it explained.

Dear Mr. Tishman:

My greetings for the holiday season! Please find, herein, nineteen (19) Polaroid photographs documenting the collection of Nora Marcus Lerner. Mrs. Lerner wishes to remind you that the pieces are the work of the artists Chaim Soutine, Amedeo Modigliani, Jeanne Hébuterne, Tsuguharu Foujita, Jules Pascin, Jean Metzinger, Sergey Mukhankin,

*and Ranko Novak, completed between the years 1910 and
1925. Additionally, one (1) photograph shows the collection
of correspondence, personal photographs, and other mementos
Mrs. Lerner had amassed during her time in Paris.*

*Mrs. Lerner and I are delighted by the Brigg Gallery's
interest in the collection, and look forward to your further
communication.*

*With warm regards,
Stanley Toynbee, Esq.*

Yale walked down to Bill's office, his legs still shaking, but Bill
had stepped out. Yale left a Post-it on the door: *I have good news
and bad news.* He went back and drafted a letter to Nora—he'd
wait for Bill's permission to send it—effusing over the photographs, saying that the sooner they began to work together, the
sooner these pieces could receive their public due. He added that
it might be best if she keep all correspondence private for now; he
hoped she'd understand this to mean she shouldn't talk to her son.
He called Fiona and left a message. "You made my year," he said.
"You and your artist-schtupping aunt." He did not call Cecily. As
she'd pointed out, she wasn't his boss. And when Bill came back,
when he stood there cooing over the Polaroids like they were
newborn kittens, when Yale told him about Chuck Donovan, his
threats and his two million dollars and the plaque he'd pried off
the Steinway, Bill puffed out his cheeks but never stopped staring
at the photos. He said, "This is a lot more than two million, Yale.
And I'm being *very* conservative. I mean, look at these. *Look* at
these. You'll figure out Cecily, you will. You're my miracle worker."

On the way home, Yale bought flowers and an apple pie. He
smiled at strangers on the El, and didn't feel the cold.

2015

Fiona slept well, from whenever Serge had brought her home until 3 a.m. She lay still a long time, not wanting to make noise and rouse Richard. Wasn't he an old man, despite everything? And then she fell back asleep and dreamed that her seatmate from the flight was swimming with her in a pool. He had something that belonged to Claire, and when Fiona found her, would she hand it over? He pulled from his swimsuit pocket, slowly, like a magician, Nico's long orange scarf.

When Fiona finally came out into the kitchen, Richard was at the breakfast table, the morning sun illuminating his computer, his hands. He typed quickly, mouthing words. "Emails," he said. "Did you ever think we'd be so buried under mountains of these things?" She sliced a banana and asked if Serge was up yet. Richard laughed. "The question should be if he's *back* yet. Which he is. He fell into bed around four." Serge had a number of boyfriends, he said, none serious. "Mostly Italians. He does pick lovely ones." Fiona knew better than to ask whether it bothered Richard. He seemed tickled by the whole situation, by Serge's youth and energy. Richard stretched luxuriously, a lion in a bathrobe, a sun king on his throne. He closed his computer and said, "Look at this gorgeous weather, just for you. I wish you could enjoy Paris. Next visit you will. I don't know when I died, but this is my Valhalla."

He told her they'd blocked off the Rue des Deux Ponts during the night for the movie shoot. She looked out the window. No crowds yet, no movie stars, but there were trucks. The sound of angry horns as drivers learned they couldn't go through. He said she might cross the bridge to find a cab. But she didn't want a cab. Even though her legs ached, she wanted to walk again. Only if Serge went with her, Richard said. He didn't want her getting lost out there. (He didn't want her passing out, was what he didn't say.)

Serge roused himself, despite Fiona's protests, to put on his jacket and come along, half the time dragging behind like a sleepwalker, half the time speed-walking ahead and deciding where they should go. She grew used to the back of his head—his dark, floppy hair, his long and ruddy neck.

Yesterday, on the back of his motorbike after the café, she'd insisted he take her on the Pont de l'Archevêché—broad and nearly empty. A bride and groom posing for a photographer, but no Claire. Of course that bridge, or any bridge, would be the *last* place they'd find her. Life didn't work like that.

Now they walked down on the quays, Fiona showing Claire's photo to every artist she saw—the ones with canvases the size of index cards for sale, the man drawing caricatures, even a clown in full makeup who sat eating a sandwich. Serge stood back to text, to light a cigarette, although his translation would have been helpful. *"Elle est artiste,"* Fiona managed each time, but she wished she could elaborate, explain that her daughter was not a pregnant teenager, not a hapless runaway. They all shook their heads, bemused.

Serge led her to Shakespeare and Company, which Fiona had known was a bookstore, but which also turned out to have beds upstairs, Serge explained, "for lonely foreigners." That made it sound like a whorehouse, but when they went upstairs she saw little cots. They were for single young people, sleeping four hours a night, caffeinating their hangovers away, engaging in passionate flings. Not a place you'd stay with a partner and a child. If she'd been in a better mood, Fiona would have fallen in love with the store, with its creaky floors and precarious tunnels of books, but as things were she just wanted to move on.

With Serge peering over her shoulder, Fiona showed Claire's photo at the counter to a young guy with a Brooklyn handlebar mustache and a Southern accent. He called a girl over.

The photo was from Claire's freshman year at Macalester, Parents' Weekend. Claire stood with one hand on her crowded dresser, half smiling, irritated but tolerant. Fiona chose it because it looked the most like Claire had in the video, round-faced from the weight she'd gained that fall. She remembered, sickeningly, the relief she felt each time she sent Claire back to school that year. Not that she wanted her gone, far from it, but she'd imagined this would be how they got along best. Claire could have her space, then she'd come home and they'd shop and eat and catch up, and soon they'd maybe even split a bottle of wine, talk as adults. It would be this way through the rest of college, and then when Claire moved to another city—Fiona always knew she would—and visited twice a year. But at Christmastime she announced she'd be spending the summer in Colorado. She came home for a week in June and then Fiona drove her to O'Hare, and when Fiona started getting out of the car to circle around and hug her, Claire said, "They'll start honking." And she quickly kissed her mother's cheek.

And that was it. That was all.

The girl shook her head. "I mean, she looks a little like Valeria." The guy said, "Is she Czech?"

Fiona said no, told them she had a little girl. The guy said, "Let me get Kate. She knows all the kids that come in."

And then this Kate was standing there, tall and British, peering at the photograph. Kate said, "I couldn't say for sure."

"She's older now," Fiona said.

"She looks like that actress from *American Hustle*."

There was a man waiting behind them to buy a stack of paperbacks, and so they stepped away, further into the store. Serge took the photo, held it by the edges. "She must miss you."

Fiona didn't know how to answer that.

Serge said, "You'll stay for Richard's show, okay? His friends mean so much to him."

"I'll try."

"No, no, promise!" Serge smiled, a smile so suddenly dazzling that it must have let him waltz through his entire life making demands like that.

"I think I'll have overstayed my welcome by that point."

"So we kick you out and get you a hotel! Promise."

"Okay," Fiona said, "I promise." She wasn't sure she meant it, but it didn't hurt to say. Another nine days away from the resale shop was too long, but in nine days she'd either have found Claire or would still be looking—and could she go home in either case?

Before they left, Fiona grabbed an English book of Paris history just so she wouldn't walk out empty-handed, the staff feeling sad for her. The mustachioed bookseller was ranting to a customer about American DVD players. Something about the frames per second. "Americans don't even care!" he said. "*That's* why I moved to Paris." He threw his hands in the air.

Fiona stopped herself from laughing. It couldn't be true, could it? That someone would uproot as easily as that? Everyone she'd ever known to leave America had done it for solid reasons: job, romance, politics. To study, like Nora. Claire and Kurt had fled the reach of the Hosanna Collective—although she'd considered the possibility that Claire was running from *her*, from some perceived childhood trauma. But what if it was nothing more than a lark? First the commune, then Paris, next a sheep farm in Bulgaria? What if Fiona had simply failed, as distracted as she was in those early years of Claire's life, to tether her daughter tightly enough to the world?

The guy looked at the price. Three euros. He told her it was on him.

By the time they circled back to Richard's in the early afternoon, the filming had begun.

It was hard to see what was going on; people had packed together as if to watch a parade. Down the street a crane loomed overhead and enormous lights glared down from tripods.

Fiona left Serge behind and wiggled through—one advantage of being small, no one ever felt you were usurping the view—and soon she was at the front, hands on the wooden barrier.

The action was a block farther down, at the corner near a crimson restaurant front, but this was the closest the crowd could get. Fiona made out a mess of chairs and ladders and people—and in front of the restaurant, a woman talked with a man. He embraced her and she walked away. Just a few yards, then she stopped, went back, did it all again. Each time, two men ran in front of her carrying white reflective sheets. A camera followed on wheels.

"I know who the *guy* is," a woman near Fiona whispered in English, "what's-his-face, the Dermott McDermott guy. But I've never heard of her."

The man she was with laughed too loudly. "Dermott McDermott. I love it."

A security guard strolled past. "We're gonna get in trouble," the woman whispered. Really, there was a constant low-level murmur all around, one that could surely be edited out if the mics picked it up.

Fiona studied the crowd on the opposite side of the street. No one there who looked like Claire. No one with a little girl. No one like Kurt. But the crowd reshuffled constantly.

Claire had talked about majoring in media studies before she dropped out of college. In high school she'd go to the Music Box on Saturdays and sit through three movies in a row. At the end of her senior year, she had a boyfriend who wanted to be a screenwriter, and Claire was going to make the films. Fiona hadn't liked that boy at all—long fingernails, no eye contact—but surely he'd have improved over time! How much better he'd have been in the end than Kurt Pearce.

Fiona had been out of touch with Kurt and Cecily for only a few years when he had walked into her store, told her he was doing some hunger activism around the city, that maybe they should be in touch. After that he invited her to occasional events, although she rarely made it. And she had no idea that the whole time he'd been battling addiction, stealing from Cecily, stealing, in fact, from some of the hunger organizations he worked for so tirelessly. That Cecily had given him one last chance, and then one more chance after that, before writing him off completely. All that news came out later, after Fiona had already introduced him to her daughter, after he'd ruined her life.

They paused the action when a plane flew overhead. Fiona remembered Julian Ames once telling her he'd rather starve doing live theater for the rest of his life than make a million dollars doing movies. Movie work, he said, was mind-numbing. Julian had paid rent by working in that blue-walled sandwich shop on Broadway, the one where Terrence first sat her down and told her Nico was sick. Julian couldn't have been there that day—she'd have remembered if he was there when she started wailing, if she'd grabbed all those napkins off the counter right in front of him—but in her mind he was the one at the register.

115

His hand forever in the tip jar. That lock of dark hair forever in his eyes.

The actress repeated her loop, and Fiona repeated her scan.

She should head back to Serge, make sure he knew she was okay. And she was beginning to do that, had just squeezed free of the crowd, when she felt a tap on the back of her head. She spun to see a man smiling down. A face she was supposed to recognize but couldn't, quite.

"I *knew* I'd run into you," he stage-whispered. She must have looked confused, because he added, "Jake. From the plane?"

"Oh!" A step backward. "It's nice to see you. Jake."

He seemed sober, but his beard and hair and the oaky scent of his clothes still suggested someone who might have slept in the woods last night.

Really, she was angry. If the laws of probability were going to allow her one random encounter on the streets of Paris, why must it be with her seatmate? This was lightning, striking only once.

He said, "I've just been wandering. My thing isn't till tonight."

"Your thing." Had he explained this on the plane?

This meeting wasn't random at all, she realized. Fiona had told him where she'd be staying, and it was a very small island. She looked for Serge, but he'd disappeared. She waved for the guy to follow, and they ducked down a connecting street—far enough that they could talk in their regular voices, but not so far that no one would hear if she screamed.

"Are you *okay*?" she said.

"What? Oh, yeah. Yeah. No, they totally found my stuff at O'Hare. They're sending it."

"Just like that?"

He shrugged. "I got a boomerang wallet. I've lost it like twelve times. And every time, someone turns it in."

"That's—unbelievable."

"Not really. It's such a clear moral test for people. They see a wallet, and it's like, *Am I a good person or a bad person?* People want to believe they're good. Same people would totally steal from work, right? But they send back a wallet, they feel good about their souls."

He was right. But how dare he? How dare he drop his things all over the globe and trust that they'd return?

He said, "This movie is a trip!"

"Did you come here to watch it, Jake?" She didn't hide her sarcasm.

"No," he said. "I was looking for you. Not, like—not in a creepy way. Sorry. I wanted to ask you something." If he weren't so attractive, she'd have run away by now. She'd have grabbed the arm of the nearest man, said, "Here's my husband!" But instead she just stood there, looking up into his face and waiting.

He said, "I was mad at myself, after we got off the plane, for not asking more about Richard Campo. Like—I don't want to sound like a stalker, but I could totally do something with him. I could pitch that *so* easy."

Fiona held up a hand to stop him. She said, "I'm missing some information."

"Sorry. I can't remember how much I said. I write culture stuff, mostly for travel magazines. You read *National Geographic*? I had a piece there last summer, on this Mayan dance festival in Guatemala."

"Okay." It all made sense—the pilot who'd been, what, fired for drinking? Or decided he wasn't cut out for that life, that there were better ways to see the world? She said, "He's been doing a ton of interviews. I don't know if that makes it more likely or less that he'd agree."

"It wouldn't really be about art, is the thing. It would be about living here, you know, like an expat artist's view of the city. Or it *could* be about the art. I don't know, whatever he wants."

Why was she even considering helping him? Maybe it was the same principle as the wallet: She wanted to feel good. Maybe it was his beautiful eyes. Maybe it was a welcome distraction. She pulled her phone from her purse and said, "I can give you his publicist's number." His publicist being Serge.

Jake adjusted his backpack, scratched his beard. He said, "That would be phenomenal."

She still had the phone in her hand, was still giving him the last digit of Serge's number, when it started vibrating.

"Oh holy shit," she said. "I have to take this!" She left him there, walked quickly for no good reason.

Static at her ear. Arnaud cleared his throat and said, "Well, they were easy to find. Mr. and Mrs. Kurt Pearce, and I have an address."

She stuck her left hand into her jeans pocket to stop shaking. "You're sure it's them?" *Mr. and Mrs.!*

"Ha, yes, he was easy to find because he was arrested last year. No prison, don't worry."

"God, what *for*?"

"Small theft," he said, before her mind could fully go to murder, infanticide, domestic terrorism. "It's—the fine he got, this was probably just some shoplifting."

"Wait," she said, "hold on. No. He'd be deported, wouldn't he?"

"Ah," Arnaud said, "okay. No, not really, and also it turns out he's an EU citizen. They *could* have, but—"

"Since when?"

Arnaud didn't know. But hadn't Kurt's father been Irish or something? Maybe he'd had dual citizenship all along. Maybe that helped explain their move to France.

Serge was across the side street, waving. He trotted to her and stood there, listening.

"You didn't *talk* to him, did you?"

118

"What I have is an address in the Fourth, just outside Le Marais. Affordable street for that area, but not dangerous or anything. You know Le Marais?"

Fiona remembered Richard implying it was a gay neighborhood, although she also thought she remembered this was where the Arabs lived, or maybe it was the Orthodox Jews. Surely not all three together, that would never work, would it? She said, "Not well."

"I'm going to stake it out. Like in the movies, okay? Just surveillance."

"Can I come?"

He chuckled. "This is not a great idea."

"So, when, tonight? You're doing this tonight?"

"Unless something comes up. I'll take photos."

"What do I do in the meantime?"

"Enjoy Paris. Your friend with the motorbike, he can take you out, yes? Go sightseeing."

Sightseeing. Lord.

"Promise you'll rest. Yesterday you nearly fainted in your omelet. Save your strength for when you need it, okay? For now, we wait. Drink some wine, rest, relax."

Resting didn't sound that bad. And she was so, so tired.

1985

Hanukkah passed, and the edges of the lake froze white. Charlie's mother couldn't fly in for Christmas because her new boyfriend was taking her to the opera. She'd come later, she said, and Yale was a bit relieved. He adored Teresa, but Charlie didn't need more stress right now.

Yale ran into Teddy at the bank. His black eye had faded to purple, but the bandage was still across his nose, a strip of white tape. Teddy claimed it had been liberating, learning he could survive an attack. Yale didn't believe him for a second. Teddy said, "Did you know you see actual *sparks*? I always thought that was just a cartoon thing." Yale said, "Yeah. I mean, I've been punched."

He ran into Fiona on the street, and she told him her family had finally cleaned out Nico's place and hadn't noticed anything missing. "Mostly because they didn't know what had been there to begin with. My cousins took all the electronics," she said. "That was all they cared about. My mom took his drawing board, but she just shoved it in a box, and I don't know what she's even gonna do with it. My dad wore *gloves*. He wore actual rubber gloves." Yale hugged her so hard her feet came off the ground.

He ran into Julian at a resale shop where Julian was trying on bright yellow corduroys, and when they were too short on him, he made Yale try them next. He said, "They make your ass look like hamburger buns. I don't mean that in a bad way." He stepped back, looked Yale up and down. "They don't do much for your front, though. And I've *heard* about your front." Yale felt himself blush, all the way down to his neck. "What," Julian said, "you think Charlie can keep a secret?" Julian bought a terrible white leather jacket with fringe. He told Yale that he and an actor friend were using their stage makeup skills to teach men with Kaposi's sarcoma to cover their lesions. "They look pretty good," he said, "from a distance."

On a gray, sleeting day, Yale went with the real estate agent to see the house down Briar. He met her on the sidewalk and she clapped like a marvelous show was beginning.

The listing price was three times Yale's salary. Better than he'd expected. Still a stretch, but doable if he kept this job, if his salary grew along with the Brigg, which it was supposed to. It was roughly the same amount Charlie had paid last year to buy the paper its own phototypesetting machine. An exorbitant amount for a piece of equipment the size of a refrigerator, but quite reasonable for a house. The purchase meant Charlie was broke, but it also meant Charlie's staff no longer had to go downtown to the typesetting company and use its machine in the middle of the night, clearing out by 6 a.m., zombified. The paper would, theoretically, over the years, pay Charlie back, bar ad by bar ad; but he was more likely to increase his staff's meager salaries than refill his own pockets. Charlie never bought anything for himself, not even food. If it weren't for Yale, he'd live on tea and ramen.

Yale hadn't mentioned the house to Charlie yet. He might balk at the cost, or even at the fact that Yale would pay most of it, but it would help Charlie feel more secure. It had to, if they owned the place together. They could get a dog then, too, and Charlie had always wanted a dog.

On the walk-through, Yale fell in love with the living room, the wooden floors, the built-in bookshelves on either side of the fireplace, the bay window. The kitchen wasn't much, but they could invest in that later. He'd always wanted to learn to tile. The upstairs was filled with afternoon light, and just standing there in the empty bedroom, looking out into the small backyard, Yale felt like he was floating. A *house*! He could already imagine the ribbing they'd get—Teddy would call them lesbian separatists— but who cared, because look at the thick glass of the windows, the solid floors!

The world sounded the same as it did from his own apartment—the hum of traffic, a car door, someone's stereo—but somehow it all felt new again. As if it weren't just a new house but a new city. This was the buzz he'd felt when he first moved here, when he spent days exploring neighborhoods, studying maps, jotting in his notebook things like, "Tell cabs take Ashland, not Clark" and lists of restaurants ("BELDEN DELI" he'd written his first week, as if he'd single-handedly discovered the place), and things he heard about but never intended to follow up on, like the fifth-floor bathroom at Marshall Field's being a tea room. He'd just wanted to know those places were there, wanted to feel at all times exactly as he'd felt in a cab flying down Lake Shore Drive. And for some reason, in this white-walled room of this little house, the city pulsed around him again.

"How much time do you think I have?" he asked the agent. "Honestly?"

She said, "Gosh, I don't know. I imagine this place will go fast."

If everything worked out with Nora's donation—and when would he know that? In a month? A year?—he'd feel, at least, secure in his job. He'd be ready. And if the house was still on the market when that happened, he'd take it as a sign.

He walked her back to Halsted, and the agent asked if he knew that the theater on the corner used to be a horse stable. Yes, he did. They stood together looking at the walled-in archway that must have been built to let carriages through. The agent said, "Imagine that."

The night of the Howard Brown fundraiser was so windy and brittle that Yale and Charlie joked about taking a taxi the quarter mile to Ann Sather. The fact that this was a Swedish restaurant, that the food would be meatballs and mashed potatoes, had seemed silly when the planning began in August, but now sounded perfect. He'd had a glass of scotch at home to warm him up for the walk, and it buzzed nicely through his hands, his feet.

Yale had been in a heightened state lately, waiting to hear back again from Nora, jumping every time his office phone rang for fear it would be Cecily. And now, on the street with Charlie, with nothing to worry about till Monday, that nervous energy had turned to pure elation. He was thrilled to walk beside a handsome man in a black wool dress coat, thrilled to give a dollar to a punk kid on a sidewalk blanket.

Every day that week, Bill Lindsey had dropped into Yale's office with more news from some Pascin or Metzinger expert who'd told him, off the record, what the works Bill described might be worth. "Not that I care about the money," Bill said, "but the farther over two million this estimate gets, the better I feel."

Bill was a "paper and pencil man" to begin with—he said it the same way Yale's uncle used to say "legs and tits man"—and he was more excited about the drawings than Yale was, but he was also particularly drawn to the painting of the bedroom, which was supposedly the work of Jeanne Hébuterne. Hébuterne, Modigliani's common-law wife, had been an artist herself, although after her early death her family hadn't allowed her work to be exhibited. Authentication would be particularly difficult, but perhaps its existence might bolster the claims on the Modiglianis. Yale loved the bedroom himself, the crooked walls and shadows.

Ranko Novak and Sergey Mukhankin were unknowns, but with a little digging, Yale found that a Mukhankin drawing not unlike the one in Nora's possession—both were charcoals of nudes—had done decently at Sotheby's in '79. Bill was taken with that piece, anyway.

The Novak works, the ones Nora was so adamant that they display, were the only disappointments. Five of the pieces—two small, rough paintings and three sketches—were his. Curiosities, but not valuable. Yale didn't mind the painting of a man in an argyle vest, the way the lines of the argyle extended beyond the bounds of his clothing, the dark depth of his eyes, but Bill hated it, and he hated the other painting, of a sad little girl, and he hated the sketches, which were all of cows. "Don't promise her this stuff's going on the wall," he said. Yale cringed and Bill said, "Well, maybe she'll, ah, pass away first. She'll never know. But look, minus these *cows*, the collection holds together. I'm a happy man. There's balance, there's contrast, there's a story, and it's just the right size. You know, it's a *show*. Someone is handing us a show." He'd clapped Yale on the back like Yale had drawn the stuff himself.

And so although the cold air had bored its way into every pore of his body, Yale was floating.

The restaurant, already festively Swedish with its folk art walls, was now a Scandinavian wonderland, festooned with Christmas lights and greenery. They headed up the stairs, fashionably late—Charlie, despite his planning role, had nothing to do with setup—and so they barely had their coats off before a dozen people ran to see them. Or, rather, to see Charlie. Not that they didn't want to see Yale, not that he wasn't their friend. But everyone had urgent and hilarious things to tell Charlie. Teddy's friend Katsu

Tatami, a counselor at Howard Brown, came bounding across the room like a gazelle. Katsu, despite being Japanese, had ended up with hazel eyes. He said, "We got like two hundred people up here! We're gonna run out of raffle tickets!" Katsu fetched them both beers, because Charlie wasn't going to make it to the bar without being stopped twenty times.

It was the regular crowd mostly. Which was comforting but always a bit disappointing: It would be nice, one day, to see people who hadn't been at the last fundraiser, and the one before that. To see an alderman, a straight doctor or two.

The silent auction wrapped the edges of the room—donated wine baskets and concert tickets and a free hotel night downtown courtesy of Charlie's travel agency—but the room was so crowded Yale couldn't make his way around to see everything.

He spotted Fiona and Julian in deep debate, Fiona talking with her hands. Bird hands, he'd told her once, and she'd fluttered her fingers up to his face, flapped them on his cheeks. He thought he should maybe rescue her; Fiona, as intense as she was herself, found Julian exhausting. "He's like a mouthful of Pop Rocks," she said once. "And I like Pop Rocks! I do! They're sweet, and he's sweet. I'm not being mean. But you don't want a whole mouthful."

Richard took photographs, as Yale had suggested: candid shots of people eating and laughing and talking. His camera was such a permanent appendage that no one much noticed—the key, Richard said, to getting great photos.

Teddy came up to congratulate Charlie on the event before turning to Yale and asking if Evanston was even colder than the city today. "You're so far up the lake!" he said. He kept rotating the pint of beer in his hand. His face looked fine, his nose looked fine. A scar right at the bridge to match the one on his upper lip. Then he said, "Have you seen Terrence?" Actually he whispered it. Yale scanned the room for Terrence's lanky frame, his wire-rimmed glasses. "It's not good," Teddy said. And then Yale saw him, and Charlie must have, too, because he gave a low gasp and turned immediately back. Yale had thought the idea was that Terrence would look bleak, maybe have lost some weight since they'd seen him at Thanksgiving. What was that, two weeks ago? But Terrence was propped against the wall like a scarecrow, his head completely shaved, his cheeks sunken in. If it weren't for the glasses, Yale might not have placed him. His skin, once warm and rich, was the color of a walnut shell. He looked barely able to lift his head.

"Bloody hell," Charlie whispered.

"I mean, he's sick," Teddy said. "He was always sick, but now he's *sick*. Like, his T cells are fucked. The Rubicon is crossed. He should be in the hospital. I don't know why he's here."

Charlie said, "He was fine! Two weeks ago he was fine!"

Yale said, "Two weeks ago he *looked* fine."

Charlie said, "And now he looks like Gandhi. Oh my God. Oh my God." Yale thought Charlie would go over to him, but he didn't yet. He headed for the bar with his empty glass.

The beer was good. He should remember to eat. He needed to talk to Terrence, needed to see how Terrence was doing, but he wasn't ready to cross the room to where Terrence now sat by the wall in a chair, Julian and some old guy flanking him. He wasn't sure he could keep a steady expression on his face, didn't know how not to look horrified. And so he headed back to the bar, where he bumped up behind a woman in a purple dress. She turned and said, "Yale!" and she breathed beer into his windpipe. It was Cecily Pearce. An inch taller than him thanks to her heels, blue eye shadow she'd never have worn at work. "I'm delighted to see you! I should have known!"

He wasn't sure what she meant, exactly, and so he said, "My partner was on the planning committee."

"Oh, is he here? I came with friends, but they're making out with each other in the coats, so I know *no* one."

Having met both sober Cecily and drunk Cecily, he was fairly sure this was the latter. Or at least the buzzed version. Maybe there was a happy medium, an ideal Cecily Pearce who would neither threaten him about bequests nor molest him.

Charlie was across the room, talking to people Yale didn't know. But just then, Julian came up and put his arm around Yale's waist, his chin on Yale's shoulder.

Cecily said, too brightly, "*Hi!* I'm Cecily, from Northwestern! It's great to meet you finally!" She squeezed Julian's hand and said, "You must be so proud!" Whether she meant proud of Yale or proud of the party, he didn't know.

Yale could feel Julian's chin press into him when he answered, his stubble move against Yale's neck. Julian said, "I am very proud. Yes. Indeed. Proud."

And because Yale could see this turning bad quickly—could imagine Cecily, on her way out of the party, telling them what a cute couple they made, with Charlie in earshot—he said, "Julian just likes to lean. Charlie Keene is my partner. He's around here somewhere. He has a beard."

Julian said, "I hate his beard, I've told him. Why hide such a pretty face?"

Cecily found this hilarious, or at least pretended to. She laughed with the desperate air of someone who didn't want the conversation to turn uninteresting lest you leave her alone with no one to talk to. Yale spotted Gloria, Charlie's reporter with all the earrings, and waved her over. "Gloria went to Northwestern," he said, and the two women started talking, and within a minute Yale and Julian were making their escape.

"Bathroom," Julian whispered right behind Yale's ear, and it didn't sound like such a bad idea. There was a lot of beer in his bladder.

The bathroom was empty. Julian, instead of heading into one of the two stalls, splashed water on his face and then stood there as if he expected to chat. He twisted his forelock. When Julian went bald someday, he'd have to find something else to do with his hands.

Yale said, "That woman is not exactly my boss, but she's not *not* my boss."

"She didn't seem so bad." Part of Julian's beauty was the way he looked at you. If you stared at the ground, you'd find that Julian had ducked down and was catching your eye from below, as if to pull you back up again. He would rub his fingers along his own ear and blush at you, and that was oddly beautiful as well.

Yale headed into a stall. No urinals here, thankfully.

Julian's voice: "Have you ever seen a snake dancer?"

"A charmer? With a basket?"

"No. Usually they're women, like belly dancers, but they let a python crawl all over them when they're dancing. Anyway, Club Baths is bringing in a guy, like this bodybuilder guy, who does snake dancing."

Yale laughed as he zipped his fly. "What could *possibly* go wrong?"

"You're no fun!"

"Sorry. That's probably the safest thing going on there." Yale came out and washed his hands. Julian looked in the mirror.

"*You* wouldn't mind if they all closed."

"Honestly, Julian—yeah, I think it might be for the best. For a while. I don't blame them for everything the way some people do, but they sure as hell haven't helped. And it's not about shame or regression or anything else. It's just, like, if there were a salmonella outbreak at a restaurant, you wouldn't keep eating there, right?"

Julian shook his head. He didn't seem inclined to leave the bathroom. "You don't even know what you're talking about. I've heard more condom propaganda there than anywhere else. You're just parroting Charlie."

"Charlie's right about some stuff."

"But Yale. After they cure this thing, there won't be any place left to go."

Yale felt a hundred years older than Julian right then—Julian, who was, in fact, examining the pores of his forehead in the mirror—but instead of saying what he thought, which was that there was never going to be any cure, he said, "When they cure it, we'll open new ones. And they'll be even better, right?"

Julian turned and gave him a sad, beautiful smile. "Can you imagine the party? When they cure it?"

"Yeah."

And Julian didn't look away. It was a small bathroom and they were only two feet apart, and the longer they stood there, the more Yale felt as if he and Julian had entered into physical contact, chest to chest, thigh to thigh. The fact that they hadn't, that the room smelled like urine, was irrelevant. It was probably just lingering guilt over the whole ridiculous nonexistent Teddy issue, but then again neither of them had moved in a long time, and really it was something else. It was an invitation on Julian's part. He'd made casual invitations in the past—whom did Julian not invite?—but there was something alarmingly sincere in the unbroken line between their eyes. This was the look, Yale realized with a jolt, of someone desperately in love.

Julian said, "Yale."

Yale glanced at the door, certain Charlie would burst through, would save him from having to think. But there was no one there, and when he looked back, Julian had taken a step forward, had shrunk the small distance between them by half. Julian's eyes were wet, his lips parted.

Yale said, "We have to get back out there."

It hit him, as he reentered the party, Julian behind him, that perhaps Charlie had been onto something after all. And he never would have said "Julian's in love with you," because that would've made it worse. What mortal wouldn't fall for that, at least a little bit? To know that someone was longing for you was the world's strongest aphrodisiac. And so Charlie made it instead about Yale, about not trusting him. There was a lot that suddenly made sense. In the twenty feet between the bathroom door and the bar, his world had shifted on its axis.

He had just enough time to refill his drink and take his place by Charlie's side before the speeches started. Cecily appeared at his elbow, and this was perfect. He could put in time next to her, clap with her, toast with her, without having to chat, without risking a follow-up conversation about Nora's son and the angry donor. Someone talked about the history of Howard Brown, and then someone came up to talk about the hotline. Yale tried not to yawn. He looked for Terrence, to see how he was holding up, but he wasn't in the chair by the wall anymore. Nico must have taken him home.

No.

No, Nico had not taken him home.

And so now, in the middle of some tedious talk about fundraising goals, Yale was suddenly, finally, drunkenly, sobbing.

Wasn't this why he'd gone upstairs the night of the memorial in the first place? To keep from crying?

Everything would've been better if he'd let it out that night. He wouldn't be a wreck right now, he'd never have scared Charlie like that, they wouldn't have fought, he'd have gotten to go to Nico's to pick out some old records or whatever.

Charlie didn't notice his crying, and Yale tried to back away before he did, before the whole night got messed up. Cecily saw him, though, as he turned, and Fiona saw him, too, so by the time he was at the top of the stairs, they were both with him, each grabbing an arm. "Come outside," Fiona said. "Come outside."

Out on the sidewalk, Cecily handed him the napkin she'd been holding around her drink. He used it on his nose, flowing even more embarrassingly than his eyes. "You'll both freeze," he said.

Cecily said, "I grew up in Buffalo."

Fiona sat on the curb and pulled Yale with her. She held his hands and said, "Let's breathe." He did, matching his breath to hers. She wore enormous silver hoop earrings that grazed her shoulders. Nico was always telling her she'd get her earrings caught on something one day, a stop sign or a passing businessman. Yale wanted to remind her of this, but instead he lost it even more. Nico had been such a good big brother; his voice always changed around Fiona, got deeper, surer. Yale dug his face into her clavicle. He tried to slurp the snot and tears back in, but he was drenching her.

Cecily said, "Here." Somehow she had a fresh glass of water for him, with ice cubes.

Yale sipped it, and he said, "I'm sorry. I've been holding things in."

"It's fine," Cecily said. And Fiona said, "It's fine."

And because Yale was a bit drunk and spewing things in every direction already, he said to Fiona: "I never got to go to his apartment. I didn't get—everyone left."

"And it was all my fault," Fiona said. "I keep thinking about that. I'm so sorry, Yale."

Cecily said, "Is this what you're upset about?"

"No, Cecily, I'm upset because I'm thirty-one and all my friends are fucking dying."

He regretted it an instant later, but then it wasn't any worse than bawling like a child, and it wasn't any worse than having cocaine in your purse on a work trip, was it?

Fiona ran her fingers through Yale's curls and didn't say

anything. Cecily, to her credit, didn't say anything more, and Yale pulled himself together. He stood.

"Do you want to just go for a walk?" Fiona asked.

"No, it's freezing." And Charlie would wonder where he was.

They headed back to the door, and Fiona slipped in first. Yale touched Cecily's arm and said, "I never meant to make trouble for you. I didn't." God, he was drunk. Sober enough to hear his words, sober enough that he'd remember them in the morning, but drunk enough to say things he hadn't planned to. He sent a message to his future self, his morning self: *You didn't tell her about the art. You didn't say anything bad.*

On the stairs she said, "Listen, Yale, I like you. I do. I want to be your friend."

Yale couldn't see himself as *friends* with Cecily, out on the town or whatever she was picturing, but still he was flattered. Nearly as flattered as he'd been by Julian in the bathroom, to be honest. When was the last time someone had made friends with *him*, rather than him-and-Charlie?

He said, "You're a good person." God, alcohol made him a sap. Why did it make some people so mean? It only made him love everyone.

Back upstairs, the speeches had finished and Charlie was holding forth in the middle of an attentive group, gesturing wildly. Yale said to Cecily, "That's my partner, right there."

"Oh, the Brit! I met him earlier!"

"I'm not surprised."

"What a perfect couple!" she said, although it made no sense; she hadn't so much as seen them stand next to each other.

And of course they weren't a perfect couple. There was no such thing. Really—and this was a drunken thought, Yale knew— Charlie was right about what was keeping them together. On some level, at least. If there weren't this monster out there, snatching up

132

guys who played the field, wouldn't Yale and Charlie have gone their separate ways? There were fights that would have done them in. There was the stress of the past few months. But no, no. They'd have reconciled. They always did. Charlie would have buried his face in his hands and asked what he could do to change, and his eyes would be desperate, and Yale would only want to hold him, keep anything else from hurting him ever again.

Charlie was saying: "The reason we don't know *all* the names, the hundred and thirty-two who've died in Chicago, is, listen, half were married, closeted blokes from the suburbs. They picked it up at, you know, the bathrooms at the train station. Commuter gays. They convince their doctor in Winnetka to tell the wife it's cancer. Okay, we don't know them, and me personally, I'm fine with that. They're hypocrites, yeah? They vote against their own bloody interest. But they're still dying. Suffering is suffering. And they're still spreading it."

Another beer had materialized in Yale's hand, the last thing he needed.

The people around Charlie looked like puppets: nodding, nodding, nodding. If someone pulled the right string, they'd clap their little hands.

For the rest of the party, Yale silently seethed at Charlie for no good reason at all. For not magically knowing he'd been outside crying. Or maybe he resented that Charlie had been right about Julian. Or maybe Yale had been mad at him a long time, an anger that only surfaced when he was already weepy and drunk, like earthworms after heavy rain.

The party wound down, and as they walked home he was stewing still.

Charlie said, "I thought it was a success, no?"

"Absolutely."

"I mean, it *was*."

"That's what I said."

At home, Charlie collapsed on the bed. He said, "I should go through ad sales."

Yale said, "Not drunk, you shouldn't." He changed into his jeans. He said, "I didn't get enough to eat. I might see what's open late."

He half expected Charlie to interrogate him, to make sure he wasn't going to meet up with Teddy or Julian or the both of them or the entire Windy City Gay Chorus. But Charlie just made a noise into the pillow.

And come to think of it, what was to stop him from going to Julian's? Yale walked up Halsted till he was just a block from Julian's place on Roscoe. That pull, knowing someone wanted you, was a powerful thing. He could duck into Sidetrack—he could hear the music out here—but he didn't need to be drunker. He turned onto Roscoe and there was Julian's building on his right. He might go back around the corner to the pay phone, call him. Say, *I'm outside, are you still up?* He was pretty sure he knew Julian's number. Or he could just ring the buzzer. But then what would happen?

Well, he could think of a few things.

He knew he wouldn't do it. He was only standing on the cliff edge to see what it felt like. He remembered in high school, sitting in assembly and becoming convinced that he might, at any second, stand up and scream. Not because he wanted to, just because it was the one thing he wasn't supposed to do. But he hadn't. And this was no different, was it? He was only entertaining a dangerous thought.

He kept walking.

He got a cheeseburger and walked back up Roscoe eating it. He went right past Julian's door again, and he thought he was going to do it after all, and then he knew he wouldn't.

2015

Fiona was jittery and she wanted to head back out, to comb the Marais, but it would be a terrible idea. She said to Richard, "Do *not* let me leave the apartment. I'll mess things up."

"We're locking you in," he said, "and we'll force-feed you."

Serge was cooking for the journalist who was coming to dinner, a woman from *Libération*. Fiona volunteered to chop something, and Serge set her up at the cutting board with a knife and six small onions. He said, "Women always like no-good men. Why is this?"

"Maybe there aren't any good men," Fiona said. And then she said, "I don't mean that."

Serge asked if she was surprised Kurt had been arrested. She supposed she was. She said, "I'm happy, actually. Is that odd? It's—maybe it's gratifying. That he got in trouble." Not that she cared if Kurt was unhappy, but she wanted Claire to see it, how she'd hitched herself to the wrong adult.

Richard excused himself to nap, and Serge put on some Neil Diamond and poured Fiona a glass of red wine she hadn't asked for.

Fiona prided herself on never tearing up over onions. A Marcus family ability, according to her father, and indeed Claire had proved impervious as well. Maybe the only thing the entire family had in common. Nora always claimed there were two distinct genetic strains in the family—the artistic one and the analytic one—and that you got one set of genes or the other. It was true that Fiona's father, who had probably wanted to hand down his orthodontic practice one day, had absolutely no idea what to do with Nico, even before his sexuality came into play. Lloyd Marcus tried to turn his son into a chess player, tried to teach him to keep score at baseball games. All Nico wanted was to trace the comics out of the Sunday paper, draw spaceships and animals. It was their mother who'd tried, in her ineffectual way, to remind Lloyd that his Aunt Nora was an artist after all, and hadn't there been a poet on the Cuban side of the family tree? But it fell to Nora to send Nico a camera for Christmas, a set of fine-tipped artist pens, a book of André Kertész photos. Nora would look at his work and critique it.

Fiona herself had no artistic skill—her strength was in the thousand logistical necessities of running the resale shop—but when Claire came along, when she started sketching realistic horses at age five, when she sat at nine to draw the downtown skyline from memory, Fiona understood she was *that* kind of Marcus. The problem was that Nora and Nico were gone, the alleged poet long forgotten. There was no one to send her to for a weekend drawing lesson. Fiona did her best, buying her charcoal pencils and gummy erasers, taking her to museums. But she couldn't give her what Nico had gotten from Nora. If Richard had stayed in Chicago, maybe he'd have filled that role.

Serge said, "Richard is glad you're here. He thinks you're good luck for the show."

Fiona scraped the chopped onions into the bowl by the stove. She said, "I think you're the good luck, Serge. He seems happy."

"Ha! Never happy. You ask him about his work, you'll see. Never happy."

"Maybe," Fiona said, "but he seems *content*."

She wasn't sure Serge understood the difference, but he nodded. He was making a stack of plates now, a stack of silverware. He said, "You can grab five placemats?" and indicated the drawer by Fiona's hip.

"Five?"

"Richard added one more journalist, someone who called today. He only does this when I already buy ingredients. American guy, I don't know."

Fiona said, "Crap," because she suspected she did know.

It was another two hours before the doorbell rang—what Serge had been cooking was a Moroccan stew that apparently took years—and yes, oh boy, it was indeed Jake, handing Fiona a bottle with a shit-eating grin, as if he'd hunted the wine down himself in the woods. She wanted to say that she wasn't the host, this wasn't her idea, this wasn't what she'd meant when she gave him Serge's number, but soon enough she *was* hosting, because Serge had to stir and Richard was still getting dressed and the other woman was running late.

She set her phone under her thigh, so she'd feel if it buzzed. Arnaud hadn't promised to call tonight, had in fact implied that he'd be in touch tomorrow morning, but surely he'd call if he saw something good or something bad, wouldn't he?

Jake—"Jake Austen, like the writer, but, you know, with a *K*. My mom was an English teacher"—had accepted a clear cocktail from Serge, and Fiona sat as far from him as possible on the couch, pointedly sipping water. She wasn't going to flirt with Jake Austen, if only on principle. She didn't want him to think he could waltz in here and expect her to be thrilled to see him, to go all girly over the way he complimented her necklace. "Are those birds?" he said. "On the sides?"

137

"Oh, it's *deeply* symbolic. Speaking of English class. Well, no. It's for luck."

He said, "You don't wear any other jewelry."

So he'd been looking at her ears, her hands. He might be referring to the absence of a wedding ring.

If she'd been in Paris for any other reason, if she'd had the time and boredom, she might have entertained the possibility of a fling. What did it matter if he was a drunk, a con artist, if she was only going to use him? And the way he kept staring at her legs, he didn't seem to mind the difference between their ages.

After the divorce, Fiona had dated so much that her friends had joked about getting her a reality show. But that was a long time ago. She'd gotten busy with the shop, with other things. And after Claire disappeared, she and Damian spent a good deal of time on the phone. It wasn't romantic, but it filled some need. A shoulder, albeit two thousand miles away, to cry on. She still dated on occasion, but the dates were rote now, and so was the sex.

It was pleasant enough, she'd grant, that Jake was sitting here talking to her about how he needed new hiking boots. It was nice that he believed she was here on vacation. And as Serge came out and almost forcibly removed the water glass from her hand, replaced it with the glass of wine she'd left on the kitchen counter, as she looked out the window to the darkening walls of a Parisian street, she could almost believe it was true.

It was seven p.m. A decent chance Arnaud would be staked out by now. Fiona took off her watch and stuck it in her pocket so she wouldn't stare at it all night.

Jake said, "Tell me the story of your life."

"*My* life," she said, and laughed. She'd never been good at that. Her life had been tumultuous, but the basic rundown always sounded boring.

She told him her degree was in psychology, that she'd started college when she was twenty-four, that she'd married her professor and then divorced him. That she ran a resale shop. She left out that it benefited AIDS housing; this was not part of the romantic, carefree version of the story, and she really didn't care to hear his follow-up questions.

He said, "Does the psych degree help you run a shop?"

She thought she felt the phone, but when she looked her screen was blank. A phantom buzzing, the vibrations of her own nerves.

She said, "My daughter was born when I was still a student. So I finished school, but things got away from me."

"Got it," he said. "Got it." Although he couldn't have.

When the buzzer sounded again, Richard rushed out to answer. The journalist—Corinne—had brought a bouquet of dahlias and an apple tart. She had silver hair, a bracelet of smooth green beads. The kind of woman who seemed made entirely of scarves. She already knew Richard and Serge, kissed their cheeks warmly. She had a digital recorder, but otherwise you'd have thought this was a purely social engagement.

"We'll speak English," Richard said to her. "Partly for Fiona, and, ah, Jacob here, but mostly—you know, if I'm going to be quoted, I want to sound smart. I'm still sharper in my native tongue." He winked at Fiona.

Corinne laughed and said, "Yes, but what then, when I translate you back to French? You're at my mercy!"

"There are worse things, are there not, than to be at the mercy of a beautiful lady?"

"You see how he does!" Serge said. "He flirts himself to a good interview!"

As they gathered at the table, as Serge carried out a basket of rolls, Richard explained that Corinne's husband was a major art critic, and that her piece for *Libération* was openly personal as well as reportorial.

139

Corinne said, "Only because I love you so much!"

Jake, thank God, was quiet. Fiona would have felt personally responsible if he'd made a fool of himself. He was still nursing his cocktail, she was relieved to note.

Fiona had snuck the phone with her, tucked it under her leg again. It was nearly eight o'clock now. Across the room, the balcony door was cracked open. It had warmed up late in the day, and now a pleasant breeze swept through.

Corinne asked Richard about his most recent work, the large-scale images that would apparently comprise half the show. A photograph of a mouth, Fiona gathered, would consume an entire wall. Fiona was surprised; she'd assumed this was a retrospective.

Serge's Moroccan stew had lamb and apricots, and its spiciness didn't hit you till after you'd swallowed.

Jake, who'd brought a notebook but left it on the couch, piped up to ask questions—smart ones—about Richard's age, though not in so many words. How his work had changed, physical limitations, the scope of his career. "It's funny," Richard said, "when I was your age, I assumed it would all be downhill after fifty. Well. Ageism is the only self-correcting prejudice, isn't it?"

Under the table, Fiona flicked open her email. A message from Damian, asking if there'd been any news in the past four hours. An update from the dogsitter.

Jake went quiet again, listening to Richard talk about his preparations, listening reverentially to Richard and Corinne reminiscing. Jake was the one person in the room to whom this was *Richard Campo*, the man from the documentary, the talent behind that iconic photo of the little girl atop the Berlin Wall, the scandalous presence behind the *Defiling Reagan* series. It was so different when you'd known the person first.

Fiona wondered what Damian would say if he saw her sitting here relaxing—if he'd wonder why she wasn't out searching, or if he'd be glad she was taking care of herself, letting the detective do his job. Progress was being made this very moment, even if she wasn't the one making it.

She tuned in to Richard joking with Jake. "You want to be my assistant? I'm constantly looking for new assistants."

"Because he's *impossible* to work for," Corinne said.

"And I promise you the pay is terrible. Even worse than journalism!"

Serge explained to Fiona that Corinne would give a party for Richard tomorrow night—or rather, her husband would, at their home in Vincennes.

"You'll come," Richard said to Fiona. Fiona nodded, but she didn't mean it.

"Can you tell me," Corinne said to Richard, "about the video installations? I do want to write about those. The world doesn't know you well for video."

"This is the fault of the world," Serge put in.

"Well," Richard said, and he looked straight at Fiona, as if she were the one who'd asked. "The irony is, the raw material's quite old. These are videos I recorded on VHS through the 1980s. In Chicago. You know, VHS was a nightmare to work with."

Fiona caught his meaning, finally, and tilted her head. The eighties in Chicago. Video.

To Corinne he said, "They're optimistic, I believe. They're full of life. I've edited them with a contemporary eye, but the subject is twenty-five, thirty years ago. The—" He faltered, and Fiona was reminded, uncannily, of Christopher Plummer in *The Sound of Music*, choking up onstage in front of those Nazis, trying to sing about his homeland. He said, "You should interview Fiona while she's here. You can interview me anytime. But her brother and those other boys, they're—" and he stopped, blinked rapidly, waved a hand in front of his face. He went into the kitchen, called from behind the counter, "Who'd like apple tart?"

"He wanted to tell you," Serge said to Fiona.

She said, "There's, what, footage? There's footage?"

"No, is not footage, is art."

"Okay." But Fiona felt her pulse in her cheeks. She'd come here to find Claire, but a recovered minute with Nico, with Nico and Terrence, with— That was something. Wasn't that a rescue, too, of some kind? She said, "I want to see it."

Corinne laughed. "So does the world! More than a week, we have to wait. And you too."

It was nearly ten o'clock, and Fiona resigned herself to the fact that Arnaud had been serious about not calling till morning.

Richard served the tart with vanilla ice cream, and the five of them carried their little plates out to the balcony railing and ate standing up, looking down at the barricaded street.

1985, 1986

The university and gallery would be closed through the New Year, but both Yale and Bill Lindsey were eager to take advantage of the Sharps being in town for the holidays. Allen Sharp was on the gallery's board of advisers and, after the Briggs themselves, Allen and his wife, Esmé, were the gallery's biggest donors. Lovely, down-to-earth people who'd rather have dinner at Bill's than be wined and dined at Le Perroquet. Yale had known them since his days at the Art Institute, where they were always keen to sponsor a party or an educational event, and he suspected they'd put in a good word for him when he applied at the Brigg. They'd insisted on Charlie's presence tonight, and so on December 30, the temperature hovering around zero, Yale and Charlie stood on the doorstep of Bill's house in Evanston with a bottle of merlot, ten minutes early. They'd walked here from the El. Charlie said, "Let's just circle the block again," but Charlie was the one with a warmer coat, thick gloves. Yale vetoed the trek, and they rang the bell.

Dolly Lindsey—Yale had met her once before, briefly—opened the door as if she'd been in a great, frantic hurry to get there, and yet the room behind her was immaculate, and the smell of tomato sauce filled the house. She'd been ready for hours. Dolly was short and plump, her hair in tight curls. If Yale was right about Bill being in the closet, then he'd chosen his wife predictably: plain, but put together; sweet enough that she likely forgave a lot. Yale hadn't mentioned his suspicions to Charlie. The last thing he needed was for Charlie to worry about a workplace affair.

Dolly said, "Get in out of that weather!" And then, as if she were delivering a line in the school play, she said, "And this must be your friend Charlie. Such a pleasure."

Charlie wasn't thrilled to be there—he felt he was neglecting work tonight, and he was worried about Terrence, who'd been admitted to Masonic with a sinus infection—but you'd never know it. "Shall we take our shoes off?" he said. "Your floors are so beautiful, I don't want to track slush in."

"Oh, they've seen worse," Dolly said. She was smiling, blushing. Charlie had already won her over, in two sentences. It helped that his accent contained a top hat and monocle.

Yale found himself planted on the couch next to Charlie with a "glass of vino," as Bill called it, watching Bill pick out records. Everything was still decorated for Christmas, candles and angels and sprigs of holly.

Dolly said, "I hope you like veal parmesan." Charlie didn't eat mammals, and they both had issues with veal, but they nodded, said it sounded delicious.

Charlie said, "If it tastes as good as it smells, I'm never leaving your house."

This sent Dolly back into a deep blush, a high-pitched giggle that would have been irritating if it weren't so genuine. She said to Yale, "I understand it's an exciting time at the gallery!"

"We're having fun at least." Even before the holiday break, the whole situation had been on ice: no further news from Nora, no angry calls from Cecily. And the surer Yale had become of the paintings' authenticity—the more he and Bill stared at the photos, the more Bill ran into his office with some new bit of detective work, the evidence that yes, Foujita had used that *exact shade of green*, look at this!—the more it hit him that it wasn't just Cecily and her egomaniacal donor he was up against, but Nora's family, a family that might easily block the transaction, might lock her in the house or intercept her mail.

"Well, it all sounds *wonderful*."

Bill had put on a Miles Davis album, and now he awkwardly bobbed his head to it. He sat in the big yellow chair across from Yale.

He said, "Roman will be here soon." Roman was one of the two PhD candidates who'd be starting as paid interns after the New Year thanks to Mellon Foundation grants. Yale hadn't met him yet, but Bill had been Roman's master's thesis adviser a couple of years ago, back when Bill's position was academic. Roman would be working with Bill again this coming quarter as a curatorial assistant; the other intern, a woman named Sarah, would work with Yale. "He phoned to say he had no running water, had to dash over to shower at the gym. The life of the grad student, no? I don't miss it. Charlie, did you do graduate work?"

"Not a day of it," Charlie said, and didn't add that he'd dropped out of university. The best Yale could reconstruct was that Charlie had stopped classes but just hung out for three years on and around the campus of King's College, galvanizing people and leading protests and being, generally, the crown prince of gay students. Charlie wasn't likely to explain this all to Bill, and Yale was relieved when he excused himself to help Dolly in the kitchen. Charlie was no cook, but he was fantastic at grabbing up a pot to scrub.

Yale said, "I think we simply have to drive up to Door County again. You and me this time. You can talk to her, and I'll talk to the lawyer." He steadied his overfilled glass; the red wine had almost splashed onto the arm of the cream sofa. "It's not like she won't be home. It's not like she'll be having a party."

"So just show up unannounced?"

"She's ninety. We don't have time to wait."

Bill sighed, looked around the room as if someone might be hiding in the corner, eavesdropping. "I want to make sure you understand what you're getting into," he said.

"I do. The worst case is very bad." It was a scenario that involved their trying to get the art but failing, or (less likely, but still possible) procuring the art and then learning it was forged. In either case, Northwestern would lose Chuck Donovan's money for nothing.

Bill said, "If Cecily gets word of what we're doing, or if it comes out badly in the end, she's going to take this higher and higher up the ladder, just to cover her own behind. It's only two million, but she's—things haven't gone well for her lately." He scooted his chair closer to Yale, and the back legs caught on the edge of the pale oriental rug, curling it over on itself. "I'm willing to *try* to take the fall for this, because they're not going to fire me. For one thing, I'm actually still tenured. But I can't guarantee what would happen. They might be determined to fire someone simply to prove a point, and that person would be you." Yale wasn't sure who *they* were, but he nodded. "I doubt they'd throw the entire gallery to the wolves, although—"

Charlie stuck his head back through the door. "I've been instructed to check your wine glasses!" Yale raised his full one and took a sip; Bill gave a big thumbs-up. It must have been clear they were talking business, because Charlie vanished silently.

Bill said, "Dolly's already on me to retire. I figure I'm putting in two more years at most. And listen, I'll stake the tail end of my career on this, and gladly. But you're a young guy, Yale. You're at the start of things. And we're shooting the moon."

A year ago Yale might have let his nerves back him out of the whole thing, but he felt ready now. He was full, the past few weeks, of an energy he couldn't name. It might have had to do with the

146

way Julian had looked at him at the fundraiser, the residue of feeling chosen—or it might have had to do with the evidence all around him that life was short, that there was no point in banking on the future instead of the present.

He said, "I want to do this."

"On a tangential note," Bill said, pointing a long finger, "let's talk about interns. Bear with me, because it's related. So, there's Sarah and there's Roman. Both excellent. You were going to have Sarah, but I've been thinking I'll swap. I want you to have Roman instead."

Yale was confused. "He's an art history guy, right? He wouldn't want to work in development."

"Well. Sure he would. We've discussed it. He's interested in museum administration. Maybe that'll be his next degree, who knows. He's the perpetual student type."

"Okay, I—"

"His dissertation's on Balthus, so he'll—well, it's not *exactly* Nora's period, is it, but close enough. He's innocent. A lovely young man. I want you to have him."

Dolly was back in the room, putting out a bowl of mixed nuts. She said, "Roman is wonderful!"

"Thank you," Yale said to Bill. He wasn't sure what had just happened, but it seemed that thanks were expected.

"And I'll take Sarah."

Dolly looked absolutely delighted. The opposite of how most wives would react to their husband bringing on a young female intern.

She disappeared into the kitchen, and then Bill said, "And if you think it might be helpful, we can take him to Wisconsin with us."

When the Sharps showed up, shrieking and laughing about the cold, Yale felt instantly more at ease. Esmé hugged him and exclaimed that Charlie looked just as she'd pictured. Yale had an excuse now to stand, to move around the room. The Sharps were only in their forties, but Allen Sharp held the patent on the shut-off device used in almost every gasoline nozzle in the world, and now they split their time between Maine and Aspen and a small place in the Marina Towers. They were odd donors, intensely interested in helping the Brigg build its collection—Allen had gone to Northwestern and Esmé had studied architecture—but with no art of their own. Beautiful people with matching chestnut hair, matching Greek noses. "I know we ought to start collecting," Esmé had said to him once, "but I don't see the point in hogging something." Yale wished the Sharps would adopt him, would give him and Charlie a room in their little wedge of Marina Tower.

Bill spread the photos on the coffee table and Yale told the Sharps the full story. Bill had instructed him to leave the Ranko Novak pieces out—and because there was no way to authenticate those anyway, Yale didn't see the harm; they weren't relevant to the conversation. Charlie and Dolly listened intently, too, and Yale realized he hadn't explained this all to Charlie, not in so many words. Well, Charlie had been so busy.

"It's incredible," Allen said. "I'm embarrassed to say I haven't heard of Foujita."

And because Bill didn't jump in, Yale said, "He was a fixture in Paris in the twenties, a celebrity. Just about the only Japanese man in France. There was an unfortunate period during the war when he moved home and made propaganda. But no one cares about that anymore."

Allen laughed. "Don't they? I think my old man would care."

Yale leaned close, like he was telling a secret. "Well, one of his drawings just fetched four hundred grand in Paris. I don't think that buyer minded."

Charlie gave Yale a look, and it took Yale a moment to decipher the look as impressed, proud. It was rare that Charlie saw him in action. If Yale had a wife, she'd be dragged along to every dinner with a donor, every alumni event. She'd wear a short dress and flatter the men and then imitate the wives on the way home. Or, well, no. Maybe if he were straight he'd have married someone like Charlie, too busy with her own life to play the nodding and smiling game.

The doorbell rang, and Bill and Dolly both jumped to answer it.

Yale had imagined that a person named Roman would be built like a soldier, but the young man who stepped inside half frozen was small and blond, Morrissey glasses magnifying his eyes. He wore a black turtleneck, black trousers. "I'm so sorry to be late," he said, handing Dolly a small poinsettia that must've been on post-Christmas sale at Dominick's. He looked like an undergrad, in fact, although Yale soon found out he was twenty-six, that he'd started an MFA in painting before switching to art history. Roman turned down a drink and perched awkwardly on the end of the sofa to chat with the Sharps about the research he'd done in Paris last summer. He had a quiet voice, kept his hands glued to his knees. He said, "My mom was worried I wouldn't want to come back."

Esmé laughed and said, "Yes, why *did* you?"

"Well. I mean, I—my education, and my—"

"She's *teasing*," Allen said. "Christ, Esmé, you've traumatized the kid!"

Roman was adorable, and Yale figured him first of all for gay—why else the strangeness from Bill?—but also for the type who didn't even know it yet himself. Yale might have wound up like that if he hadn't, sophomore year at Michigan, gotten Mark Breen as his macroeconomics TA—older, beautiful, confident, persuasive. Five minutes in Mark's apartment, and Yale couldn't remember his own past or anything else he'd ever felt.

Dolly asked Roman if he'd gone home for Christmas.

"Yes, well, we—I've got six brothers and sisters. So we all converge on the house. Northern California."

"Seven kids!" Esmé said.

The family, it turned out, was Mormon.

Yale could sense Charlie appraising Roman too. He wasn't Charlie's type, but Charlie did have a thing for glasses. Before he got so insecure, they used to play "Who Would You Screw?" at the beach or at the airport (one of them would identify three men, the other had to pick one hypothetical lay, and *only* one, and the other would guess which he'd chosen) and Charlie always went for men with glasses. Yale teased him about his Clark Kent fetish.

Charlie said, "So you'll be working in the gallery?"

"Actually," Bill said, "he'll be working under Yale."

Dolly invited them all to the table, and when Charlie went to wash his hands, Yale followed him around the corner and down the hall, touched his arm outside the bathroom. He whispered. "Bill just sprang that on me. The intern thing."

Charlie smiled thinly.

"I wonder if Dolly made him switch," Yale went on. Everyone was finding seats back in the dining room, exclaiming over the good smells. "Do you think? It was so sudden. It was weird."

Charlie whispered too. "It's okay. You expect me to freak out?"

Yes. He did.

"I'm not some monster, okay? I'm not going to flip my lid every time you come in contact with someone."

"I know," Yale said. "I didn't mean it like that."

At the table, after the Sharps had both drunk a fair amount of wine, after they'd grilled Charlie about his newspaper and asked him for travel recommendations and raved over Dolly's cooking, Yale looked for his moment. He turned the conversation back to the donation and the plans to visit Nora again (leaving out that

150

they hadn't been invited, leaving out the entire issue of Nora's family and Chuck Donovan and the development office) and said, "I want to float something a little unorthodox."

Esmé said, "I *love* unorthodox!"

"This donor has no assets beyond the collection. She can't pay for authentication, and she can't endow maintenance on the works. Sometimes there are grants for restoration, but not authentication. Because—"

Esmé nodded. "Because it's a gamble."

Allen rested his fork on his plate.

"Now, I have no idea if this would be acceptable to her," Yale went on, "but she doesn't seem to have an ego. I'm thinking if someone wanted to endow those things, we might put two names on the collection. Not a quid pro quo, but, you know, an *in honor of your generosity* deal."

Bill said, "The Lerner-Sharp Collection, for instance."

Esmé and Allen glanced at each other. "We're intrigued," Esmé said.

"This is putting the cart before the horse a bit," Yale said.

Esmé raised her glass. "Well, here's to the carts. May the horse catch up."

On the way to the El, Charlie said, "If you have to have a hot intern, at least it's a Mormon virgin."

Yale laughed.

"No, wait," Charlie said, "not a virgin. He has a girlfriend, a little blonde girlfriend who lives, conveniently, three hours away. Sweater sets and pearls. Sees her every other weekend."

Yale said, "She can't figure out why he won't propose."

"Republican. *She* is, at least. And her parents. He pretends to be. He doesn't actually vote."

"But his work is on Balthus!" Yale said. "Do you know who that is? All these naked young girls. Really controversial."

"Exactly."

"Exactly what?"

"You have one confused turnip on your hands."

Yale, because the street was completely empty, swung Charlie around to kiss him.

Charlie had arranged to take the paper's staff out for a year-end lunch the next day, before people headed to their various New Year's Eve celebrations. Charlie and Yale were planning to visit Terrence at Masonic instead of partying. He'd called yesterday and said he was ready for visitors. Apparently they did a good job celebrating holidays on the new AIDS unit, but Terrence didn't expect them to make a huge deal of ringing in a year few of them would see to the end. New Year's was his favorite, though, and he wanted to do it right. Or at least as well as he could. Fiona would pop in early, but then she had to head back to her nanny job so the parents could go out on the town. "I need you guys too," Terrence had said. "It doesn't have to be midnight. I just want my party." Yale could have used a real celebration, some pure stress relief—but the staff lunch counted, he supposed. He liked these people. They would celebrate now, and tonight Yale and Charlie would stay sober and walk to Masonic together. They'd sidestep puddles of vomit on the way home.

At noon, twelve staffers plus Yale crowded around smashed-together tables at the Melrose. They passed around yesterday's issue, containing Richard's photo essay. The write-up of the fundraiser had appeared last Monday, but Richard had needed more time. This was art, not reportage. As the paper made its way toward the bench where Yale was sandwiched, he felt irrationally uneasy, as if Richard had managed a photo of him and Julian gazing at each other in the bathroom. But no. Here, instead, was a shot, snapped from below, of Yale and Charlie listening to the speeches, Yale looking emotional. It must have been taken right before he broke down. There was a shot, too, of Cecily laughing with two men—presumably the friends she came with. "What's her deal?" Gloria asked and reached over to point. "She was cute."

Yale said, "Straight. And confused. She kind of hit on me once."

They all found this hilarious. Charlie called down the table, "Women used to hit on me all the time. Before I started losing my hair." And, good employees, they clamored their protest.

Yale knew most of the staff well, although there'd been some turnover. Nico, for one. And two others of the original crew were sick now too. "Is it terrible that I want to replace them all with women?" Charlie had said that fall. "It's insurance. Dykes won't die on me. They won't even take maternity leave." Yale had answered that yes, it was terrible. "Blessed be the dykes," Charlie said, "for they shall inherit all our shit."

Yale mentioned to Dwight, the copy editor, that he was about to head up to Door County again, and Dwight, who'd grown up vacationing there, had all sorts of advice for him, most of it seasonally inappropriate. Dwight was a tedious person, but Yale hadn't caught a typo in *Out Loud* all year. Dwight also told him about the German POWs who'd been sent to the peninsula during World War II to pick cherries, and how many of them had stayed and married local girls. Yale logged this away as fodder for the ride up.

Down at Charlie's end of the table, though, something was wrong. Charlie had his head in his hands, and he'd gone white, and he was saying, "Fuck, fuck, fuck."

"I'm so sorry," Rafael was saying. "I thought you'd know before I would."

Yale said, "What?" and Charlie shook his head urgently. It was something to be dropped. Something to talk about at home. Meanwhile, no one at Yale's end seemed to have heard whatever was said. They dutifully found conversations to cover the awkward silence. Dwight asked to taste Gloria's tomato soup. But then Charlie was up from the table, heading out the door to the pay phone without his coat. Through the window Yale could see him dialing, listening, hanging up, retrieving his quarter, dialing again. Four times.

When he came back, he didn't sit down but reached across the table to Yale. He handed him his credit card and whispered: "Take care of everyone, okay?" And then he turned and walked out.

The people sitting at what had been Charlie's end of the table didn't seem shocked, just chagrined, as if they'd made a horrible mistake. Yale squeezed his way off the bench past Gloria and went to fill Charlie's vacant chair. He said, quietly, "What just happened?"

The two men on either side—Rafael and a new guy—both started to talk and then stopped. Rafael finally said, "It's Julian Ames."

"Oh. Fuck." Yale felt faint, felt himself go as pale as Charlie had. "No," he said. "Fuck."

But they weren't contradicting him, weren't saying, "No, we only meant he broke his leg. We only meant someone beat him up." He looked at them, and they looked at their plates.

Yale's breath wasn't coming on its own.

And, terribly, half his horror was selfish. Had he actually considered going up to Julian's apartment? He hadn't actually done it, had he? He hadn't gone up there and then blocked it out, and here he sat in denial? He really hadn't. He'd had vivid dreams about it since, but he hadn't done it.

No, more important: Julian, beautiful Julian. Julian, who kept talking about the cure. Yale wondered if this was in fact what Julian had been trying to tell him in the bathroom. A confession of illness mistaken for a confession of love. He said to Rafael, "You heard this firsthand?"

"He, um. It was his birthday present to himself, to get tested. That's kind of all I know. Not from Julian, from Teddy Naples."

Julian's birthday was December 2. The Howard Brown fundraiser had been—it had still been Hanukkah, hadn't it? The thirteenth. So no, he wouldn't have had the results by then. Unless he already wasn't feeling well. Unless that was the reason he'd finally done it.

The new guy said, "I mean, if it's just the virus, he could have a long time. Years!"

Rafael said, "What I heard was they called him on Christmas Eve. He woke up because the phone was ringing, and he thought it was his mom calling for Christmas. And it was the nurse, saying to come in for his results."

The whole table was listening now, satisfying their own curiosity. No one seemed personally upset, just concerned for Yale. Either they didn't know Julian well, or Yale and Charlie were the last to hear.

Yale reached for Charlie's half-full glass of water and watched his own hand shake. He should call Julian, but that was clearly what Charlie had tried. He should chase after Charlie, figure out where he was going—but Yale was the one with the credit card, and people still had food in front of them. Rafael said, "Let's take this down the street. Let's get you a beer."

Charlie wasn't at the apartment when Yale got home two hours later. He felt disappointed, to an extent that surprised him. He'd wanted to talk it over, to lie there on the bed together staring at the walls and swearing and rehashing any details they'd picked up. But there was more to it: By holding Charlie, Yale could begin to atone for ever thinking of starting up with Julian. The tighter he held Charlie, the more he could take it back.

At nine o'clock, Yale headed to Masonic alone with some

magazines and a paper party hat for Terrence. He hadn't been up to the new AIDS unit yet, and he took the wrong elevator, had to wind his way through the pulmonology ward, but then there it was. Christmas lights and streamers on the nurses' station. A nurse who looked like Nell Carter asked Yale if he wanted sparkling cider. Sure, he said, and she poured it into a little Dixie cup. "He's got a new roommate in there today," she said. "Angry guy, but he's out cold now. Terrence is awake."

Yale tried to peek at this new roommate as he walked in, tried to see if it was anyone he knew—but it was dark on that side of the curtain, and all he could see was the bottom of someone's chin, stubble and purple lesions on a hollowed jawline.

Terrence was eating a chocolate pudding with a plastic spoon—a cannula in his nose for oxygen, an IV taped to his wristbone. He looked even thinner than he had at the fundraiser, but better too. Happier, at least. "Hey," Terrence said. "You want to eat this for me?" His voice was rough, strained.

"I'm tempted," Yale said, sitting down, "but those artificial flavors are for *your* health and recovery."

Yale asked if Charlie had been in. Terrence said no, just Fiona. "Why? What's wrong?"

"Nothing. We just got our signals crossed." He said, "Hey, don't talk, okay? I'll talk. This place is nice. Seriously, you got a TV lounge out there? This is Club Med."

"Club Dead."

"No, no talking. I made your veggie chili on Christmas. It turned out okay, but I'm no expert."

Terrence said, "You know the hardest thing about having AIDS?"

It had quickly become an old joke, but Yale still laughed. "Yeah," he said, "telling your parents you're Haitian."

"No." Terrence cracked a wide grin. "It's actually the dying

156

part." He started laughing, and then he started coughing. But it was okay, it was okay.

Yale remembered, so vividly: Terrence carrying Fiona down the hall of the suburban hospital where Nico's parents had insisted on moving him, carrying her like a baby as she sobbed on his neck. She had stubbornly refused to go into Nico's room without Terrence, and all the social worker had managed to broker was an hourly changing of the guard: Mr. and Mrs. Marcus, to whom Fiona wasn't speaking, would spend an hour at his bedside while Terrence and Fiona sat in the ICU waiting area, and then Terrence and Fiona would get half an hour while the Marcuses went down to the cafeteria. Yale and Charlie and Julian and Teddy and Asher and a rotation of Nico's other friends filled in the gaps. Yale was the one there with Fiona and Terrence—the three of them were stepping off the elevator—when the terrible nurse with the spiky hair came toward them, told Fiona she should go in there now, that this was the time. "Can I bring Terrence?" she said, and the nurse looked put out and said she could maybe get the social worker out of his meeting, and Fiona said, "I'm not going in without him."

Fiona sat down then on the bench, and Yale didn't know whether to look at her or to look at Terrence, who was shaking, his hands on the windowsill, or if maybe he should just leave—if this was the point at which he didn't deserve to be here anymore. And after thirty seconds, Fiona stood up and said, "I'm so sorry, Terrence," and ran down to Nico's room.

Yale strode over to the nurses' station, said, "Yeah, let's get the social worker here. This is not okay. This is not okay."

But while they were waiting for him, Fiona came back out, looking both twelve and a hundred, but not twenty-one. She was convulsing, sobbing so hard that she made no noise. Behind her, Mrs. Marcus started wailing. The doctor came out of the room and toward Terrence, and Yale prepared to catch him as he fell.

But Terrence, once the doctor had confirmed what they knew he would, did not collapse.

He said to the doctor, in a voice like hollow stone, "I'll be back in two hours. You're going to clean him up, right? And they'll have their time. And I will be back in two hours." His knee was still hurt from running into the cleaning cart that morning, but he scooped Fiona up like she weighed nothing and walked straight out of the hospital. Yale stayed back to call Charlie and everyone else from the nursing station phone. He found out later that Terrence had carried Fiona around the outside of the hospital for twenty full minutes until she was ready to come back in and call for a ride. That someone, concerned that a black man was carrying a sobbing white woman around the parking lot, called the police, and an officer showed up and trailed them slowly, until Fiona shouted that she was fine, that it wasn't illegal for a person to carry another person, was it?

And now it was Terrence in the bed, and at least this was a much better place, but did it matter in the end? And soon it would be Julian.

Terrence's eyes had closed, and Yale sat there a long time, relaying gossip. Yale sang him "Auld Lang Syne," croaky and off-key, till Terrence whapped him with the back of his IV-free hand to make him stop. The whole time, Yale thought Charlie might show up. But he didn't.

Terrence opened his eyes. "Is it midnight yet?"

"It's 10:40. But we could watch the ball drop in New York. Can you hold out twenty minutes?" He got the little TV in the corner working, showing a Times Square that Terrence would never visit again.

Terrence watched the ball, and then he said, quietly, "I made it. 1986, man." He closed his eyes and fell asleep.

Yale didn't feel he should go yet—or maybe he didn't want to—and so he sat there a few more minutes. The door opened and

Yale thought it might be Charlie, but it was just a nurse, checking that everything was alright.

Yale squeezed Terrence's thin hand as hard as he dared. He said, "You can't die of a fucking sinus infection."

Charlie wasn't at home, either.

Yale left a long message on Julian's answering machine, shamefully relieved that he hadn't picked up. "I want you to let us know what we can do," he said. "Some people—I mean, Nico and Terrence had each other, you know? And if you don't have anyone—which isn't what I mean—you have all of us."

He wondered how Teddy was doing. Teddy and Julian had been on and off for years, and he must be terrified, on top of devastated. Yet Teddy, despite all his time in the bathhouses, all his time in the back rooms of clubs doing things that made Yale squeamish to imagine, seemed perfectly healthy so far. (He could hear Charlie and Asher both, chastising him for that line of thought. From Charlie: *It's not about the numbers, it's about the condoms.* From Asher: *If we had* more *bathhouses, we'd have less illness. You know why? We'd have less shame.*)

Once, Teddy had drunkenly whispered to Yale, like it was the best secret: "You know why I don't have it? You can't get it if you always top." And Yale had tried to give him data, had said that was like girls who thought you couldn't get pregnant in summer. That you couldn't apply rules to a virus this random. Yale said, "Look, you ever get soap up in there? Things go both ways." If Teddy didn't already know, deep down, that he had it, he had to know now. They were human dominoes. How could Teddy not know he was the next domino in line?

It wasn't till two in the morning that Charlie walked in the door. Yale had been sleeping in sweatpants on the couch, by the lights

159

of the small Christmas tree. Charlie's face was pinched, and he moved like a broken puppet. Yale asked, as gently as he could, where he'd been, and Charlie said, "Walking." He sat on the couch, and Yale sat up and put his head on Charlie's shoulder. Charlie's body gave off cold like an open refrigerator. Yale took the blanket he'd been using and covered Charlie with it too. Charlie said, "It was just the final straw. Not that it's final. That's the thing. It's a straw, and it broke me, but I know there'll be more."

And Yale understood, because that was how he'd felt the night of the fundraiser. He put his hand to Charlie's face, and Charlie shuddered. "Sorry," Yale said. "I wasn't—I just want to make sure you're okay."

"What, are *you* okay?"

"Of course not. But this seems to be hitting you harder than most."

Charlie snorted. "Most."

It was easier to talk to Charlie when they were both looking at the Christmas tree than when they were looking at each other. Yale breathed deeply and said, "I want to reassure you. I've said this before, and I shouldn't have to say it, but I know for some reason it was always a concern for you. And you need to know that Julian and I never touched each other."

Charlie jerked away and looked at Yale wild-eyed.

"I'm sorry, I thought maybe—I thought that might have been on your mind."

Charlie stood, throwing the blanket off like it was covered with spiders. He said, "Bloody fucking hell, Yale."

"Okay, I shouldn't have brought it up. Come back. Come here. Come here."

Charlie did, and he cried for a while into Yale's chest hair, and then he fell asleep there.

2015

Arnaud had asked her not to call till 10 a.m., so Fiona called at 10:01. He didn't answer and so she tried again, and then she killed time by showering. At 10:26, he answered.

He said, "You got some rest?"

"*Tell me*," she said.

"I have photos, if you'd like to see."

"Was it them?"

"Yes, yes."

"Was there—did they have—was it *just* them?"

"Two adults. Listen, I can describe these forever or you can look for yourself."

They agreed to meet at noon at a place in Saint-Germain called Sushi House—not really Fiona's idea of Paris, but at least she pronounced it easily for the taxi that took her there. And when they sat down and she made herself look at the menu, kept herself from diving across the table to rip open Arnaud's messenger bag, she could also understand the food being described: *sake nigiri, ikura, miso*.

Arnaud told her he'd waited in his car till eleven, and at last Kurt and Claire had come walking past his window, hand in hand.

Arnaud held his phone out over the table. "You ready?" he said.

She didn't understand at first. She'd been expecting him to pull out a stack of glossy 8 × 10s. But the photos were on his phone; of course they were.

The first was just of Kurt, a close-up.

"It's him," she said. She waited to be overwhelmed with rage at the sight of his face, but instead she felt just the buzz of recognition, the click of encountering an old friend—which, after all, he was. Fiona couldn't ever see him without also seeing the kid he'd been, the smart, nervous boy who would rattle off facts about German submarines and spy planes.

The phone was still in Arnaud's hand, and so she said, "Okay, I'm ready. Next?"

But the next photo showed both Kurt and a tall woman with thick black hair. They were hand in hand, and the woman held a plastic shopping bag. It was not Claire.

She yanked the phone from him, scrolled to the next photo and the next. They were taken in rapid succession, so it looked like a flip-book as the two figures moved down the sidewalk.

"No," she said. *"Fuck."* She was angry at Arnaud, which made no sense. *"No."* She felt trapped in the booth, suffocated under the yellow lights and quiet music.

"It's not her?"

"How does that even *remotely* look like her?"

"She could have dyed her hair."

"What, she dyed herself a different nose too? She dyed herself taller?"

"Okay," he said, "calm down. It's good, yes? This means she's not with him anymore."

She smacked the phone facedown next to the soy sauce, grabbed her purse.

"Where are you going? Order some food, okay? So, we have some more steps to take. We need to plan those out. Here. Drink water."

She put the glass to her forehead instead of drinking from it, and when the waitress came by Arnaud ordered for her.

"Let me see again," she said, and Arnaud unlocked his phone, handed it back.

Kurt's hair was pulled into a bun, his face shaved. He looked maybe half Hosanna. Hard to tell with the woman. Long hair parted down the middle. Fiona couldn't see, washed out as this woman was by the streetlights, if she had makeup on. She wore a coat, but her legs were cut off by Arnaud's camera. Fiona studied each shot again, as if clues would be lurking in the background.

Arnaud said, "Does the group have—do you say *polygamy*?" He pronounced it like a French word.

"Yes. I mean, yes, that's the word. But they don't, actually. Thank God." Was she really thankful? It meant Claire didn't live in that apartment. That she might not even be in Paris. But wait, no, the video. The video was in Paris, and Kurt was in Paris. So Claire had *been* in Paris, at least. "If Claire left him," she said, "she probably left France too. She's—how does immigration even work? You can't just stay somewhere, right? If you're not a citizen?"

Arnaud shrugged. "Plenty of people stay illegally."

What if, the very day Fiona got here, Claire had decided to show up at her door in Chicago? What if she'd knocked, went away, came back, figured Fiona had moved? What if she'd come by the store, asked around, was told that Fiona was out of the country? Fiona should call a neighbor. She should have left a note for Claire, clearly marked and taped to the front door. But no, she was being ridiculous. Why would Claire choose that exact moment to come home? Fiona hadn't felt this urgency a month ago; it was only the video that had made everything seem so immediate. She hadn't left town since Claire went missing, but she'd been gone all day plenty of times, and some nights, when she stayed over at a date's house or, once, crashed at a downtown hotel for a wedding. And the world hadn't fallen apart any further than it already had.

Their food had arrived, and Arnaud gestured with chopsticks.

"I can—for a little extra money—I can gain entry to the flat. Maybe find some more information."

"Like, pick the lock?" There was avocado roll in front of her, and she was so hungry she went for it with her fingers.

He laughed. "No, like bribe the landlord."

"Why not just approach Kurt?"

"Because if he doesn't cooperate—then we're through. But if we look around first, then we know more, and we can still talk to him later. This neighborhood, I'm sure we can bribe our way in. It's not kosher, you understand? This is why the extra money. I'm not trying to rip you off, but for something like this, a little extra. Just one hundred euro."

"I understand."

"Plus the cost of the bribe. So one-fifty."

"Can I come with you?"

Arnaud looked exasperated. He stuck a tuna roll in his mouth.

"Sorry," she said, "I know, I know, but you don't even know what to look for. If I'm there, and I see something that used to be Claire's—I'd recognize it. You wouldn't."

Arnaud exhaled slowly. Invisible smoke from the pipe he ought to have had. Or at least a cigarette. And a trench coat. Today he wore a bright yellow V-neck tee and jeans. "I might only have ten minutes to get in and out."

Fiona said, "Wouldn't the landlord be more likely to let you in if I came too? If we explain that my daughter's missing?"

"No," he said. "But look, yes, okay, if I can get in, I'll bring you. You won't meet the landlord, but you can come in the flat. Okay?"

She promised she'd keep her phone on, be ready to fly across the city. But not yet, not yet. Arnaud had to learn Kurt's schedule, find the landlord, etcetera, etcetera. It would take a couple of days.

1986

Yale had the place entirely to himself. Bill Lindsey and the gallery registrar had both called in sick; the art handler and the bookkeeper were both part time. Yale blasted some New Order and ate a sloppy turkey sandwich at his desk and worked. He scheduled dinners and researched grants and followed up with the Sharps. He called Nora's lawyer again, got a message saying the office was closed for the holidays. God, it was January 7. He prepared to leave a message, but the tape let out a shrill beep that didn't end. He wrote to both Nora and the lawyer saying they'd be driving up next week unless he heard back that they shouldn't. He poured himself into reimagining the official gallery brochure.

When he showed up the next day and the office was still empty, he decided to call people to invite them up to see the place. It would help keep his mind off Julian, how close he'd come to Julian's apartment that night. Teddy and Asher were the two who were available, and they showed up in the afternoon. Yale was glad it wasn't Asher alone; he wouldn't have known how to act. And for totally different reasons, for Charlie reasons, he was glad it wasn't just Teddy. Yale showed them the current exhibit—twelve Ed Paschke portraits that made him dizzy every time he walked through—and then they sat in Yale's office and Teddy used Yale's

MoMA mug as an ashtray. He smoked alarmingly fast, a puff every couple of seconds.

They talked about Julian, which was at least better than *thinking* about Julian.

"He's been out every night," Asher said.

"Doing what?"

"Drinking," Teddy said. "Finding other infected guys to fuck."

"He told you this?"

"He was joking about Russian roulette." Teddy might have sounded more concerned—this was a sometime lover he was talking about—but then Teddy's love of gossip generally trumped all. He said, "Did Fiona tell you she found him on her couch last week with no shoes or coat? He traded them for like five quaaludes and a joint."

"And this is in the house where she *nannies*," Asher added. Asher was playing with Yale's four-color pen, clicking the colors down in rotation.

Yale felt out of the loop. How had all this happened in a week? Well, it had been cold; he hadn't gotten out much. Charlie had been throwing himself into the paper harder than ever since New Year's, as if articles about housing laws and drag shows would magically generate a vaccine. If he wasn't at the office or at meetings, he was working at home, his Macintosh humming like a life support machine. He'd joined Asher's effort to bring the Human Rights Ordinance back up for a vote, something he'd formerly wanted to stall on. They knew it would fail, knew city council had zero interest in their rights, but it was a starting point; they'd get in the *Trib* and on the evening news. Charlie talked about it, suddenly, with the zeal of a religious convert.

He'd been too tired for sex, or too stressed for sex, or too moody for sex. On Saturday night they'd gone to see *The Color Purple*, and when they came home Charlie couldn't stop ranting about

166

how Spielberg had watered down the lesbian plotline to a single kiss. "I have more contact with my *dentist*," Charlie said. Yale had unbuttoned Charlie's shirt, tried to lead him to the bedroom. Charlie buttoned his shirt back up and, pinning Yale to the wall, ran his lips along his collarbone and then knelt and gave him an efficient blowjob that would have felt disturbingly perfunctory if it hadn't also felt good.

Teddy lit another cigarette. He said Julian was planning to refuse any antibiotics, any vitamins, even the papaya enzymes Terrence was always talking about. "There's the combo of the two drugs from Mexico, right? I know a guy who brings it up. And Julian doesn't want it."

Yale said, "I thought he believed they were about to find a cure," and Asher said, "Belief is a fragile thing."

Asher kept leaning his chair back on two legs, and Yale worried it would tip.

Yale said to Teddy, "You look good. Your face. You can't even tell."

Teddy raised his left fingers to the bridge of his nose.

"I want him to sue the school," Asher said. "He won't listen."

"Well it doesn't even make sense! Everyone wants me to be madder than I am. Charlie wants me to write a thing, a personal account. I just—it doesn't feel like that big a deal."

Asher said, "Teddy, you were attacked. It's nothing compared to people dying, but it's something. And it's related. It's not like it isn't related."

Teddy laughed and said, "Remember Charlie yelling at Nico? Outside Paradise?"

It was before Nico was sick. Nico had said, "I think we'll have to worry less about getting beaten up, you know? People are afraid of blood. I mean, they might throw something, but no one's going to punch you in the mouth coming out of a bar now, right?" And Charlie had said, "Are you fucking kidding me? Attacks

167

are up threefold. You should try reading the paper you draw for. *Threefold*, Nico." They'd all imitated him the rest of the night. *Threefold! I shall now consume threefold beers, forsooth!*

There was a knock, then, on Yale's open door, and he jumped. It was Cecily; he'd left the gallery unlocked when he let his friends in.

He hoped she'd take Teddy and Asher for donors or at least artists, but she might well have recognized them from the fundraiser, and Teddy, at least, in his duct-taped Docs and his stained white T-shirt, cigarette at his mouth, looked like he'd just blown in from the after-party of a Depeche Mode concert. She clearly thought nothing of interrupting them, because she walked right in and said, "I hope you had a lovely holiday."

"Several of them, in fact. And you?"

"I want to check that we're still in a good place."

Asher raised his eyebrows and pointed at the door. Yale shook his head.

He said, carefully, "I mean, you tell me. Has Chuck Donovan complained anymore?"

"Nothing recently."

Yale said, because it was technically true, "Nothing from Wisconsin lately either." He could keep his voice steady when telling a technical lie in a way he couldn't with an outright one. It was one of the things that had always made Charlie's paranoia so bizarre; Yale was a horrible liar.

"Well, good," she said. "Great."

Asher needed the bathroom before he left. He was going to give Teddy a ride back south in his Chevette, a car so loud you had to shout your conversations. Yale and Teddy waited for him in the hall.

Teddy said, "Did you hear they're discharging Terrence?"

Yale hadn't heard. "Is that even a good idea?" he asked, and

Teddy shrugged. He said, "Look, Teddy, aren't you gonna get tested now? I mean, I know how you feel about the test, but if there are things that can help—don't you want to do those? Some clinical trial? Wouldn't *you* take the Mexican pills?"

Teddy said, quietly, "I did get tested. We went together. That was the deal—for his birthday, he wanted both of us to get tested. It was my present to him, that I agreed. I'm negative. I mean, I told you. I always told you."

Yale said, "Jesus Christ, Teddy. I'm happy for you, but Jesus Christ."

The next day, Bill finally returned, suspiciously tan, and there was at least more noise around the office. That following afternoon, Roman the intern started. He sat in the Northwestern crest chair across from Yale and held his black backpack in his lap. He twitched his foot.

Yale said, "I know you probably thought you'd be doing more curatorial work. I hope this isn't a disappointment."

"No, I mean—I'm up for anything. I don't have experience talking to people about money, but I guess that's good to learn, right?"

There was no way Roman would be talking to donors—he'd be listening in, at most—but Yale didn't point this out. If nothing else, he'd join them in Wisconsin next week.

Yale said, "Listen, I'm an art lover myself. I wasn't a money guy who fell into museums. I'm an art guy who's good with numbers."

Roman brightened. "Did you do grad work?"

Yale said, "Let me rephrase that. I'm an art lover who majored in finance."

"Got it." Roman nodded. "I mean, it's not too late."

Yale couldn't help laughing. "I've gotten a pretty good education along the way."

"Cool," Roman said. "Cool." He took his glasses off and wiped them on his sweater.

Yale set him to work on the Rolodex, which was still a mess. There was an extra table in the front corner of the office that made a decent desk, so long as no one opened the door. And, if Yale was honest, it improved his view. When he wanted to look at something nice, there was the window behind him, or there was Roman, hard at work, in front of him. In another life, Yale might have let himself fantasize about filling another kind of mentor role for Roman, teaching him things in and out of bed. But at the moment, the thought was almost revolting.

Before he left for Wisconsin, Yale bought a big bag of stuff from the deli—egg salad, pasta salad, cold cuts—and put it all right at the front of the refrigerator for Charlie. He made him promise to sleep enough.

Charlie said, "I don't deserve you." He was looking into the fridge like it held King Tut's treasures.

Yale said, "Remember that, next time I leave the window open and it rains."

The whole trip north, Bill told stories about former interns, at the Brigg and elsewhere—promising ones and shy ones and the one who'd had a mental breakdown. Yale got the distinct impression that many of these young men had been more than interns to Bill Lindsey, and that Bill wanted Roman to pick up on the fact. Bill wasn't the kind of older man Yale had been imagining for Roman. For one thing, he was sixty. And a closet case wasn't any kind of model for someone young and nervous.

"So," Roman said. He rode in the backseat, as if he were Yale and Bill's child. "We're just walking right up and knocking on the door?"

"That's the idea."

Regardless of whatever ancillary motives Bill had for bringing Roman, the idea was basically a good one: Roman could talk about the student perspective, the benefit to the school. That he looked like an undergrad might remind Nora of her husband's time at Northwestern. And Roman proved, on the way up, a handy navigator. He even pumped the gas.

Yale said, "The one thing I'm going to ask is that we *don't* bring up money. Not even if we're alone with Nora. Not even words like *value* or *worth*, okay?"

Roman said, "I don't mean this in a bad way, but—why is she doing this? Like, why *us*?"

"I guess her husband had a really good time at Northwestern," Yale said. "And I know her grandniece." He felt guilty, not mentioning Nico.

They stopped first in Egg Harbor to check in and unpack at the bed and breakfast, where Yale strategically chose the middle of the three rooms, feeling he should protect Roman from the possibility of a late-night Bill Lindsey advance. They met back in the front hall, and the couple who ran the place—it was cherry-themed, with paintings of cherries and cherry trees, the promise of cherry cobbler for breakfast—loaded them with advice on what to see if they had "a little extra time."

Yale felt queasy as they pulled into Nora's driveway. Even though this had been his idea, he deeply hated springing things on people. He'd often told Charlie that he'd never throw him a surprise party, because his heart couldn't take the pressure.

A yellow station wagon was parked beside the two Volkswagens this time. And before they were out of the car, a small boy ran around the corner of the house, looked at them, dashed back.

"Shit," Yale said.

Bill said, "Hey. This could be good. This could be a good thing."

Yale didn't see how that was possible. It crossed his mind that maybe Nora had died, that these people were here for some kind of visitation. That they were five days too late.

Patches of snow dotted the lawn, reflecting sunlight. They were halfway up the walk when a young woman, not Debra—red-haired, bundled in a blue parka—rounded the corner holding the boy's hand. She said, "Can I help you?"

Yale said, "We're from Northwestern University."

He was about to explain, to ask if Nora was home, but the woman asked them to wait on the screened porch. She and the boy vanished inside, and a few seconds later a stout, bald man appeared. He stepped out in a polo shirt with no coat, leaving one finger hooked around the knob of the cracked door.

"This isn't a great time," he said.

Yale extended a hand. "Yale Tishman," he said. "Are you Nora's son? Frank?" Best-case scenario, he could win the guy over. Have him call off his dogs.

"You can't come up here and harass her."

"I apologize. We didn't have a phone number, and I knew she wanted to meet the gallery director. This is Bill Lindsey"—Bill nodded—"and we've brought one of our graduate students." Yale was talking too fast. The man looked them up and down, and Yale couldn't even imagine how they appeared to him: three fags of various ages, shivering in dressy coats and scarves.

In the house, Nora was talking. Yale heard her say, "Then why didn't I hear the doorbell?" He thought of calling to her, of ducking under Frank's arm and through the door.

Frank squinted down. He was up a step. He said, "You're trespassing. This house belongs to me, not my mother. If you're gone by the time the police get here, I might not have you arrested." And he closed the door.

Bill started laughing, a thin, helpless laugh. They walked back to the car.

The air around Yale had taken on a migraine density, a pink, oppressive haze. Frank was surely on the horn already to his donor friend, who would call his lawyers and Cecily and the president of the entire university.

They went to a café in Egg Harbor, the first place they found open, to regroup.

"I'm sorry." Yale directed this at Bill. "This was a phenomenal waste of time."

He suspected Bill felt otherwise, though, the way he'd been pointing things out to Roman like a tour guide, even as they'd fled the scene. Bill was ordering coffee now, wondering if he was hungry enough for a sandwich. He'd warned Yale: He himself had nothing to lose. And with Roman here, Bill didn't seem to notice Yale circling the drain, didn't notice the pallor Yale was sure had overtaken his face.

Yale said, "What if—what if we drop in on the lawyer? If he's back from his very long holiday. And have him call her. Or give us the number. We can't just leave." It was too late to give up; they were going to suffer the consequences now regardless.

Roman slurped his coffee and said, "The mailbox was by the road, right?"

"Yeah. With the house number."

"I mean—it's two p.m., so maybe they've picked up the mail, maybe they haven't. Probably the redhead got it when she was out with her kids. But what if we put a note there for Nora? We make it look like it came in the mail. Fake return address, whatever, just as long as Frank doesn't see us. It could ask her to call us at the bed-and-breakfast. I mean, I don't know. I've been watching too many spy movies, but I think it could work."

Bill said, "Isn't he great? Intern of the year."

Yale watched his hand stir his coffee. "It's not a bad idea," he said. "And we can visit the lawyer in the meantime."

They found a gift store that sold greeting cards, and inside a "Thinking of you!" note with butterflies, they wrote Nora a letter saying they apologized for dropping in, but they'd been unable to reach her, and right now was the best time to meet the gallery director. They addressed the letter and even dug up a stamp, rubbed some ink on it so it looked mailed. They drove slowly down County Road ZZ, and when they neared Nora's mailbox Yale rolled down the passenger window and stuck the letter in with the magazines and bills that were, in fact, still there. They sped away laughing like teenagers who'd just egged a house.

Bill and Yale dropped Roman at the B&B, where he was to wait by the house phone in case Nora called, and found their way to the offices of Toynbee, Ball, and O'Dell in a converted Victorian outside downtown Sturgeon Bay, the kind of place that might as easily have been turned into an orthopedist's. It was open, and Stanley looked happy to see them. He was working in a blue sweater and khakis, and seemed to have no pressing engagements.

"You probably did the right thing," he said, "coming up. I worry for her, with that family. They're not locking her in, nothing like that, but half the time I call, they won't put her on. And she's sharp. She knows what's going on."

"But she lives alone, right?" Yale said. "I thought the others just visited."

There was a huge clock on the wall behind Stanley, one that must have reminded most visitors of his hourly fee but that to Yale served only to count down the hours till Frank Lerner's phone tree reached Cecily.

"I don't think Debra's left in months. Let me tell you about her father, Nora's son. Frank." He leaned back in a desk chair he was too tall for. "She had him when she was thirty-two, which—you know, back then that was late for a first child. Only child, actually. She thinks it's all her fault that he's a bully. Has a decent amount of money, and he thinks he's a wine connoisseur. An oenophile. You know that word? I just learned that word. My daughter gave me this word-a-day calendar for Christmas." He tapped the little block of paper attached to a plastic easel on his desk, turned it toward them. Today's word was *avuncular*. "Yeah, he's a big *oenophile*." He chuckled. "Sounds dirty, right? My point is, he's not about to starve if she gives away that art. He didn't even know about it till five or six years ago."

Yale said, "That was his wife, at the house today? With kids?"

"One day she'll wake up and realize she's married to an old man. She's what, half his age? Beautiful lady, though. Phoebe. An *aerobics instructor*." He waggled his eyebrows.

Bill said, "What are the odds of his contesting the will?"

"Decent. But winning is another matter. And I'm on your side in this. I want whatever Nora wants, and Nora wants to work with you."

Yale said, "If she could donate while she's alive, we wouldn't be worrying about a will."

Bill said, "You can't contest a donation from a living person, can you?"

"Well," Stanley said. "It's been *done*. You know, let's say an old woman with dementia suddenly announces she's giving her entire fortune to her nurse. But you're right, in this case it would make things a hell of a lot easier. My advice, regardless, is to have your own counsel present. I'm there, your counsel's there, it's pretty airtight."

"Is Nora amenable to donating right now?"

Stanley half smiled, bobbed his head from side to side.

Yale had a ridiculous vision of the three of them walking back through the doors of the Brigg tomorrow with armloads of art, of Cecily seeing these Modiglianis—and Chuck Donovan's two-million-dollar check, his little piano donations, falling away like gnats.

The secretary, the one who'd shown them in, rapped on Stanley's half-open door with one knuckle. She said, "We have a call for your visitors."

Roman's voice was ecstatic, breathless: "She called. She wants to see us. She said bring the lawyer."

And so an hour later there were eight of them seated around Nora's dining table, an awkward board meeting. Nora sat at the head of the table in a wheelchair—"Not my first time in the chair, but it never lasts long," she said—the sun setting behind her head. Yale took a seat between Frank and his daughter Debra, so that Bill, Roman, and Frank's wife were mixed together on the table's other side. Less adversarial this way. Stanley sat at the other end, opposite Nora. Frank's children—a boy and girl who probably should have been in school, but maybe it was still Christmas break after all—had been sent to the basement to watch TV. Yale had called Northwestern's general counsel, who'd promised to drive up as soon as he could get out of the office. It was unlikely he'd arrive before eight p.m., but even if that was after Nora needed them out of the house, they could get everything done in the morning.

Yale felt he should start things off, break the tension that was causing Debra to fold her arms over her flat chest and Roman to twitch his foot so hard that it shook the floor—but Nora piped up, clearing her throat pleasantly and saying, "I'm *thrilled* you're here. Frank, not a word from you. It's good for you to know my plans, but I'm not looking for advice."

Frank snorted and leaned his chair back. He was close to sixty, and what remained of his hair was silver, but there was something about his wet, dark eyes that made him look like an overgrown child.

"The Polaroids are remarkable," Bill Lindsey said. "And

depending what artifacts you have, what photographs of Paris, letters, and so on, those might be put on display as well."

Nora looked taken aback, but then she said, "I don't suppose there's anything so private in there. I'll have to look through."

Debra said, "Wait, Nana, you're giving away the papers too? Did we know this?"

"Well the papers go with the artwork, dear."

Frank rolled his eyes, made a sound to go with it.

"So you liked *all* of it?" Nora said. "The Novak pieces too? Because I do want those appreciated."

Before Bill could say something that sounded less than enthusiastic, Yale said, "I'm really drawn to the man in the argyle vest."

Nora laughed, closed her eyes as if the painting were inside her eyelids.

Debra whispered, but for everyone to hear: "Ranko was her *boyfriend*."

"Ahhhh," Bill said. "That makes sense." And he shot Yale a look.

The only thing Bill's intern Sarah had been able to find out about Novak was that he'd been one of three students to share the prestigious Prix de Rome in 1914—a detail footnoted with the fact that the outbreak of the war prevented their traveling to Rome that year, and so the award was postponed. But that seemed to be the end of his historical trail.

Bill talked about his vision for an exhibit. "We could always accept the pieces on loan and mount something temporary," he said, "but in that case we couldn't raise the endowment for authentication and restoration." He was speaking out of turn—Yale had never intended to bring up the possibility of a loan—and Yale tried in vain to catch his eye.

Yale said, "We'd like to be able to promise that we'll care for these works in perpetuity."

Nora turned to her son and said, "You do understand, don't

you, Frank? That it's costly. Nothing's framed, and everything will need preserving." She coughed wetly into her hand.

Frank said, "Am I allowed to talk? Listen, I know a guy who used to work in the art world, a gallery up in Toronto. He'd do that authentication part for free. A personal favor."

Yale shook his head. "You might be thinking of appraisal rather than authentication, but even so—"

Frank was insulted now, Yale could see. "Look," he said, "I hate to bring this up, but I have a close friend who, let's just say he's *very big* at Northwestern, and—"

"Mr. Donovan has been in contact with the development office," Yale said. "It doesn't concern us right now."

Frank opened his mouth as if to yell at Yale, but then he turned to Nora instead. "Mother, I'm paying for this house. Have you considered that? You're cutting me and my children out of this money, and you're sitting here in a house *I own*."

Nora said, calmly, "Are you planning to evict me?"

Before Frank could answer, his wife put her hand on his arm. "Frank," she said, "why don't you go out back for some air?"

Frank stood, presumably to do that, but then there was a shriek and crying from the basement and Frank and Phoebe ran down to see what had happened, and then Roman asked where the bathroom was, and soon people had dispersed all over the house. Which was fine by Yale. He followed as Nora wheeled herself into the living room, and she invited him to sit on the same couch where he'd sat with Cecily. He picked the middle this time, less awkward but also less comfortable. The seams where the two flattened cushions met dug into his tailbone. Bill—when Yale nodded at him that this was good, that a one-on-one with Nora would help—went out on the front porch for a smoke, and when Roman finished in the bathroom, he scurried out to join. Stanley stayed in the dining room, listening from a distance.

Nora said, "I need you to know that I'm dying. I have this congestive heart failure. My heart is simply weak, and I'm not a good candidate for surgery, as you can imagine. They don't suppose I've got longer than a year. You'd think the doctors would know more. The funny thing is, I'm hardly struggling, but apparently my heart believes otherwise. What's likely to happen is I'll die in my sleep. That's not so bad, is it? I always imagined I'd get lung cancer, and this is what I get instead. You don't smoke, do you? Nico was always smoking, and I hated it, though I don't suppose it mattered in the end. I stopped when I was forty, and look where it got me. Now, Frank and Debra know about my *condition*, but they hate me talking about it."

Yale couldn't figure out what to say. He'd had recent practice with this very thing—someone looking at you and telling you they were sick—but in every other case he'd been able to wrap his friend in a bear hug, to sob, to say, "I'm so fucking sorry." None of these would be appropriate. He managed to nod, to say, "I'm sorry to hear that. You look fantastic."

She laughed. "I don't know about fantastic. You should've seen me at twenty-five. Hell, you *have* seen me at twenty-five. Didn't I look fantastic?"

"You did."

"Now you and I have work to do, because I don't just want you to have the art, I know you need *provenance*, and my memory is still perfect. I can tell you when and where every one of those pieces was done."

"That would be invaluable." He could hear Frank and Phoebe yelling at their children in the basement. Debra was angrily washing dishes. Yale told Nora about the Sharps, about their willingness to help. "If we got the ball rolling," he said, "these works could be hanging in the gallery while you're still around to see it."

"Well, I like that. I do. What needs to happen?"

Heavy footsteps ascended the basement stairs. He told her, quickly, about needing professional shots of the work for authentication, how there were separate experts for each artist. "And eventually they'll want to see it in person. If you're willing to put the pieces in our hands," he said, "then they'd come to us. We'd handle it all."

Frank was in the doorway. Nora said, "That seems smart, doesn't it?" Yale wished Bill and Roman would come back inside, but then he didn't want anything to break the spell. The whole room felt like a soufflé that had just risen, like the slightest shake would destroy it.

Frank pressed both hands into the doorframe. He said, "You're giving away millions of dollars." His voice a cyclone in a bottle. "Your grandkids won't be able to *go* to Northwestern if you do this."

Nora said, "Stanley, won't you come in here?"

"I would consider this undue influence," Frank said. "Is that the legal term, Stanley? Undue influence?"

Stanley had entered the room, and he gave Yale a wary look. "This is where you want your own counsel present. Just—so you don't have to deal with any of this a year from now, two years from now." Yale checked his watch. Only 4 p.m..

Frank said, "Then I want *my* own counsel present."

"You're welcome to that," Yale said.

Roman was back, reporting that it had started to snow.

Nora said, "You certainly do bring the weather, Mr. Tishman!"

Yale squinted at the window. Had this been predicted? They'd had the radio off the whole drive up. It was falling steadily, thickly. A mixed blessing, at best: Frank might not be able to send for his own lawyer from Green Bay, but this would slow the Northwestern counsel down significantly. The Northwestern counsel, whose name, for Pete's sake, was Herbert Snow. A cosmic joke.

180

"May I use your restroom?" asked Yale, and Roman, who'd already found it, pointed through the dining room. Yale passed the polished table, the curio cabinets, and entered the kitchen—the kind of kitchen every grandmother ought to have. Herbs on the windowsill, shelves of cookbooks. An oilcloth on the small table, patterned with little picnic baskets.

A hand clamped down on Yale's shoulder, meaty and cold. Frank said, "Stop right there."

Yale said, "I understand you're upset. Family is always—"

"My kids use that bathroom."

Yale tried to catch up.

"I know who you are," Frank said. "I know where you're *from*. You are not unzipping your trousers in my house."

The hand was still on his shoulder, and Yale bent his knees to duck out from under it. He was a good six inches shorter than this man, but he had better posture. He had a sharper chin, and he leveled it at Frank's neck. He said, "Where I'm from is Midland, Michigan."

"Feel free to head back there."

Yale could have said terrible things then. He imagined that Terrence, in the same situation, would have assured Frank he'd use the guest towels when he jerked off. He imagined Asher or Charlie lighting into him, calling him a coward and a bigot and worse. But he was himself, and he couldn't afford to anger this guy any further, and so he said, "I'm healthy. If that's what—I'm not sick." But his voice cracked on the last word, which didn't help.

Frank looked revolted, as if the words themselves were contaminated. He said, "There are *children* in this house."

And you're one of them, Yale didn't say. He said, "Maybe it would be best if we met Nora at the bank in the morning, to finish this up. At the safe deposit box."

Debra appeared behind Frank. "Everything okay, Dad?"

"Gallery boy's leaving now," Frank said.

Yale and Roman and Bill put their coats on in the living room, and Yale took a pencil from his pocket to copy the number off the tag on Nora's phone.

Debra would drive her to the bank at 10 a.m. Stanley promised he'd be there too.

"Me three," Frank said, and his wife scratched his neck soothingly with her pink nails.

At 6:30 that evening, Herbert Snow called them at the B&B: He'd gotten as far as Waukegan and turned around. He'd start again in the morning. "Can you be here by ten?" Yale said. Why the hell had he turned around? Why hadn't he just stayed there and saved an hour tomorrow? "You'll need to leave around five thirty, is the thing."

He said, "I'll do my best."

They went to dinner—"To celebrate!" Bill said, though Yale felt it was a terrible jinx to say so—and wound up ordering three bottles of wine. They were the only people in the restaurant until a wedding party came in—not for the reception but simply to eat after the reception, which had just been cake, as Roman learned and reported back after he'd stumbled over to congratulate the bride and groom— and the two parties both stayed so late that the waiters, by the end, were scrubbing the same nearby tables over and over, clearing their throats. Bill told Yale and Roman a story about Dolly's father, a concert pianist who had once courted one of Rachmaninoff's daughters. He kept refilling Roman's glass the second it was halfway empty. Bill got drunk enough that soon he was doing all the talking, and all of it was directed at Roman anyway, so Yale was free to lean back and stew. He was relatively sober; he'd be the one driving.

The art, he reminded himself, *might still be forged*. Even if everything worked out, there was still the possibility, however remote, that their trouble getting into the house today, and all this protestation, were part of some long, crazy con behind which Frank was the mastermind. But what in the world could these people gain from it? Not money.

Yale had never been able to take good fortune on its own terms. His fear of being tricked went back to at least sixth grade, to the day the basketball roster was posted and a classmate added Yale's name to the list in careful mimicry of the coach's handwriting. Yale showed up for practice unaware he'd been cut, and the coach looked at him and, with no trace of meanness, said, "Mr. Tishman, what are you doing here?" Behind him, the team had laughed and coughed and pounded each other's backs. While they ran laps for punishment, the coach asked Yale if he'd like to be the equipment manager. He didn't look surprised when Yale said no.

This had been followed by a thousand small cruelties over the next seven years of school, a thousand baits and traps. And all the while, Yale had tried, hopelessly, to trick everyone around him about the biggest thing of all, hoping against hope that they'd fall for his professed crush on Helen Appelbaum, his ogling of the girls' volleyball team. But they never did, and Yale understood that he would always be the tricked, never the tricker. It was why part of him had assumed, the night of Nico's memorial, that he was the victim of some coordinated meanness. And perhaps it was for similar reasons that Charlie had assumed even worse things that night. Charlie had it worse growing up, English schools being what they were.

But Yale was a grown man, and even if the world wasn't always a good place, he reminded himself that he could trust his perceptions now. Things were so often exactly what they seemed to be. Take Bill Lindsey here, leaning across the table to Roman, talking about the art professor who "really opened me up, if you know what I mean." Take the snow out the window, falling so deliberately. Take the waiter, checking his watch.

2015

Fiona covered as much ground as she could that afternoon, figuring that even if Claire was no longer here, someone who'd known her when she *had* been here could be helpful. She tried art supply stores, yoga studios, every vaguely approachable person on the sidewalk.

Shrugs, sympathetic smiles, confusion. Two people took pictures of the photo with their phones, copied down her number.

She ought to be back in the States, where Claire was most likely to be. But after they searched the apartment, she could lasso Kurt, with or without Arnaud's help. Enormous as he was, she could sit on him till he talked.

She ended up back on the Pont de l'Archevêché. Mostly empty, again. Sections of it were still covered in padlocks, as they'd been in the video, but some panels of chain link had been cleared and covered with plywood. A giant heart sticker was affixed to the sidewalk, an English message printed in white on the red: "*Our bridges can no longer withstand your gestures of love.*" In the heart's right atrium, a crossed-out lock.

On the other side of the bridge, a man leaned over to stare at the tour boat passing below.

She rested her back against the railing, facing not the water, not Notre Dame, but the width of the bridge itself. It was a cold day, foggy and damp. How long could she stand here, waiting and watching, before someone worried she was a suicide?

When no other pedestrians were on the bridge, she called Claire's name down the river. Because it wouldn't do any good, and wasn't it nice, for a change, to do something she *knew* would do no good? She was tired and hungry again, and she ought to get back to the apartment and call Damian, who'd be up by now. She needed to call the store and make sure Susan was running everything smoothly.

She shouted for Claire ten times. It felt like a lucky number.

Beginning in fifth grade, Fiona was in the habit of taking the train nearly every Saturday to see Nico while her parents thought she was at Girl Scouts. The leaders never cared if you showed up, so she made sure to put in just enough appearances (the first meeting of the year, the last, the field trips) that she remained on the troop's roster. But most Saturdays, she'd take the Metra to Evanston, and then the El all the way down to Belmont.

She'd carry a backpack filled with things she'd filched from the cupboards and refrigerator up in Highland Park. Half a carton of cottage cheese, a stick of butter, leftover chili, a sleeve of Ritz. Spoons, once, when Nico didn't have enough. Items from his room, so slowly her parents wouldn't notice: socks, photographs, tapes. She wished she could bring his records, but they wouldn't fit in her backpack—and besides, his roommates seemed to have plenty. It dawned on her only years later that they hadn't needed any of the things she'd brought, not really. They could have stolen spoons from a restaurant. Between them, they could have afforded food.

There were five of them, sometimes six or seven, living in one room above a bar on Broadway. Almost all of them teenagers. She found out only years later, as Nico was dying, that some of them had been hustling. Nico had a job bagging groceries, and between that money and Aunt Nora's money, and the few dollars Fiona managed to sneak him (she'd steal change all week to pay for her train tickets, give him what was left), he managed to stay off the streets. At least this was what he'd maintained to the end. She didn't imagine he'd tell her, though, because then she'd have felt it was her fault, that she hadn't done enough, back when she was only a kid and was doing all she could.

She would knock on the door and he'd fling it open and say "Feef the Thief!" and scoop her inside. It was Christmas every time, watching him open the backpack, remove the items one by one. His roommates would crowd behind him, cheer for things like the spoons. Once, she managed a bottle of wine. They couldn't believe it. One of them—was it Jonathan Bird?—made up a song about her. She wished she could remember it.

Nico had his own place by the time she moved to the city after high school, but a lot of those guys were still around, still called her Feef the Thief, loved to tell these stories right in front of her. "This kid was *Robin Hood*!" they'd said. James, Rodney, Jonathan Bird. She might not have remembered Jonathan Bird, except that he was the very first to die. So early that he didn't die of AIDS, because there was no such acronym; he died of GRID. The *G* stood for gay, and she'd blocked out the rest. Jonathan had been healthy one day, and the next he had a cough, and a week later he was in the hospital, and the next day he was gone.

It hadn't occurred to Fiona till just now, her hands gripping the cold bridge railing, that her mother might have known where she was going all those weekends, all those years. As she got older, when Girl Scouts wasn't a legitimate excuse, she'd made up stories about skating parties, study sessions. Maybe her mother had left her purse unguarded for a reason. As she called Claire's name one last time into the wind, as the city returned her voice on the wet air, Fiona remembered her mother calling and calling for Nico in

186

the yard when they were kids. Had she ever stopped calling for him? Had she ever stopped leaving coins around, hoping they'd find their way to her boy?

After Nico died, their mother spent twenty years drinking. Fiona knew she was crushed, but she couldn't forgive her. They had done this to Nico, her mother and father. Her mother had stood there, crying, arms crossed, the night their father kicked Nico out, but she hadn't done a thing to stop him. She hadn't even given him any money. She'd gone and found his duffel bag in the basement, as if that were a favor.

Over the years, Fiona visited them less and less. She withheld Claire.

And maybe Claire would have been better if she'd had grandparents, a safety net, extended family.

Our bridges can no longer withstand your gestures of love.

Well, fuck.

She peeled her fingers from the railing.

She walked back to Richard's, climbed the stairs toward the smell of browning garlic.

1986

In the morning, they ate their too-sweet cherry cobbler, and Bill nursed his hangover, and they watched the snow fall. "He won't make it, will he," Roman said. "The counsel."

Yale said, "I'm more concerned the *rest* of them won't. They'll say they have to delay because of the snow, we sit around three more days, it all falls through."

Even one extra day might mean more interference from Frank, an intervention from Cecily, a telegram from the president of the university.

"Good God," Bill said. "Who called in the doom brigade?"

Roman stammered an apology. His hair, still wet, hung in clumps. One clump had left a spray of water across his glasses. He said, "I mean no one's called yet, have they? That's good. It's a good sign."

The three of them were there at 9:50, waiting in the car until the bank unlocked its doors. At ten, they stood in the lobby trying to warm back up. Yale cursed himself for wearing Nico's shoes, which had gotten wet in the snow and let the slush onto his socks. But they'd brought him luck last time, and he was superstitious. Why couldn't he have claimed Nico's scarf instead? It might even have smelled like Nico, like Brut and cigarettes. It was Nico's favorite joke to try to convince people that Carly Simon's song was about him, about his apricot scarf. "And I *am* so vain!" he always said. "So you know it's true!" ("That scarf is not apricot," Charlie always responded. "It's orange and gray." Nico would reply that British men were known to be color-blind.)

Yale tried not to look at the clock above the counter. Despite the snow, despite Nora's obstructive family: If this didn't happen today, it would be *his* failure, his embarrassment. It was a magnification of how he felt when he was the one to pick the movie out of the listings: Although he couldn't control the action on the screen, he was the one who'd set it in motion, and if anyone had a bad time, it was because of him. Instead of simply watching the movie, he'd watch it through Charlie's eyes, glancing over for the reaction, listening for laughter. And right now he wanted Bill Lindsey thrilled. He wanted to give Roman the experience of a lifetime. He wanted these curious bank tellers to keep watching, with fascination, as art history was made.

The snow continued falling in huge, lacy chunks.

Roman said, "I'm worried the roads are getting worse."

But just then Debra walked in, wrapped to the eyeballs in a brown coat, a blue scarf. She said, "One of you has to help Stanley unload that wheelchair." Yale felt something unclench in his lower back, a muscle he hadn't even felt cramping.

Bill went out to the van while Debra talked to a teller, and by the time Stanley and Bill came back through the doors with Nora and her chair, everything was in order. The whole group—Frank hadn't arrived yet, thank God—followed the teller into the safety-deposit room.

"Our counsel is on his way," Yale said to Stanley. They could proceed without him if need be. But then . . . but then, but then.

They started piling their coats on the long table in the middle of the room, but Bill needed it clear for inspecting the work. He handed out the white gloves they'd optimistically brought from the museum. Debra refused hers.

Nora wheeled herself up to the table. She said, "This is just ideal, isn't it? Now we have to tell you, I've absolutely bought Debra off."

Debra didn't respond, just nervously twirled her key ring. Her fingers were red from the cold.

Nora said, "There's more in here than art, and we've decided it's time to hand some of that over. Jewelry, you know." Yale wondered why this would be a compelling payoff when Debra could just as easily wait for Nora to die. Maybe it was a matter of everything passing through Frank, the possibility of Frank giving necklaces to his wife instead.

Yale was afraid to bring it up, but he said, "Where's your father?"

"We killed him," Debra said. "I smothered him with a pillow."

Nora burst out cackling. "Well, that would solve things, wouldn't it? Don't scare them, dear, they'll think you really did it. No, what Debra's done for us is promise her father that nothing will get signed till this afternoon. A lie, but a white one."

"I promised him too," Stanley said.

Debra said, "He's sleeping in."

But it was 10:15, and Yale imagined that when Frank woke up fully, when he looked around the empty house and thought about the fact that everyone was at the bank without him, he'd show up. Or worse: He had let them leave only to wait on the front porch for the lawyer he'd asked to speed down from Green Bay. Or he was polishing his shotgun.

Debra's hands shook as she tried to settle the key in the lock. She looked not just annoyed but terrified. Like someone who'd cut her losses and sold out her father, her rather vengeful father, for what was left of the pie. Yale was still struggling for a response when Roman touched Debra's elbow. "You did the right thing," he said.

Debra said, "Okay, there's two boxes, but I can never remember which is which."

The teller helped her slide out the first large container and carry it to the table. It held the shoebox—Yale carefully lifted the lid and took in the edges of envelopes and folded pages and white-rimmed photographs—plus some velvety jewelry boxes and a large envelope that, when Debra opened it, seemed to contain birth certificates and old deeds. Yale replaced the shoebox's lid, resisting the temptation to paw through.

They held their breath for the second container, and when Debra opened it and reached in herself, gloveless, Bill made a noise like a frightened bird. He said, "Please, let me, let me." Nora, at eye level to the tabletop, couldn't have seen into the box yet. She sat still, hands folded across her lap, taking long, patient blinks. Yale wondered how long it had been since she'd seen the pieces in person. Stanley stood beside her, attentive.

The drawings and sketches were contained—dear God—in two crumbling manila envelopes. Below those, unprotected, lay the Foujita watercolor, Nora in the green dress. Yale was looking for paper quality, damage, rips. He was no expert, but things looked both appropriately old and in decent shape. The oil paintings, the alleged Hébuterne and Soutine and the two Ranko Novaks, were rolled and secured with rubber bands. Bill slid the bands off slowly, evenly, in a way that reminded Yale of a man carefully dealing with a Trojan. He called Roman to help, and together their gloved hands unfurled the canvas at an excruciatingly slow pace and held it, by the corners, to the table. It was the Hébuterne, the bedroom.

Nora said, "Goodness, this is like being pried open, isn't it? What an odd feeling." She leaned forward to see the work. Yale could hear her wheeze, fast and thick.

Yale couldn't read Bill's reaction yet, didn't want to say the wrong thing—what if Bill was busy noting that this was acrylic paint, not oil, that it couldn't be legitimate?—but something needed to be said. "Nora," he managed, "we're so grateful to you."

Bill motioned for Yale to come take his place, to be the hands that held two corners down, while he himself stepped back to view it from a distance. And then he let out a sigh—a postsex sigh, a sigh of extraordinary contentment.

Nora said, "Well, I like that sound."

"These are phenomenal," Bill said.

"Yes, and you believe me now, don't you? Your skepticism did not escape my notice!" This was directed at Yale.

Yale said, "We can't thank you enough."

But now that the art was here, where was the general counsel? It was 10:35. If Herbert Snow didn't arrive by noon, Yale decided, he'd go ahead with the paperwork anyway. But maybe he should do it sooner. Because what if Frank burst in?

Bill rushed through the Novak paintings—the man in the argyle vest was smaller than Yale had imagined, the size of a notebook page, while the sad little girl was enormous—and lingered over the Soutine portrait. "That one," Nora said, "I'll have you know I stole it from him, which is why it's not signed. He was going to burn it along with a heap of others. And it's of *me*! I couldn't let myself be burned! Such a strange man."

After the paintings, Bill no longer needed people to hold down corners; everything else was flat. He worked as carefully as a surgeon, removing the sketches from the manila envelopes. Yale stepped away, but kept the white gloves on. Like Mickey Mouse, or a butler. Bill asked Nora about dates for the ones that weren't signed. "I'll really have to think," she said. "Ranko's pieces are earliest. Those are the only ones from before the war. Nineteen thirteen, I'd say. But not the portrait with the vest, of course! No one wore argyle before the war!" She laughed as if this were obvious.

Bill nodded, bemused.

Yale went to where Debra leaned against a wall. He said, quietly, "We really appreciate your help. I do understand your side of things."

"I doubt that's true." She never moved her mouth much when she talked.

"At least I know I'd be unhappy in your position."

Over at the table, everyone else was making noise about the writing on the back of one sketch, flipping it over and holding it an inch above the table. Debra whispered: "She had an amazing life. I'm bored out of my mind, and I'm giving up my freedom to take care of her, when she had these wild years in Paris hanging out with, like, *Monet*, you know? And she could've given me just a little bit of that. But she didn't."

Yale had to give her credit—he'd thought it was all about the money, and maybe it wasn't, after all. He said, "If it makes you feel better, there are absolutely no Monets in there."

"Listen, just tell me. How much do you think it's all worth?" She closed her eyes, waiting for the blow.

"Oh," Yale said. "God, it—I don't know, it doesn't really work that way. The art market is so weird. It's not like a diamond, where you could say there's a certain weight and—"

"But, like, how much do you *think*?"

He couldn't tell her. In part because it would make everything worse, right when they'd gotten her help. And partly because he didn't want this poor woman dwelling on it for the rest of her life. He said, "They're mostly just sketches, you know? A painting by Modigliani would be one thing, but—what's valuable to *us* isn't necessarily worth a ton of money."

"Okay." Her face relaxed. Relief, but maybe a touch of disappointment too. Yale wanted to hug her, beg her forgiveness.

"Debra," Nora called to her, "look through the jewelry whenever you'd like."

Yale helped her spread it across the empty end of the table. He was almost as fascinated by these necklaces and earrings as he was by the art. They weren't laden with gemstones, but everything was Deco and chic and bright, stuff out of an Erté print. Yale watched Debra pick things he could never imagine her wearing. A sunburst haircomb, chandelier earrings, a scarab-beetle brooch. There was a necklace with what looked like a real emerald, not that he'd know, and he moved it to her Keep pile. "This could be worth something," he said.

When the remaining jewelry had been packed back up, when the art had been replaced in its rubber bands and envelopes (Bill had neglected to bring anything better for storage), the general counsel was still not there. It was 11:20. Debra was spinning the key ring again.

Roman said, "Should I phone someone? At Northwestern?"

They sent him to call the bed and breakfast from the lobby to see if there'd been a message. He came back shaking his head.

But meanwhile, Nora had opened the shoebox of papers, started sorting them into stacks. She said, "There's more than I remembered."

"The more the better," Bill said.

"Yes, but I wanted to go through it with you—really I have to—and I don't see how we'll get it done." Stanley leaned over and pulled out half an inch of papers with bare hands, and Bill inhaled sharply. "Sit down," Nora said, and Yale and Bill and Roman all did, on the cold metal folding chairs. Yale sat at her left elbow. Debra paced. "This one here," Nora said, "now you see it's signed 'Fou-Fou,' and I'm sure you could figure out that was Foujita, but look." She showed them a small sketch of a ragged puppy next to the signature. "You wouldn't know that this was because he called me 'Nora Inu.' Nora means 'stray,' you see, in Japanese, and he thought this was wonderful, that I was a stray who'd found my

194

way across the ocean. 'Nora Inu' is 'stray dog.' That sounds like an insult, I suppose, but it wasn't."

"Amazing," Yale said, and he met Bill's exuberant eyes. "That—details like that, I think, will help a great deal with authentication. Maybe we could record you, what you're saying—"

"Well yes, someone should be taking it all down. Isn't that what *you're* for?" This was directed at Roman.

"I have a notebook in the car," he said, helplessly. And when they all kept looking at him, he bounded from the room to fetch it.

"Well," Nora said, "my point is you're going to need these stories. And I don't see how we're going to do that if you take this all back to Chicago. And I'm going to want to sort things too. I can see now they're out of order. Couldn't you stay up here a week or so?"

But they couldn't, not right now. They had meetings, they had a gallery to run—plus as soon as the papers were signed, they wanted to get the art away from Frank. They hit on the idea that Roman could take the shoebox to the public library that afternoon, along with a load of dimes, and Xerox everything. The originals of the correspondence could remain in Wisconsin for now. "Not in the house, though," Yale put in. "So much more could happen to the papers there."

"Yes, yes," Nora said. He didn't need to spell it out.

They'd leave it all at the bank, and next week Yale and Roman would come back up, help her sort through.

When Roman returned, out of breath, Yale felt a knocking on his knee. Knuckles. He understood that he wasn't to jump or ask what Nora wanted. He looked down as subtly as he could at her closed fist. When she raised it slightly, he put his palm beneath it. She was passing him something. She let it drop into his hand, and he closed his fingers around a complicated object, metal and pointy. He could feel a chain. A necklace.

He didn't understand, but he shoved it into his trouser pocket, shifted so the sharp part dropped next to his groin.

195

She said to them all, "Listen, I feel dandy today, but I don't know how I'll feel next week, and if nothing else I want you to take this down." She pointed at Roman. "Everything I read about Modigliani says he drank himself to death. That's bunk. He died of tuberculosis. The drinking was only to cover up the illness, because there was such a stigma. He'd be at a party and start coughing, and he'd pretend to be falling-down drunk and take off. Now, he really was a *bit* of a drunk, that's why it worked. He was trying to save his dignity, isn't that funny? I don't think he imagined that decades later people would still be saying he drank himself to death. It makes me terribly angry. Did you write that down?"

Roman read from his notebook: "Modigliani died of tuberculosis, not alcohol."

"Ha. Well, you missed a bit. Next time, a tape recorder. Now I need to tell you about Ranko, because you won't find anything in a book."

But the teller was back at the door. She said, "There's a man here who'd like permission to join your party."

Yale stood. His adrenal glands did strange and unwelcome things.

But the man stepping into the room was not Frank. It was someone Yale had never seen before—a tall, older black man brushing snow from his trench coat and looking horribly peeved.

"Herbert!" Bill said, and rose to shake his hand, a big, manly shake.

And while everyone was turned that way, Nora tapped Yale's arm. "For Fiona," she said. The necklace.

Yale nodded and walked to greet Herbert Snow. "This is our general counsel," he said to everyone, to himself, to the universe.

Yale and Bill and Roman whooped and sang all the way back to Egg Harbor.

At the inn, Yale called Charlie.

"That's good," Charlie said. "I'm really happy for you."

"You're *really happy for me*? Come on, this is huge! That's like what you say when you see your ex on the street, *Oh, you have a new boyfriend, you lost weight, I'm really happy for you*. This is a huge thing! Like, the art is literally *in Bill's room*. I'm taking you out to dinner. Tomorrow, because we have to stay one more night. We have Xeroxing to do, and the roads are bad. Where do you want to go? For dinner?"

"I'll think about it." There was a pause, and then Charlie said, "I really am happy for you. I'm just tired."

Yale almost said something then about the house, about how there was this house he'd been wanting Charlie to visit, and this was the sign, this was the right time—but that could wait. He'd bring it up tomorrow, when they'd had some wine.

He called Fiona next, and she shrieked gratifyingly. He told her he had something for her, told her to come by the gallery to see the art. She said, "Oh, Yale, this was *supposed* to happen, don't you think?"

On the ride back the next morning—art packed and padded in the trunk, sheaves of Xeroxes on the backseat, papers signed and dated and witnessed—the three of them talked at full speed.

"I do feel bad for the family," Yale said. "We're not terrible people, are we?"

Bill said, "That man would take the pieces to the wrong restorers, the wrong appraisers, he'd get ripped off, and nothing would ever get authenticated, let alone into the catalogs. A lot of the world's great art has been lost thanks to folks exactly like Frank."

"And this will *make* the gallery," Yale said. "I mean—I'm sorry, the gallery's already in tremendous shape—"

Bill laughed to reassure him. "But we don't yet have four Modiglianis."

Roman spoke from the middle of the backseat: "This is a hell of a first week."

It hit Yale halfway home: If Nora weren't donating everything, she might well have willed a piece to Fiona. A single sketch could have paid Fiona's way to college. And certainly Fiona knew it. And she'd never said a thing.

2015

When Fiona got back to Richard's, Jake Austen was on the couch talking to Serge. She wanted to be angry at the invasion, she let herself be angry, but maybe she was a little relieved too. No one would ask her, yet, how her day had gone. Still: She hadn't imagined this guy would *embed* himself. His eyes were red, his shirt undone one button too low.

She put her purse on the counter, slid her shoes off. Both men waved, and Jake pointed dramatically to his phone, which lay on the coffee table. He was recording. Fiona made herself tea as quietly as she could.

Serge was saying, "He finds the space between the action and the resting. He doesn't want the photo of action, and he doesn't want the photo of rest, okay? Yes? He looks for the moment between." Fiona was unclear about whether Serge worked as a publicist for anyone else anymore, or if giving interviews about Richard had become his life.

Jake tapped his phone, and the two men relaxed. "How'd it go?" Jake said. "They, ah, they filled me in, I hope you don't mind. Is everything okay?"

"Christ," she said. "I don't know." Well, there went her little fantasy of looking like a normal person on a normal trip. *Poof.*

Fiona hadn't had dinner yet, but she wanted to go straight to bed. She should call Damian, though, and not forget to ask after Karen with something like concern. She ought to call Cecily and tell her that yes, Kurt was definitely in Paris, even if Cecily wouldn't want to hear it. Or maybe it could wait. Was it even Fiona's responsibility to tell her? She'd always had a bad sense of who fell under her jurisdiction and who didn't. Cecily had known why she was coming here, wished her the best. Fiona hadn't told her, though, about the little girl in the video. Why do that, when nothing was certain?

She said, "I think I'm done for the day."

"This is perfect," Serge said, "because you can come to the party! I convinced Jake to join already."

"Party?"

"At Corinne's, remember? We take the Métro to Vincennes at seven, okay? We get you home early, don't worry!"

"Oh. I—"

"Lots of important artists there. And you need to meet Corinne's husband. You need to see his beard."

"His beard?"

Serge laughed. "Trust me. Just trust."

Fiona called Damian from her room, and he wanted every detail repeated three times. It sounded less hopeless in the retelling, more like progress.

"This is great!" he said. "This is huge!"

She pretended, for his benefit, that she believed him.

Karen's radiation started on Monday; otherwise he'd hop on a plane, he hoped she knew that. "I haven't been to Paris since that conference in '94," he said.

"And you left me home with a baby. I never forgave you." But she knew he could hear her smiling. "I don't know what to do with myself," she said. She told him about the party.

"Go!" he said. "You get to hang out with artists in Paris! Go and have a good time."

"It's not exactly *hanging out with artists*," she said. "We're not sketching at the café."

He said, "Listen, try to retrace your great-aunt's steps while you're there. Didn't you always want to? What about her boyfriend, the dead one?"

"Ranko Novak?"

"Try to track him down."

"What, his grave?"

"I don't know. Sure."

"You're sweet, Damian."

"Go to the party." And then, "Ciao," which was something she used to find charming, back when he was her professor and she didn't know better.

Well, getting ready for a party was an excuse not to call Cecily. And she really didn't have it in her to call Cecily yet.

Fiona wished Jake weren't with them, weren't holding the Métro bar with two fingers and looking down at her. Richard and Serge sat behind her speaking rapid French, so Fiona had no one to talk to but Jake, and no way to talk to him but quasi-flirtatiously. The one dress she'd brought, a pale blue wrap, was low cut—and although she had a light coat, the buttons were broken and it hung open. Jake was staring straight down her cleavage.

When they disembarked in Vincennes and walked through the dark, quiet streets, past shops and restaurants and then beautiful, narrow houses, Jake got close to her ear and said, "So is this the Evanston of Paris?" and she couldn't help laughing. She stopped herself, though, so he wouldn't think he'd earned it.

He smelled of gin, and she wondered if he'd been drinking at Richard's or before.

She checked her phone, although she'd just checked it two minutes ago and the ringer was on. And there was no reason Arnaud would be calling yet. But she couldn't help refreshing her email, clicking on her empty voice mail.

It struck her that she could get rid of Jake by fucking him. It would be fun, she'd get it out of her system, and then he'd do the inevitable and graciously disappear. If he lingered, if he showed up tomorrow, she could always pretend she was in love, ask when they could see each other back in Chicago. "You know," she could say if the situation got desperate, "there's a chance I'm still fertile."

Would he even be able to perform, drunk as she assumed he was? He held each syllable a bit too long ("Check out that mooooon"), held her gaze too long, moved his feet too slowly. Not enough for Richard or Serge to notice, apparently, but enough to irritate Fiona. Why was he allowed to go through life drunk? Why was he allowed his boomerang wallet?

And then she was stuck with him at the damn party. Both of them hung by Richard and Serge in the entryway at first, where Corinne (in a yellow tunic dress and a necklace of enormous wooden beads) greeted them warmly, made sure they had drinks, beckoned her husband from the next room. Fernand Leclercq's beard was, as Serge had promised, prodigious: chest-length, as snowy and curled as the beard on a Claymation Santa. Importance radiated off him, a buzz that filled the foyer. "Feel free to look around," he said, and she couldn't figure out why she'd need or want such an invitation until she realized the house was filled with incredible art, that guests were sticking their necks into corners and back halls and even upstairs to glimpse Fernand and Corinne's acquisitions. A Basquiat hung outside the bathroom; a Julian Schnabel plate portrait dominated the dining room.

People made an effort to speak English to her at first—Corinne, Serge, the German writer they introduced her to—but soon everything was a whirl of French, and she was left talking to Jake. They wound up in a sunroom at the back of the house, a room that filled and then emptied every few minutes as guests popped in to make sure they hadn't missed any trays of food, buckets of champagne, seminal works of cubism.

He said, "I've been studying his work online. Richard's. It's weird how many photos I didn't even know were his. Like, famous ones. That triptych thing, I've totally admired that before. No idea it was Campo. And I saw one of you, I think. Yeah?" Despite the drink in his hand, he seemed soberer now than he had on the Métro. She wanted him to disappear.

"Was I wearing a flowery dress?"

"No, you were next to a guy—you were curled up next to someone in a hospital bed."

Fiona attempted to drain her champagne, although it hurt her nose when she swallowed. "You're asking about private things," she said. "It's art, but I was *there*. Those were my friends."

"I—hey, I actually didn't ask anything. I don't think I asked a question."

"Fair enough."

"What were you afraid I was going to ask?"

She thought. "You were going to ask me who that was, in the bed."

"Hey, do you want to sit down?"

"No." She looked at the group hovering in the sunroom door, but they were speaking French and hadn't glanced her way.

"Can I—listen, I just have one question, and it's not about that picture, it's about the triptych."

"Christ. What."

"Sorry! Sorry. Let's find food."

She was stressed about things that had nothing to do with Jake Austen and his invasion, but he was a convenient punching bag. And so she stepped too close to him, spoke too loud. "That was Julian Ames. In the triptych. He was a beautiful person, an actor, and Richard took the first photo when everything was great, and he took the second when Julian was freaking out because he knew he was sick, and then he took the third when he weighed like a hundred pounds."

"Hey, I'm sorry, I—"

"My brother died in this stupid hospital where my parents put him, this place where everyone was scared of him and no one knew what the hell they were doing, and Julian came up there every single day. He wasn't the smartest guy, but he was loyal and he felt things more than other people. *You*, you numb out with alcohol, right? Some people actually *feel* things. And there was this nurse who'd come around with the menu, but she wouldn't bring it into the room. Not that he could eat anything anyway."

"That's awful."

"Shut up. So half the time it didn't matter, because Nico was out of it. What we realized at the very end was he had lymphoma of the central nervous system, and these idiot doctors missed it and gave him steroids, which was the worst thing. But it reduced the brain swelling at first, so for a couple days he had these lucid windows. He'd reemerge for ten minutes, and then he'd be gone again. So he's lucid one day and the nurse comes and stands there, and she's got this smug little face, and she starts reading the menu from the doorway. Julian's in there with me, and Nico's alert, and the nurse goes, 'Spaghetti with meatballs.' So Julian stands at the foot of Nico's bed and repeats it in this *theater* voice, like he's playing a Shakespearean king, and then he does—it was somewhere between pantomime and an interpretive dance. This whole thing about spaghetti, twining it around his fork, slurping the noodles.

204

And the nurse just has this look on her face, like, *This is why you're all sick, look at this faggy behavior.* Julian goes right up and peers over her shoulder at the menu, and he announces the next thing, which is chicken salad, and he does a chicken dance. He does the whole menu like that while the nurse stands there."

"That's awesome."

"No. It was sad and awful. It was the last time my brother was awake."

"Can I ask what happened to him? To Julian?"

"What the fuck do you *think* happened?"

"Fiona, you're—"

"He was an actor with no family and no health insurance, and he could've gotten some decent support at least if he'd stayed in Chicago, if he'd stuck around till the drugs came out, but instead he took off and died alone and I don't even know where."

"You're bleeding."

"What?"

"Your hand."

She looked down. The empty champagne flute, which she'd been holding tightly, was cracked. A droplet of blood ran down her right wrist and another ran down the outside of the glass. When she peeled her hand back, the whole glass fell apart, shattering onto the floor.

The room went gray at the edges, and voices closed in. Corinne was there, holding a towel under her hand, guiding her to a wallpapered little bathroom with golden faucets, sitting her on the closed toilet.

Now Corinne's husband was kneeling in front of Fiona with a pair of tweezers, slowly picking out the shards embedded all over her palm.

"I'm so embarrassed," she said when everything was back in focus, when Corinne had left to clean up the mess.

"This is not allowed." His voice was phlegmy and deep. There was something regal about the top of his bent head, his gel-combed white hair. *Fernand*, she reminded herself. *Fernand the important critic.* Nothing here was recognizable as her own life. This man, this room, this blood.

He massaged the meat of her palm gently, peered at her hand through his glasses.

"Thank you," she said. "Have you done this before?"

"I'm just finding the bits of light."

Fiona imagined her palm littered with a thousand slivers of reflective glass, ones she could carry with her forever. Her whole body ought to be like that. Her skin ought to cut the people who touched it.

She wanted to say nice things to him, but didn't want to sit here endlessly repeating her thanks. "Do you paint, too? Besides the critic stuff? Your hands are so steady."

"I studied painting." He looked up and smiled, and she felt she could stay in the bathroom forever, being taken care of. "Terrible idea. Critics shouldn't know how to paint."

Jake appeared in the doorway. She didn't have the energy to send him away.

Fernand daubed more antiseptic on her skin with a flat circle of cotton. He said, "I attended the Académie des Beaux-Arts. Very, ah, old-fashioned."

Fiona perked up. "Are you still there? Do you teach?"

"No." He laughed. "Not for me."

"I just—" she stopped while he dug into the base of her middle finger with the tweezer point "—my family's always been trying to track down this one artist who was there. He was my great-aunt's boyfriend, and he died young."

"What year?"

"Oh, *way* before your time! I didn't mean you'd know him, I just—I don't even know why I'm asking. I'm a little woozy. He won the Prix de Rome, but then he died right after World War I."

"Ha, yes, that's before my time!"

"His name was Ranko Novak. We were just always curious."

"You're trying to find what, records? A picture?" He turned to where Jake still hovered. "Do you have a light on your phone?"

Jake turned on his phone's flashlight and, grimacing, held it above Fiona's palm.

"I tell you what," Fernand said. "I have a friend there. You write the name down before you leave tonight, I'll ask him."

"That's so kind!"

"Well, you nearly severed your fingers at our house. This is so you won't sue!"

Fiona held a glass of ice water in her gauzed hand because it felt good, even if the condensation made the gauze wet. She'd found Richard in the dining room, holding court over platters of smoked fish.

She could barely follow the conversation, and only thanks to Richard's occasional translation. ("Marie is his wife." "This was the Gehry retrospective last year." "She's talking about her daughter's work.") Fiona wanted codeine. She wanted to find a pharmacy. And then what? Maybe walk around Kurt's neighborhood till morning.

Richard said to her, "Paul here was asking how fame changed me. I'm explaining that I've only been famous a quarter of my life! Such a short time!" And then he spoke French again to this Paul, who had a giraffe neck and tiny teeth. Back to Fiona: "I was saying that my very first patron was a collector named Esmé Sharp, do you remember her? And she just emailed last week asking for a first look at some stuff before Art Basel this spring. Nothing changes! I'm still making work for the same audience."

Jake had disappeared but now he was back, lingering outside the circle. He had rolled up his sleeves; his arms were all muscle and vein. At his left elbow, the bottom of a tattoo.

The name was a distant bell to Fiona. Esmé Sharp. Someone circling Richard when his career took off, someone she might have met when she was driving back to Chicago from Madison on weekends, pregnant or with a newborn Claire. Or maybe she'd met her after they moved back to the city in '93, Damian teaching at U of C and Fiona going out of her mind, bored to death in the place she'd once found endlessly vibrant. The early nineties were a haze; Claire had been born in the summer of '92, and Fiona was in the throes of what anyone today would easily spot as extended postpartum depression, on top of the PTSD she'd carried with her from the '80s. She'd lied to her doctor that everything was splendid, and he hadn't pushed further. She tried taking graduate classes at DePaul, but couldn't bring herself to complete a single paper. She watched morning television, interviews with celebrities whose names she didn't know. She sat on benches while Claire circled playgrounds and dug her fat fingers into cold sandboxes and got herself stuck on top of slides. It wasn't till Claire started preschool and Fiona began working for the resale shop—around the time Richard left for Paris—that everything came clear. It was as if someone had handed her new glasses around 1995, turned up the color, unmuted the city. Just in time for Fiona to realize how unhappy she was with Damian, his little lectures, his teeth-licking. She began fucking a man she met at *yoga*, for the love of God, and even as it slowly eroded her marriage, it helped her wake up. But by then Richard was gone. Esmé must have been from that lost time, a boat in a foggy harbor.

"*Et qu'est-ce que vous faites, dans la vie?*" a woman asked Fiona.

She said, "*Je—j'ai une boutique. En* Chicago." God, she wanted to leave. Richard rescued her, talking quickly; she assumed he was disabusing the crowd of the notion that Fiona sold fancy shoes. She heard "*le SIDA*," which she'd always found a prettier acronym than AIDS. Well, everything about AIDS had been better all along in France, in London, even in Canada. Less shame, more education, more funding, more research. Fewer people screaming about hell as you died.

She sidled up to Jake and whispered. "Help me find more gauze," she said.

"You want me to ask the hosts?"

"No. Just come with me."

If she could ride around on a scooter like a teenager, she could act like one in other ways too.

He followed her into the front hall, empty but for the coat tree. She said, "You don't happen to have any good pain meds on you?"

"I wish."

"Do you have a cigarette?"

"No, but I could use one."

"Do you have a condom?"

"A what?"

"Listen." She checked her phone; nothing. She dug her coat out from under the others. "You're drunk, right?"

"Not really." He followed her out the door; the streets were empty.

"Do you think you're sober enough to find the Métro again?" She turned left, although she wasn't sure that was the way.

"I said I'm not drunk. I was a little stoned when we got here, but it wore off."

"You're a shoddy alcoholic. Not even drunk."

She walked fast and he worked to keep up.

"Who said I was an alcoholic?"

"Some guy on a plane."

They stopped at an intersection and waited for the crossing light, although the streets were empty.

"You're what," she said, "thirty?"

"Thirty-five. Why?"

"I don't want to sleep with an infant. Thirty-five should work."

It was clear from his face that he couldn't tell if she was joking, and also clear that he wanted her not to be.

She'd had the wrong amount of wine for self-analysis. One more glass and she might be sitting on the sidewalk, spilling her life's secrets, wondering aloud why she tended to weaponize sex. One less glass and she'd still be next to Richard, nodding along to a French conversation. As things stood, she'd had just enough to be aware of how narrowly she'd missed both these possibilities, and also just enough not to care. She was drunk enough to want a man on top of her, but not so drunk that she'd fall asleep as soon as she was horizontal. Once they'd crossed the street, she put her hand on Jake's ass, slid her fingers into his back pocket.

He swung toward her and gave her a *look*, some combination of vulnerable and predatory, and then he cupped the base of her skull, pulled her mouth onto his and her tongue toward his and her pelvis toward his. They walked another block and he did it again, and then another block, and he did it again.

He smelled like smoked meat, which was not something she minded. They made their way to a pharmacy for condoms and ibuprofen and then back to Richard's house, and in her crisp guest bed, they had sex. Fiona remembered only once, riding on top of him, that she was most likely someone's *grandmother* now. Mostly she felt no self-consciousness at all; Jake was so beautiful, the skin of his upper arms taut and goose-bumped, that it was easy to be lost. She ran her left hand through his chest hair, as thick as his beard, and kept her gauze-wrapped right hand tight on the bed frame. It would hurt worse in the morning, but she didn't care.

Jake finished with a long, helpless caveman grunt, and then he lay next to her and slipped his fingers between her thighs, which she didn't think would work, until it did.

She imagined Jake would go to sleep afterward, but instead he propped himself up on one elbow and told her about his first college girlfriend, a woman who tied him to the bed and left him there an hour, which was something he thought about all the time, and he hated her for it, but it was also the reason he still wasn't over her. Pillow talk, good God. Fiona wanted to kick him out, but it was only ten o'clock, and she couldn't imagine Richard and Serge returning for a couple more hours. She'd need him gone before then; not that Richard would judge her, but he wouldn't pass up the opportunity to tease her, either. And she was fifty-one, and she didn't quite believe Jake was thirty-five, and she couldn't bear for the age difference to be a topic of prurient interest.

Jake said, "Tell me about your first."

"What," she said, "are we *bonding*?"

He laughed, not hurt. "This is one of the best parts. It's like, there's foreplay, and there's afterplay."

She rolled toward him. What the hell. "I lost my virginity to my cousin's science teacher. I'd already graduated high school, just barely. Different school."

"Damn."

"I don't know, all my friends were much older. They were my brother's friends, and then they were mine. It was hard to get excited about someone with acne."

"Did you ever sleep with your brother's friends?"

The laugh that escaped her was embarrassingly gooselike. The idea of her younger self with Charlie Keene or Asher Glass! She'd been madly in love with Yale, but that was different. Without expectation, without hope, a crush could remain pure and platonic. It was never lustful, never selfish. She was always just looking for excuses to touch him, talk to him, lean her head against his arm.

"Not so much?" he said.

"Not so much."

"So what I don't understand about that triptych, about the guy in the triptych, is that—"

"My God, shut up. Come here." She tried to kiss him, just to stop him from saying another word, but he pulled back. "Didn't I already cut my hand over this? You're being kind of . . . *vampiric*."

"Sorry," he said. "Sorry. I'm being a journalist. But also, like, isn't it something you should talk about? To process it?"

"I've been processing for thirty years," she said. "I've been processing since you were watching Saturday morning cartoons in your pajamas. I have a shrink for this stuff. I don't need a journalist."

"But you don't have sex with your shrink. I mean, do you? Because seriously, when you talk after sex, it's different. I think it's why Freud had everyone lie down."

"Did Freud sleep with his patients?"

"I think so."

She rolled her eyes. "Okay. Fine. Julian died—God, I don't even know how long ago. You know, depending how close you were to someone . . . There were some people who drew you in, leaned on you, and you spent more time with them in those last months than you ever had before. And there were people where if you were outside their closest circle, they shut you out. Not in an unkind way, it's just they didn't need you. You'd have been an interruption, you know? And I wasn't in Julian's tightest circle. And anyway, in the end, he shut *everyone* out."

Jake looked like he didn't follow. "Okay," he said.

"There was this competitive grieving thing that could happen. People would crowd into the hospital and stand around for days,

212

sort of *posturing*. That sounds terrible, but it's true. Not that they had bad intentions, just ... you always want to believe you're important in someone's life. And sometimes, in the end, it turns out you aren't."

Jake ran his tongue down her ear and then along her clavicle. "One more time," he said.

She didn't like the way he looked at her, staring deep like he was trying to get their pupil dilation synced up. The point had never been for him to get more attached, especially not with everything else going on.

There were sounds out in the apartment.

"Shit," she said. "If it's just Richard he'll go to bed soon. You can sneak out then, okay?"

"Alright," he said, and closed his eyes. "I'm not an alcoholic. That was a joke."

"How is that funny?"

"I don't know. I was drunk."

Fiona must have fallen asleep, because she was on a bus in Chicago with Richard, looking for Corinne's house. Her hand was on fire.

When she rolled over in the middle of the night, Jake, thank God, was gone.

1986

Bill had decreed that everyone had the afternoon off. Yale lugged his bag on the El, and then to Briar and up the two flights. He'd been away long enough to induce that wonderful coming-home-after-a-long-trip feeling, the way you're hit with the smells of your own building, the dimensions of your own hallway, which have somehow readjusted themselves so the place feels dreamlike, off by a few vertiginous inches in every direction. He was hungry, late for lunch. He thought he might make a grilled cheese, and he wondered if there was tomato soup in the pantry.

When he opened the door, Charlie's mother stood there in a gray dress, her feet bare. He'd thought she was coming next week. Yale dropped his bag and said "Teresa!" and went to hug her. As he did, he heard the bedroom door shut. He assumed Charlie was coming out to see him, closing the door to hide the unmade bed from his mother. But Charlie didn't appear. He'd gone in, not out.

And when he pulled back from Teresa, she had the strangest face. She smiled, but only with her mouth, and she said, "Yale, we need—Shall we go for a walk?"

He felt as if the room might tip sideways, or already had.

"What happened?" Charlie was having a breakdown. Julian had died. The paper had folded. Reagan had—

214

Teresa put her hands on his arms. He still had his coat on, his dressy coat. "Yale, we ought to take a walk."

"Why would I want to do that? Teresa, what the hell?"

Her eyes were filling, and he saw now that she'd already been crying, that her face was a mess. Her hair was a mess.

He put his hands into his coat pockets. Fiona's necklace was there, transferred from his pants, and the wings stabbed his palm. It was a cameo with birds on each side, birds holding up the frame of the cameo. Sharp metal wings. Something was very wrong.

Teresa drew a breath and very quietly said, "Yale, I'm going to walk you to the clinic and we're going to get you tested."

Yale started to say, I can't believe he's doing this again, I can't believe you're listening to him, I can't believe he thinks I'd do that to him, and we just got tested this spring.

But he sat on the floor and put his head between his knees.

She was trying to tell him something different, something about Charlie, and Yale couldn't work out the pieces. But yes, oh God, he understood. Needles shot through his arms and legs and abdomen, pinned him to the moment. A dead bug on a foam square.

He could hear Charlie in the bedroom, walking. Moving things. Yale squeezed his ears with his knees. Teresa had crouched in front of him. She put her hand on his shoe. Nico's shoe.

She said, "Yale, can you hear me?"

Yale was shocked to find that he wasn't crying, even though Teresa was. Why was he not crying? He whispered: "Teresa, what did he *do*?"

"I don't know." She shook her head. "He won't tell me. Listen, Yale, even if he has this—these—*antibodies*, that just means he's been *exposed*. It doesn't mean he has the virus."

"That's not true. He knows damn well that's not true. Did he *tell* you that?" His compulsion to whisper might have come from practice—not discussing someone's disease when the guy was within earshot. Or maybe he wanted to deny Charlie his reaction. He could have screamed, couldn't he? He could have broken down the bedroom door and held him, or punched him, instead of sitting here thinking about his own body, his own health, his own heart.

He might vomit. He *wanted* to vomit.

If Charlie were out here, saying all this himself, he could think about Charlie, about what this meant for him. But all he had was a closed door and this message, this messenger.

What the hell had happened? He looked at the ceiling, which was still, improbably, just a plain white ceiling.

He said, "When did he call you? When did you come?"

"He got the results yesterday. I flew in this morning."

Today was the sixteenth. So Charlie would have gotten tested what, the very beginning of the month? The very end of December?

And Yale was on his feet, hurtling toward the bedroom. "Charlie, did you fucking sleep with *Julian*? *With Julian*? What the hell did you do, Charlie? What the fuck is *wrong* with you?"

He kicked the door, and he kicked it again.

It hurt his foot, but not enough.

Those were the dominoes that had fallen: Julian, and then Charlie. And maybe Yale.

Charlie going pale at lunch. Charlie at the pay phone. Charlie walking around the city on New Year's Eve while Yale visited the hospital alone.

When Yale took too much of his inhaler, his hands would buzz and tingle. They did this now, and they were hot.

Teresa pulled him back by the waist, and he heard sobbing through the locked door. She said, "We need to get you out of here, Yale. You don't have to get tested right now. We can just go to a—a pub. A friend's flat."

216

Julian skipping out on Thanksgiving. Charlie not wanting to see *Hamlet*. Charlie grilling Yale (*What did Julian say? What did Julian do?*) every time he mentioned seeing him.

He wheeled on her. "It would do me zero good to get tested right now. Do you understand?" He was shouting, so Charlie would hear. "It takes three months to be sure. You have to wait three months from the last time you were exposed."

"But you might feel better," she said weakly.

When was the last time they'd had sex? There was the blowjob on Saturday, but when was the last time Charlie had so much as removed his own pants, let Yale unbuckle his belt? God, not since New Year's. Yale had to give him that much credit. He'd pushed him away again and again. But before that, yes. Christmas, etcetera. And Lord knew when he'd slept with Julian, how many times, over how many weeks or years.

He shouted, close enough to the door that he could feel his own breath bounce back and hit him in the face. "How long were you doing this, Charlie? Is this why you were so paranoid? Because you were looking in the goddamned mirror?"

"Honey, stop," Teresa said. He shouldn't have said any of this in front of her, but he didn't care.

"You at least could've let *Teddy* fuck you!" Yale shouted. *"He's not sick!"*

Something crashed into the door. Teresa said, "Yale, *stop*." And he had to listen to her. Her son was dying. Charlie was dying. He sank to the floor again and put his head between his knees again. He thought about getting up again and kicking furniture, but no, he was going to stay here and breathe.

This wasn't about Yale, at least not yet.

When they got tested together in the spring, Yale had imagined that if they were infected, they'd hold each other and sob and then they'd go out for a good meal and make jokes about fattening up, and they'd order the most expensive bottle of wine, and it would be a terrible night, but they'd be heading into this together. Dr. Vincent had counseled them, together, before their tests. "Let's discuss what a positive diagnosis would mean for you," he'd said, and he'd explained that these things went better if you thought through your reaction, your options, ahead of time and with a clear mind. He said, "Who would you turn to for support?" They'd pointed to each other. Charlie had said, "And we have a tight circle of friends. And my mother." Yale felt all those people falling away right now like dust. If he didn't have Charlie, he didn't have Teresa. And he didn't have their friends, who'd all been Charlie's friends first. He was fairly sure he didn't have Charlie. Apparently, Charlie had Julian instead. And who knew what else Charlie had been up to.

He picked up his overnight bag and stuck in a bottle of scotch from the cupboard. He kissed Teresa—missing her face, grazing her ear—and he said, "I'm so sorry." He said, "I didn't do this to him."

"I know," she said.

And then he was out on the street with no idea which way to walk. He wandered to Little Jim's and sat there staring at the bottles behind the bar and drank vodka tonics because they were on special. He might have been pounding them down, if he'd felt like moving his arms, which he didn't. Despite his heart rate, despite the unhelpful primal signals telling him to scramble up a tree for safety. Porn was showing on the big TV: A guy watched, tentatively, from behind a shower wall as two other men went at it. The camera kept panning back to the voyeur's face. He was never going to join in. It wasn't that kind of movie. Yale felt nothing, watching. Or, nothing besides what he already felt: nausea, paralysis. He'd torn a little plastic straw to shreds.

No one bothered him. Surely they could tell something was wrong.

It wasn't the cheating that bothered him most. He articulated this, mentally, down into his glass, thought it at the melting ice cubes. And it wasn't *only* the disease, the exposure, although that was most of it. But the thing screwing itself into his heart right now was that he'd let himself be so cowed by Charlie's demands. He'd been walking on eggshells for this man, and meanwhile Charlie, behind Yale's back, had just been throwing the eggs straight at the wall. He felt, more than anything else, *stupid*.

By the time he walked out the door it was late, past dinner, although the clinic would still be open. But why do that to himself right now? He should wait three months. No, three months minus—today was the sixteenth. Three months from New Year's. So, the end of March? He couldn't manage the math. The antibodies *might* show up faster, but that wasn't exactly reassuring. He'd be walking into either a meaningless negative and more purgatory, or a death sentence. He thought about going to the gallery, sleeping on his office floor. But the security guard would freak out. He thought of Terrence, who was home from the hospital. Someone ought to be at Terrence's anyway. He could be the person at Terrence's, the person taking care of Terrence.

He walked to Melrose and buzzed. Then he felt awful at the thought of Terrence having to get up to answer. They weren't best friends or anything. He'd been closer to Nico. He had no right to Terrence's energy reserves. He was about to walk away when Terrence said hello. He said, "You can come up, Yale, but I'll be honest. It smells like shit."

It did. Terrence's face had hollowed, his skin was shiny and taut, but in the hospital he'd grown a patchy beard, and he hadn't shaved it since. How had his body found the energy to produce hair? Why was it growing a beard instead of T cells?

Roscoe, Nico's old gray cat, rubbed against Yale's leg. "Does he need food?" Yale asked.

"No," Terrence said, "but you're welcome to clean his litter." He wasn't joking. "I'm not supposed to do it without rubber gloves, and I ran out. Not supposed to have him here at all, really." The box in the kitchen was disgusting. Yale knelt on the kitchen floor and got to work, with Roscoe head-butting his thigh. Doing this felt right. Yale could spend the rest of the night scooping out dung and islands of dried piss, and it would feel like he was in exactly the correct place. "You know his doctor doesn't want you here," he whispered to Roscoe. "And he's allergic to you too."

Once he was on Terrence's couch, a glass of his own scotch in his hand, he found that he couldn't tell him anything true. He couldn't say, "Charlie's sick," and he couldn't say, "Charlie cheated on me." It was humiliating, and the first part wasn't his news to tell. He couldn't go spreading word that Charlie, who had advocated safe sex in *Out Loud* before anyone else, was a hypocrite. Not that most people would see it that way; they'd more likely take Charlie's side, interpret anything Yale said as blame, as vindictiveness.

Terrence was in his big green armchair, his cane beside him. He said, "Yale, you okay?"

He didn't feel sick, hadn't noticed anything strange. He knew that before he slept tonight he'd check himself in the mirror for spots, check his lymph nodes, check his throat for thrush. It had been a compulsive nightly ritual before the tests came out, one he'd been free of for less than a year. Now it would be back. But Terrence wasn't asking if he was sick, only if he was about to burst into tears, which in fact he might be. He said, "Charlie just kicked me out. I think we're done."

Terrence puffed air through his lips, but he didn't look surprised. He tucked his ratty quilt around his legs.

Yale said, "Wait, Terrence, do you know something about this?"

"About what?" Terrence was a bad liar, or maybe he just didn't have the energy.

He shouldn't have said it, but he said, "The—Charlie and Julian."

Terrence grimaced and then nodded, slowly.

"Does *everyone* know?"

"No. No. It's just that after—okay, after the memorial?"

"Oh, fuck."

"After the memorial, when we went to Nico's, he couldn't find you and he was pissed about something, and he got drunk. Like, *really* drunk. Julian was in the bathroom with him, taking care of him. I figured he was puking. But they were in there a long time. I went in to see what was up, and they were—you know, they were at it. And a little later they left together. No one else noticed. I called Julian the next day, and he was torn up. Seriously, it was a one-time deal. Julian wouldn't want to hurt you. Neither would Charlie. I know that. You know that."

"No way it was one time," Yale said. "No way. Things don't work that way." That was the plot of some educational filmstrip, not real life. *One time is all it takes. Don't even hold hands, you might get syphilis.* But could it have been true? Was the universe that horribly vengeful? That precise?

Yale was suddenly reeling back to the night of the Howard Brown fundraiser. Dear God, this was what Julian had been trying to convey, standing there by the sinks and staring into Yale's eyes. Julian wasn't in love with him. He was *sorry*. Maybe he thought Yale knew, or figured he'd find out soon, or maybe he was trying to salve his own conscience. Like an idiot, Yale had felt flattered.

And right on the heels of those thoughts, Yale was blaming himself, ridiculously, for having gone upstairs at Richard's after the memorial. If he hadn't done that, if he hadn't scared Charlie, maybe none of this would have happened. If it had truly been an isolated thing, then the moment he climbed those stairs, he'd killed Charlie. And maybe himself.

Yale let out a shudder that might have been half a sob, and he said, "He's got the virus, Terrence. But you can't tell anyone."

"Fuck. Oh, Yale." Terrence looked like he wanted to get out of his chair, like if he had the energy he'd come sit next to him so Yale wouldn't feel so small and alone on the big couch. "I knew about Julian, but I didn't know about Charlie. It—somehow it didn't even cross my mind. I don't know. Maybe it was all Charlie's stuff about rubbers, all his safety stuff. Yale, if I'd thought of it, you have to believe me that I'd—"

"Okay," Yale said. "Okay."

"God."

"Look, no one knows, and you can't tell. It was just that stupid test. If it weren't for the test, we wouldn't even know. We'd be out to dinner right now."

"Fuck. Yeah, but we need that test, right? You might not get sick. Because of the test."

"I'll know that in three months."

"Listen, you get the Fuck Flu? You been sick? Stomach flu, fever, like you got steamrolled but the steamroller was full of wolves, and the wolves were made of salmonella?"

"Not everyone gets that. And, like, I was probably sick in the summer, I just can't remember. Maybe I was sick in the spring."

Charlie had been under the weather in December. So maybe the whole thing was true; maybe it had been a one-time lapse. Or maybe the Julian thing had *started* that night, and kept going. Yale's head spun.

He said, "It's like the world's worst logic puzzle."

"I'm sorry, Yale."

"Stop it. You're not allowed to feel sorry for me."

"I think I am."

Yale poured himself more scotch. He still hadn't eaten dinner, but he wasn't about to ask Terrence for food. Roscoe jumped up on the couch beside him and fell promptly asleep.

Terrence said, "You can stay here tonight if you want, but believe me, you don't want to stay longer. I'm gonna wake you up with my morning sickness." He rubbed his concave belly and said, "This baby must be a girl. She's such a drama queen."

Yale said, "Until about one o'clock, this was the best day of my life." And although Terrence might well have been hinting that he was ready for bed, he couldn't stop himself from talking. He told Terrence about Nora's artwork, or at least the bare details. Modigliani, etcetera. It felt now like a tremendously hollow victory. He'd lost his lover and possibly his health, his life, but he'd brought some old drawings from Wisconsin to Illinois. Pieces of paper.

He said, "The whole time we were up there, I kept thinking, *This is too good to be true. There's something I'm missing. I'm being tricked.* Maybe it was my subconscious. You know? I knew inside something was off, something wasn't right. Red flags. Only I got it all mixed up."

Terrence was quiet and then he said, "This is a weird question, but are those Nico's shoes?"

He'd forgotten. "Oh, God. Yes. I'm sorry. Do you mind?"

"No, it's fine. I mean, maybe you could leave them by the door, actually. I just don't want germs tracked in."

Yale slipped them off, put them on the welcome mat, and then he washed his hands, even though he'd already done it after changing Roscoe's litter. He said, "Tomorrow before I leave I'll run errands for you, okay?"

"Yeah."

Yale lay on the couch that night, listening as Terrence tossed in

223

his sheets, as he whimpered through his night sweats. Yale closed his eyes and watched himself, the night of the memorial, from high up in Richard's house near the skylight. He watched himself talk to Fiona, talk to Julian, sip his Cuba libre.

Again and again he watched himself take in the beginning of the slide show, then turn and put his foot on the first step. He watched himself climb the stairs.

2015

Fiona woke up late, not with a hangover but with a raw throat that was already spreading its ache into her chest and sinus. Her hand flashed with pain every time her heart beat.

Serge took her to his doctor in a cab, no appointment required (no insurance either), and the doctor swabbed her with iodine and bandaged her up sleekly and gave her pain pills and a prescription for an antibiotic. The bill was twenty-three euros, which Serge insisted on paying.

"You take the day off," he said. "Promise, okay? You feel like going out, maybe you come to Richard's studio and he give you a tour. He can show you the videos on his computer, so you see before the show!"

But Fiona couldn't do that, not yet. Watching this footage was a great thing to do tomorrow, but not today. Never today. She *could* take a few hours off, though, as defeating as the notion was. She could wait for Arnaud to call, see how sleepy these pills were going to make her. If Claire wasn't even in Paris, it made more sense to search online for "Kurt Pearce + arrest + Paris" (fruitless) and "how to move to France American citizen" (semi-informative) and "Hosanna Collective Paris" (also fruitless) than to wander the streets.

When Serge took off for the studio, she told him she was too tired. It was chilly out, but she opened the balcony doors, dragged a chair over, and listened to the sounds of the film crew. If she angled herself right, she could see the crowd, the lighting fixtures, the crane. She'd need to learn the movie's name before she left town, so she could see this thing when it came out.

But she had no idea how long she'd be staying, or what her next step even was.

She held on her lap the book of Paris history she'd bought. She was too distracted to read, but the photos were lovely, evocative: women with fur stoles, men crossing a flood by stepping across café chairs, a nightclub entrance made to look like a monster's gaping mouth.

She remembered what Nora had said once: "For us, Paris wasn't even Paris. It was all a projection. It was whatever we needed it to be."

This conversation had happened at the wedding where she'd told Nora to get in touch with Yale, where she'd written down *Yale Tishman, Northwestern, Brigg* on a cocktail napkin. It was her cousin Melanie's wedding, north of Milwaukee, and Melanie had specifically invited Nico and Fiona but not their parents. She didn't include Terrence—it would've been a step too far, maybe, for 1985 Wisconsin—but her loyalty was to her own generation. Fiona and her brother had walked in together, like dates.

Nico had lost weight, but Fiona thought nothing of it. He danced with Fiona, and he danced with the bride, and with their terrible cousin Debra, and he sat and entertained Nora. In his car on the way home, he rolled up the side of his shirt to show her a stripe of vicious red bumps, ones that made Fiona's eyes water. "It's shingles," he said.

And when she freaked out, he said, "It itches like hell, but it's the same thing as chicken pox. Anyone who ever had chicken pox can get it. The virus lives under your skin forever."

He hadn't been to his own doctor, she learned later, just to the ER, where they'd given him calamine lotion and a leaflet.

A month later, he and Terrence were shopping, and Terrence asked how much cash he had, and Nico spent a long minute staring at the ten dollar bill in one hand, the five dollar bill in the other hand, unable to add them together. And six weeks after that, he was gone.

She looked at the pigeon that had landed on the balcony rail. She was not ready to look at Richard's videos, but maybe she could work her way there by looking through Richard's photo albums. She closed the balcony, poured a glass of milk, took a few deep breaths.

There were probably twenty albums on the shelf, a fact Fiona hadn't absorbed that first day. Rows of black leather, brown leather, colored canvas. Boxes full of slides, as well, but she wouldn't mess with those.

When she pulled a thick red album off the shelf, though, a paper slipped out and landed on the floor. Fiona attempted to clutch the album closed before anything else fell, but she dropped the whole thing, and now there were papers everywhere. Cream-colored sheets folded in half, small cards, a lavender page with a grainy photo of a man. They were funeral bulletins and prayer cards. She got on her knees and started stacking them up. This wasn't a photo album at all, she saw when she opened it to an old clipping from *Out Loud Chicago,* an obituary of someone who'd danced with the Alvin Ailey Theater.

Jesus.

She opened the album at the beginning, and tried to slide the papers back into the empty spots. A man named Oscar, no one she remembered, had died in 1984. A clipping about Katsu Tatami from 1986. Here was the bulletin for Terrence Robinson, Nico's Terrence. How odd—she must have put this bulletin together herself, but she didn't remember it. Jonathan Bird. Dwight Sumner. There were so many of them, so impossibly many.

In her current life, it happened at least once a week that someone would wander into the store and then, when they discovered its mission, say something like "Oh, I remember that time!" Fiona had learned to check her temper, to push her toes into the floor so her face didn't change. "I knew someone whose cousin had it!" they'd continue. "Did you ever see *Philadelphia*?" And they'd shake their heads in dismay.

And how could she answer? They meant well, all of them. How could she explain that this city was a graveyard? That they were walking every day through streets where there had been a holocaust, a mass murder of neglect and antipathy, that when they stepped through a pocket of cold air, didn't they understand it was a ghost, it was a boy the world had spat out?

Here, in her hand, a stack of ghosts.

She looked through Terrence's bulletin. They'd read a Psalm, apparently, although the book and verse numbers didn't mean anything to her now. Asher Glass had sung. She remembered that.

Asher would speak at ACT UP meetings with a voice like a politician from a black-and-white movie. He'd break into city council with his bloody handprint banner. He and his friend chained themselves to Governor Thompson's fence one summer, got arrested for the millionth time. Asher was still around, Fiona knew, living in New York. She'd seen him in a documentary a while back, a "three decades of AIDS" thing. He looked as healthy as anyone, was so muscular you couldn't believe he had the same virus she'd seen carve men into skeletons. His hair had grayed and he had jowls, and surely he was dealing with early osteoporosis or the other landmines of being HIV positive over age fifty, but in that movie he'd looked ready to jump through the screen into Fiona's living room to help her lift boxes.

It wasn't true, what she'd said. They weren't all dead. Not all of them.

On October 13 she'd held her own quiet memorial, alone in her house, for Nico. Candles and music and too much wine. Thirty years. How could it possibly have been thirty years? But that was just the start of the worst time, when the entire city she'd known was turning into lesions and echoing coughs and the ropy fossils of limbs. And although it made no sense at all, she'd never fully been able to shake the ridiculous, narcissistic feeling that the whole epidemic was somehow her fault. If she hadn't mothered Nico (she'd recently whined this at her therapist), if she hadn't taken care of him in those early years, brought him his allergy medicine on the El, let him see that she was doing alright—wouldn't he have gone home sooner or later? Vowed to date girls? He'd have been miserable, but it wouldn't have lasted long. A couple more unpleasant years at home, like every other gay man on the planet. And maybe he wouldn't have been exposed. He wouldn't have died.

She had so much guilt about so many of them—the ones she wished she'd talked into getting tested sooner, the ones she might have gone back in time to keep from going out on a particular night ("Let's agree that we know this is illogical," her shrink said), the ones she might have done more for when they got sick. The night that, for no reason, she'd told Charlie Keene that Yale was with Teddy. Why on earth had she done that? It was an honest, drunken mistake, but everyone knew what Freud said about mistakes.

She felt, sometimes, like some horrible Hindu god, turning all she touched to ash.

The painkillers were making her swimmy.

She could stay here, with this paper graveyard. And who knew what other landmines Richard's shelf contained?

Or.

Right now, maybe a ten-minute walk away, there was footage of Nico she could look at. Nico alive. She was terrified; it would be so much stranger than a still photo. Was there sound? When was the last time she'd heard Nico's voice? When he was alive, she figured. If anyone had ever taped him—well, that would have been Richard. These would be the tapes.

She had to do it.

Serge had told her the corner for the studio, but she hadn't paid attention to the street number—and it wasn't like Richard had a sign out front. Fiona looked at the doorways, the storefronts, as if she could figure it out by squinting. Nothing looked right.

Was she glad? She found herself at least partly relieved.

And then she spotted Serge's motorbike parked on the broad sidewalk, propped against the wall of a building.

She steeled herself and said, "Okay, then."

She felt her phone before she heard it.

"Yes?" She was shouting, and she didn't care. She plugged her other ear.

"Hey, calm down," Arnaud said.

"I'm calm. *What*."

"Can you get to Le Marais? I think we have a couple hours."

She spun around to look for a cab. If nothing else, this timing was a sign, wasn't it? She wasn't meant to go in there and dwell on the past. She was here for Claire, not Nico. She left Richard's studio behind like it was on fire.

1986

Yale nearly forgot to go into work the next day. He'd somehow believed that it was Saturday, that after he went to the grocery store and the GNC for Terrence, after he packed up and tiptoed out of the apartment, all he had on his agenda was finding a place to stay tonight, maybe buying a clean shirt. But at ten o'clock, walking down Halsted with a headache, he saw a guy in a necktie and realized it was Friday.

At least it gave him somewhere to be. He already had his overnight bag, so he just got on the El, his clothes wrinkled from Terrence's couch. As the doors closed, someone came running at them, as if he'd fit through the inch of space left. He stood there, desolate, as the train pulled away. A thin man with dark hair. Yale thought for a moment that it was Julian—but that wasn't his chin, and Julian wouldn't be up yet at ten in the morning. Yale wondered what he'd do if and when he ran into Julian. Would he hit him in the face, or embrace him? It wasn't Julian he was mad at, somehow. It was only Charlie. Halfway to Evanston, he decided that if he saw Julian, he'd probably just cry on him.

Roman was already in Yale's office, collating and labeling the copies he'd made in Door County at the library. The entire contents of the shoebox.

Two messages from Bill Lindsey on his desk: one saying the Sharps were coming after lunch to see the pieces, the other reading, "Campo said yes—thank you!" It took Yale a few slow seconds to remember that he'd given Richard Campo's number to Bill in the car yesterday morning, suggesting he could shoot the 8 × 10 photos they needed to send to New York, that maybe he'd do it on the cheap.

Yale went into the restroom to shave and brush his teeth. He hadn't done it at Terrence's, because Terrence was curled on the bathroom floor by the time he woke up, and again, or maybe still, when he got back from his errands. Terrence had promised he'd be fine, that Asher was coming by later. Yale sprinkled water on his shirt now to iron out the wrinkles by hand.

Maybe the test was wrong. Wasn't it possible to mix up the files? There were no names on any tests, just—what, numbers? Codes? So the code could be off. Which still left him with the fact that Charlie was a louse and he himself was a fool, but all that would seem like nothing if the results could somehow be undone. And the test was so new. Teddy was always saying he didn't believe everyone with the virus would get the full-blown disease. It was part of some larger conspiracy theory Yale couldn't remember the details of. Something about there being no longitudinal studies. Christ, was this the bargaining stage of grief? But he hadn't even moved on from anger yet! He looked at his face in the mirror, crumpled like a child's. Portrait of a sucker.

Back at his desk, he stared at papers he couldn't read. He hadn't eaten since breakfast the day before in Sturgeon Bay, not counting his liquid dinner last night. He should have bought himself a banana when he'd picked up Terrence's groceries. If he was infected, the best thing he could do was gorge, get fat while he still could. Eat six burgers tonight. Maybe by dinner he'd magically have an appetite.

But where was he even going to eat dinner? Some miserable restaurant. And then what? He couldn't put Terrence out again. And he couldn't go anywhere they would ask questions. He thought of Richard's house, that big guest room, but the thought of that house made his stomach clench. Once upon a time, he might have stayed at Nico's. Maybe his apartment was still empty, unrented, but where was the key? There were old friends from the Art Institute, some who didn't even know Charlie, but no one he could impose on.

He felt ill. Feverish, dizzy, an ache in his joints. He'd reminded himself when he woke up this morning that he would probably convince himself he was sick. Knowing this didn't help much.

At noon, he slowly dialed his own number. He imagined Charlie had gone in to work—Charlie would work through a tornado—but he thought maybe Teresa would pick up, could give him more answers.

Really, no, it wasn't that. He wanted to cry at her, wanted her to tell him everything would be okay. If Teresa picked up, he'd send Roman out of the office. But she didn't. And they didn't have an answering machine, because Charlie was convinced that the day they got one it would be filled with panicked messages from his staffers.

He called *Out Loud Chicago* and, in a voice he hoped didn't sound like his own but wasn't odd enough to attract Roman's attention from across the room, asked if the publisher happened to be in today. "No," said a young person Yale couldn't identify, "Mr. Keene is out on personal business." He tried the travel agency, too, and was told that Charlie would be in on Tuesday.

It was a tremendous relief when one o'clock hit. He had something to do now, a script to recite. When he got to Bill's office, the Sharps weren't there but Richard already was. Yale hadn't heard

233

him come in. Had he been asleep? He felt like maybe he had. Richard wore all black, except for the yellow sweater he'd knotted around his shoulders, and he moved like a cat around the room, crouching low to adjust the lights he'd brought. He had the Foujita green-dress watercolor laid out on Bill's table.

"The man of the hour!" he said, and blew a kiss at Yale before turning back to his lights.

Yale managed to say, "Thanks for doing this." He tried to remember if he'd seen Richard since the night of the memorial. Yes, several times. At the fundraiser, for instance. Still, Richard seemed to have walked straight out of Yale's nightmares. The man had done nothing wrong. He'd thrown a great party. He'd made a beautiful slide show.

Richard didn't talk as he worked, didn't require Yale's conversation, and soon the Sharps were in the doorway, grinning like parents about to meet their adopted child.

Bill made introductions—Esmé, Allen, Richard Campo, Allen, Esmé—and shut the door behind them all. He said, "Truly, this is the most extraordinary find of my career, and I can say right now that I'll retire happy. We could get this up next fall, is what I'm hoping. Well, maybe that's a bit optimistic. But a spectacular show."

Bill showed them the Foujita, still on the table.

"That's her," Yale said. "That's Nora."

"She's lovely!" Esmé leaned over the paper, entranced.

Bill opened the cover of the giant portfolio he'd moved the smaller pieces to, and Esmé held her husband's arm. Richard looked, too, from behind. Yale said to him, quietly, "It's Nico and Fiona's great-aunt." The portfolio was open to one of the blue-crayon Modiglianis, not that it looked much like anyone at all.

Richard laughed, delighted. "Spectacular genes in that family."

Maybe he could ask Richard, after all, for a bed tonight. A different bed. Would that be so terrible?

Allen said, "I don't want to wake up and find I've invested in restoring some frauds."

"Well," Yale said, "we could hold off till authentication comes through." His voice was made of tin. "But we have strong corroboration for provenance, and we'd love to get restoration started to prevent further damage."

A painting was a thing to which you could prevent further damage. You could restore it, protect it, hang it on a wall.

Bill looked at Yale expectantly. There was something else he was supposed to say, but he was blank. Bill cleared his throat and said, "One option is, we could wait for the *first* authentication to come through. Let's say the Pascin people verify his work, for instance." He flipped to the nude Pascin sketch. "Wouldn't that reassure us about the rest as well?"

Allen bobbled his head side to side. Noncommittal.

Bill said, "Well, go get Roman! Go get the copies!"

And so Yale did, and as Richard continued working at Bill's desk, the rest of them gathered around the chair where Roman deposited the stack of papers. Yale half listened as Roman read them a letter Nora had written home about Soutine and his wretched table manners.

Bill, meanwhile, had come up behind Richard, who was putting white gloves back on, ready to pull one of Ranko Novak's cows out of the portfolio.

Bill whispered: "Not those."

It wasn't as if there were some Ranko Novak expert out there to mail the photos to.

Bill said, "The artist was not overburdened with skill."

The cow sketches weren't *bad*, but the three were nearly identical, and there was something too neat and too simple about them,

235

like images from a "how to draw animals" book for kids. Still, Yale didn't fully understand Bill's contempt. Well, no one ever got to be a gallery director through egalitarianism.

Richard shrugged, turned carefully to the first Metzinger sketch.

Allen looked agitated, scratched behind his ear. He said, "Look, what I'm thinking of, I'm thinking of those fake heads they found in the river." The summer before last, someone had dredged a canal in Italy hoping to find the carved heads Modigliani had allegedly thrown there in his youth after a harsh critique from friends. They found three heads and rushed to display them, but a few weeks later some university students came forward to say they had carved the pieces themselves and tossed them into the river as a prank.

Bill took the letter Roman had been reading from, put it back on the stack, kept his hand there. "It's true everyone's hackles are up. There's a high bar to clear, for Modigliani in particular. But listen, we're tremendously confident. The point is, authentication could take ages. And why not get things moving?"

Out of nowhere, Yale was frozen by the memory of Charlie and Julian driving down to a protest in Springfield that summer. Charlie said there were other people in Julian's car, but Yale hadn't seen that himself. They'd said they were staying with some National Gay Task Force people. They'd said they didn't get arrested at the protest but that Julian got a speeding ticket.

Yale looked over at Esmé, who was watching Richard work, standing back so she wouldn't make a shadow on the art. He could see from her face, the way she leaned over the Metzinger sketches as if she wanted to dive in, that she was sold on the whole thing: the story, the collection, the exhibit.

Esmé said, "How did she go from art student to model? I'm only asking because—weren't the models, you know, *ladies of the night*?"

Yale said, "We'll be going back up to Wisconsin, getting the whole narrative."

And yes, that was where he could go, not tonight, but soon. He could stay up there. He could drag it out. He could leave this city, keep driving north, put a great, frozen expanse between himself and Charlie.

Bill said, "What do you think? This is the Lerner-Sharp Collection."

Allen drew a deep breath. He said, "We trust your instincts, both of you."

Yale doubted anyone should follow him anywhere, since he was, himself, the world's biggest fool. But he nodded. "You won't regret it," he said.

Back in Yale's own office, Roman stared at him expectantly, a border collie awaiting command. Yale said, "It's been a long week. I'll see you Monday."

He thought, as Roman walked out the door with his backpack hanging by one strap, of calling after him to ask if he had a spare futon. But that was just sad. He couldn't handle his intern looking at him with pity.

He tried calling home two more times, and no one picked up. Maybe Teresa had taken Charlie to the doctor, or maybe he was lying in bed listening to the phone ring.

Time passed strangely. Five minutes spent staring at his empty bookshelves took around five years of psychic time, while the twenty minutes he spent talking to Donna the docent out in the gallery flew by too fast, and then he was at his desk again, staring at infinity.

Richard poked his head in after he'd finished. He grinned and whispered: "He doesn't remember me."

"Who?"

"That old queen. Your boss. He used to skulk around the Snake Pit, eight, ten years ago. Just sat there at the bar *watching* everyone."

"Are you serious?" Yale was simultaneously entertained by this and aware of—grateful for—the distraction. Which is to say, he wasn't fully distracted. "Why would he remember you?"

Richard cocked a shoulder, batted his eyes. "Ten years ago, I was the belle of the ball!"

Yale waved him further into his office and whispered. "Listen, is there any chance I could crash at your house tonight? Charlie's mother's in town, and she snores."

"Well, I have a date. We'll be making a lot more noise than Charlie's mother."

Yale laughed, as if he'd only asked on a lark.

Richard said, "Are you alright? You look like hell."

He tried to make a humorous face. "She's a *very* loud snorer."

The sun was setting and Bill had gone home. Yale pulled out both his scotch bottle and the Yellow Pages. There were hotels right near campus. He had about eight hundred dollars in his checking account. A hotel would eat that up quickly, but he couldn't think about it right now.

Someone rapped on his door, and he remembered Cecily, that certainly she'd be coming today to light into him. Didn't she always save him for the end of the day? This was the thing he'd been dreading most two days ago. And now, it was nothing.

He said, "Come in," and he pulled two coffee mugs down from his bookshelf, and without even looking at her, he poured scotch into both.

She stared for a long time at the mug he held out to her, and then she took it and sat down. She looked more drained than furious, and he felt, suddenly, terrible for her. He'd originally planned to call her in the morning, or better yet to send a memo over, some kind of apology or heads-up or both, but whatever his plans had been yesterday, they were dust under the freight train now. Cecily wore a yellow pantsuit that washed her out. Her hair had gone limp.

She said, "I suppose you know what I've been doing all day."

"How's Chuck?"

"Furious. Yale, it's not the money. Maybe your art is really worth two million dollars, but the point is, there's fallout for me. He's got the new president's ear, and he's giving me a list of all the trustees he's going to complain to. They won't pull their bequests or anything, but it makes things very bad for *me*, for my job."

He said, "I really am sorry it turned out this way."

"I thought we were friends."

Yale could think of nothing to say, and so he held out his own cup to click against hers. He assumed his face was ravaged enough that she couldn't mistake this for celebration. She sipped her scotch and sank back.

"Plus I'm sorry," she said, "but most of the trustees, they don't care about the art. They can't build a new fitness center with art. They can't give scholarships with art."

Yale said, "The media will be all over this. Tell them we just *made* this gallery. In five years, they won't care."

He felt dizzy, glad to be sitting. Food. He'd forgotten food again.

"Am I correct," Cecily said, and now she sounded sharper, less self-pitying, "in my understanding that you still don't even know if these pieces are authentic?"

Yale put his forehead on his desk, softly, because it was the only place his forehead could go. He said, "If they're not real, I'm the one who's getting fired, not you. Not Bill. If they're mad right now, just tell them to fire me. Blame it on me."

"Are you being passive-aggressive? What is this?"

"I'll quit if I have to, alright? I'll sign a thing. I'll tell them."

She said, "You don't seem okay, Yale."

"I'm about to pass out, Cecily. And I don't care about my job anymore. I want to go to sleep now. Can you leave?"

There was a long pause and then she said, "No."

Later, he didn't quite remember them leaving his office, but he must have explained that yes, he meant that he wanted to sleep in his office, and no, he couldn't go home. He remembered walking down Davis Street, an arm around Cecily for support. She was telling him about her couch—that it pulled out but might be more comfortable folded.

The cold air had revived him enough by then that he was able to wonder if this was a terrible idea, if she'd again offer him cocaine and rub his thigh. But she was saying something about her son, how he'd already be home. The Door County behavior must have been the freak-out of a stressed single mother with the rare chance to misbehave. And if she hadn't gotten the message that he really was gay when he sat outside the Howard Brown party snotting up Fiona's shoulder, something was wrong with her.

She said, "Your feet must be freezing. Don't you have boots?"

"These were my lucky Door County shoes. They worked at first. My luck has turned."

He was glad Cecily didn't press for details. Maybe she'd gotten the impression he was prone to tears and didn't want him melting down. She said, "How do you feel about Chinese?"

His stomach responded before his head could, a tidal wave of hunger. He said, "It's on me. For putting you out."

Cecily lived on the second floor, in a two-bedroom place with a living room half the size of Yale's office. Her son, Kurt ("He's a latchkey kid," she'd said on the walk), was sprawled on the couch when they arrived, homework spread on the coffee table.

He looked straight through Yale—maybe Cecily brought a lot of men home—and said, "Mom, I finished my math for the whole weekend, can I watch *Miami Vice*?"

"This is Yale," she said. "He works with me."

"But can I? I'll go to bed at nine."

"We have a guest," she said.

Yale said, "I don't mind. I like that show."

So after they ate—Yale scarfed down helping after helping of mu shu and lo mein, glad he'd paid for it—and after Yale had mindlessly asked Kurt about his classes and sports and friends, they sat and watched Don Johnson and his five o'clock shadow chase a smuggler around an eerily blue swimming pool. Kurt cheered as if it were a live sports match. This was how Yale needed to spend his days, if the next three months were going to pass with any speed. He needed to watch TV and go to movies, mindless entertainment that would keep coming at him. No neurons left for hating Charlie, missing Charlie, obsessing over his own health.

After Kurt went to bed, Yale pulled out the scotch again and Cecily brought two glasses from the kitchen, little red ones with white silhouettes of Greek athletes around the sides. He told her, in detail, what had happened. Because he needed to tell someone, and because she wasn't part of Charlie's circle, and because, maybe, it was an offering of sorts. Having ruined Cecily's life, he could at least lay his own ruined life on the table in front of her.

She sat there nodding, nicely horrified at the worst parts. She was a good person. She showed no sign that she was thinking anymore about her own job, her anger, her terrible day. He was developing a theory about Cecily: The hardness of her outer shell was only to protect a very soft core.

Yale said, "I can leave, if you want."

"Why would I want that?"

"I mean, you have a kid and everything. If I've been exposed to— You know."

Cecily looked affronted. "I don't imagine you're going to have sex with my son." Then, quickly, "That was a joke!"

"I know."

"I don't see how else it could be a problem. I'm fairly educated on the matter. I'm not worried about you sharing the orange juice."

Yale said, "Thank you. I can't believe you're being this good to me."

"Look, I know how I can come off. To get by in my job, as a woman, I have to be a certain way. But I genuinely like you." She refilled his scotch, and he was glad.

He said, "It's been a long time since I had a day that just cuts your life in two. Like, this hangnail on my thumb, I had it yesterday. It's the same hangnail, and I'm a completely different person."

The scotch was helping him talk. He wasn't sure why he trusted Cecily, but he did. They'd done nothing but embarrass themselves in front of each other. Well, wasn't that how fraternities made kids bond? If they puked enough beer on each other, they were tethered for life.

Cecily said, "I've had days like that. Nothing this bad, but before-and-after days." Yale didn't know what path Cecily's divorce had taken, but he imagined it was true. "A change of scene is probably good. You're not around everything that reminds you. You know, if he'd walked out—"

"Right."

"Then you're left with all his things."

Charlie was the one surrounded by *Yale's* things. Charlie was sitting on the bed they'd shared, and beside him was Yale's pillow, and in the closet were Yale's clothes. But Yale didn't feel pity, just gratification. Let him be miserable. Let him hate himself as he publishes hypocritical articles about condom distribution. He couldn't quite get to *Let him be sick.* Of course he didn't want that. Maybe he wanted Charlie to suffer before the doctors came back and said it was a false positive. He wanted him to worry for six months until the researchers suddenly announced a cure.

He said to Cecily, "This disease has magnified all our mistakes. Some stupid thing you did when you were nineteen, the one time you weren't careful. And it turns out that was the most important day of your life. Like, Charlie and I could get past it, if he'd just cheated. I'd probably never find out. Or we'd fight and make up. But instead, an atom bomb went off. There's no undoing it."

She said, quietly, "Doesn't he need you? I mean, when he gets sick, don't you think that might change things?"

"I could get sick before he does. This thing doesn't follow a predictable timeline. And if I do, I don't know that he's the one I want holding my hand."

"Fair enough."

It was something he hadn't known for sure until he said it aloud.

Cecily said, "You can stay as long as you need. A few days, a few weeks. Kurt could use a male figure around. Lord knows his father isn't much of one."

Before bed, he called home. The first five times, there was no answer. The sixth, Teresa picked up. She said, "I'm sure you have much to say, Yale, but unless you're calling to smooth things over, this isn't the day."

"No, I'm pretty sure it is." But he was slurring his words.

"Today was hard enough already, and he's asleep."

He worried that if he waited, his anger wouldn't be at its peak. He needed to yell at Charlie now, not when he'd calmed down, had time to think. Except he wasn't calming down. Every few minutes, it would hit him fresh. Every few minutes, his blood pressure rose.

*

The next day, Saturday, Yale went to the movies. He saw *Spies Like Us* and *Out of Africa*, but they weren't as distracting as he'd hoped. He was more absorbed with the people around him, the couples and teenagers and solo film buffs having perfectly normal days. He'd had thousands of normal days himself. It seemed such an alien concept now, to have a *normal day*. To walk around oblivious, just participating in the world. It seemed unreasonable for anyone to be allowed a normal day.

That night he played Battleship with Kurt and insisted on doing the dishes. As he scrubbed, Cecily said, "Do you want me to call my friend Andrew? He and his boyfriend were the ones I went to the Howard Brown thing with. He lost a lover, and he's a counselor now."

"Thanks. I'm not ready." Yale could think of two Andrews, and wondered if this was one of them. Hadn't Andrew Parr lost someone? The out population of Chicago had always been small enough as it was, and now they'd lost more than a hundred men. And who knew how many they'd lose this year. Soon there would only be one gay Andrew left in the whole city. No last names needed. Even now, the odds that Cecily's Andrew knew Charlie were high.

Yale said, "I can't get my thoughts straight. I feel like—like my head is full of oil and vinegar, and someone's shaken it all up."

Kurt, painting a model airplane at the table, said, "Your head is salad dressing."

"Sure."

"Salad head."

2015

Fiona met Arnaud outside the Saint-Paul Métro. He had the key to the building's front door already, and right around now, he hoped, the landlady would be unlocking Kurt's apartment. She'd call Arnaud to let him know it was done.

He checked his messages. "Nothing yet, but we have to walk anyway." Fiona had imagined them breaking into Kurt's in the middle of the night, or at least in the dark, but that made no sense. They had to do it when he and his wife were at work. And she had assumed this landlady would want to be present, to make sure they weren't stealing anything, but no—it was more important that she wasn't around to be implicated.

Fiona looked at every face they passed, and it wasn't, this time, to find Claire—it was to check for Kurt, make sure she didn't have to duck behind Arnaud, pull her hair across her face.

"You need to calm down," Arnaud said.

"Ha. Well. I'll try."

The neighborhood was relatively swank at first, but slowly, as they walked, the streets—which were indeed full of both falafel places and rainbow flags—grew dingier. This side street in particular had what looked like either a sex club or peep show. She couldn't quite decipher the signs, but that was the gist. Arnaud stopped at a newsstand and bought *Le Monde*. He said,

"It's around the corner. While we wait I'll buy you a whiskey."

"It's not even two o'clock!"

"You need a whiskey to calm you down."

"It's one fifty-four!" she said, but she followed him. Her pain-killer was wearing off, and she was fighting this cold, and wasn't whiskey basically medicine? They found a café that was really more of a bar.

Arnaud sat Fiona with a whiskey at a tiny round table in the corner. He read his paper and drank a beer, the foam sticking to his lip.

This wasn't the worst thing. She'd be less likely, now, to jump if the floorboards creaked, to shriek if she saw a spider. She held the glass with her left hand, kept her bandaged right hand in her lap. She still couldn't uncurl her fingers without sending white-hot pain up her arm.

She was the one facing the windows, and she watched the side-walk the whole time.

At the only other occupied table, a couple argued quietly in French over their espressos. The man looked a good deal older than the woman, although what French woman between fifteen and fifty didn't look twenty-six? This is how she and Damian must first have appeared to the outside world: the young student and her professor, the fifteen-year gap just small enough that no one took them for father and daughter. And how could they, the way she used to hang on him? They'd been eating once on the top floor of the Edgewater Hotel in Madison, a place with windows looking out over Lake Mendota. Bobbing docks and angry gulls. When Damian got up for the restroom, a white-haired man approached the table and in a thick, slobbery accent said, "You are the mistress, no?" Fiona had the presence of mind not to engage, not even to deny this; she just signaled the waiter, who came right over, and the man left. But she'd laughed about it with Damian for weeks.

When she answered the phone he'd say, "You are the mistress, no?" She wasn't. Damian had never been married, never even planned to get married until suddenly, that next fall, Fiona found herself pregnant. It was the start of her fourth year at Wisconsin, and she was twenty-seven.

She said to Arnaud, "Can you just *call* the landlady?"

"I tell you what, I'll call in ten minutes. But we'll hear before then."

She appreciated his confidence as much as she resented it.

The couple at the other table, she realized, had switched to English. Odd, because they didn't speak it well.

"I pay for the flat," the man was saying. "I pay, and this is how you do!" He glanced at Fiona and she pretended to read the front of Arnaud's newspaper, just inches from her face. She imagined the man assumed they were French—*Le Monde* probably helped—and thought English would be the safer language for communicating his anger.

The woman said, "What I'm supposed to spend my day? I should sit there?" She looked frustrated, but defiant too. Was she a *kept woman*? Something worse?

"Yes," he said, "you sit, you read a book, I don't care. You watch a film." He had wild, thick eyebrows. He was furious.

Arnaud had gone still, moved his paper to the side to get a better look.

Fiona wanted to write the woman a note ("Leave him *now*!") but there was no way to get it to her without the man noticing. Had someone seen Claire and Kurt like this in Boulder and done nothing? Had anyone seen Claire and the other Hosanna women walking together on a rare trip to town, arms covered, faces down? Did anyone ask if they were alright? If they needed a ride to the airport and three hundred dollars?

The woman was crying, and Fiona managed to make eye

contact with Arnaud, who gave a small shrug. The man picked up his own half-empty glass and poured his remaining water into the woman's. He checked that the waiter had his back turned, and then he wiped the glass with his napkin and shoved it into the woman's purse.

The woman whispered in French, a protest, and he whispered back. Was this how they furnished her apartment, one pilfered dish at a time? The woman stood, miserable, and picked up her purse. They left quickly.

"Wow," Fiona said. Her whiskey was gone.

Arnaud folded the paper, shook his head. "Some women are very stupid."

"Excuse me?"

"What, you think she's a genius?"

"You don't know what it's like to be with someone manipulative." Though really, she didn't know either. Damian had been older, sure, and he often turned professorial, lecturing and pontificating, but he never manipulated her.

Damian had supported her finishing school that year after the baby was born, and when Fiona had class she'd drop Claire off with a bottle at his office, where she was the little princess of the sociology department. She'd come back two hours later to find the room full of grad students cooing over Claire, holding a rattle for her. Damian was never anything but solicitous; the marriage's failure was her fault, entirely. She'd offered once that if any new girlfriend called her up, she'd testify to his character, explain how she was the one with commitment issues. How her heart was too battered for anything like real love. When he got together with Karen, Fiona had repeated the offer. "It's okay," he said. "She knows."

Arnaud said, "I see this all the time. What do you think I investigate? Half of it involves, okay, *not-so-genius* women in trouble with a man. I turn down jobs every week from guys like that who want women followed."

Fiona told herself not to yell at Arnaud, whose assistance she didn't want to lose. She said, "I've known men in that situation too. Men manipulated by women. Or by other men."

Arnaud looked at his phone. "She texted."

"Oh," she said. "Okay. Okay." And suddenly she was all nerves again. She tipped the chair back getting up, had to grab the table's edge, nearly tipped that over as well.

Under other circumstances, it might have been an adventure. Watching for neighbors, scampering inside. But it was terrifying, nauseating. In the worst case, they'd find something horrible. Fiona didn't believe Kurt would hurt Claire, but did you ever know a thing like that? She remembered something her own mother had told her one of the last times they'd really talked, right before Nico died. Fiona had been blaming her for not standing up to her husband, for letting him kick Nico out. They were in the hospital cafeteria. Her mother said, "You'll never know anyone's marriage but your own. And even then, you'll only know half of it."

The apartment was dingy and poorly furnished. A dead-rat-in-the-wall smell, rotting sweet. A big, divided room with an unmade bed at one end, a threadbare blue couch at the other. A small kitchen area, two empty bowls in the sink.

Arnaud had made her promise not to touch anything, and so she stood, helpless, in the middle of the place, turning circles as he explored. "The other closet is coats," Arnaud announced, "but this one is dresses." He stood at an open door near the bed. "You recognize any?" If she did, they'd have to be from Claire's freshman year or earlier. She'd completely given up on the idea that Claire lived here with Kurt, but it couldn't be ruled out. Maybe the woman with dark hair was just someone Kurt was having an affair with! She stood at Arnaud's side and peered in. Pastel colors, which Claire hated. Nothing familiar. But there were sundresses and cocktail dresses in here. Not Hosanna clothes.

Arnaud held a whole dress out from the rack, the way you would at a store.

"Way too long to be Claire's," she said. This thing would drag on the floor. And there were no toys around, no child's bed.

There were bills for Kurt Pearce on the small coffee table, and an empty greeting card envelope addressed to a Marie Pearce.

"*Marie*. She could be French," Fiona said.

"Sure. Could be from New Zealand for all we know."

Fiona looked in the bathroom. A medicine cabinet missing a door. Nothing abnormal inside, no antipsychotic drugs. Vitamins, ointments. A packet of birth control pills. The Hosanna did not believe in those.

To the right of the sink, a photo of a little girl had been tacked up in a plastic sleeve.

Oh, God. About three years old. It had to be the girl from the video. Had to.

Fiona felt something like an allergic reaction—tight in her throat, her chest—even as she wanted to sing, to grab Arnaud and waltz him around the apartment. Golden curls, eyes—eyes like Nico's. Not much like Claire herself, who had resembled Damian even as a child: wan, glowering, lips thin and tight. When Damian was her sociology professor, Fiona had imagined his face suggested soul, a life of wisdom dearly earned. She'd never imagined it might come down to genes. But this little girl! She was a Marcus. Nico's hair had started blond, had grown dark right as he sprang up tall, right as his voice dropped. Fiona grew suddenly shy around him that year, didn't know how to relate to this strange, giant boy. And really she never learned again how to be his sister, because within a year or two she'd turned into his accomplice, his thief, his occasional mother.

This child: If you cut her hair, if you dressed her in the boy clothes of the 1960s, she was Nico.

With just her good left hand, Fiona pulled out the tack and drew the photo from its sleeve. There was nothing on the back. She wanted to take it. But she couldn't do that.

"Look," she said to Arnaud.

He grabbed it by the edges and said, "Ta ta ta ta ta! Don't get fingerprints!"

Well, what had he been doing, touching everything, then? He laid the photo on the bed and took a picture of it.

He said, "It's impossible not to get a spot of light."

"Will you send me a copy?"

"Sure," he said. "Sure."

They didn't find much else. Arnaud said, "Ten years ago, we'd be looking for an address book. Not so easy anymore."

He opened the cupboard above the stove, rifled through boxes and cans. "What do you think of this?" He held out a brown cereal box on which a cartoon dog leaned over a bowl of chocolate flakes. Chocapic, it was called. The box bragged, *C'est fort en chocolat!* "Maybe for the little girl?"

"Well," Fiona said. She didn't want to let herself get too excited. A man who lived in an apartment like this, she thought, might eat those for dinner. But then she remembered that Kurt had always been a health nut, that the Hosanna Collective believed in biblical grains. He might have left the cult, but it would be odd to rediscover chocolate cereal in your forties. She opened the refrigerator, and although there wasn't much, it was health food: plain yogurt, bottled green drinks, what seemed to be the French version of Tofurkey.

"Expires next spring," Arnaud said, still looking at the box. "It can't be so old. That's good, yeah?"

The cereal did reignite some small hope, but she didn't want to admit it.

Arnaud took more photos. Fiona sensed it was for show. What good would a picture of the sink do?

As they left, she fought the impulse to leave something deliberately askew, to bump a lamp or scrawl a question mark on the wall.

"We were never here," Arnaud said. He turned the lock and closed the door behind them. "Goodbye, Kurt Pearce's flat."

Fiona wandered the Marais a long time, feeling awkwardly American here where there weren't as many tourists. She showed Claire's photo, with slightly renewed optimism, to waiters, to shopkeepers.

She showed it to a scraggy-haired man waiting on a corner with a long, narrow box. He turned out to be a Brit, and she was fairly sure he was stoned.

He looked at the picture a long time, and then he said, "Not everyone wants to be found."

Fiona walked away insulted, and didn't feel like talking to anyone else.

She circled back too close to Kurt's apartment. Here was the place she'd had the whiskey earlier; she stopped to use the bathroom, feeling she had more right to do so here than elsewhere.

When she emerged, she hoped she'd see the fighting couple out on the street. Really, she hoped she'd see just the woman, alone, leaning against a window and crying. Fiona would wrap her up, take her back to Richard's. She could save one woman, even if it was the wrong woman.

But the street was—as she'd known it would be—empty.

1986

Sunday was the day. Charlie would be working, even if he'd taken Friday off; *Out Loud* published on Mondays, which meant the paper was put to bed late Sunday night.

Early Sunday morning, Kurt's father picked him up for hockey practice. He greeted Yale stiffly and whispered something to Cecily. The ex was a big man, big with both fat and muscle, in possession of a remarkably uncharming Irish accent. Yale could see the man in Kurt's upturned nose, wide mouth. He wondered if it was best, in this situation, to come across gay (as in, not involved with Cecily) or straight (lest the man get deranged ideas about Yale's interest in the eleven-year-old). He tried to act natural, which was probably on the gay side.

He did his laundry in the building's basement, and then he took the El into the city. His feet, Cecily was right, were slowly dying in those shoes, even with socks. There was slush today on all the sidewalks, and in no time it had soaked through.

It was one o'clock. He walked, with the numb determination he imagined assassins felt, down Belmont, through the door next to the taco place, up the flight of stairs that led to a dentist and an insurance agency and the *Out Loud* offices. Dwight, who worked out front, looked up and waved. Nothing amiss.

Charlie was in his office talking with Gloria. Yale walked in

253

as he'd done a hundred times and sat in the chair by the door. Gloria gave a little wave and kept talking, didn't seem to notice that Charlie had stiffened. Yale felt like a ghost, visible only to one person. Only Charlie saw this specter at the door. Only Charlie felt the chill.

Gloria said, "You want me to come back?"

And Yale said, "Keep going! I'm happy to wait." As if he were dropping off Charlie's sandwich.

He hadn't seen Charlie's face since he'd left for Door County. The last time he'd looked at Charlie, it had been with complete trust.

Charlie hurried Gloria out, said they should meet after layout was done. He shut the door behind her. He said, quietly, "Jesus, Yale." He looked everywhere but into Yale's eyes.

Yale knew his own silence was a kind of power. He stayed in the chair, arms crossed. There were at least five things he planned to say, and several answers he intended to demand, but not quite yet.

Charlie went back and sat in his desk chair, and for a moment it looked as if he were going to collapse sobbing. In a way, it would have been the only appropriate thing. But instead his lips thinned, his nostrils flared. He said, "I didn't know how to reach you."

"You could've called my office."

"I meant yesterday, or today."

"What did you want to say?"

Charlie put his elbow on the desk, then his forehead in his hand. "I needed to tell you that Terrence died."

Yale only stopped breathing for an instant, because it wasn't true. What the hell was Charlie trying to pull?

"No he didn't."

"Actually, he did."

Was he trying to prove that Yale wouldn't know if a thing like this had happened?

Yale said, "Sorry, but I was just there. I *stayed* there, at his place. On Thursday night. He's fine."

Charlie's voice was suddenly patient. "That might be true, but they took him to the hospital late Friday morning. He died Friday."

Yale didn't believe him. But then why did he find himself crying? His tears were hot and fat and they rolled silently into his mouth.

Charlie said, "I'm glad you were with him."

Terrence had looked so sick on New Year's, had seemed about to go. But not on Thursday. Not on Friday morning. He'd been on the bathroom floor, but that was *normal*. And Yale had left him there. Yale had kept him up talking, the night before. Yale had tracked germs into his house. He felt like tearing the air around him to shreds. He couldn't think.

He said, "Where's Roscoe?"

"Who the hell is Roscoe?"

"The cat. Nico's cat. Terrence had him."

"*That's* what you're concerned about? I'm sure Fiona has it."

Yale said, "I was with him at the hospital on New Year's."

"That's good. I'm glad."

"Where the fuck were *you* on New Year's?"

"Yale, don't start. The thing is, the service is at three."

"*Today?*" How many days had passed? Two? This seemed even less plausible, even more of a horrid joke than the actual death. He said, "Wait. So he what, he called an ambulance on Friday? Or someone found him? What time?"

"I don't know the details, Yale."

"How is this happening *today?*" He was asking the wrong questions. Watching Julian's production of *Hamlet*, he'd been struck by Laertes' response to Ophelia's death. "O, where?" he'd said when he heard the news. But yes, look, it was right: The details were what you grabbed for.

"Fiona's organized it." Of course; that was part of the whole

255

power of attorney thing, dealing with the body. Charlie said, "It'll be odd if we aren't there together."

"*Will* it."

"I just mean we shouldn't burden Fiona with this right now. You can sit beside me. It won't kill you."

Yale had never hit anyone in his life, not *really* hit, but he wanted to right then. He wanted to grab all the gay weeklies from around the country that Charlie hung on those pretentious racks behind his desk and crumple them, one by one, in his face.

But Charlie looked so tired. Blue moons under his eyes.

Yale said, even though he knew it was ridiculous, "Where did you even have this testing done?"

"Yale. It's positive. I was exposed, and it's positive. One plus one is two. I'm dead." He flung out the last word like a hand grenade.

And if Charlie had broken down right then, if his face had crumpled—Yale might have softened, gone around to him, held him in his arms even as he stared out the window conflicted. But Charlie's face didn't change.

Yale had come here planning to yell, and the fact that he wasn't yelling was concession enough.

Charlie said, "Would you please just sit near me at the bloody church so we don't have to explain this to everyone?"

The thing was, Yale wasn't ready to explain it either.

"I'll need a suit. Fuck. Is Teresa in the apartment?"

"I can call and send her on an errand."

"Yes, please do."

"It's at the Unitarian place. You've got, what, two hours?" This was the same church where they'd held services for Asher's friend Brian. A gay-friendly church right off Broadway, and thus—recently—Funeral Central.

Yale said, "I don't even understand. I don't get—" And he stopped talking, wiped his face with his sleeve.

256

Charlie said, "I'm sorry you're so torn up about *Terrence*."

"Okay, Charlie." Instead of screaming, he walked out of the office. He closed the door, really believing that Charlie would call him back, chase him down. Had this truly been their first and only conversation since Yale had called him, jubilant, from Wisconsin? He'd talked to Charlie so many times in his head that it didn't seem right.

And how had he left without making Charlie apologize, beg forgiveness, explain?

He got angrier as he walked. He'd felt deflated in the office, but the cold air, the sun, every step away from Charlie, filled him again with indignation. Charlie had not, for an instant, expressed concern for Yale, for his health.

But then had Yale said, at least, "I'm sorry you're infected"? Maybe they were both terrible, prideful people. Maybe they deserved each other.

He tried to imagine the kind of man who, faced with the news that his jealous lover was, in fact, making a fool of him and had blithely exposed him to a fatal disease, would say it didn't matter, would stay calm and supportive and sign up for months, years, of bedside care and devastation. Who would do that? A saint, maybe. A patsy. It had taken ages for Yale to learn to stick up for himself—after those boys on the basketball team tricked him, hadn't he gamely sat with them at lunch the next day?—but apparently, somewhere along the line, he'd figured it out.

He knocked first to make sure Teresa was gone, and he turned the key slowly. He hated the version of himself that had stood here last, ready to share the details of his amazing trip, oblivious to the coming ambush. He hated that if the Yale from three days ago could see the Yale of right now, he'd misinterpret the scene, think he was coming home from lunch somewhere, a little bedraggled but happy, normal.

Everything was slightly out of place. Teresa's pillbox sat on the table next to a *New Yorker* he hadn't seen yet. A stack of cassette tapes stood balanced on the arm of the couch, as if Charlie had been sorting them or looking up lyrics. Yale found his own mail stacked neatly by the phone. Some alumni thing, a postcard from his cousin in Boston. No utility bills, thank God, or he'd have torn them up, left the scraps on the floor. Yale usually paid the rent, but the apartment was in Charlie's name; he'd been living here when they met.

Yale changed into his suit, and then he found a decent-sized box on top of the refrigerator—Charlie had bought a carton of grapefruit right after New Year's for some fundraiser—and filled it: his passport, his grandfather's watch, two shirts, a pair of khakis. His checkbook, and a mug of CTA tokens. He put Nico's Top-Siders in there, but shoved the other clothes he'd been wearing into the laundry hamper for Charlie or Teresa to deal with. He put his dress shoes into the box for later, got his snow boots from the front closet. He padded the rest of the box with socks and underwear and draped the whole thing with a sweater. He'd have taken a suitcase, but the only big one was Charlie's.

In the refrigerator were cold cuts he'd bought before his trip. They ought to be long expired, from a different decade, but they were still fresh, still fine. He made a sandwich with turkey and Muenster and stood at the counter to eat.

It felt too normal—as if Charlie were down the hall, ready to step out of the shower with a towel around his waist, everything fine. He could put his hand on Charlie's chest, feel his heart through his wet, warm skin. The truth was his body missed Charlie, or missed Charlie's body. Just the presence of it. Not sexually, not yet, although surely that would get worse, on nights when he lay alone and awake. The tensed muscles of Charlie's thighs, the way he bit Yale's ears, the taste of him, the impossibly slick smoothness under his foreskin. Well, here it was, then: longing, missing. The most useless kind of love.

He was rinsing his plate when the door opened. Teresa said, "I thought you'd have left."

"I can. I should."

She put her purse on the counter and walked toward him as if she planned to hug him, but she didn't. Her face looked terrible, dry and deeply creased. Her chin, her jowls, had dropped. Her eyelids were swollen. She said, "Yale, are you alright? Have you been tested yet?"

"It would be pointless."

"You'd feel better. *Charlie* would feel better."

"Charlie's feelings aren't my concern."

She looked pained. "I don't see why you boys have to fight. You love each other." Yale wondered if that was true. Teresa picked up his hand in her own, stroked the back of it. She said, "If you'd come home, I could take care of *both* of you. I've been cooking, you know. And not just soggy British food! Did I tell you I took an Italian cooking class this fall? I have a wonderful meatball recipe now, only Charlie won't eat beef."

"I'm fine," he said. "I'm going to be fine."

"He made a mistake. It was the first thing he said when he called. He said he'd made a mistake, and he couldn't fix it."

"That is true. He cannot fix it."

"Yale, I'm worried if he's upset he'll get sick faster. He'll wear himself out worrying."

Yale marveled at this turn of logic, the idea that he was now the one making Charlie sick. He could sit here and explain things about AIDS that would make Teresa's head spin, or he could say that Charlie hadn't uttered a word of apology, but what good would it do? He told her he was meeting Charlie at the funeral,

259

and this seemed to appease her. She said, "Be gentle with him, won't you?"

So that he wouldn't be seen walking down Halsted with the box, Yale turned east and took the long way around—a route that took him past the house he'd toured. He should have kept walking, but he stopped to look. A masochistic gesture. Because even if he wasn't sick, even if he got some enormous raise and could afford the house all on his own, he'd never buy a place down the street from Charlie. Even if Charlie were *gone*, he couldn't live so close to where they'd been happy together, couldn't walk past their old apartment on his way to the El.

But did he truly believe Charlie would ever be gone? It was still a hypothetical in his mind, like a tornado hitting the city. Did he believe, as foolishly as Julian used to, that someone was about to announce a cure? He didn't think that was it. It was all just a rock that hadn't sunk yet, that was still hitting the surface of the pond.

The "For Sale" sign was still there, the phone number glowing in the late sun, runic writing that no longer held meaning. In the window of the place next door, a cat slept. Someone played the piano.

Yale dodged the people congregating in the church lobby and ducked down a back hallway to find a place for his box. He put it behind a beanbag chair in what must have been a youth group room, a place where the kids had painted the walls with daisies and frogs and Beatles lyrics.

Then he straightened his suit, damped his hair down in the bathroom, found Fiona, and helped her with the flowers she was carrying. He gave her the necklace from Nora, said she mustn't ever wear it around her cousin Debra, and Fiona held up her curls so Yale could fumble with the clasp behind her neck. "I've never done this before," he said, and Fiona, for some reason, found that hilarious. He helped straighten the chairs in the sanctuary. Yale appreciated the chairs: less ass-numbing than pews, less likely to dredge up negative childhood memories.

By the time Charlie arrived, the front of the place had filled. Charlie was trailed by some of his staffers—Gloria, Dwight, Rafael, Ingrid. They must have changed at the office, then walked here together. They'd be walking back together too, while Yale wandered off alone. Yale caught Charlie's eye, and a minute later Charlie was there beside him, smelling like aftershave.

The minister spoke about community and friendship and "the family you choose," tremendously aware of his audience, obviously practiced in this sort of thing. How many of these funerals had he personally overseen? Fiona got up and told a story about the day Nico introduced her to Terrence. "He warned me that Terrence had a *sense of humor*," she said. "And so I was terrified. I kept waiting for him to put a whoopee cushion on my chair or something. But he didn't crack a single joke. At the end of lunch he looked at me and he said, 'You've taken care of your brother your whole life, and I—'" Her voice had run into a wall. She tried again but no sound came out. She said, "It would've been easier if he'd said something funny." They all laughed, just to add their voices to the room, to get her through this. "He said, 'You've taken care of your brother all your life, and I want you to know I've got it from here.' And he did. He didn't know what he was signing on for, but he was with Nico to the absolute end. And now he's taking care of him again." She barely got it out. A girlfriend walked her down from the lectern, rubbing her back.

One of Terrence's teaching colleagues read a poem Yale couldn't focus on. The minister led everyone in a meditation. Asher, who was a classically trained baritone, sang the "Pie Jesu" from Webber's new requiem—a song Yale had only heard a soprano recording of, but that worked just as well for Asher, for the cello Yale had always imagined living in Asher's throat. Yale, no more Catholic than Asher was, reveled now in the sound of Latin, those pure, liturgical vowels, the crunch of *Q*'s and *C*'s. The song wasn't just a lamentation; it was a wringing out. Yale was a wet washcloth, and someone was squeezing everything out of him over a sink.

He didn't look at Charlie. He could hear him breathing, hear him blowing his nose. At Nico's vigil, they'd held hands.

He did look back at the rows behind him. Seven teenagers sat together, without parents. Yale imagined they were students who'd somehow gotten word. Behind them sat Teddy and Richard. Teddy drummed his left hand on the chair back. Some of Terrence's family sat in the rear. Or at least he assumed they were family. A tall young man who looked remarkably like Terrence, three young black women. No one who looked the right age to be Terrence's parents, but one woman old enough to be his grandmother.

When it was over, Yale and Charlie walked out together, and they each hugged Fiona.

Yale spotted Julian across the church lobby. He hadn't seen him in the sanctuary, but here he was now by the coatrack, eyes wide and glassy. He'd lost weight. Yale didn't imagine it was the virus; the odds of Julian getting sick precisely when he learned he had the thing were low.

He realized Charlie was staring, too, and for an instant Yale and Charlie were aligned again, communicating telepathically.

Yale whispered to Charlie, "Did you tell him?"

"No."

And then they were apart once more, thinking completely different things, and Yale knew Charlie was remembering whatever he'd done with Julian, memories Yale was forever—mercifully—locked out of. Yale took off down the hall to the youth room for his box.

But when he'd picked it up and turned around, Charlie was there in the doorway. Just looking at him.

Yale said, "For whatever it's worth, I'm sorry you're sick. But beyond that, I have very little sympathy for you right now."

The lights were off in the room. Streetlights through the windows, but that was all.

Charlie said, "I think I've figured out why I did it."

"Oh, do tell." Yale held the box in front of him, a barrier.

"This might not make sense, but I think I did it because I was tired of being scared."

"You were terrified of a disease, so you went out and *got it*?"

"No. *No.* I was scared of you leaving me, of you cheating on me with someone younger and better looking and smarter. I know it's fucked up, but somewhere in my mind it was like, if I did the worst thing I could think of, then every time I saw you flirt with someone else I'd almost hope you *would* go for it, so it would even the score."

"You thought this all through."

"Not at the time, no. I was blotto, Yale. And Julian had these poppers he'd stolen from Richard's house."

"Poppers last all of ten seconds."

"That's not what I meant, I mean what we did in bed, I wouldn't have—"

"*Jesus*, Charlie."

"I wouldn't have let him."

"I think your little self-analysis is way off. I think you were absolutely trying to get sick." Yale was yelling, and he didn't care. "*Why* is the question, but that's for you to figure out. Maybe you hate yourself. Maybe you hate me. Maybe you want the attention. There's no good reason, is there? When you *know* the risks. You're not naive. You're the fucking condom czar of Chicago."

Charlie was shaking his head. Charlie never seemed to cry

263

actual tears, but his eyes would turn pink and puffy. He hadn't come far into the room, was standing near the doorway as if he might run out. He said, "We used a rubber. We did. We were in Nico's apartment at first, when things, you know—and we were in the bathroom, and it was dark, and before we left I asked Julian if he had a rubber, and he said, 'I bet there's one here somewhere.' And he groped around the medicine cabinet, and he put a couple in his pocket. And then we went back to his place. But later, before I left, I saw the wrapper, and it was lambskin."

"Holy fuck, Charlie. It was probably old too."

"Probably."

"I don't even believe you. Really. You used a rubber, but it was dark, and oops, it was *lambskin*? Why would Nico even have lambskin? For what? To prevent pregnancy? You can come up with a better story. How many times did he fuck you *really*? I was willing to believe you. I was almost ready to believe you. And you come up with *lambskin*."

"It was one time."

"Just one great postfuneral fuck. Why not make it two? He's out there right now. Have at it."

"Yale."

"Teddy fucks half the city and gets nothing, but the *one time* you mess up, *with* a rubber, you magically get sick. You should go on the talk show circuit. You should go into high schools and give them the scare talk. Tell the Republicans! They'll *love* you!"

"Yale, *stop*." Charlie was shouting now too. "You know it doesn't work like that. You know it's random."

"Are you aware that you haven't apologized? Has that crossed your mind? You're making excuses and stories about lambskin, you're coming up with theories about your motivation, and you haven't once asked if I'm okay. You have not once acknowledged that you've blown up my entire life."

Charlie opened his mouth, but Yale kept going.

"You spend five years playing up this monogamy thing, putting a fucking *leash* on me, and meanwhile you're doing whatever the hell you want. You know what? It's all greed. Our relationship was about *you*, and whatever the hell you did, that was about *you*, and your refusal to consider anything but your own feelings right now, that's definitely about *you*."

Charlie put his hands on his head. He said, "That might be true, but I cannot begin to deal with your emotional needs right now. My mother is draining me enough."

Yale pushed past him with the box, rammed the corner into Charlie's chest. He said, "At least you have her. I have no one."

He went down the hall and past a woman he didn't know, and then past Teddy and Asher, who were close enough that they'd probably heard the shouting.

Back at Cecily's place, all the lights were off. She'd given Yale a key, and he opened the door quietly, the box balanced on his hip. A latchkey kid, like Kurt.

He changed in the apartment's only bathroom. Cecily's makeup and face creams and curling iron littered one side of the sink; the other held just Kurt's red toothbrush and an egg timer. Yale took his shirt off and checked his chest, his back, the smooth, pale skin on the insides of his upper arms. Not that there weren't a thousand other ways the virus could manifest, not that it wouldn't wait, invisible, for years. When Terrence was first diagnosed he'd said, "It's like putting a quarter in the toy machine at the grocery store. You know the possibilities, but you have no idea what you'll get. Like, will it be pneumonia, or Kaposi's, or herpes, or what?" He mimed opening one of the plastic balls. "Ooh, look, toxoplasmosis!"

How many times had he and Charlie had sex between Nico's

memorial and New Year's? Only slightly less often than usual. Maybe ten times. Maybe Charlie had put his faith in that lamb-skin, if it was even real. Or in Julian not being sick. Julian had looked so healthy. Still, Charlie could have made excuses, could have said his back was out. He could have gotten tested, although maybe he'd been waiting for the three-month mark, the same way Yale was now. But then when he heard about Julian, he went ahead and did it. And lo and behold, early antibodies.

Yale put his T-shirt on, and when he went back out, Cecily was in the kitchen, pulling a tea bag out of her mug. She wore a robe and slippers, and she looked (Yale had learned this his first night there) like an entirely different person without makeup.

She asked how he was feeling, and then she said, "I'm afraid there's a problem."

"Oh."

"It's my ex. I guess—you know, the other night, I mentioned my friend Andrew in front of Kurt. Kurt's so smart, and he notices more than I think. He misunderstood, though, and he thought *you* were sick. He doesn't mind. He knows Andrew and everything, and—"

"He told your ex I have AIDS."

"I explained that you didn't. Basically I told the truth, I said you'd been exposed to the virus. But Bruce freaked out, and he's saying he can't believe you're staying with us, eating food with us. It's ridiculous, but this is what he's like."

"It wouldn't help for me to talk to him, would it?"

"The thing is, we haven't always agreed on custody details, and he thinks he could use this somehow in court." She bit her top lip with her bottom teeth.

He felt suddenly exhausted. "Got it. Honestly, he probably could. If he got the right judge." Yale looked down at his sweat-pants, his bare feet. He said, "If I stayed one more night, do you think that would be okay?" He felt terrible asking. He'd

266

compromised Cecily's career, and now he was upsetting her family. This woman barely had it together, and Yale was stomping across her life.

"Of course! But then—"

"I'll clear out in the morning."

"I'm sorry, Yale. And Kurt feels terrible. He knows he messed up. What's funny is Kurt didn't even mind, he just thinks it's *interesting*. He's been hearing about it on the news."

"He didn't mess up. Can you let him know that?"

"This was the last thing you needed."

Yale said, honestly, "It means more that you would take me in than that someone wouldn't want me here."

"Kurt's worried about you. I told him you aren't sick, but he's worried everyone's going to be mean to you."

"Well, I *might* get sick."

She nodded, serious. "I feel so strongly that you're going to be okay."

"Are *you* okay?" he said. "Your job?"

She hesitated. "As long as those paintings are real, I'm probably fine." Her face was pinched, and he wasn't convinced she was giving him the whole story. "Even if they're not, it's just a job, Yale. This has reminded me of that, you know? There are more serious things."

In the morning, Yale was dressed and shaved and out the door with his stuff before Kurt and Cecily's alarms went off.

2015

She didn't have Arnaud's permission to do this, but what the hell did she care about Arnaud? Arnaud wanted to stretch things out. Arnaud was getting paid.

Plus when Jake showed up at Richard's flat late the next afternoon, she wanted to hustle him out of there. If he was there to bother Richard, he needed to leave, and if he was there to bother her, he could do it elsewhere. So before Serge could invite him to sit down, get him a drink, Fiona grabbed his arm and said, "I need your help with something," and dragged him outside.

"I know where he lives now," she said. "The guy, the one who roped her into the cult. We're going back there."

"We?"

"You're bigger than me. You're not as big as him, I should warn you. But he's not an athlete or anything."

"Oh. Great."

But he followed, got in the cab.

She said, "So you're really not an alcoholic?"

"I don't know. I've taken some of those online tests. Here's what it is: In America, I'm considered a heavy drinker. In France, I'm completely normal."

She laughed, felt her pocket to make sure she hadn't left her phone at Richard's. "If I dropped you into the eighties, into my group of friends, you'd be a monk."

"Lots of parties?"

"We *all* had drinking problems. Every single one of us, except some of the ones with drug problems."

"And you survived!" he said. "You're still here!"

God, she hated him right then.

She said, "Listen, when we get there, don't talk. You'll be scarier if you're silent."

"Sure," he said. "I'm the muscle."

She brushed his hand away before it even made contact with her knee.

Fiona hoped, as they knocked, as her stomach did painful gymnastics, that the wife would answer. That she'd invite them in, and Kurt would return from work to find them all on the couch, drinking tea. But it was Kurt who answered, stared blankly. He looked more at Jake than at Fiona until, finally, he turned to her and his eyes went wide, his hand went to his ponytail.

"Ohhhhh," he said. "Hey. I— Oh, wow. Hey. Fiona."

Fiona said, "We're coming in," and she ducked under his arm and into an apartment that—with grocery bags on the counter and an open laptop on the couch—looked significantly fuller and warmer than it had yesterday.

Fiona had spent an inordinate amount of her adult life engaged in two different ongoing fantasies. One, especially lately, was the exercise in which she'd walk through Chicago and try to bring it back as it was in 1984, 1985. She'd start by picturing brown cars on the street. Brown cars parked nose-to-tail, mufflers falling off. Instead of the Gap, the Woolworth's with the lunch counter. Wax Trax! Records, where the oral surgeon was now. And if she could see all that, then she could see her boys on the sidewalks in bomber jackets, calling after each other, running to cross before the light changed. She could see Nico in the distance, walking toward her.

The other fantasy was the one where Nico walked beside her everywhere, wondering what the hell things were. He was Rip Van Winkle, and it was her job to explain the modern world. She'd done it at O'Hare on her way here. Focused as she was on Claire, on getting to Paris, she'd suddenly had Nico beside her on the moving walkway as it rolled past a sign advertising "a firewall for your cloud." How could she even begin to explain why a cloud needed a wall of fire? And once he was in her head, he was following her all around the terminal—ordering food with her off the iPad at the pizza counter, jumping at the autoflush toilet, reading the scroll at the bottom of CNN and asking what Bitcoins were. He asked why everyone was staring at calculators. "You're living in the future," he whispered. "Feef, this is the future." And when she saw something he'd fully understand—a baby crying for a dropped pacifier, a McDonald's, a whole wall (was it still possible?) of pay phones—she felt the world had been set right.

And there were times, too, when she simply narrated for herself what was happening around her, things that *sounded* as if they could have come from another era. Right now, for instance, she told herself she was sitting here with Kurt Pearce, that she and Kurt Pearce were having a conversation. That Richard was off at his studio, and she needed to give Cecily a call later. A description that would have made perfect sense in 1988.

Except Kurt would be an adolescent, not this enormous man sitting opposite her, his legs reaching halfway across the floor. Jake wouldn't have been standing against the wall, arms folded across his chest in an attempt to look like a bodyguard.

Kurt seemed sober, lucid. He spoke quietly, his voice impossibly deep. "I don't know how much I can tell you. I don't know if you're going to try something."

"*Try* something!" Fiona said, and then stopped herself. She shouldn't get emotional.

"I always thought she was way too harsh on you. You did the best you could. And you're making an effort. I get it."

He seemed so young. This whole time, she'd hated him for being closer to her own age than to Claire's—and he was just a kid, a hippie doofus.

He said, "Look, I wish it had worked out differently. I messed up pretty bad for a while. But everyone's fine. We're all doing okay. Hey, what happened to your hand?"

"Are they here in Paris?"

"I can tell you everyone's safe and healthy. But beyond that—it's not my place to tell you stuff. I'm lucky to be back in their lives. I'm lucky Claire allows that."

It was all Fiona hoped for, herself—to be allowed back in. She hadn't messed up as badly as Kurt—she hadn't been arrested, at least—but maybe she'd messed up for longer. And maybe it was harder to forgive your mother than a man. She'd always figured that her own failings would make more and more sense to Claire as she grew up—that an adult would understand an affair (such a garden-variety mistake!) in a way a child couldn't have. Shouldn't Claire know the messiness of the human heart by now?

She had too many questions for Kurt, and no good starting point. And she couldn't give away that she'd spied on him, been in this apartment yesterday. She said, "I understand you're married."

He looked back and forth between Fiona and Jake, and then he said, "Yeah, she's a good match. It's healthy."

"Well, I'm happy for you. I've always wanted the best for you, and I just wish—" She wouldn't be able to express how much fondness she'd always felt for him, or at least for his memory, at the same time that she loathed him with all her being for taking

271

her daughter away. She said, "You're clear of the, the *group*, right? The Hosanna people?"

Kurt laughed. "You can call them a cult. That's what they are. Yeah, I was happy to put an ocean between us."

"So you soured on them."

"Hey, can I get you a beer?" Fiona shook her head. "Can I get *you* a beer?" he said to Jake, and thank God Jake said no. He wouldn't have looked nearly as effective with a bottle in his hand. Kurt got up and fetched himself one, sat back down.

"*She* soured. I was never that big on them, but I was in love."

"How does being in love mean you have to join a cult?"

"It was what she wanted! She—at the beginning, she cared more about them than about me, that was obvious. If I made her choose, I knew who she'd choose, and it wasn't me."

Fiona glanced at Jake, but he was still just standing there. This made no sense. "You were the one who lived in Boulder," Fiona said. "You were the one who—you found the cult."

"Nope. Nope, nope, nope. She met this guy in the kitchen of the restaurant where she was working, and at least I knew it wasn't romantic, because he had this terrible skin and he was sort of emaciated, but he invited her out to a party at the compound, and she brought me along. I thought the whole thing was ridiculous. Tambourines and drums, right? There's this girl named *Fish*, I swear to God, who just latches on to Claire and talks to her all night. They give me this tea that's laced with something. They weren't into drinking, but man, would they lace your tea. And we end up crashing on the floor. It seemed like a laid-back place, until they got their claws in. And Claire wanted to go back, night after night. She was about to lose her apartment at the end of the month, and I'd offered to let her move in with me, but then Fish told her there was a room we could both stay in. It really—I mean, they got to me, too, after a while, don't get me wrong, they have a way of doing that, but Claire's the one who pulled me down the rabbit hole. I'm not just trying to make myself look good here."

Fiona found that she believed Kurt, but still she wanted to scream that he was lying, that her daughter would never fall for something like that, because the people who got suckered by cults were the ones who'd never really had a family to begin with, the ones who, under other circumstances, might have joined a gang. Or at least that was the thing you told yourself to explain why bad stuff happened to someone else's kid, but your kid would be okay. But a battered woman, she could understand. A woman so under the sway of a domineering man that she had no choice but to go along with it. Although she'd never wished that on Claire, wasn't it the story that let Fiona herself off the hook?

Fiona said, "And you gave them all your savings?"

"I didn't really have savings. And actually they helped me close out my credit cards. I only owed a couple thousand dollars, but they paid it all off so I could shut them down. Which, at the time—I was like, *I'll take it*."

The bill for Claire's MasterCard had continued to show up in Fiona's in-box, and she'd kept paying the annual fee this whole time, hoping sooner or later Claire would charge something, giving a clue where she was. She never had.

Fiona was ready to ask it now. "Why did they pick her? How did they know it would work? Because you could try that on a hundred people, and ninety-nine would walk away."

Kurt shrugged. "I guess they have practice. Listen, if we get all psychological about it, she was already drawn to an older man, right? She was looking for parent figures."

Fiona had wanted him to say it out loud, so she could hate him. She said, "Damian was a big part of her life. Look, you were a child of divorce, too, and back when it was less common. It doesn't mean you walk around damaged."

Kurt stood. He stretched and put his palm flat on the ceiling. He said, "I can't judge, but one of the first things she ever told me, in Boulder, was that the day she was born was the worst day of your life. She told me you *said* that to her."

"That's not true."

Was it possible that *this* was the stone in Claire's shoe? That it wasn't about Fiona's affair, the divorce, at all? Her hand was throbbing, taking all the ache that should have been in her head, her gut.

"She grew up knowing she'd ruined your life," Kurt said. "What do you think that does to a person?"

Fiona stood, too, and Jake took a step into the room, like he was getting ready to dive between them. "First of all, I *never* said that to her. It was something *Damian* told her, in the middle of the divorce, to poison her against me. Second, yes, that was *one of* the worst days of my life, although lord knows I've had lots of them, but it had nothing to do with Claire. This isn't some huge secret. It was a terrible day, a shitshow. That doesn't mean I didn't want her, and it didn't change the way I raised her."

"Hey. I'm not saying—I remember that day too. I was—"

"You don't think that's more than a little fucked up, that you *remember the day your girlfriend was born?*"

"She's not my girlfriend." He held his hands up, an unattackable Buddha. "I'm trying to help you out here. You want to make things right with her, this is the swamp you have to wade through, okay? Claire is—she's not a happy person. I don't think she'd ever have been happy, no matter what you did. It's like bad astrology or something. She's just a fundamentally angry human. You weren't a bad mother."

But why did it hurt so much, if it wasn't true?

"Listen, I need to ask you to get out of here before my wife gets home. She's not a fan of the Claire drama."

"Does she know Claire?" Fiona said.

Kurt opened his mouth but then stopped. He'd caught her trick. She said, "Can you at least pass a message on?"

He shook his head slowly. She had fully expected him to say yes. "I'm barely in her good graces. I bring this to her, and maybe she takes it out on me. If she finds out I talked to you, let you in ..."

Jake said, "What about an email address?" Fiona didn't mind him talking; it was time to team up.

Kurt went to the door, opened it for them, though Fiona didn't move. "Here's what I can give you: Everyone's okay, everyone's safe. You want to leave me your number? I can promise I'd call you if anything bad ever happened."

"You'll tell me if she *dies*? How thoughtful."

"That's not what I—"

"Look, what about the little girl? Is she yours?"

Kurt put an enormous hand not on Fiona's shoulder but on Jake's, and steered him effortlessly through the doorway. Like guiding a toy boat. Fiona quickly fished a pen and her old boarding pass from her purse, wrote her number down.

She said, before she walked out the door, "You're a father. Think about what this feels like. Use your imagination. I know you used to have one."

Out on the street, Jake wrapped Fiona in a hug, pressed his beard and lips to her forehead. He said, "I can tell you're a good mom."

Fiona worried he would ask where she was going, ask if he could tag along, but she told him she needed to be alone—she was well practiced at shaking men—and she got in a cab and asked the driver to take her to Montparnasse. She didn't want to go back to Richard's, she knew that much, even though her hand felt like it was touching a live wire and she'd forgotten to bring the pain-killers. "Promise me you'll practice self-care," her shrink had said to her before she left, and she didn't imagine Elena had meant fucking vagrant former pilots. She could have a nice dinner; that was one thing she could do.

She wound up at La Rotonde, the place Aunt Nora used to talk about, the place, if Fiona remembered right, where Ranko Novak lost his mind. Or was it Modigliani? In any case, she sat inside where it was warm, and she ordered *soupe à l'oignon gratinée* and wished she weren't surrounded by so many English-speakers. There were no scruffy, drunk artists, no absinthe-drinking models, no great expat poets.

Well, how would she know? Maybe that table in the corner was full of them.

She'd asked Nora once if she'd ever met Hemingway, and Nora had said, "If I did, he didn't make an impression."

But she imagined that in the intervening decades, the avant-garde had changed its meet-up spot.

If this was really where Ranko Novak had lost it, it seemed an odd place. Everything was warm and red and magical, and the soup was so good.

Well, if you were going to be miserable, you could be miserable anywhere. She'd known that for years: the way one person could starve to death at the banquet, the way you could sob through the funniest movie.

The waiter asked if she would like dessert. She ordered another soup instead, exactly the same as the first.

1986

After the gallery closed, Yale brushed his teeth in the bathroom. He shaved again so he'd look okay in the morning, and he changed his shirt. He left his things under his desk.

Evanston was not a town where places stayed open all night, and he thought he'd have a better chance in the city, so he went back down on the El. His plan was to stay pretty south on Clark, where Charlie wasn't as likely to be. He started down at Inner Circle, which was dead, and then he headed up toward Cheeks to see if the cute bald bartender was working. He was a block away when he saw, in front of him on the sidewalk, the back of Bill Lindsey, his loping gait. Yale froze and figured he'd backtrack, but then Bill looked over his shoulder and stopped and called to Yale, gave a giant wave that Yale couldn't pretend not to have seen.

When Yale caught up, Bill said, "You live near here, yes? It's not an area I know too well."

"Bit north of here."

"Well, this is serendipity! I have something in my car that I forgot to bring to the office today. You're going to be *thrilled*."

And so Yale found himself following Bill to his Buick, the same car they'd all ridden triumphantly back from Wisconsin in. Bill was parked right outside Cheeks. He didn't seem embarrassed at all, except that he was talking faster than usual.

"Look!" Bill said, and thrust an enormous book at him. Yale rested it on the car's hood.

Pascin: Catalogue raisonné: Peintures, aquarelles, pastels, dessins. The second volume. Bill said, "Page sixty. Tell me what you see."

"Oh." A woman in a chair, blonde waves parted far to one side, a nightgown falling off her shoulders, pooling in her lap. The pose was exactly the same as in Nora's supposed Pascin study. The face was the same. The only difference was that here she wore clothes. Yale said, "That's great news." He felt like laughing. That his luck should be so good only at work.

"I can ask her about it," Yale said. "I can take this up there with me."

"What I want you to do—before you get all her stories, and I know that's what she wants—is to see if she can remember what paintings might've been done from the sketches. Because this one, for instance—Yale, this is in the Musée d'Orsay! Maybe they'll have interest in the sketch, you know? Display it beside the original. Not to sell," he said, seeing Yale's face, "but a loan or exchange. I can send the catalogs with you to Wisconsin. Of course there's no Hébuterne catalog, or Sergey What's-His-Face. And no *Ranko Novak* catalog, ha! But we're going to load your trunk with books."

"And you're sure you don't want to come?"

"I have so much to do for the Polaroids." The Polaroid show didn't open till August, but Bill was dealing with loaned Ansel Adams and Walker Evans pieces, and every time he talked about the exhibit he wound up flapping his hands in frustration. "I want you back up there very soon. You and Roman. He's a fine specimen, no?"

Yale had no idea how to respond. "He seems like a quick study," he said.

As he got in his car, Bill winked.

*

278

Yale sank onto a barstool in the darkest corner of Cheeks and pried his feet loose from the stickiness of the floor and ordered a Manhattan. It was a safe place to spend time, and they wouldn't close till four, and he kept seeing faces he vaguely knew. The receptionist from the gay-friendly dentist on Broadway, Katsu Tatami's ex, the tall Canadian Nico had once been obsessed with. He had a long purple lesion on his left cheekbone. A former staffer of Charlie's came up to say hi, and one of Julian's theater friends, the one who'd played Fortinbras in *Hamlet*. The place was oddly full for a Monday; some kind of bat signal had been sent up, apparently. The cute bartender wasn't there, but the one on duty had a generous pour. A dusky guy in a ripped T-shirt dropped a matchbook in Yale's lap, and when Yale opened it he found a phone number on the flap. It occurred to Yale that he was essentially single now, that he could go home with someone, take advantage of a warm bed and a shower, a distraction. The problem was he wasn't sure he remembered how to flirt. It had been too long. That, and the fact that all he could think about were germs and bodily fluids. The whole bar looked to him like a petri dish.

Despite the number of people, everyone seemed subdued, just kind of nodding their heads to the Bronski Beat and standing in little groups. Maybe because it was so cold out that the frost blasted in every time the door opened. The whole cruise-with-your-shirt-off thing worked a hell of a lot better in L.A.

Someone squeezed the back of his neck and he looked up to see Richard, the silver waves of his hair catching the bar lights. He got close to Yale's ear, spoke loudly. "This is a rare sighting! Yale down here in the Deep South, slumming with the likes of me!"

"I just needed somewhere to go."

Richard nodded like he understood. He said, "Museums should

stay open all night, for this very reason. You could wander around the Field Museum. No one would dare assault you in front of a sarcophagus."

"We should move all the museums to Boystown."

Richard laughed. "If we moved the museums to Boystown they'd just turn into bars. That's why I don't move there myself."

"You'd turn into a bar?"

"No, a raging alcoholic."

He told Richard about running into Bill Lindsey outside. Richard said, "Start watching for him and I bet you'll see him crouching in the corner every time you're out." He was surveying the room. "I want to shoot some video in here," he said. "It's so viscerally sleazy."

Yale said, "Are you *kidding*? You'd be banned for life."

"Mr. Technicality."

"That's my job. To suck the soul out of art."

Richard said, "You either need more booze or less. Shall we get you more?"

The door opened again and more icy wind flooded the room. A new cluster pushed in, loud, already drunk. Julian was in the midst of them. Of course he was.

He hoped Julian wouldn't see him, but Richard was waving him over—Richard had always had a thing for Julian, was always asking him to pose—and now Julian was heading straight toward them. He put both arms around Richard's neck and hung there like a huge, drunk necklace. He wore a hat and a sweater but no coat. He slurred what sounded like "Richard, I can live in your house." It might have been something else. He sounded like an old man who'd forgotten his dentures.

Richard said, "Julian, what are you on?"

Julian fell between Richard and Yale, caught himself on the

bar. "It's *kid* stuff. We were at Paradise! Let's go back to Paradise! I didn't wanna leave. Oh, Yale." He put out a hand and touched Yale's chin. "Yale, I had to *tell* you something."

"No, you don't." Yale wanted to hate him, but he couldn't. He was so pathetic. How could he hate someone this pathetic?

Julian reached up and took off his hat, and Yale coughed in surprise, struggled to recover. Julian's head was completely shaved, albeit badly, his beautiful black hair—his unicorn lock—reduced to patchy stubble and scabs.

Richard ran his fingers along the top of Julian's scalp, horrified.

"Why did you do that?" Yale said.

Julian made a phlegmy noise, a sick animal noise.

"Whoa," Richard said. "Hey. We need to get you home."

"I lost my key."

"Yale, can you take him to your place?"

Yale blew out a mouthful of air and almost said, "I told you about the snoring," but instead he said, "Charlie and I split up." Because he'd have to say it sooner or later. Charlie couldn't coerce him into sitting together at every event, putting on the couple show.

Julian, to Yale's horror, began to cry. He put his face on Yale's chest and didn't get him wet but just sort of heaved there, his whole body shaking.

Richard said, "I didn't know, Yale. I'm sorry. He can—Julian, don't cry. Julian, you can come to my place, okay?" And Julian nodded, without taking his face off Yale. "Yale, where are *you* staying? Are you alright?"

"I have no idea. I mean, I'm fine. I was kind of gonna sit here till four."

"Oh, *Yale*. Come with us, then. Is that why you asked me the other day? I'm a dolt."

Yale said, "You're not. And I shouldn't. I can't." Not if Julian would be there. He couldn't wake up sober in the morning and eat eggs with Julian. He couldn't take care of Julian vomiting in the night.

Richard said, "My friend owns a little hotel on Belmont. It's in a beautiful old house. We'll walk you there, okay?"

It seemed as good an option as any.

Richard hugged the hotel's owner, an older guy in a bolo tie and aviators, and gave him a fifty-dollar bill and asked him to take good care of Yale. As the owner showed Yale the elaborate key system (one for the front door, one for the upstairs hall, one for the room), Richard and Julian took off.

In the morning, there was coffee and powdered doughnuts. There was a little dog that lived downstairs—a fluffy white thing named Miss Marple—and a TV that broadcast two channels. Yale came back the next night with his bag and his box, and reserved his room for the rest of the week. It would deplete his checking account, but if he had to dip into savings, he would. What the hell was he saving for, exactly?

On Friday Yale went to the Laundromat, and there was Teddy, pulling his clothes from the dryer, peeling apart his staticky shirts. He said hello—coldly, Yale thought—and went back to his folding. But as Yale was starting the washer, Teddy came up and stood there, arms full of clothes. Of course Teddy couldn't just *hold* clothes; he bounced them in his arms like a baby.

"Listen," he said, "There's something I need to say."

"Okay?"

"After you left the church on Sunday, Asher and I went in there and found Charlie in a pretty awful state. So let me just start by saying I know what's going on, I know he's sick."

"Alright." Teddy didn't say anything, so Yale looked around, saw no one was listening, whispered. "Well, no, he's not sick, he just has the virus. Do you know how he *got* the virus?"

"No, and I don't want to. That's where judgment and blame come in, and I want no part of it. I mean, what, we're gonna make an infection tree? A flowchart? Come on. Everyone got it from someone. We all got it from Reagan, right? We're gonna blame someone, let's be productive and blame the ignorance and neglect of Ronald Fucking Reagan. Let's blame Jesse Helms. How about the Pope? Here's what I know. I know your lover of—what, five years?—is scared shitless, and you decide the appropriate response is to *walk out* and leave him alone with his terrified mother, and then to *yell* at him at the fucking funeral of your friend."

Yale said, "Wait. Wait. He kicked me out." Although that wasn't precisely true, was it? How had it even happened?

"Yeah, he'll be acting irrationally for a while. Come on."

He wanted to ask if Asher was mad at him, too, if every gay man in Chicago had heard Charlie's side of the story, if Yale's name was being mentioned around town in the same breath as Helms and the Pope.

"Teddy, he doesn't want me there. And he's the one who should be crawling to me."

"The sick don't do the crawling."

"Is that a philosophical tenet?" Yale tried to lower his voice; the woman at the counter was staring now.

"Sure."

"So you're out there tending the ill? Walking the streets and giving out morphine shots? You're running the clean-needle exchange?"

"As a matter of fact." Oh, God. Yale had stepped right into it. "As a matter of fact, Julian just moved in. I'm taking care of Julian."

Teddy and Julian hadn't been an item, a *real* item, in a year

283

or two, but there had always been that possibility, a thread left hanging.

"When?"

"Two days ago. Richard called me Wednesday morning. He said you were out cruising together when you found him."

"Jesus. I was not cruising, I was homeless."

"Anyway, he's at my place now, and one of the things I'm realizing is how much I love him, how much I always have. When you're going to lose someone, it puts things in a new light."

"You're back *together*?"

"Well, not physically. Not yet, but it could happen. The point is, you have to take care of the people you love."

Yale considered blurting out that Julian was the one who'd infected Charlie, but what was the point? It would get around, it would hurt people. And if Teddy was so happy to take care of Julian, why throw a wrench in the works?

He said, "You must be a better person than I am, Teddy. I wish you all the best."

2015

Fiona had the door to Richard's only half open when Serge flung it wide. He grabbed her arm and drew her in. He said, "I look for you an hour! Your phone is, ah, asleep."

Fiona pulled it out of her purse. How had she let it die?

"He's here!" Serge said.

"Who is?"

"Your detective. He's very, um, excited? Yes?"

Richard appeared behind him. He said, "Serge was out combing the streets for you! Your guy found us. I mean, that's a decent detective, to track us down here."

Fiona looked back and forth between them. "Excited" could have meant agitated, coming from Serge. It might have meant alarmed or panicked. Or happy.

Serge said, "He uses the bathroom! One second!" and then he vanished down the hall.

She said to Richard, "*What*, tell me!"

"Well, I'll mangle it, dear. Be patient."

And here came Arnaud, tucking his shirt back into his jeans.

Arnaud said, "Ah, okay, hello! Yes! Your phone was dead all day! But I have double good news. She's ready to meet with you."

"She's—what? Who, Claire?"

"Ha. I'm good, right? Fast. She's here in the city. Well, she lives in Saint-Denis, not a very nice suburb. But she works at a bar-tabac in the eighteenth."

Fiona found herself leaning against the wall.

She said, because it was the first question she could think of, "How did you do it?"

"I cut the Gordian knot! I asked the wife. I walked up and down the street early this morning, and when she comes out I say, *Are you Claire Blanchard?* When she says no, I say Claire owes a parking ticket, does she know her place of work? So she sends me there."

Fiona said, "Oh my God. You went there? You saw her?" She was vaguely aware of Serge and Richard grinning at her. Kurt must not have told his wife about the visit or she'd have been on guard.

Arnaud said, "Yes. A couple of hours ago. She's fine. A little thin but fine. She didn't look, ah—not like she was in a cult. Little bit of lipstick, you know. Not so bad."

"And the girl?"

"No. I mean, I didn't see the girl. But yes, that is her daughter. I verified. It's her daughter with Kurt Pearce. She has the girl."

"She does!"

"Nicolette. I didn't see her, but she told me."

Fiona's whole face stung. "Her name is what?"

"Nicolette." He enunciated. "You want me to spell it out for you?"

"We—" She couldn't talk. She couldn't look at Richard. She finally managed: "What am I supposed to do?"

"Well. You pay me. Ha. And I'm going to give you the address. After that, it's up to you." But Claire didn't want her coming by till tomorrow. Arnaud said, "She wants, you know, some time. To prepare. She was a bit shocked."

"You don't think she'd leave?" Fiona said. "What if she runs away?"

"Well. I have no idea. But this was not my impression."

She wanted to go right away to the address Arnaud had just handed her, but why? It could only do damage.

Arnaud had to leave; this was not his only case, and he'd spent all day tracking her down. Serge took her dead phone out of her hand to charge it, said he'd bring some food to her room. She was shaky, and she must've looked it.

It was too early to call Damian in Portland, but not too early to call Cecily.

Cecily must be at least seventy now, but in Fiona's mind she always looked as she had in the mid-1980s. Shoulder pads and gelled hair, her face bright and unlined. She'd seen Cecily only once since Kurt and Claire first joined the Hosanna Collective. Cecily was in the process of packing up her Evanston house then, getting ready to move to the Upper Peninsula, and she sat with Fiona at the table in her otherwise empty kitchen. She expressed concern for Claire, for Fiona, but said she'd written Kurt off long ago. She said, "I could've told you. I *would* have told you. If I'd known you were introducing them. He's his father all over again. Well, no, he's smarter than his father. But that doesn't help. He thinks himself in circles and he acts impulsively. It's a cycle, the overthinking and the compulsion. I've tried. Fiona, I've tried. He's an adult, and I've made my mistakes, and I can't unmake them anymore." This was when Fiona learned that Kurt had stolen more than twenty thousand dollars from his mother, that he'd lied his way through rehab, lied his way through the counselors she'd paid for.

Now Fiona listened to Cecily's phone ring, and when it went to voice mail she tried again. Serge was back in the room with a tray: toast, grapes, some wedges of soft cheese. A tall, thin glass of water.

Cecily finally answered, her voice dry, tired.

Fiona said, "Well, I have news."

"Is it news I want to hear?"

"Yes," Fiona said. Serge put the tray on the little bedside table and sat on the foot of the bed, listening. Fiona didn't mind—it gave her someone to make eye contact with as she talked. "Kurt is fine. I talked to him even. He seemed clean. As in sober. And healthy and everything." She told her that he was living with someone, not Claire, but didn't say married. She didn't say that he'd been arrested. And then she said, "We've found Claire. I'm seeing her tomorrow. This might be premature, but you ought to see about flying out."

Cecily sighed, a long, tired sigh. Fiona imagined her in a bathrobe. She said, "I understand why you need to be there. I love Kurt, but he's a grown man, and I don't consider myself a mother anymore, not in the same way. There was a season for that, and the season is done."

Fiona said, "Yes. But I need your help." She dug her fingernails into her knee. She said, "And we have a granddaughter."

1986

It was a relief to head to Wisconsin on Monday, all his stuff in the trunk, Roman in the passenger seat. The roads were slick, the trees black against a white sky. They were headed, in a rented Nissan that smelled like artificial pine, to 1920s Paris. Yale tried imagining that every hour they drove took them fifteen years into the past. They'd reach Sturgeon Bay in time for the Hindenburg. They'd pull up not to Nora's house but to a café lit by gas lamps.

Yale had circled the date of January 26 in his pocket calendar at some point—he didn't remember doing it, which meant he'd probably been drunk—and he'd recalculated several times in the past weeks. And today was the twenty-seventh. Twelve full weeks and one day since Nico's memorial. If that was truly the night Charlie had been infected, then Yale could have been infected soon after. He could wait till the end of March, three full months from the last time he'd had sex with Charlie, or he could pull the trigger now. Because even if he hadn't been infected till that last time, any antibodies were, according to two different people who'd answered the Howard Brown hotline on two different nights, 80 percent likely to have shown up by now. And some doctors believed transmission rates were highest right after infection—he knew, thanks to several helpful articles in the newspaper of the asshole who had possibly murdered him.

Yale tried to get Roman talking, asked him about his childhood. "It's not what you think of when you picture California," Roman said. "Truckee is where the Donner Party got stuck."

"They got stuck in *California*?" It hit Yale as absurd.

"Cannibals and skiing. That's what we've got."

Yale asked if he still considered himself Mormon and Roman grimaced, hesitated. "They make it really hard to leave. It's like trying to quit Columbia House."

"Ha! They send you sheets of stickers?"

"Yeah," Roman said. "You get eleven years of guilt for only a dollar."

Yale asked why he'd be *inclined* to leave the church, but Roman only shrugged. "I have trouble with some stuff," he said, and Yale decided he shouldn't press further. He remembered the feeling of suspecting someone was on to you when you weren't even able to admit things to yourself, and he didn't want to inflict that on Roman. There had been one old-lady cashier at the grocer's who, when Yale was a teenager, would look at him like he was the saddest thing in the world. He'd question his purchases—would gum make him seem gay?—and after a while, he made excuses to drive to the store six miles south instead. And there was Mr. Irving, his guidance counselor, who cautiously, forehead scrunched, asked Yale if he planned to look for a college with "a cosmopolitan feel." The assessment of those two hit him harder than the judgment of the peers who simply called him a faggot, who stuck Kotex to his locker. Because that happened to other kids too. Anyone could have their underwear thrown into the pool, anyone might have to use, night after night, a chemistry textbook that had once been drenched in piss. But only real fags got looked at with pity by adults. And so although Roman was hardly a teenager—he was only a few years younger than Yale, really—Yale dropped the subject.

"Our biggest priority," he said when they stopped for gas in Fish Creek, "besides any connection to full paintings, is *dates*. Can we help her figure out the year, at least, for the undated works. I know what she wants is to tell us stories, but Bill's gonna be peeved if we come back without a timeline." Plenty of the pieces were signed, but few were dated. The Modiglianis, frustratingly, were not.

"I do have to be back by Friday," Roman said.

But it was only Monday, and although Yale wanted to stay in Wisconsin forever, away from Chicago, away from Charlie, he said, "I only think it'll take two days. Big weekend plans?"

"She's really dying?" Roman squeegeed the windshield while Yale worked the pump. Roman wore a black coat and black jeans—Yale had never seen him in anything but black—and out of the context of the city, he looked odd, depressed.

"Congestive heart failure is apparently a waiting game. We have to assume each visit could be our last. So, big picture first. Colorful details later."

Back in the car, Roman said, "I want to know how you made her trust you that fast."

Yale considered feigning ignorance, but instead he said, "I think I remind her of her grandnephew. We were good friends. He died in October."

"Oh."

"He had AIDS."

Roman looked out his own window. "I'm sorry for your loss."

They had dinner in Egg Harbor and checked in at the bed and breakfast. Nora had told them the morning was her "best time," and so—without the influence of Bill Lindsey and his endless bottles of wine—they settled in early. Through his bathroom wall, Yale could hear Roman brushing his teeth, spitting out water. The sinks must have backed right up to each other. He could say "good night" right through the wall, but why make things strange?

They found Nora sitting in front of a meager fire. She was holding a plastic spray bottle, no wheelchair in sight. "Let's get you some coffee," she said, which sent Debra clomping to the kitchen like an underpaid waitress.

"Roman," Nora said, pronouncing it "Ro-*mahn*," as if he were Spanish, "would you be a dear and help with this?" She meant the spray bottle. "Debra doesn't think it will help. It's peppermint water, for the mice." Yale and Roman both scanned the room. Yale didn't see any rodents. "It keeps them away. Could you spray along the floorboards? The windowsills too."

"I—sure," Roman said, and left his notebook and pen on the couch next to Yale.

Yale had wanted to ease into things slowly, logically; he'd thought of several ways to frame the conversation, none of which had to do with mint-bombing rodents. He searched his folder for the list of the works, but Nora was already talking.

"I've been in quite a state," she said, and then stopped and looked at Yale as if he should know exactly why. "Those papers we signed. I should have asked Stanley to explain more."

"Oh! Is there—"

"Everything we *said*, about making sure the work was all displayed equally, it wasn't in there."

Roman stood by the fireplace twisting the nozzle of the spray bottle, trying to get the mist right. Yale could hear, in the kitchen, the coffee percolating, Debra banging around.

"Right. Right. That's okay. Occasionally someone might do a tailored gift agreement, something with specifics, but they're a lot of trouble. I can assure you I haven't forgotten your wishes."

"Listen," she said, "I'm no fool. I know Ranko's work isn't something you'd normally feature. But it's not *bad*."

"I love the two paintings!" Roman said. He was spraying beside the record shelf. "The perspective is way off, right? Sort of tentative and haphazard at the same time. But in a good way, like he was on the verge of figuring something out." Roman had never said this before, and Yale wondered if he was lying or if he'd just kept quiet about it around the gallery, knowing Bill's opinion.

"I *like* your intern," Nora said. "Your boss, I'm not so crazy about."

"I'm your advocate in all this," Yale said, and he was gearing up to say more, but Nora spoke again.

"I'm going to tell you about Ranko. I know you have your own agenda, but you can find out about Soutine at the library. The art historians can tell you more than I can about most of those pieces. You're not going to find much of anything about Ranko, though, and I need to do it while I have the chance." And then, as an afterthought, "Sergey Mukhankin too."

Yale said, "We can go through the works chronologically, and when we get to Ranko's you could give us those details. I have some catalogs in the car that—"

"No." She shook her head like an obstreperous little girl. One who happened to be in charge. "I'm going to tell you the most important stories first, and then the next, and so on. And the first is about the time before the war, when Ranko was locked away for the Prix de Rome."

"Locked away?"

"Don't move any furniture," she said to Roman, "but if you aim it under the couch that should do."

Yale lifted his feet while Roman did so.

"He was a Serb," she said. "But born in Paris, raised there." Roman was supposed to be the one taking notes, but since he was busy, Yale grabbed the notebook. The air smelled like peppermint now, pleasantly antiseptic.

"We were at different schools. Now, my father was French," she said, "and when I decided to study art he took it seriously, and he

293

thought there was no point to studying in Philadelphia." She spoke quickly but paused between sentences for breath—a swimmer coming up for air. "The big school in Paris, as I'm sure you know, was the École des Beaux Arts, but they didn't admit women, and even if they had, they were *fusty*. I wrote to two schools, and one was the Académie Colarossi. And"—she laughed—"I'll tell you what impressed me most: They were going to let me draw from nude male models. This was the excuse for keeping women out of most schools, you know. *We can't have women here, there are nude men!* So it was set for me to go to Colarossi"—she spelled it for Yale, who'd seen the name before but was still two sentences behind—"and my father took me over. It was 1912, and I was seventeen."

Roman crouched to spray the threshold to the dining room, the back of his black T-shirt riding up.

"I was meant to stay with my father's aunt, Tante Alice. She was senile and never left her bed. The idea was her nurse would keep me in line, but the poor nurse had no idea how. She'd make me toast in the morning, and that was the extent of her supervision. That fall there was an anatomy class at Colarossi that was open to the public. You know, the interior workings of the knee and so on. Beaux-Arts had similar courses, but this was a special deal, someone was visiting to teach it, so a few of those students came."

Roman was back, like a relay runner, to grab the pen. Yale returned to his own list, the hopeful empty spaces for dates beside each piece, but he found he had nothing to add to the timeline but *1912—arrival in Paris.*

"And next to me was a man with dark, curly hair—quite like yours, Yale, although his face was longer—and as he sat there, he made himself a crown of paper clips. Linked them in a circle and put it on his head. He sat there like it wasn't the least bit unusual, the sun glinting off him. I wanted to paint him, that was my first thought, but the next instant I was smitten. I'd never understood it before, how artists fall for their muses. I thought it was just a bunch of men who couldn't keep it in their pants. But there was something about the need to paint him and the need to possess him—they were the same impulse. I don't know if that makes sense, but there it was."

Yale tried to say something, but didn't know how to begin. It had to do with a walk he once took with Nico and Richard around the Lincoln Park lagoon, the two of them sharing Richard's Leica. It struck Yale that day how they both had a way of interacting with the world that was simultaneously selfish and generous— grabbing at beauty and reflecting beauty back. The benches and fire hydrants and manhole covers Nico and Richard stopped to photograph were made more beautiful by their noticing. They were *left* more beautiful, once they walked away. By the end of the day, Yale found himself seeing things in frames, saw the way the light hit fence posts, wanted to lap up the ripples of sun on a record store window.

He said, "I get it, I do."

Roman, meanwhile, was sweating, his face shiny. Yale wondered if it was this talk of love that made him nervous, or if he was getting sick. The way he shifted on the couch made Yale suspect the former. Well, the last thing Yale himself needed right now was a love story.

"Ranko was hosting a picnic the next day and he invited me along. And that was it, I was lost. He *smelled* right, like a dark closet. So much of sex is in the nose. I do believe that. And he was in love with me too." She stopped, held a finger up, appeared to concentrate on breathing. Yale was tempted to ask a question, just to fill the silence, but here was Debra, with big white mugs of coffee for both Yale and Roman. No sugar, no cream: just coffee so thin you could see the cup bottom through it. Roman took the mug awkwardly, rested it straight on the coffee table. Debra leaned against the doorframe, arms crossed, a statue of bored impatience.

"Is this still about Ranko?"

Yale nodded. Roman said, "We're at the paper clips."

"He's the entire reason she gave you the art. You know that, right?"

"I don't deny it," Nora said before Yale had to decide how to respond.

Roman asked what she meant, but Debra laughed loudly. "Seventy years is just a really long time to be obsessed with someone," she said. "Don't you think? Like, I'm sure he was a great guy, but he's been dead forever, and she's still choosing him over her family."

Roman said, "I don't get why that means she had to give the Brigg—"

"Debra," Yale said. And then he found he had no idea what to say next. He'd just been desperate to break the tension, to change the subject. "Is there any sugar?"

And when she stormed back to the kitchen, Yale got up to follow, signaled Roman to keep writing.

Debra opened the refrigerator and stared into it; this surely wasn't where the sugar was kept, but Yale hadn't really wanted any, anyway. He'd been hoping Debra didn't hate him as much as she once had. She'd be a valuable resource after Nora passed away.

He said, "It has to be so stressful, taking care of her."

Debra didn't answer.

"Emotionally and financially, both. Hey, look, if you want to get that jewelry appraised, I'd be happy to introduce you to the right people. You don't just want to go to some shop up here. If you're interested in the monetary value—I mean, you might be surprised. I know someone in Chicago who would even drive up here. As a favor to me."

Debra turned. She was holding, for some reason, a bottle of mustard. She had tears in her eyes, but they must have been from a minute ago. She said, flatly, "That's sweet of you."

"It's no problem."

"You know, I've never been mad at you *personally*. It would be easier to hate you if you were an asshole. This is how you get stuff from people, isn't it. You're nice. And it's not even fake."

Yale used to believe he was nice, but Charlie might say different. Teddy would too. He shrugged and said, "No, it's not fake." To his great amazement, Debra smiled at him.

Nora was telling Roman, when they returned, about moving in with a divorced fellow student from the Académie. "We were in a little flat over a shoe repair shop on Rue de la Grande Chaumière. Oh, dear," she said to Roman, "do you speak French?"

"I do, actually. I've—my dissertation is on Balthus, and I've—"

"Ha! That pervert! Well, good, you can spell. The husband supported her still, sent money every month. I bribed my aunt's *bonne* with a few francs, and my poor aunt was too far gone to notice I'd left."

Yale sat, tried to skim Roman's notes, but he hadn't written much. Debra pulled a dining room chair in.

"So those were my student years. Drawing, painting, being with Ranko. Those cow sketches are from that time, from a trip we took around Normandy. March of 1913, I'd say."

Yale jotted the date next to the three Ranko Novak sketch slots. The absolute least important of the details he'd been sent for. If he returned with only the cow sketch dates, Bill would think it was a prank.

"We wanted to get married but we needed to wait, because in April, Ranko entered the Prix de Rome. It wasn't just a prize, it was a contest for students, a yearlong thing, and they'd eliminate you one by one. It was like Miss America, the way each round they send those poor girls off crying. And—can you guess?—it was only open to unmarried men. You had to be French, and of course another student raised some nonsense that Ranko wasn't truly French—it was his name, I suppose, the fact that he wasn't named *Renée*—but they let him go forward anyway. It upset him, though.

"He was quite fragile. And strange! Now, he's one who should *not* have been at the Beaux-Arts. It was the establishment, you know, and they wanted to tame him. It was the age of the bohemian, and the last thing you'd want was a pat on the back from the old standard-bearers. He was always tamping down his oddness for them. It worked, unfortunately, in the end. He sanded his work down till they loved it."

Roman said, "Those two paintings don't seem sanded down."

"Well, *exactly*. Those weren't ones his teachers ever saw. The one of the little girl—he did that around the same time, dashed it off. It was supposed to be me; he was painting me as he imagined I'd looked as a girl. He got it all wrong, I'm afraid, but still that piece has a soul. The work he did for them, though, it was polished and flat and religious. And he was an atheist!

"He progressed and progressed in the contest, and the end of the whole ordeal was that they sequestered you in a studio in the Château de Compiègne for seventy-two days. Seventy-two! Can you imagine? And they gave you a theme to paint on. First you had twelve hours to sketch, and then you had the ten weeks to paint, and you weren't allowed to vary from the sketch. Whoever decided an artist shouldn't change his mind? So for seventy-two days he was locked up, and there I sat pining away."

Roman said, "Could he write you letters?"

"No! It was the worst time of my life. Now, I say that, but really I fell more in love every day. What's more romantic than waiting for a lover who's locked up in a chateau? I lost twenty pounds.

"I can't remember what theme they gave, but what he produced was this stiff *pietà*. It looked like a bad Easter pageant, is what I thought. And he won. *Three* students won, in fact, which was a scandal. They hadn't awarded the prize the year before, and someone before that had to give his prize back for some silly reason, so there were three spots open at the Villa Medici in Rome, which is where the contest winners were sent. Any other year, to be honest, Ranko wouldn't have won. Everyone knew it was really third place, and he knew it too.

"So you can imagine: The love of my life sequesters himself for months, and his prize is three to five years in Rome. And we can't get married *now*, because there's no room there for a wife. He was elated, and I was just devastated."

"This is the thing," Debra interjected. "I understand devoting your life to the memory of someone great, but he was a jerk."

Yale had to silently agree. Maybe Ranko hadn't been a bad guy—the prize sounded like the opportunity of a lifetime—but if a young Nora had come to Yale for relationship advice, he'd have told her to cut her losses and move on.

"Then that summer, two things happened. One you already know: That terrible man had to go shoot the Archduke and start the war, and I could have just kicked him. But the other is that my father died suddenly. So in one instant, Ranko's travels to Rome were put off, and in the next, I was called home."

Roman made a sympathetic noise, underlined the word *died* in his notes.

"Everything was chaos, you can imagine. I wasn't going to leave, I was going to stay with Ranko. I was almost happy for the war, in a horribly selfish way. But Paris was becoming dangerous, and my father's death meant I had no money to stay in school—and then, in August, Ranko broke it to me that he was being mobilized. I hadn't even known it was a possibility.

"I cried for two days straight, and I decided I'd go. I had a hell of a time getting out, what with everyone booking passage at once. I went back to Philadelphia, where my mother was, and I taught drawing classes to some insufferable children."

"But you came back," Roman said. "All the other pieces, they're later, right?"

"Yes," she agreed, and then she launched into a deep, wet cough that rocked her whole body. Debra shot out of her chair and vanished into the kitchen, and Yale stood, not knowing what to do. He'd become used to the PCP cough, a dry bark he'd heard on the streets and in the bars, a cough that made him think of a more medieval type of plague. He remembered Jonathan Bird, Nico's old roommate, saying, "I just wish that with all this hacking I could cough something *up*." Whereas Nora sounded like she was drowning. Debra was back with a paper towel and another glass of water.

Yale stepped into the dining room, signaled for Roman to join. They could give Nora space, at least.

Roman whispered: "He died in the war, right? Ranko Novak?"

Yale shrugged. "I mean, I don't feel like this story has a happy ending."

"It's so beautiful," Roman said. "Doomed love."

Yale laughed. "Is it?" And then he couldn't stop laughing. Which was terrible, because Nora was still coughing and Roman looked hurt. But the moony expression on Roman's face, his voice, had hit the darkest spot of Yale's humor. How beautiful, the doomed love! How gorgeous and ambient, the ways we abandon each other! The lovely wars we die in, the poetry of disease! He wanted to be able to call Terrence up, to say, "*You were like Romeo and Juliet! Romeo and Juliet die puking their guts out. Tristan and Iseult at ninety pounds with no hair. It's beautiful, Terrence. It's beautiful!*"

Roman said, "Are you okay?"

Nora's cough was finally dying down.

"Maybe we should leave," Roman said.

And then Debra was in the doorway, suggesting the same thing. "This is way more than I should have let her do," she said. "What about tomorrow?"

It sounded lovely: the guarantee of another night up here, away from the city, away from everyone he knew. If only he could stretch it into a week, and then a month. No posters up here urging him to get tested. He could stay in Nora's house, send Debra off to live her life.

In the car, Yale said, "If she dies in her sleep tonight, just shoot me, okay?"

"Now that you said it, she won't."

The seats were frozen, and the steering wheel sent waves of cold through Yale's gloves. "I'm not sure I have that kind of power over the universe."

Roman said, "When you think a specific bad thing is going to happen, it never does. I don't mean like if you think it looks like rain it won't rain, but like if you think your plane will crash, it won't."

Yale shook his head. "I want to live in your world. Doom is beautiful, and you can control your fate." Although probably it was a belief system Roman desperately needed. Why mess him up? Yale couldn't tell him anything the world wouldn't eventually teach him on its own.

They stopped for a late lunch at the same place they'd eaten the night before, and Yale had the same batter-fried fish plus a couple of beers.

When they walked back into the bed and breakfast, Mrs. Cherry ran toward them, flapping her hands. "Oh it's *terrible*, isn't it? Now, your rooms have NBC and CBS, but ABC doesn't come in too clearly. PBS you'll get, too, I think, but you never know if they'll show the news. I'd try CBS, myself."

Yale was opening his mouth to ask what she meant, to say they hadn't been near a TV all day, but Roman was already asking what channel CBS was and nodding in agreement as Mrs. Cherry said again how *terrible* it was. She didn't seem that upset, though—it couldn't have been the end of the world. "Now let me ask you," she said, "do you fellows drink wine? A young couple checked out this morning, and they left a full bottle right on the floor. Hold on and I'll grab it."

They only had time to look at each other in bemusement before she came back with local strawberry wine, cough-syrup red, the bottle itself somehow already sticky when she pressed it into Yale's hands.

"Or you can take it back to your family," she said, and Yale thanked her, assured her that they did indeed enjoy wine, that they'd put it to good use.

Yale was heading to his own room, but Roman beckoned him from two doors down. "You don't want to know what's on CBS?"

Yale did, and furthermore he didn't want to find out alone if it was something like Russia declaring war. He carried the wine into Roman's room. He said, "What's going to be worse, the news or the wine?"

There was a basket on top of the bureau with a corkscrew and napkins and plastic cups. Yale poured them each a glass—hard to gauge with cups this shape how much wine it was—and they clicked a toast. Yale expected a mouthful of syrup, but this stuff had an untamed acidity under the sweetness, so that it was both far too sweet and not sweet enough.

He took a seat on the end of Roman's bed. Roman's suitcase, down on the floor, spilled black clothes like lava.

Roman had gone to the TV to turn it on—it was just a couple

302

of feet from the end of the bed, perched on the bureau—but now he was blocking the set. Yale had nothing to look at but his back and his ass.

"Oh," Roman said. "Oh, wow."

"What?"

"The, ah, the space shuttle. It blew up."

"Shit. Move over."

Roman sat beside him, cross-legged. He took his glasses off and put them back on.

Dan Rather was explaining, in the studio, that something went wrong one minute and twelve seconds after liftoff. Live at Cape Canaveral, a man at an outdoor desk tried to explain what had happened, talked about the big pieces of the craft that had fallen into the ocean. They showed the shuttle taking off this morning, and things went well for long enough that Yale was almost hopeful nothing would happen after all. And then it burst into a ball of smoke, two spiraling plumes.

"My God, they had that teacher on there," Yale said.

"What?"

"You know, there was that contest for a teacher to go to space. The woman. Oh God."

Roman said, "Huh. Yeah, I don't really watch the news."

Yale wouldn't have been as aware of it all himself if Kurt Pearce hadn't been talking about it the other day—how now we were going to go back and forth to space all the time, how Kurt planned to live on the moon by the time he was twenty.

Roman's left knee was touching Yale's right knee, or at least the cloth of his black jeans was brushing Yale's khakis. Yale wondered if it was intentional, wondered if he would hurt Roman's feelings by shifting away.

Yale said, "Well it was a really big deal. Fuck."

"Do they have other space shuttles?" Roman said.

"What do you mean?"

"Like, do they have a fleet of these things, or is there just the one?"

"There's—" It seemed like an easy question, but Yale found he wasn't sure of the answer. "There's one at a time, right? This was the current one."

Yale found himself gulping the wine. It was only afternoon but it felt later. Roman's curtains were all drawn, the blinds down behind them.

Roman flopped back on the bed, legs still crossed, knee still pressing toward Yale, and balanced the wine on his belly with the aid of a finger hooked onto the cup's rim.

Yale took time to think out the whole thought, in words: He was not going to sleep with Roman. Not now, and not ever. Not now, because he might have been infected. Not ever, because he was supposed to be this guy's mentor. He wasn't sure what rules existed about grad student–professor relationships at Northwestern, but he imagined they *did* exist, and he imagined he'd be held to the same standards. Not ever, because he wasn't interested in helping some confused virgin work out his sexuality. Not ever, because Roman, despite his pending PhD, wasn't the brightest bulb, and that kind of thing mattered to Yale.

"It's hubris," Roman said. "That's what it is. Like, you listen to Nora's life—that was so recent. She's taking ocean liners over there, you know? And now we think we can just run buses back and forth to space."

Yale wanted to ask if the astronauts could have staved off disaster by fearing it would happen, but that would have been unkind. This was so horribly sad. *Everything* was so horribly sad. He said, "You know what's worse than something bad happening, is when something was supposed to be really good, when everyone expected it to be wonderful, and then instead it's bad. Why is that so much worse?"

The newscaster was saying that Reagan had cancelled the State of the Union address that was scheduled for tonight but would surely address the disaster. Yale missed Charlie suddenly, desperately. He wanted Charlie there to shout at the TV that what Reagan would "surely address" wasn't always so logical. A handful of dead astronauts and Reagan weeps with the nation. Thirteen thousand dead gay men and Reagan's too busy.

When the news went to commercial, Yale took the opportunity to rise from the bed, lower the volume a bit, refill his glass, sit back down farther from Roman.

Then the TV showed the schoolchildren who'd gathered to watch the launch. It showed the ground crew handing the teacher an apple. It was hard to look away, and harder to look. The wine was affecting him more than he'd have thought. Well, the beer plus the wine. And the darkness of the room, and the horrible plumes of smoke.

Roman said, "When I think about death, I start questioning everything."

Yale did not want to talk about death. He said, "Sometimes questioning is good."

"I keep thinking about Ranko. How *romantic*. I mean, he's literally shut away in a castle. And she's out there waiting for him."

"It sounded awful, to be honest."

"Don't you envy what Nora had, though? There was so much disaster, but it was like she *belonged* to something, you know?"

Yale was careful. "I mean, you can—you can find that in Chicago. That belonging."

"Maybe that's my problem. I'm stuck in Evanston looking at paintings."

"I didn't come to the city till I was twenty-six," Yale said.

He had the sudden inspiration that he should hook Roman up with Teddy. Teddy was healthy, after all, and he'd consider Roman a fun project. A puppy to train.

"Listen, you need to come down to, you know, to Lakeview. You'd have a lot more in common with people down there than in Evanston. Good bars, fun people. A little more laid-back."

"This ceiling is weird," Roman said, and without willing his body to do it, Yale lay down next to Roman, his legs still hanging off the end of the mattress. There was nothing particularly odd about the ceiling. It was just stucco. Roman had finished his wine; he tossed the plastic cup to the floor. He said, "I'm messed up."

"No, you're not." Yale turned his head in that direction, hoped Roman could see the earnestness in his eyes.

Roman reached out and, with just his fingertips, touched Yale's neck, his green sweater. Yale stopped breathing, just watched Roman's face flickering blue and yellow in the television light. He should tell him to stop. He should get up. But maybe this was the first time Roman had ever done something so bold. Maybe, if Yale rebuffed him, it would be the last. And while he lay there paralyzed, Roman ran his fingers down Yale's arm and onto the outer seam of his Dockers. Yale felt pinned to the bed with sugar, with alcohol, with afternoon languor. With, to be honest, an erection that was now straining against his boxers and his left thigh.

Roman looked terrified, and so young, and Yale took the hand off his leg but instead of letting it go he held it, twined his fingers through Roman's long, pale ones. They faced each other now, and Yale realized no one had touched him, not really, since his life had fallen apart. Teresa had hugged him when he came home from Wisconsin that day. Fiona had hugged him at Terrence's funeral. That was it. And being touched was Yale's weakness, always had been. People joked sometimes about not being held enough as a child, but in Yale's case it was so terribly literal, like a vitamin deficiency.

Roman whispered: "I don't know what I want." He was shaking, or at least his hand was. His glasses, pushed up by the pillow, framed his face unevenly.

Not fifteen minutes ago, Yale had had reasons nothing should happen, but what had they been? Well, he might be infectious. There was that. But did that rule out everything?

He wanted the television off. He knew that much. This required moving, which he did: He dropped Roman's hand, propelled himself off the bed, hit the power button with his sweaty thumb.

His feet felt unsteady on the carpet. He remembered the night in December when he'd kept walking past Julian's apartment. It had maybe, maybe saved his life.

And yet, right now, he wanted to do the opposite of everything he'd ever done before. He looked at the door and expected to find himself walking toward it—but instead he was sitting sideways on the edge of the bed, one leg up and one leg down. Roman sat up, leaned back against him, so that the back of his head nestled under Yale's chin. Yale moved his hand down Roman's shirt, found his fly, found his way into the fly. Just his hand, just his right hand, drawing Roman out of the top of his briefs, and then his left hand on Roman's chest, holding him in place, feeling Roman's heart shake his ribcage. He rubbed him slowly, until Roman began rising to meet his strokes, and then Yale sped up, squeezed harder.

When was the last time he gave a full hand job? Charlie wasn't much of a fan, although certainly Charlie had been the last, but it might have been a year, two years. With the angle—Roman pressed close against him, gasping, almost choking, their shoulders aligned, hips aligned—it wasn't all that different in technique from doing it to himself.

"Relax," he whispered, and Roman leaned back into him more.

Yale's own erection pressed into the base of Roman's spine, but really that wasn't the point. The point was, Roman seemed to need this—how much, Yale couldn't know, but he could guess—and Yale needed it too.

Roman braced himself, his hands on Yale's knees, and with a low wail he came onto the front of the dresser, onto the shallow drawers and brass pulls, right below the television.

And then before either of them could even exhale, Roman bolted up and grabbed a black T-shirt from the floor and began wiping at the dresser drawers like he was terrified someone would walk in and see it. "Sit down," Yale said, and he took the shirt from Roman's hand and mopped things up himself. When he finished—rolling the shirt into a ball and tucking it into the corner of the suitcase—Roman was facedown on the bed, arms out crucifix-style.

Yale said, "Do you want me to stay, or go?"

He had no idea which he'd have chosen himself, but Roman said, into the sheets, "I think I want to be alone."

Yale went back to his own room and turned on the shower and thought, vaguely, of jerking off, but by the time the water had warmed up, he didn't want to. He felt his groin for lymph nodes, decided he was too dizzy to be in the shower, lay in bed and thought about trying to find a TV station that wasn't about to show Reagan's giant head. He fell asleep without eating dinner.

Yale was at a small, round table in the breakfast room—hung over, his temples throbbing, his mouth fuzzy—when Mrs. Cherry greeted Roman at the door, ushered him straight to the seat across from Yale. Roman looked at the ground, and then he picked up the *Door County Advocate* and hid behind it.

Yale had been asking himself all morning what the hell was wrong with him, what he'd been thinking, but he figured it was his job to act normal, to signal that everything was okay, that healthy gay men did not need to wake up the next morning consumed by self-loathing. He said, "We have to get the details today. As fascinated as we all are by Ranko trivia."

308

Maybe he should've said something else, something kinder. Maybe Roman thought Yale was avoiding the subject too. But it was dawning on him how long the rest of the visit and the ride home would be, how awkward work would be next week. He'd been so distracted by questions of infection, so satisfied with his answers to them, that he'd forgotten, last night, the more mundane issues: remorse, attachment, expectation, embarrassment.

Mrs. Cherry brought them toast. She said, "Wasn't it beautiful last night, what the president said? It was just poetry."

Yale said, "I'm sure it was."

"You didn't watch?"

"*I* did," Roman said. "You're right. Poetry."

Roman stared out the side window all the way to Nora's house. Yale thought of apologizing. But it could plant the seed that he had abused his power. And worse: It would reinforce whatever notions Roman had that sex was something to be ashamed of, apologized for. It could put the kid back five years.

Was it Roman's inexperience and guilt that had sucked Yale in? Or would he have succumbed to *anyone* in that moment? He didn't think he would have. He wouldn't have been drawn to someone who could hurt him.

How funny that Charlie had thought Roman was safe precisely because he was so virginal. Maybe Charlie didn't know him at all.

"You can't make her talk too much today," Debra said. Yale assured her all they really wanted were the missing details. Debra went and perched on the staircase landing with knitting; she was just visible through the doorway. Yale wished he'd eaten less breakfast. Or maybe *more* breakfast, to absorb whatever strawberry wine was still sloshing in his stomach.

Nora did look tired. Her skin, always pale, had a bluish cast, and her eyes were pink. When Yale told her they really had to get a time frame on the other works, she didn't object. "It's all before '25, I'd think," she said. "I wasn't modeling much at the end. By '25 I was engaged to David."

Roman sat on the couch with Yale, but as far away as he possibly could. He had the binder of Xeroxes, and he'd spent last week collating, labeling, chronologizing, building an index. Nora suggested they sort the letters by correspondent. "Then I can patch it together." So while Roman leafed through for the few Modigliani letters first, Yale took the notebook and pen and asked Nora if she remembered exactly when she'd returned to Paris.

"I'd say mid-spring of 1919. I was twenty-four, and I felt terribly adult. In Philadelphia, I was considered an old maid."

"What happened to Ranko?" Roman said, and Yale wanted to throttle him. Yale did actually want to know, but not until everything else was settled. It slowly came back to him that he'd *dreamt* about Ranko last night, about Ranko locked away in his castle. Yale was trying to phone him, trying to get him to come out and see Nora before she burned his paintings. The number he'd been dialing, Yale realized, was the number of the *Out Loud* office.

"Well," Nora said, "that was the question. I hadn't heard a word, not a single letter. I'd find myself hoping he'd died, so it didn't mean he'd rejected me, and then I'd hope he hated me, if it meant he hadn't died. Don't imagine I stayed in love the whole time. I had a few gentleman friends in Philadelphia, though no one I wanted to marry. The boys I'd grown up with had gone off to the war, so I was stuck with—oh gracious, there was a *shoe salesman*. After all those wild young artists. I was bored out of my mind."

Yale started to ask how she began modeling, but he was too slow—the brain fog didn't help—and she was off again.

"You have to understand, we didn't know who was alive or dead. My friends from Colarossi, even professors. And on top of the war, there was the flu! Sometimes you'd get a letter, *So-and-so was wounded in action. And later you'd hear he'd died in the hospital camp, and you didn't know if it was the wounds or the flu. But mostly there was no news at all.* You really won't find too much Modi in there, dear," she said to Roman. But Roman kept looking. Yale wondered if he was hiding behind the binder, avoiding eye contact.

"I got back to Paris, and Paris was gone. Not the city, just the—I don't know if I can explain. The boys were gone, our classmates, or they were missing limbs. There was an architecture student who came back intact, only he'd lost his voice from mustard gas, never said another word. Everyone that spring just wandered. You'd find a friend in a café, and even if you'd hardly known them you'd run and *kiss* them, and you'd exchange news about who was dead. I don't know how you could compare it to anything else. I don't know how you could."

Yale had missed a step. "Compare what?"

"Well, *you*! Your friends! I don't know how it's like anything other than war!"

Roman froze—Yale could see it in his peripheral vision, Roman's fingers stopping on the pages—and Yale wanted to assure him he couldn't have contracted anything from Yale's hand. Or maybe Roman was worried Nora's "you" included him.

Nora said, "That's why I picked you, why I wanted you to have all this! The instant Fiona told me about you, I knew. I understand Mr. Lindsey's in charge of the show, but you're the one who's going to make sure it's cared for the right way."

This wasn't true in any official sense, but Yale nodded. "Of course," he said.

"Because you'll understand: It was a ghost town. Some of those

311

boys were dear friends. I'd studied next to them for two years. I'd run around with them, doing all the ridiculous things you do when you're young. I could tell you their names, but it wouldn't mean a thing to you. If I told you Picasso died in the war, you'd understand. *Poof*, there goes *Guernica*. But I tell you Jacques Weiss died at the Somme, and you don't know what to miss. It—you know what, it prepared me for being old. All my friends are dying, or they're dead already, but I've been through it before."

Yale hadn't particularly thought of Nora having current friends. Somehow he'd always thought of friends as the people you met early and stayed bonded to forever. Maybe this was why his loneliness was hitting him so hard. He couldn't imagine going out and selecting a brand-new cohort. How unimaginable that Nora had lived another seven decades, that she'd known the world this long without her first adult friends, her contemporaries.

Nora said, "Every time I've gone to a gallery, the rest of my life, I've thought about the works that weren't there. Shadow-paintings, you know, that no one can see but you. But there are all these happy young people around you and you realize no, they're not bereft. They don't see the empty spaces."

Yale wished Roman weren't in the room, that he and Nora could sit and cry together. She fixed him with her wet eyes, held his gaze as if she were squeezing it.

Roman said, "And Ranko wasn't around?"

Nora blinked. "Well. No one knew *where* he was. Some of my friends were still at Colarossi, but I didn't have money to go back; I'd only saved enough for the trip. I stayed with a Russian girl who'd been a classmate, a *terrible* influence.

"There were paid evening classes for the public, and some of the instructors would let us sneak in. I thought I'd skip around town and paint things, but I was at such loose ends. I wanted to paint boys who'd lost arms, but I couldn't bring myself to. So in the

312

midst of all the chaos, there I sat drawing fruit. The same brainless exercises I'd given those children in Philadelphia."

"And you met these artists then?" Yale prompted. "That year, or later?"

"That summer and that fall."

Roman took the notebook from Yale, flipped to the back. "Modigliani returned to Paris in the spring of 1919," he said. He'd made a timeline in there, color coded and everything. "With Jeanne Hébuterne and their daughter." Yale could smell Roman's sweat from here—not a bad scent, but one he'd been up close to yesterday, one that accosted him with its familiarity.

"Fantastic. Well, and he was dead himself the next January. So that must give you a time frame, no?" She looked pleased with herself. "Modi had studied at Colarossi, and he would come back to strut around. He looked like an opera villain, and he was already famous. Terrible breath, terrible teeth, but when I saw him I was starstruck. He was in the hallway with our instructor, and I found some excuse to ask a question. He was the first to ask me to model.

"The thing is, I wanted to be a *muse*. It had to do with my own art, the way it wasn't expressing the losses I felt. And if I couldn't paint it all myself, maybe someone could paint my soul. It was a stab at immortality, of course."

Yale had a million questions, one of which was whether being a muse involved sex, but what he asked was, "So this was spring? Summer?"

He tried to imagine someone, sixty years from now, pinning him down on the minute details of his life: *Which happened first, the test or the hand job? Who died first, Nico or Terrence? Where did Jonathan Bird live when he got sick? When did Charlie die, exactly? Where were you when you heard? When did Julian die? What about Teddy? Richard Campo? When did you first feel sick?* He'd be the

313

world's luckiest man to stand there at the end of it all, to be the one left, trying to remember. The unluckiest too.

And then Roman screamed. It was shrill and it came in pieces, a rapid machine-gun scream that didn't stop. Yale understood as soon as Roman's legs were off the floor and he was kneeling up on the couch. Debra must have understood, too, because she was down the stairs with a broom already in her hand. "Where'd it go?" she said, and Roman waved his arm in a general way toward the wall, the shelf, the dining room.

"I'm sorry," he said, "but I *hate* mice." Yale did, too, but Roman's overreaction was allowing him to underreact, to ask calmly if he could help. As Debra looked around, hit the broom handle against the record shelf to see if anything would scamper out, Roman said, "I don't know what's wrong with me. I didn't sleep last night."

"Just let the poor thing go, dear," Nora said to Debra.

But now that Roman said he was fairly certain he'd seen it run behind the hutch in the dining room, Debra enlisted Yale's help in moving the hutch away from the wall.

He was dizzy when he stood, the hangover still grabbing at him. He wanted to be home sleeping. Well, *somewhere* sleeping.

"Get your fingers under the ledge," Debra said. The hutch was tall and enormously heavy, and he couldn't manage a decent grip.

He'd read in a magazine that hangovers exacerbated feelings of shame—that you'd feel worst about whatever you did the night before when you were still hung over. He hoped it was true, because the thought of going back to the B&B tonight, of sleeping in the same *building* as Roman, was bringing a wave of nausea. Or maybe that was the heavy lifting. They walked the hutch a foot forward, one end at a time. There was a lot of dust back there but no mouse, no nest. In the living room, Roman had calmed down; he and Nora were talking in what sounded like normal voices.

"Just leave it," Debra said. "I should vacuum." She redid her ponytail, which had come loose. "I guess it's good we don't have the art here. It's a pigsty."

Yale needed a glass of water. He needed the bathroom. He said, "Ha. Yeah, the dust bunnies wouldn't hurt, but you don't want mice around two million dollars of art."

Debra's hands stopped in her hair. *"Excuse me?"*

He was so out of it, so distracted, that he thought he'd offended her by bringing up the very mouse she'd been chasing.

She said, "Did you say two million dollars?"

"Oh. I just—" He tried to say something about that simply being the amount Chuck Donovan had brought up, but he couldn't think fast enough to form a coherent sentence, besides which he had no excuse for lying to her. He said, "Yeah, more or less."

Debra's face grew so red, so pinched, that he thought she might spit at him. She whispered, which was worse than if she'd shouted. "I was on your side. For like half a minute, you had me on your fucking side."

"We *are* on the same side," Yale said, ridiculously.

"I *defended* you to my dad. Does she know? Does my grand-mother know how much she gave away? I thought we were talking about hundreds of thousands. That was bad enough. You *lied* to me."

There was a slick side of Yale that sometimes emerged, magic and unbidden, in tricky professional moments, and he waited for it now, hoped something placating would come out of his mouth.

"You need to leave," she said. "This house belongs to my father. I was willing to keep this visit from him, but you're going now." She folded her arms across her stomach, a gray X of sweater.

"Sure," Yale said, although his voice barely came out.

Nora and Roman didn't seem to have heard a thing. "We were talking about those poor astronauts," Nora said when Yale came back to the doorway.

"They're going to leave," Debra said, "and let you rest."

"Oh! But they'll come back tomorrow?"

"You have the doctor tomorrow." Debra was already holding their coats. "They're going back to Chicago."

Yale didn't look at Debra. He wanted to swear, to yell at himself, to hit his head against the wall. He said, "We'll get right back up here."

He couldn't imagine that was true. But they'd work something out, maybe just phone conversations.

Nora stood and slowly joined them near the front door. She said, "I fear I haven't gotten it across at all. If only we had a time machine, I could take you on the most wonderful tour!"

Yale said, as he fumbled with his coat buttons, "I was just thinking about time travel on the way here."

She laughed. "Time travel is so easy! It's devastatingly easy! All you have to do is live long enough!"

Roman stopped with his arm halfway down his sleeve.

"Listen," she said. "When I was born, the streets weren't paved."

Yale was still thinking about that when Roman said, "But Ranko. We never heard the end."

Debra opened the door, let the freezing air in. "He showed back up, and his hand didn't work right, and he killed himself," she said. "That's the end of the story."

Yale and Roman said "Oh" at the same time, Roman an octave higher.

Nora said, "Right in front of me, I'm afraid."

Debra opened her mouth, and before she could make things worse, before she could announce what an enormous mistake Yale had made, he walked out the door, made sure Roman was following.

Outside Milwaukee, Roman turned off the radio and said, "It's great that he killed himself."

316

"Are you being sarcastic?"

"It's a better story this way! And the better the story, the more likely Bill is to include his stuff. If it's just some random guy, then they're just cow sketches. But if it's her *love*, and he *killed himself*, then it's, like, the main story of the collection. When we go back, we'll get the details! Do you think he shot himself? He must've, right?"

Yale's stomach was a mess, and he needed to put his head down and sleep. He didn't want to break it to Roman that he'd quite possibly never get the end of the Ranko Novak story, at least not firsthand.

Roman said, "Did you know that when Jules Pascin slit his wrists, he wrote a message for his mistress with his blood?"

"How romantic."

A minute later Roman said, in a quieter voice, "You know that's not—last night—that's not the kind of thing I do."

"Okay." Yale kept his eyes on the road, tried to act completely neutral.

"God, I'm so messed up."

"I don't think that's true." He tried to remember why he'd let it happen, who had initiated it all. The heavy stickiness of that room was still with him, but none of it made sense anymore.

Roman's face was turned completely away. What good could he even be to this kid? It was January 29, three days past the circled spot on his calendar, and he was heading back to the city, to real life, with everything he still owned in the back of a rental car he'd have to return before dinner. He had a few dates jotted down for Bill, but no scoop on any artists besides Ranko Novak. And he might have just burned their one bridge to Nora. He had no idea where he was spending the night. Roman might have needed a role model, but it sure as hell shouldn't be Yale.

He said, "If you don't mind, I'm going to turn the radio up."

2015

Starting when Claire was eight, she would come in on Saturdays to help Fiona in the resale shop. Fiona had just been made manager, and she still needed to spend twice as long as she would in subsequent years with the balance sheets, the payroll, the ancient and temperamental computer. She'd pick Claire up from ballet and head back to work as the store was closing. Claire would wander, dusting and straightening. She'd come and tell Fiona if a bulb was burnt out, and Fiona would give her a notepad and tell her to write down which one.

Or sometimes it was Claire and a friend, some girl who thrilled at the prospect of walking around an empty store as the streetlights came on outside, pretending to be trapped in an old mansion.

The store was chic and sparse and curated, two floors of artfully arranged living rooms and dining rooms and closets. Sometimes Fiona would ask Claire to straighten up the ladies' shoes, and Fiona would emerge from the office an hour later to find the high heels sorted by color into rainbow stripes. Just as often, she'd find Claire sitting on one of the couches, staring into the middle distance, not having done a thing Fiona had asked. It didn't matter much—she'd really just been inventing tasks—but this, Claire's teachers said, was what she did at school too: Sometimes she'd do her work and sometimes she'd stonewall them, just sit silently drawing trees, impervious to threats of lost recess.

Once, that year, there was a tremendous snowstorm, and Sophia, the friend they'd brought back to the store from ballet, worried she wouldn't be able to get home. Or at least she and Claire enjoyed *pretending* to worry. "You can sleep on the stripy bed upstairs," Claire said, "and I'll sleep on Soft-more." Soft-more was her name for a particular leather couch that had been in the store for more than a year. Sophia said, "We'll have to change into new clothes in the morning. We'll have to pick outfits."

Sophia lived only six blocks away, though, and at seven o'clock Fiona called Mrs. Nguyen and said she'd be happy to walk her home. She told the girls it was time to go. Sophia whined a bit but Claire was silent. It wasn't till they'd dropped Sophia at her door and were back on Clark that Claire sank to the snowy sidewalk and shouted, "*I hate you!*" Not crying, just seething in a little ball, angry and red.

The affair Fiona had started with Dan from yoga was, right then, at its most confusing point. Dan would email her every day on his lunch hour, and on days when he didn't—as he hadn't today—she'd invent all kinds of scenarios wherein he'd suddenly reconciled with the wife he was divorcing, or had abruptly, in the middle of the morning, grown sick of Fiona. She was convinced that she loved him, that she'd never loved anyone more, but then when she did see him, when he managed to slip away from the home he still shared with his ex and their kids, meet her at a hotel or at the store—where, lights off, they'd make love on top of a blanket on that same couch Claire adored—she'd remember that he wasn't all that special. A brown-haired guy with nice eyes, average intelligence. He could have been in an insurance commercial. That winter, though, he had her in a permanent haze, and when Claire dropped to the sidewalk, Fiona could only stare at her.

If they'd been home, she might have called Claire out for her language. But here, an upset Claire could decide to take off into the street or onto a city bus. Fiona stood a long time between Claire and the road. The few people who passed smiled sympathetically. The wind hurled snow in everyone's face.

Eventually she put her hand on Claire's back, and Claire screamed. How had she even felt it through her parka? She yelled, "Leave me alone forever!"

Someone had stopped behind them, a woman who bent down and asked Claire, in a Jamaican accent, if this was her mama.

Claire, caught off guard, said yes.

The woman stood and said, "Just pick her up and carry her. Last time she little enough for that."

And although Fiona expected Claire to kick, to bite, she bent and scooped her from beneath, a compact mass. Claire clutched her own legs to her chest but did nothing to fight. A block later she was sobbing into Fiona's chest, and by the time they reached home, she was shaking so hard Claire worried it was some kind of seizure.

Why hadn't she thought to pick her up in the first place? Why did it take a stranger to tell her this?

She laid Claire on the bed and zipped their coats off and curled up around her, and Claire didn't elbow her away, didn't act, for once, like Fiona was touching her with ice hands.

In the hospital, when Claire was born, Fiona had been so flooded by hormones and panic and grief and fear and guilt and revulsion that when Damian brought her the baby, impossibly small and alien, its body a lurid pink, Fiona told him to take it away, to keep it safe from her. She had some horrid, febrile vision of a mother animal smothering its young, eating it. In fact Fiona did have a fever, as it turned out, and when she emerged from its fog, five hours had passed, and Claire had been given a bottle in the nursery. Fiona was furious—all the books had said not to do this—but when they brought Claire to her for a supervised feeding, nothing worked properly anyway. The baby wouldn't latch, and Fiona had no milk yet. The nurse assured her this was how you *got* the milk, by letting the baby try. Fiona was crying so much, sweating so much, that she couldn't imagine her body would ever secrete anything but saline.

"You have so much else going on," Damian said. "I'm sure it's partly mental."

He'd meant it to be reassuring, but to Fiona it was an indictment: This was her own fault, not just a failure of the body.

And in fact the nursing never worked, despite the best efforts of three lactation consultants. Claire was underweight, Fiona was bleeding and then her breasts were dangerously infected, and in the end it was in everyone's best interest to stop trying.

Not that it should have mattered! Whole generations turned out fine on bottles. Fiona hadn't bought all the La Leche stuff about bonding. But as she lay on the bed with eight-year-old Claire, what she remembered far too clearly was her resignation to the idea that this baby would never be able to take comfort from her—that Fiona had nothing left of herself, that first day or ever since, to give.

And what she remembered *now*, staring out Richard's window toward the afternoon sun, was the absurd feeling back then, when Claire was eight, that they'd already missed the boat forever. That the damage had been done sometime in the past, not the present, and they were living in its aftermath. That the best they could hope for was good scarring.

1986

Yale didn't say anything to Bill about messing up with Debra. He told him Nora had given a few general dates, provided some context, but that she wasn't great on specifics. "Roman will type it all up for you," he said. "Including a lot of stories about Ranko Novak!" He felt gross going for the cheap laugh; Ranko had grown on him.

He had a message waiting on his desk from Esmé Sharp, and when he called her it ended up spilling out that he had no place to stay, and so at her insistence, he spent the night at the Marina Towers in the fifty-eighth floor apartment Esmé and Allen let lie empty all winter when they were in Aspen. "Stay as long as you like!" she said. "You can water the jade plant."

It was far enough from Boystown that he wouldn't run into Charlie. He did want to see Charlie soon, wanted to yell at him all the things he hadn't yet yelled, but only when he was prepared. He didn't want to bump into him at the ATM.

Esmé insisted he could take the master bedroom, but instead he set himself up in the smaller guest room, which had its own half-balcony and featured a shelf of architecture books. In the kitchen was a rack of wine that Esmé said "better be drunk up the next time I check." In the living room was the best stereo system Yale had ever used, and a shelf of classical CDs and opera and

322

Broadway and Sinatra. Left to his own devices, he'd have been listening to The Smiths, which wouldn't have helped a thing; and if it turned out he only had a few years to live, shouldn't he be listening to Beethoven? He could see the river and the Sears Tower from the windows. At night, the city below him turned to constellations of yellow and red.

Back when Charlie had first taken him to the Bistro, right up the street, he'd been fascinated to see the two Marina City towers up close, the way each flower petal projection was really a curved balcony. And now, from the inside, he was terrified by how low the balcony railings were, how easily someone tall might lose balance and pitch over, how easily someone could step up and jump.

He wouldn't do this, not even if he tested positive. Because the test didn't mean you'd get sick this year or next year. If he ever went blind, he thought, he might end it then. If he couldn't get through the day without shitting his pants. He and Charlie had met a guy in a bar that summer who'd sat there telling them about his lover, how this guy had vowed to kill himself when he couldn't dance. And then when he couldn't dance he'd changed it to when he couldn't eat. And when he couldn't eat, he'd said, "*When I can't talk.*"

"He never did it," the guy said. "He fought for his last breath. And what does that tell you? What does that tell you?" Yale and Charlie hadn't offered an answer, and neither had he.

The days were ticking by, the odds of a reliable blood test increasing. Good news still wouldn't be definitive, but bad news might be making an early debut. And then at least he'd know. It was the kind of decision he'd have loved to bounce off a friend, if the ones who knew about Charlie didn't hate him, and if the ones who didn't know could be told. He hadn't seen anyone, really, since he'd run into Teddy at the Laundromat. One evening Yale was

323

coming out of the dentist on Broadway—an appointment he'd made in another lifetime—and Rafael from *Out Loud* was passing with a friend. Rafael, drunk, kissed Yale on one cheek and bit him on the other—but they hadn't had a real conversation.

After Wisconsin Roman had kept to his normal schedule, coming in both Wednesday and Friday afternoons—and, mercifully, the first time he entered Yale's office, Janice the cleaning lady was in there with the vacuum, making any greeting other than a silent wave impossible. Roman went about his normal business, albeit more nervously. About twice an hour, he put his forehead down on his desk, and Yale didn't dare ask if it was over some frustration in transcribing Nora's letters or in the grant applications Roman was assisting with, or if it was a more existential crisis, one to do with Yale himself, one to do with Roman's own soul. In any case, Roman was the last person on earth Yale would confide in about his fear of infection.

On Sunday evening Yale saw Julian at Treasure Island. He could have gone to the Jewel right near Marina City, but he hated figuring out the layout of a new store. And maybe he'd been hoping to run into someone after all. Julian was buying a plastic-wrapped roast beef sandwich. He looked better than he had two weeks ago, or at least he had more color in his cheeks. He froze when he saw Yale, stood there like he'd been punched in the gut, and it wasn't till Yale stepped closer and squeezed his shoulder that he relaxed, said hello.

"Teddy's been feeding you," Yale said. "You look good."

Julian glanced down the aisle. He whispered. "Teddy's suffocating me. Have you noticed that he never stops moving? Like, ever. And he's in my *face*, like I open my eyes in the morning and *there he is*. Listen, don't say anything till it's done, but I'm getting out of here. Out of the country."

Yale wasn't sure he believed him—Julian was prone to overstatement—but he acted as if he did. He said, "Where?"

"I got a passport two years ago, and I never used it. Seriously, I'm not going back there. I have my stuff." Julian turned to show Yale his backpack. "I don't even know where I'm going. I gave up my apartment."

"You're not going to *Thailand* or something, are you? You're going to be careful?"

"Listen," Julian said, "I heard a rumor that you've got a place. What if—I just need like three nights, just to get my shit together before I leave. If I stay at Teddy's, he's gonna sedate me and tie me to the bed, I swear. I know you hate me right now. I know that. Why wouldn't you hate me? I hate myself. You should—you should let me stay with you, and then you should throw me out the window. You can say no. I can't stay with Richard again, it's too weird there. I could pay you."

It was humiliating how happy Yale was to say yes. Julian was almost the last person he wanted to spend time with, but it was *someone*, and he wouldn't be staring at the TV alone for the next few nights. He wondered how much he'd wind up babysitting, wondered what drugs Julian had in that backpack—but it felt like a triumph to be asked. A year ago he'd have thought about germs, but he was over it. "Do you need any more of your stuff?"

"I can't go back there. Not for a second. And you can't tell anyone where I am, okay?"

So Julian helped Yale carry his grocery bags all the way back to River North on the El, all the way up the very fast elevator and into the apartment.

They ate pizza and drank beer at the dining table, and turned off the lights so they could look out the windows at the city. Julian said, "This is like *The Jetsons*. Like, a flying car should pick you up outside your window."

It had been nearly two weeks since Julian had shaved his head, and at least you couldn't see white patches anymore. Still, it was all wrong. His ears stuck out, his forehead looked broad and pale.

Yale said, "I want you to know I'm not mad at you. I'm mad at Charlie, and I'm mad at the world, and I'm mad at the government, but you're hard to be mad at."

"It's because I'm so *pitiful*. No, really, it is. I've learned this recently. When you're a sad sack of shit, no one feels anything for you but pity."

"I don't think you're pitiful," Yale said.

"Just wait till I weigh eighty pounds. I mean, you won't ever see that, 'cause I'll be gone. That's my point. I hate being pitied. I wish you'd just be mad at me. I wish you'd kick me in the head. No one's willing to be mad at me but God."

"For Christ's sake," Yale said. "You can stay over, but Jerry Falwell can't, okay?"

"I can't shake the feeling that God chased me up here from Georgia. I tried to make my life perfect, and I came up here and everything was beautiful, it was so good, and I should have known. I should've been waiting for this."

"I understand, but that's—you're internalizing a lot of bullshit."

"Did I ever tell you about Disney World? Not when I worked there, the first time I went."

Yale said no, got them more beer.

"They have this thing called Grad Night, when they keep the park open all night long for kids about to graduate high school. And Valdosta's right across the border, so the Parents' Association got us buses and bought us all tickets. You could go on any ride, no lines, and there were bands playing. You just had to stay awake all night. Everyone had a flask.

"And at first I was sticking with my friends, all these theater girls who thought they were gonna marry me, and then I start noticing these three guys from some other school. *So* beautiful. And so gay, like dripping with gay. Which wasn't something I'd really seen in Georgia. We're waiting behind them for Space Mountain, and one of them, this kid with an earring, starts talking to me and says they're getting food next, do I want food. So by the time we get off the ride, I'm following these guys, eating ice cream with them, and my friends are gone. And the guy with the earring wants us to do the PeopleMover. It's not even a ride, really, it's like you go in this little box along an elevated track, but slow. So his friends go in one car, and he and I go in the next one, even though we could have squeezed together. And at this point in my life, just being in the same space as this guy is the most thrilling thing I've ever done. I'm terrified.

"So the ride goes through some buildings, and at one point it goes into the dark. And it's only supposed to be a few seconds, but the ride gets stuck there. In the dark. Everyone's shouting and laughing."

Yale wasn't sure if the story was about to turn pornographic or romantic or terrible, so he just said "Oh God," which covered all three possibilities. "What did you do?"

"Nothing. The kid got down on his knees and unzipped my fly and sucked me off. It was the most amazing two minutes of my life. I mean, I was terrified they would turn on the lights, but I didn't really have much mental space for that. The ride started moving again like half a second after I zipped back up."

"That's—wow."

"Well, yeah. And my takeaway from the whole thing, besides the fact that I was *definitely* gay, was that there were good places and bad places in the world. Disney World was a good place, and Valdosta was a bad place, and I had to get back to Disney as fast as I could. Which I did. And then after a couple years it was about getting to a real city, so I tried Atlanta, and then it was about getting out of the south, getting to a bigger city, a bigger theater scene. Like, the more steps I took away from Valdosta, the safer I'd be. It was a ladder that just went up and up and up, right? And it ended in some kind of mansion in San Francisco. But look at me. I feel like such an idiot. That I ever thought I could have a really good life."

Yale said, "You'll have a better life if you stay here than if you go. You need to stay where people love you. Aren't you falling into the same trap again? Thinking there's some better place out there?"

"I mean, there are *warmer* places. I'll say that. If I'm gonna die, I want to die with the sun shining on my face."

"Fair enough."

Yale made sure Julian had towels in the master bathroom. He imagined the Sharps coming home next month to find an entire fifty-eighth-floor refugee camp of the recently diagnosed. Sleeping bags and cots, vitamins and protein shakes.

On Monday morning, the heat in the office was broken. Yale walked straight back to the El, relieved he wouldn't have to see Roman but dreading an empty day, one in which he now had no excuse not to get the test over with. But when he got off the train he just stood there by the pay phone, because he wasn't even sure where he was going.

He thought of calling Dr. Vincent, but it was as if Charlie had inherited him in the breakup, the same way he'd inherited most of their friends. He couldn't imagine walking in there and awkwardly trying to figure out how much Dr. Vincent already knew. And maybe Dr. Vincent had known for months, for years, that Charlie was cheating. Maybe he'd been treating him for gonorrhea, telling him to be careful. Yale couldn't face him, his sweet, watery eyes. He thought of calling Cecily, but he'd caused her enough stress as it was, and he didn't want anyone connected with the university believing he might be sick. He thought of going back to Marina Towers, but seeing Julian would scare him out of going through with it. What had the test done for Julian but wreck his life? He considered calling the Howard Brown hotline, but the thought of some kind lesbian talking him through his options—reading to him off a *form*, cautiously choosing her words—made him ill. Worse, Teddy's friend Katsu might answer, might recognize Yale's voice. Plus the hotline wasn't open till evening, and it wasn't even 10 a.m. So although he knew better, although she was the last person who needed to be put through all this again, he called Fiona Marcus.

After three rings he started hoping she wasn't home, but she was. She'd been about to bundle up her charges and take them to the zoo. Did he want to come? Yes, he did.

They met by the big cat enclosures, Fiona in a bright blue parka that made her look more substantial than she really was. The two girls circled her, spinning, yelling. Fiona reminded him that the little one with the pink hat was Ashley and the five-year-old was Brooke. Their father was high up at United Airlines, and their mother, according to the stories Fiona told, mostly occupied herself with tanning. Brooke announced that she wanted to visit the penguins and polar bears. "Because those are winter animals," she said.

"Hold on," Yale said to Ashley. "Let me straighten your ears first." He gently tugged one up and the other down. "Much better," he said, and the girls giggled and looked smitten. It was his only line for kids, but it always worked.

Fiona said "How *are* you?" and then, as they walked, "I've heard contradictory rumors. I mean, I know about Charlie. But I decided I wouldn't believe anything else till I heard it straight from you."

"Thank you," Yale said. "That's refreshing."

"Spill."

329

The zoo was nearly empty, just a few well-insulated stroller-pushers and a sole jogger.

He told her the entire story, more than he'd even told Cecily, in part because there was more to tell now. He told her about the fight at Terrence's funeral, about Roman, even, and about the circle on the calendar a week and a day ago. He left out the part about Richard's house. Why make her blame herself when Charlie might have been lying anyway? He said, "Your cousin Debra hates me now," but left out how much money was involved. He told her about Julian crashing with him.

"God, this is depressing," Fiona said, although she wasn't talking about Yale's issues. They were in front of the penguin enclosure and you could hardly see through the grimy glass. "Are they even in there?"

"Look, look, look!" Ashley pointed to a small, wilted bird right at their feet. If the glass hadn't been there, Yale might have walked right over the thing. The girls ran back and forth, trying to get the bird to follow.

Fiona said, "So, the intern. You like him?"

He knew she was trying to start on the least stressful part of what he'd just told her, but the thought of Roman made him feel as nervous as the rest of it.

"Oh God, not really. He's so young. Not literally, he's an adult, he's just *young*. I'd say it was only sex, but it wasn't even sex. And even if it were—like, sex is never going to be just sex again."

Fiona laughed. "Welcome to the club."

"I don't mean emotional stuff."

"Good God, Yale, I don't either. This is what women have lived with since the dawn of time. Babies can kill you or ruin your life. And all kinds of shit gives you cancer if you're a woman. A guy, you get some jock itch, they give you a powder. A woman, you get cancer. Or you get something that means you can never

330

conceive, or *if* you can conceive, your baby goes blind because of something some jackass gave you at senior prom. And it's not like we can't get AIDS. It's not like that's not an issue. Oh, Yale. What. I'm sorry."

He realized he had a horrible look on his face. He said, "No, I just—I was thinking how—"

"Look, I'm sorry. I'm not clueless, okay? I'm not some asshole who doesn't get it."

He knew that was true.

The girls were ready to move on, and Fiona stopped to re-Velcro Ashley's boots. "It's a long way to the polar bears," she said. "Are you sure?"

Brooke said, "Come *on*, Fiona!" and pulled her by the hand as if she were a disobedient dog.

"You guys run to that garbage can," Fiona said, "right up there, and we'll meet you."

She never took her eyes off the girls, even when she talked to Yale. It must have been exhausting, all that vigilance.

"I'm sorry," she said again.

"A few months ago, someone was saying to me how we used to be fun." His hands were deep in his pockets. "And it's true, there was this tiny window where we were safer, and happier. I thought it was the beginning of something. When really it was the end. Julian had the same—I used to think Julian was so naive. And I just realized we're the same."

"You're a lot smarter than Julian," she said.

"He only plays dumb. I don't know. I keep thinking that maybe they'll start over, you know? The next generation of baby gays, when we're all gone. But maybe they won't, because they'll be starting from scratch. And they'll know what happened to us, and Pat Robertson will convince them it was our fault. I was living in the golden age, Fiona, and I didn't know it. I was walking around

331

six years ago, living my life, working my ass off, and I didn't know it was the golden age."

"What would you have done, if you'd known?"

He had no idea. He wouldn't have run around having more sex. In 1980 he'd been perfectly free to do that, and promiscuity hadn't appealed to him much. He laughed. "I'd have made up a song about it or something."

They trekked slowly north, following the girls, and every time they caught up, Fiona would send the girls a few yards farther on, to wait by a bench or a tree.

"You'll make a great mom," Yale said.

"Ha! Sure. Maybe that's my next move." There was something horribly bitter in her voice. He shouldn't have brought up family. Nico's death hadn't made her any closer to her parents, and now even Terrence was gone. She had these girls, but only until they started school. A husband and a baby—those were the only ways Fiona would ever really have a family again. Not that Yale was better off himself. Who the hell did he have? But there was something so *alone* about her, her gloved hands tucked into her armpits, the wind batting her hair into her face. He'd felt guilty about calling her, about leaning on her, but maybe it was a good thing. Maybe he was doing her a favor.

Yale had never been up at the north end of the zoo, hadn't seen the polar bears. You could look into their space from above, but you could also go down below, which is what the four of them did, to peer through the glass into the water. It was dark and warm down there, no wind, and Fiona plucked the hats off the girls' heads.

"There's Thor!" Brooke shouted. "That's Thor!"

"How do you know?" Fiona asked. Another bear was lying on a rock up out of the water.

"He's the friendly one! He's the one that always swims!"

The bear in question zoomed past the glass, a furry torpedo.

"I want to say something," Fiona said. Behind and above the girls, it felt as if they could have a completely private conversation. "I have never liked Charlie."

Yale burst out laughing at the absurdity of it. Everyone loved Charlie. Everyone told him, constantly, how much they loved Charlie.

She said, "He was really good to Nico, and he does all this great work, and he's, you know, he's *important*. I think he's one of these people where—he's just so *there*, and people respond to that. But I never feel like he's listening to me. He's always just waiting to talk again."

A month ago, Yale would have had to pretend to be deeply hurt by this, even as he recognized the truth. But now he was able to nod. "How do you know that when other people don't?"

"Maybe they do know. Maybe it's how everyone feels. He reminds me of one of those girls in junior high, the ones who are so popular just because everyone's scared of them."

"You're saying he's an eighth-grade girl."

"I'm saying he's a *bully*. I mean—I'm sorry, I shouldn't say that. But listen, I never liked the way he treated you. He was always asking weird questions about where I'd seen you, who you were with. It seemed a little controlling."

"That's fair."

"I thought about it, and I wonder if that's why I told him you were with Teddy, at the memorial. Like, it felt good to finally throw something in his face. But I don't know. I was drunk. I don't mean—"

"It's okay." He didn't want to hear it. He couldn't handle being mad at her.

"I hate that he's wearing Nico's scarf. I saw him out with it, he was way down the street, and there was this second where I—"

"You saw Nico."

"Yeah. And if it had been *you*, someone I wanted to see, that would've been different. I want to get it back."

Thor swam straight up to the glass, pressed his nose and one huge, scraggly paw flat against it, just inches from Brooke and Ashley's faces. The girls squealed, and Fiona stopped Ashley from beating the glass with her little fist.

"He's such a ham," Fiona said. "You're right, Brooke, that's definitely Thor."

"The other one is his wife!" Brooke said.

Yale said, "I didn't know polar bears could get married. It's good to hear you say that, about Charlie. I was feeling like the only person in the world who could see through him."

"*Yale*." She turned and put her hands on his biceps, gave him a mock-serious stare that maybe was actually serious after all. "You deserve someone who adores you. Charlie only ever wants an audience."

"But," Yale said. "But. What if that's the last boyfriend I ever get?"

"No way. You'll outlive Thor here. You'll outlive the elephants. Don't elephants live forever? Turtles. You'll outlive the turtles."

"Cockatoos live for sixty years!" Brooke chimed in.

"Hey," Fiona said, "were you eavesdropping?" Although what had they said, really, that a kid would understand?

Yale said, "I won't be getting a cockatoo."

"You'll feel better after the test. I tell you what, after you get your results, I'll take you out and buy you a goldfish. One of the big ones that lives for decades and you eventually have to buy it a swimming pool."

Yale said, "You're the one who has Roscoe, right?"

Fiona didn't say anything, just stared at Thor through the glass. She looked strangely frozen.

"Your brother's cat. Roscoe."

She jerked her head to stare at him, lips parted.

He said, "What."

"Holy crap. Holy crap."

"I mean, Terrence had him, and then—"

"Holy crap."

"Wouldn't his family—"

"No. They haven't set foot. They haven't— Oh *my God*. Yale."

"But the landlord, right? Wouldn't they have moved his stuff out?"

"People don't just run in there and get their hands all over someone's stuff. They wait and get it, like, fumigated. And they might not even know he's gone. Who even told them he was dead? *I* didn't. Teddy was the one who went in there to get his suit, for the—"

The girls were looking up at them now, ignoring the polar bears. Fiona unwound her scarf like it was strangling her.

It was Monday the third. Terrence had died on January 17. More than two weeks. Yale might not have remembered it so precisely if he hadn't been staring so much at his calendar lately.

Yale said, "Well, let's—shit, can we go up there? We can go right now. Let's go."

They ran back through the zoo, past the animals, past the yellow placards that told their scientific names, the girls crying that they hadn't even seen the gorillas yet.

Fiona had a key to Terrence's apartment, but it was back at her place. She had to drop the girls off anyway—their mother was home and knew what Fiona had been going through and wouldn't mind sparing her for an hour or two. Yale waited on the street while Fiona ran the girls inside. By the time she was back with her keys, he'd flagged down a cab.

"I'll go in first," Yale said on the way. "You should wait in the hall."

"Nope, no, no, no. We're going in together." She asked the cabbie if he could rush. He gestured at the red light and muttered in Polish.

Yale admitted to himself, as they finally got out, as they mounted the front steps, as they climbed to the second floor, that this was a welcome distraction. It had been so long since he'd had a clear course of action, an easy decision with an obvious answer. They were going to go up there and find the cat. Or better yet, they wouldn't find the cat.

Fiona puffed out her cheeks and stuck the key in Terrence's lock. She stopped suddenly and knocked, put her ear to the wood. Yale held his breath, hoping she'd hear new tenants, a cleaning crew, frantic meowing. But she shook her head, turned the key.

The living room smelled horrible. Yale couldn't remember if it was the *same* horrible—medicine, vomit, cat litter, sweat—as two weeks ago, or if it was something new. Terrence's furniture was still all in place. A neatly folded sheet still lay on the couch where Yale had left it two weeks ago.

Fiona called, "Roscoe!" Quietly, like she was afraid of the answer.

Yale went to the kitchen and checked the litter box, which had indeed been used, but not as much as you'd hope. Roscoe had a double plastic bowl—food on one side, water on the other—and both halves were empty. Yale had refilled it himself the morning he left—intentionally overfilled the food side, a mountain of Meow Mix, enough to last a while. The water was the bigger issue. Yale said, "Roscoe?" He ran the faucet to see if the sound might attract him. He looked behind the garbage can, in the cupboards, beside the refrigerator. Fiona was calling still, moving through the apartment. "The toilet's open," she called, and Yale understood she meant the cat had a water source if it was smart enough, if it had good balance.

There were bottles of pills lined up along the kitchen windows. Painkillers, vitamins, more vitamins, old antibiotics. All half full (he shook a few), all useless. He could grab them for Julian maybe. Or himself. A spider plant wilted on the counter in a little blue pot, and Yale held it under the tap, soaked the soil. Why not.

He looked behind the garbage again. In the garbage. Out on the fire escape.

Fiona was in the doorway, her face red and wet.

In her arms she held what looked like a deflated stuffed animal. A fur pelt. Roadkill.

"He's still breathing," she said. "I think."

In the waiting room at the vet, Yale paged through an old *Life* magazine with a feature on the Mafia. Fiona held a ball of Kleenex in her lap, and although she'd stopped crying she still had the hiccups, and every few minutes she heaved a single sob, leaned forward into the tissues. They'd given Roscoe a kitty IV, and the vet had promised he'd update them soon. He had so clearly considered them a couple, Yale and Fiona. He'd directed every question at both of them, even after Fiona made it clear that Roscoe was her brother's cat. She'd told a short version of the story, said her brother had died and the cat had been neglected. "You did the right thing," he said to both of them.

Around them in the waiting room, dogs strained against leashes and the slickness of the tile floor. A cat paced circles in its carrier. Fiona said, "So last week, I went to get a massage. And the woman goes, 'Were you in a car accident?'" She did a Russian accent for the woman. "And I'm like, 'No, I'm just really stressed right now.' So like five minutes later she goes, 'But maybe a long time ago? A car accident?' Feel." She put Yale's hand on the back of her neck, and he pressed into what he'd already guessed to be muscle as hard as marble.

He said, "That's not good."

"And I'm like, I have honestly never even been in a fender bender. And she goes, 'Yes, but sometimes we forget.'"

Something about her delivery, the Russian *baba* wisdom of it, cracked Yale up. Or maybe it was the fact that he'd felt like this himself all month, like someone had injected cement into his deltoids and locked him in a meat freezer.

An assistant came out and told them Roscoe was doing well, and they exhaled as if he were their child.

Yale would take the cat, if it survived. Obviously. How could he ask Fiona, of all people, to worry about one more thing? He told her he'd figure it out, and she nodded slowly, already somewhere else, her head framed by an informational poster about feline leukemia. Her skin was dry and tight; she was too thin. He was about to ask if she was taking care of herself, if she was thinking about going back to school next year, if it wasn't maybe time for a break—but then she looked at him and said, "What if you went to Dr. Cheng?" Dr. Cheng had been Nico's doctor, and during the couple of weeks last summer when Nico was allowed to be at home, he'd visited every day to check in. He'd shown up once when Yale and Charlie were there, and ordered and paid for a pizza—not for himself or for Nico, who couldn't hold down food, but for Yale and Charlie, who'd been there all afternoon. "Just to get his advice," she said. "It'd be better than some helpline. I can call him. He *loves* me, I don't know why. I could get you in today. I really could."

Yale had the instinct to stop her, to tell her she wasn't allowed to take care of him, too, that she couldn't do that to herself. If she called Dr. Cheng, was it the start of something? Would she be the one changing his bedpans in the end? But he was already agreeing, because the thought of Dr. Cheng, of his slow voice, was so overwhelmingly comforting.

*

Fiona called right from the vet reception desk, and when they left an hour later—Roscoe would need to remain on the IV at least overnight—it was to walk to Dr. Cheng's office on George Street. Yale chastised himself for letting Fiona escort him there, for letting her get further embroiled in everything. She should be home, taking a nap. Eating something. But she must have felt she'd failed Nico today, failed Terrence. She'd cried into the cat's fur the whole way to the vet. Was it so bad to let her do right by him?

Dr. Cheng's office was in what used to be a house. Incense in the waiting room, a nurse who came around the desk to give Fiona an enormous hug. There was no one else there, thank God, no hollow-eyed stranger sitting like the ghost of Yale's own future, no acquaintance with whom he'd have to make small talk.

"It's a day for waiting rooms," Yale said.

Fiona said, "Better magazines here." On the coffee table sat a stack of old *Esquires*. He had forms to fill out, though: family history, medications, surgeries.

He said, "You don't have to wait."

"I want to say hi to Dr. Cheng. If I go back home, I have to watch the kids. Trust me, this is vacation." She must have been lying. She'd probably passed some of the worst moments of her life in the same worn green armchair she was sinking into right now.

Yale said, "I'll let you stay if you promise something."

Fiona's look was a cross between wary and indulgent.

"What are you doing for yourself these days? What's your plan for next year? You're twenty-one. You're smart. Don't you think that now—don't you want to go to college?"

"You mean now that Nico's gone."

"Well—yeah. And Terrence. Here's what I don't want. I don't want you to adopt me next, and then whoever else gets sick, and then the next guy, and before you know it you're fifty and you're living in a ghost town surrounded by all our old clothes and books."

"I won't adopt the next person. Just you. Nico loved you, and you were so nice to me when I was a kid. Do you remember when you walked me through the Art Institute?"

"Yeah, you set off the alarm."

"I'm just saying: We could both use a friend right now."

"We're friends, Fiona, I just—"

"Well let's be *best* friends. Don't laugh, I don't mean like ten-year-olds! I mean like family. Let's just say we're family now. Let's say we call each other when we're sad. And I'll get you a birthday present, and everything."

"Okay." He couldn't say no to her. "But we were talking about college."

"Oh God, Yale. I really don't see myself enjoying the frat party scene. I'm going to, what, sit there in class with eighteen-year-olds?"

The distance between eighteen and twenty-one seemed laughably small, but he didn't say so. Besides, Fiona's twenty-one might as well have been two hundred.

"You could take classes here in the city. It wouldn't be going off to *college*, with dorms and, like, drunk guys playing guitar at you. Just think of it as the classes, the degree. You don't want to be a nanny forever, do you?"

He regretted the words once they were out. But only half his brain was in the conversation. He was wondering, at the same time, if he would let Dr. Cheng talk him into doing something today. He didn't want that. He wasn't ready.

He said, "Would your parents pay?"

"They *would*, but I'm not taking a fucking penny from those people. Whatever they leave me when they die, I'm giving it straight to AIDS research."

340

She'd have taken money from Nora, though, Yale imagined. She'd have accepted a sketch. At least it was only a matter of pride; the money was there for her, it sounded like, if she ever truly needed it. But Fiona was stubborn. She'd never crawl back asking favors.

"I'm supposed to call up my old high school teachers and ask for recommendations? I hardly even went to class."

"I'm sure they remember you. I'm sure it happens all the time." The nurse stood, but it was only to reach something from a high shelf, and then she sat back down. "I'll write a letter myself. An extra one. I do work at a university, technically. I mean, I oversee students."

Fiona busted up laughing at that, which is what he'd hoped for.

And then the nurse was calling him back.

Dr. Cheng had a framed photo of Mount Kilimanjaro on his wall, and the room smelled more like soup than rubbing alcohol. He looked right at you when he talked, paused deliberately every three sentences as if some superior had taught him in med school to do so. He went over Yale's medical history, did a short physical exam. No paper gown, at least, but still, it felt like too much, like the start of something official. The thought came to Yale, as Dr. Cheng listened to his lungs, that this could be the man presiding over his final days. That in walking through this door, he'd potentially chosen a partnership more permanent than any other in his life. Till death do us part.

"I understand you have some concerns," Dr. Cheng said.

Yale spat everything out so fast that he worried the doctor would think he was lying.

Dr. Cheng slowly repeated the story, wrote things down, made sure he had the dates right. He said, "You're concerned that you were infected back in December."

"Or sooner."

"December or sooner. In early January, did you experience any fatigue, fever, loss of appetite?"

Yale shook his head.

"Any rash, sore throat, headache, muscle ache? A cold?"

"No."

"Have you noticed swollen lymph nodes?"

"I wasn't checking. But not now."

"I want to hear your questions and concerns about the test," Dr. Cheng said and folded his hands across his knees.

Yale said, "I'm not sure I want it today. I don't want results that mean nothing." He picked the cat hair off his sweater, piece by piece.

"You know, if you contracted this a month ago or more, I'd say your results would be pretty solid. Would I want you to get retested three months from now? Absolutely. Do I need you to promise me you'll avoid behaviors that would put yourself or others at risk? Yes."

He stopped and leaned forward, waiting until Yale started to talk.

"I don't know why I'm more scared this time. The first time, last year, it was like we'd gone back and forth between assuming we had it and thinking we were safe. But most of the time, deep down, I thought I did, you know? I'd check my tongue every morning for thrush. When we went in, it was—maybe it was a relief. It doesn't feel that way now."

"It's harder alone."

"Sure." Yale managed to keep his voice steady.

Dr. Cheng scooted closer. "Listen: You were exposed, yes. That's not as definitive as it might feel. I've treated guys I *slept* with, Yale. And that was before the test. I assumed I had it too. And I don't. Let's not fall apart over something that hasn't happened yet. We'll get you the test today. You'll feel better, I think, in the meantime.

And we'll make an appointment for the results"—he wheeled himself over to his desk calendar—"two weeks from today, the seventeenth."

"Doesn't the first test only take a few days? I want you to tell me if that's positive. I want to know."

Dr. Cheng shook his head. "I can't do that. Any positive would be preliminary. A positive ELISA gets repeated, then sent out for the Western blot. Lots of reasons you could have a false positive on the ELISA. Syphilis, for one. Drug use. Multiple pregnancies."

It wouldn't have been funny if Dr. Cheng's delivery weren't so deadpan, but Yale found himself looking up, smiling. He could deal with this guy at his sickbed.

"A negative ELISA is pretty damn negative, but I can't tell you I'll call you with that, because then if you don't get the call—right? You understand."

"You think I'd jump off a bridge."

Dr. Cheng asked if Yale would like to talk to a counselor—no, not yet—and told him they'd give him a slip of paper with a number on it. A corresponding number would go into the chart. "I don't even write down that we're running the test," he said. "I put a special symbol. If my records were seized, all they'd see is some funny shapes. This isn't a shame thing, I want you to understand. Sometimes we associate secrecy with shame. This is simply about protecting you. Do you have questions about confidentiality?"

Yale didn't need the shame lecture, but it was a nice delay. He tried to think of a question that would take some time, but he couldn't.

Dr. Cheng said, "I'm going to stay in the room while Gretchen draws your blood," and he did just that. Yale looked away; he always had a problem with his own blood, watching it rise up the vial. "We have some party favors," Dr. Cheng said and presented Yale with an opaque plastic bag of rubbers. "You've got five different kinds in here. Several of each. Do you know how to use them?"

Yale said he did. He'd put one, laughing, on a banana, at one of the meetings Charlie had organized in their apartment. Charlie had introduced him to the group as "my spokesmodel for prophylactic application!" But he'd never actually worn one. He'd had a couple used *on* him, before he was with Charlie, and he hadn't particularly appreciated the feeling. Yale wondered if he'd ever use these, or if they'd languish in their bag as he spent the rest of his life, long or short, celibate.

Gretchen was done. Yale walked back to the waiting room, his sleeve still rolled up, and when he saw Fiona—God was he happy to see her—he pointed to the bandage in the crook of his elbow, the cotton ball.

Her eyes were red, but she said, "I'm going to buy you a lollipop. I am! There has to be one around here somewhere. I'm buying you a lollipop."

2015

Fiona chose her outfit carefully: gray slacks, blue blouse, black heels.

She could have taken the Métro, but she didn't want to worry about changing lines, getting smelly. So she crossed the bridge away from the movie set and took a taxi all the way to the eighteenth, to an address that turned out to be at the bottom of Montmartre.

Cecily had said, "Remember that you have time. You don't have to solve it all at once." But Cecily didn't know Claire—the way one wrong move might make her vanish. And Cecily, although she'd been hungry for the few details Fiona could provide about their granddaughter, hadn't wanted to come to Paris. "I'd make things worse," she said. Since when was Cecily the expert on anything?

Fiona hadn't been sure what to expect from a "bar-tabac," but really it was just a bar. A cozy dive you might as easily have found in Rogers Park. Film posters, little Christmas lights running along the shelves of bottles. It was just before noon, and there were a few patrons, mostly men, mostly alone.

She couldn't feel her feet.

Fiona held her shoulders back and approached the woman at the bar—definitely not Claire—and said, "*Je cherche* Claire Blanchard. *Elle est ici?*"

The woman looked at Fiona, an *Oh, you're her* look, and said something quick that Fiona couldn't follow. She disappeared through the door at the end of the bar.

And then: Claire. Pushing the hair from her face. Taking a huge, bracing breath.

Those were Claire's eyes, the dark lashes. The marbled brown of her irises.

The other woman stood behind her, peered at Fiona. She asked Claire something quietly, and Claire nodded.

She looked thin but healthy—her cheeks pink, her hair back in a sloppy twist—and startled, caught off guard. Which she couldn't have been.

Fiona had imagined a thousand conversations they might have, a hundred ways the morning could end, but she hadn't thought through what to do with her face, her body. Claire smiled tightly, an embarrassed smile.

What Fiona said, eventually, was "Hi."

Claire came around the bar and gave her a brief hug, the kind of hug you'd give a distant aunt. She said, "It's good to see you."

Fiona felt, of all things, angry and ridiculous. That she'd spent this time and money and despair to find someone who would hug her so casually, who wouldn't collapse in her arms and ask to be rescued. This strange *adult* standing here, so collected. Her hair had darkened a bit, and her face had changed in ways that had nothing to do with her thinness; the bones had settled, the eye sockets deepened. She didn't look at all like a college freshman, and not like the sun-washed, pixelated young woman in the video either.

Fiona said, "Can we go somewhere to chat?"

"I thought we could stay here." She said it firmly, as if she'd practiced. As if the woman behind the bar were going to make sure Claire wasn't abducted today.

They sat in the corner under a TV showing a soccer match. The scattered patrons looked in that direction, but it was at the game, not at Fiona and Claire. Fiona wished for something to drink or eat, something to anchor them to the table. Something to lend this meeting the timeline of a meal, guarantee it would last longer than a minute.

Fiona said, "I need to know that you're okay." She wanted to touch Claire's hands, to feel if they were rough now, or still soft. She wanted to tuck her hair behind her ear.

Claire said, "We're fine."

"You have a little girl."

Claire smiled. "I'm teaching her English, don't worry."

"That wasn't really my concern."

Claire pulled a phone from the pocket of the apron Fiona just now registered her wearing—a white apron around her waist over a black skirt, a black shirt. "Hold on," she said, and she thumbed the phone and then placed it on the table in front of Fiona. A little girl on a three-wheeled scooter, curls blowing in her face.

Fiona wanted to snatch the phone up, scroll through the pictures one by one, see how far back they went, how far forward. Instead she said, "She's beautiful."

"Kurt got married. He watches Nicolette sometimes while I work."

She'd pronounced it the French way, Nee-co-lette, and Fiona couldn't bear to ask yet if the child was named after Nico, after the uncle Claire had never known but in whose shadow she'd grown up. She feared both answers equally. She said, "Is she in school?"

"She's only three."

"You had her in Colorado?"

Claire got up and grabbed a cocktail napkin off the bar to blow her nose. Fiona worried she wouldn't sit back down, but she did. She said, "Yeah, well. That was the beginning of the end. They—it was a home birth, and it didn't go very well."

"Oh. Oh God, honey."

"I was bleeding a lot, like a *lot*, and they wouldn't let me call an ambulance. So Kurt stole the car—there was one car—and he drove us. I nearly died. I was in the hospital for a week. They took us back though, after that. I think they figured we could've sued them."

Your mother was supposed to be there when you had a baby, was supposed to yell at doctors for you and make sure you were resting. If Fiona had allowed her own mother in the hospital, would things have gone differently? Would her mother have insisted on putting baby Claire on her chest, making sure they bonded as they slept? The thought hit her hard, right in the abdomen, and so did the realization that what Claire had done to her was exactly what she'd done to her own mother. She hadn't even thought to call her mother till Claire was two days old. She'd—oh, God.

"How did you pay the hospital bill?"

"Um. We didn't pay it, actually. Like, we got out of there before they tracked us down."

"That's when you left?"

"Nicolette was a month old. We waited around and gathered some cash. I mean, we weren't supposed to have our own money, but Kurt would run the till at the farmers' market, so. And he wrote to this friend in Paris who helped us. Which is who he ended up marrying."

"Honey," Fiona said, "I'm just glad you're out." She meant both things—the cult and the relationship.

Claire said, "I was working in an art supply shop for a while." She smiled. "You would've liked it. It's been around for two hundred years. Monet bought his brushes there."

"Which one?"

Claire looked at her strangely—why would Fiona know the names of art supply shops in Paris?—and instead of telling her

348

she'd searched them all, looking for her, Fiona said, "Aunt Nora might have shopped there."

Claire said, "It was a good job. And then Kurt stole from the store. He came in when I was closing up, and he took stuff, a bunch of times. I didn't know he was doing it. I still got fired. But I didn't get arrested. *He* did. Which is when we broke up."

"Is he on drugs?"

"He's totally clean now. I wouldn't let him watch Nicolette if he weren't."

Fiona gave her a look.

Claire said, "Mo-o-om." An imitation of a whiny teenager. It would have been funnier if she hadn't *been* a teenager the last time Fiona saw her. She said, "What brings you to Paris?" No irony in her voice.

Fiona said, "I just thought it would be fun to spend three years and several thousand dollars tracking down my daughter. You know, and see the Eiffel Tower too."

"Oh." Claire looked annoyed, but also like she was trying to hide that she was pleased. "You didn't need to come all this way."

"Claire, you have a kid now. Do you not get it? Wouldn't you—if your daughter—" Fiona couldn't bring herself to say the child's name. It would be an invasion, a privilege she hadn't been invited to enjoy.

Claire said, "That's different."

An accusation, maybe, but instead of taking the bait, Fiona said, "Your dad is fine."

"I know."

"How?"

"I mean, we have Google here. You can see when he's doing lectures. And your store seemed okay, so I figured you were fine."

Fiona wanted to ask if she understood that she had denied her parents the right, for the past three years, to know if she was alive or dead. She wanted, at least, to know *why*. But that was something to work out down the road. In this conversation, it would be a bomb.

She said, "Karen has breast cancer. That's why he's not here. She's starting radiation."

Claire looked only mildly concerned. "Is it bad?"

"I mean, it's *cancer*. But it sounds treatable."

"She's gonna get way too into that pink ribbon stuff, isn't she. She's gonna go on all the marches and never shut up about it."

Years ago, Fiona might have admonished her—she'd always been careful to speak respectfully of Karen, maintain good relations—but she let herself laugh, and it felt wonderful.

Fiona took an envelope from her purse and wrote Damian's number on the back. "He's going through a lot," she said, "and if he could hear your voice I know it would help."

Claire accepted the envelope noncommittally, stuck it under the band of her apron.

Fiona whispered. "Are you here legally?"

"It's complicated. I'm not about to get arrested or anything. I've overstayed. But I can get it sorted out."

"Why not just come home? To Chicago?"

"Tell me you didn't keep my bedroom preserved."

She hadn't, thank God, or that would have stung. Claire's bed was still there, and her dresser and her books, but right after she first took off for Colorado Fiona had moved the sewing table in there, and then things had spread.

Fiona said, "I'll be here another week or two. Do you remember Richard Campo?" It was a silly question. A photo that Richard had taken of baby Claire crying in Damian's arms was one of his more canonical works. It still hung in MASS MoCa. Claire wrote her college essay about that picture. "He has an opening at the Pompidou on Monday. I'm staying with him." She was tempted to imply that this was the main reason she'd come over, that Claire was secondary, but why? For pride? It had been her failing with Claire all along—pretending not to love her as much as she did. Trying to steel herself against a broken heart, the way she would with a boyfriend. (The first time she and Damian had gone to couples therapy, the therapist had finally said, "What are you afraid will happen if you open yourself up to him completely?" And Fiona, already crying, had shouted: "He would die!" It clearly wasn't what the therapist had expected to hear. He hadn't been a very good therapist.)

She said, "I'll be here at least that long, to see his show. I'd like for you to come home with me, but—" she put up a hand to stop Claire's wide-eyed protest "—if that's not an option, I'd like to stay a while. Maybe I can help with the baby. Will you give me your number at least?"

"She's not a baby. She's three."

"I'd love to help, sweetie."

Claire would *not* give Fiona her number, but Fiona could come by again in two days, they agreed, and they'd take things from there.

The woman behind the bar called to Claire, pointed at her watch, and Fiona wondered if this wasn't prearranged: *Call me back after six minutes unless I give you the signal.*

Claire said, "I don't mind you being here, but we're fine."

"I know you're fine. I can tell. You were always going to be fine."

Part of her actually meant it.

1986

Yale kept wishing Julian would leave the apartment, but Julian didn't want to risk being seen. He wanted to hide here till Sunday, when his flight would leave for Puerto Rico. He had a high school friend out there to stay with—and after that he wasn't sure, except that it would be somewhere warm. "Maybe Jamaica," he said, and Yale said, "Julian, they kill people like us in Jamaica." And Julian, disturbingly, had shrugged.

Julian spent most of his time locked in the master bedroom, or else working out in the Marina City gym in exercise clothes he'd dug out of Allen Sharp's dresser. As far as Yale could tell, he was staying clean—but then he didn't know what went on during the day. At 6:30 each evening, Julian would appear in the living room to turn on *Wheel of Fortune*, which Yale wondered if he even enjoyed; he never made any effort to guess the answer. When the winner went shopping in the little showcase after each round, Julian would wonder aloud if the person would choose the Dalmatian statue. That was the extent of his engagement.

After work on Tuesday, Yale saw Asher Glass at the Hull House pool. Asher was already toweling off when Yale got there. Yale jumped in and talked to him from the water. He felt scrawny next to Asher, pale, and the water was a good cover. Asher had heard that Yale was living down in River North. Yale said, "In the corncob towers. I keep trying to think of a good cornhole pun, but I've got nothing."

Asher didn't laugh, just looked at him with concern. He said, "If you need legal help getting what's yours out of your old place—or anything financial—I'm just saying, this is what I do, and I'd be glad to help."

The water clung to Asher's shoulders and chest hair in perfect spheres.

"It means a lot that you'd say that."

He hadn't thought much about the things he'd left behind at Charlie's. He'd been wearing Allen Sharp's sweaters for several days now, and Allen Sharp's very soft bathrobe, and he had all the music and furniture and dishes he needed, for now. But the fact that Asher would help him instead of helping Charlie—it made his skin warm in the cold water. After Asher left, he sank to the bottom of the pool and looked up at the streaks of pale blue light.

Fiona called Yale at the office on Wednesday to say Roscoe was ready to be picked up. Yale didn't ask about the money, and Fiona didn't mention it either; he paid the 360 dollars. He brought Roscoe home in the cardboard carrier they gave him.

Yale hadn't mentioned the cat episode to Julian—because it was upsetting, and because he didn't trust himself to tell the story without also telling the story of getting tested—so when Yale opened the box, when Roscoe took a tentative step out, Julian stared bewildered from the couch. Yale said, "Remember this guy?"

It took only a second of blank confusion before Julian was down on the floor, clutching Roscoe like a long-lost security blanket. "Where did he *come* from?" he said, and—mercifully—didn't give Yale time to answer. "Hey, buddy, you're living in the penthouse now! Is he gonna stay? Can he stay?"

"If he doesn't have another social engagement."

He worried, the way Julian was holding that cat, that now Julian would never leave either. But Julian's ticket was purchased, and he seemed antsier every day. Yale went back out and bought Roscoe a litter box and some food and a dish and a cat bed. Halfway out of the store, he turned and went back to buy him a toy, a purple ball with a feathery tail.

On Thursday, a Foujita expert came in—he'd flown from Paris— to meet with Bill. Yale wanted to listen outside the door. He wanted to spend the rest of his life building Nora's Paris out of sugar cubes, brick by brick. He wanted a one-way ticket to 1920. He thought about Nora's idea of time travel. What a horrible kind of travel, that took you only forward into the terrifying future, constantly farther from whatever had once made you happy. Only maybe that wasn't what she'd meant. Maybe she meant the older you got, the more decades you had at your disposal to revisit with your eyes closed. He couldn't imagine ever wanting to revisit this year. Well: In eleven days he'd have his results. And maybe then he'd long for this purgatory, the time when he could sit at his desk clinging to some small splinter of hope.

When Yale got home that night, Julian was at the table reading the *TV Guide*, even though he was nowhere near the TV. It was an old one, from the last time the Sharps were here. Roscoe was on his lap.

Julian said, "This is funny. They pretended to interview Kermit and Miss Piggy."

"Yeah, I saw that."

"He insists they're not married, and she thinks they are."

"Hilarious. You doing okay?"

"I'll be out of your hair in two days."

Yale sat down. If Julian really was leaving, Yale could ask him. He ought to, before he left. He said, "I want to say again that I forgive you for what happened with Charlie. I should be poisoning the coffee, but I'm just not mad at you. But you have to tell me something. I need to know whether that was really the only time."

Julian flipped the magazine over, open, as if he didn't want to lose his place. He held Roscoe up to his chest. A shield. "Okay. So . . . yeah, pretty much."

"Pretty much?"

"He blew me once. About a year ago. But in terms of—if that's what you're asking, then yeah, only once."

"He blew you about a year ago." Yale was trying to do mental math, trying to remember what had been going on in their lives last winter. Charlie's paper was struggling. The test hadn't come around yet. He wasn't surprised, but then why was his heart pounding?

"But listen, Yale—like, if you really want to know this stuff?" Yale nodded. "He was definitely getting around."

Yale controlled his breath. He said, "I need you to be more specific."

"What would happen—he kept it so bottled up. I mean, you know how I feel about monogamy. He's this *pillar of the community*, or whatever, and then every six months or so he'd snap. I'm not saying it was constant, but—you know how if you haven't eaten all day, your body takes over and eats a whole cake? I just know there was a lot of, like, dark corner sex. Train station bathrooms, the forest preserve, that kind of stuff. He used rubbers. At least he said so."

Roscoe came in and out of focus. Julian's face came in and out of focus. Train station bathrooms were where guys from the suburbs went, furtive men with wives and kids, the "commuter gays" Charlie used to rant about. People who could match his guilt, his self-loathing. Yale didn't believe for an instant that Charlie had used rubbers. What Charlie was doing was suicide. You don't use condoms for suicide. He said, with the last of the breath that had already escaped him, "Fuck."

"For what it's worth, I think he stayed away from, like, our community. He wasn't picking up guys at Paradise or anything."

Yale wondered if Charlie had been protecting his reputation, Yale's feelings, or both. He couldn't have thought those guys from the suburbs would be safer.

"You gotta understand," Julian said, "this was why I didn't feel so terrible about it. I mean, I *did*, but it wasn't like I was breaking something unbroken, you know? And I wasn't sure if you guys had more of an understanding than you let on. I guess not."

"How do you even know all this?" Yale wanted to ask who else might have known, but he wasn't sure he could handle the answer. Terrence had really seemed to believe he'd witnessed an isolated incident. But if Julian knew, surely Teddy did. He wondered about Asher, Richard, Charlie's staff.

"I mean, he always sort of confided in me. One time I saw him at Montrose Street Beach, like full-on knocking on some guy's Audi window. After that he'd tell me things. He wasn't bragging or anything, just unloading. He wasn't happy about it. Like, why does anyone do that stuff? Either you're having a blast, or you do it because you hate yourself, and I don't think he was having fun."

Yale felt a lot of things clicking into place, pieces he hadn't known were scattered around the recesses of his brain. He said, "And you didn't tell me. You knew, and you didn't tell me." If Fiona was right, if no one really liked Charlie, why had they all protected him for so long?

"I just—I wouldn't want people talking about every mistake *I* made. That's the sex police, you know? I'm not the sex police. Hey, I'm really sorry, okay? I'm really, really sorry. You're not—you're not infected, are you?" Julian's eyes filled with something like panic, as if the thought had only just occurred to him.

Yale said, because it was true in the loosest sense, "I tested negative." As of May. Well. He'd been negative, and lord knew how long Charlie had been exposing him to stuff. He stood up, made Julian stand up, hugged him. If Julian really was leaving on Sunday, he didn't want their friendship ending in a fight. He could be angry later, on his own. He could draw targets on the wall, pictures of everyone who'd betrayed him, and he could throw darts at their faces. But he could also hold Julian tight for a second. It felt good. He said, "Sex police would be a great Halloween costume."

He was awake till three. The odds of Charlie becoming infected after only one encounter, and *then* Yale becoming infected after only a few encounters with Charlie, would be minuscule. But now his statistical padding had disappeared. He knew that the virus didn't care about fairness, about probability—but that didn't make him any safer.

Yale wondered suddenly if Charlie had even gotten tested at all, back in the spring. They'd been counseled together but their blood had been drawn separately, and they'd been called back separately for their results. Nothing was beyond Yale's imagination now, no level of deceit. Charlie might have been too chickenshit to go through with it, might have convinced himself he was okay until he was presented with the undeniable fact that someone he'd slept with was indeed infected.

When Yale got to work on Friday, still half asleep, he had a note to "call Alfred Cheng." It took him a moment to recognize this as Dr. Cheng, the Dr. Cheng who wasn't supposed to phone for another ten days. His throat flipped inside out. He wanted to call back instantly just as much as he wanted to wait a hundred years, but he couldn't imagine phoning from the office. And he couldn't call from the apartment either. Julian had planned to stay in all day watching soap operas and playing with Roscoe. It was probably nothing—an issue with the bill, a follow-up question. It was far too soon for the results, and what bad news could there be besides the results? Maybe something else had come up in the blood work. Cholesterol. Flat-out cancer.

In the late morning, Teddy called to ask if Yale had seen Julian. "I haven't," he said, "but I'm sure he's fine."

"Why would he not be fine?" Teddy said. "I only asked if you'd seen him."

Yale wanted Teddy to figure it out, to realize Julian would rather spend time with him than suffocate under Teddy's watch. He wanted to ask if he'd known Charlie had been out whoring around like a teenage drug addict.

At noon, exactly noon, he walked over to the concert hall without his coat. There were pay phones in the lobby. His hands shook too much to be efficient with his quarter, too much to flip carefully through the address book he'd shoved in his pocket. He cursed himself as he dialed for waiting till lunchtime; the whole office was probably out. Someone played the trumpet somewhere—fast, agitated music, which didn't help.

But the receptionist answered, and a minute later Dr. Cheng was on the phone. "Well," he said, "I lied!"

"I'm sorry?"

"I lied, about not calling you for the ELISA test. You're negative."

"Oh." Yale floated somewhere between the floor and the ceiling. "How—how negative?"

Dr. Cheng laughed. "Very negative. There's no such thing as a false negative. This is definitive."

He might die right here, in the lobby.

"You seemed so nervous; I didn't want to give you another restless week for no reason. Now listen, you can't tell anyone I did this, because then—"

"I get it. I get it."

"And when we test you *again*, in three months, I'm absolutely not calling you early. No joke. This is a one-time thing."

Yale wondered if that was true, or if the scene would repeat, with another vow that it was the last time.

"Now, official disclaimer, this means there are no antibodies *now*. You said the last time you were intimate with your partner—"

"Ex-partner. December. So I'm really not clear till March, right? Can I come back in March?"

"Sure. I'd normally say three months, but we can do March. And I'm going to caution you to use protection in every situation until then, even with an uninfected, monogamous partner. *But*— the odds of the antibodies showing up that late are slim. If I were you, I'd rest easy. Celebrate, okay? Responsibly."

"And you're *sure*? I mean, your coding system, and everything."

"I'm sure. Listen, I think it would still be a good idea to come in for counseling. I know I dealt with a lot of guilt myself when I tested negative."

"I'll think about it."

How *did* he feel? He kept his hand on the receiver after he hung up, as if the phone could feed him the proper emotion. There was elation, certainly—and a sober sense of having dodged, once again, a bullet that was still flying straight at his friends—but in what proportion? Mostly he felt sheer adrenaline.

Two students came into the lobby with violin cases. Yale bummed a second quarter from one and called Fiona. She wasn't home but she had an answering machine.

He said, "Just calling because I'm in such a negative mood. Feeling really, really negative over here." She would hear his grin. "Just awash in negativity. Thought you'd want to know."

Back in the office, Roman was leaning with his whole upper body on a three-hole punch. Yale said, "Let's turn some music on." His

New Order cassette was still in the tape deck. He sat at his desk, beating time with his ballpoint pen. Roman stared with what seemed like genuine alarm, but then when the chorus began he joined in, hitting his table like a bongo drum. When the chorus came back a third time, they both sang along.

Yale stayed late at the office so he wouldn't have to spend time around Julian. He couldn't bear it, couldn't stand to look him in the eyes knowing Julian was sick and he was healthy. He'd done it before—hadn't he been fine with Nico, with Terrence? But this was different.

When he got off the El that night, instead of going back to the apartment he went down Hubbard Street where there were a couple of gay bars and an unmarked bathhouse. He had no plans to enter the bathhouse and wasn't sure about the bars either—it was just nice to walk there. To know there were other groups of friends in other parts of the city having their own crises and affairs and redemptions. To be outside, feeling healthy. He stood across the street from Oasis and watched people coming and going. How lovely not to recognize anyone. How lovely not to know which of these men were dying.

Around the LaSalle corner came a group with all the noise and buzz of a night in full swing, and for a second Yale wished he could join, blend in and follow them—until he realized that in front of them all was Charlie. Charlie, who never usually came down here. Gesturing broadly, mid-debate. In his "FRANKIE SAY RELAX" shirt, jacket open. Yale stood there, an additional lamppost, not breathing much.

As the group turned toward the door, Yale saw another guy—no one he recognized, at least not from this distance—whisper something into Charlie's ear, then turn back and look straight at Yale. But Charlie never turned.

Yale's feet stuck to the ground quite a while. The emotions he'd have felt if this had happened yesterday were mitigated by the fact that he wasn't infected. It hit him now that he'd outlive Charlie, that he'd be the one looking back on this in fifty years, telling Charlie's story to someone just as Nora had told Ranko's to him. With less longing, granted. He couldn't imagine he'd see this as the great lost romance of his life. He wanted to be invisible so he could follow Charlie into the bar, see if he was drowning himself in beer. Instead he walked home, straight into the wind, and by the time he got there his skin was numb.

Yale spent Saturday feeling awkward around Julian, finding excuses to leave the apartment. He'd catch himself thinking about how he'd been *spared*—and if he'd been spared, what did that make Julian? Chosen? Then he'd sit there beating himself up, and Julian would ask what was wrong, and Yale would say nothing was wrong. Then he'd realize how dumb that sounded, when really everything was wrong—just not as wrong as it might have been.

It was still dark when Yale woke to what sounded like the apartment being robbed, but it was just Julian shoving things into his backpack. Yale stood in the doorway and watched Julian by lamplight, bent at the waist, a white strip of skin above his khakis. Roscoe stood on the bed, kneading the comforter.

"What time is your flight?" Yale said, and Julian dropped the whole bag on the floor, zipper side down.

Julian said, "Shit, shit, shit." Yale picked up the bottle of eye drops that rolled to his foot, scooped up some of the shirts and socks too.

"Hey, take a deep breath, okay?"

Julian sat on the floor, the backpack between his legs.

"You're not missing your flight. What time is it?"

"I just need to get out of here."

Yale said, "Okay. Are you *on* something?"

Julian didn't answer and Yale took it for a yes. He handed Julian the eye drops, and Julian looked at them like he'd never seen them before. "Listen, you have your ticket? All you need is ticket, ID, cash. Show me your ticket." Julian removed it from the backpack's outer pocket. A United flight that wasn't till 9:14 a.m. Yale checked the clock on the nightstand. "You've got more than an hour before you need to leave. Let's—look, let's sort your stuff out."

Yale sank down beside him. It was like helping a small child, one too winded by his last tantrum to make decisions. They folded the three T-shirts into a stack, laid the toiletries in a row, found the wallet—held together with frayed duct tape, thick with coupons and video store cards and gym passes. Julian pulled them all out one by one and laid them in front of Yale. "This one's for a free fries. Give this to Asher."

Yale knew that one of the warning signs of suicide was the divestment of belongings, the careful bestowal of objects—but there was that ticket on the floor by Julian's knee. He'd be getting on the plane. He'd make it that far, at least.

Julian picked up a white trapezoidal dental floss container and held it in his palm. He said, "Why do I have this?"

"To—I mean, it's important, right? The whole plaque thing?" He was hoping Julian would smile.

"No, Yale, really, why did I pack this? I'm never flossing again."

"Sure you are."

"I'm telling you that I have decided not to. Like, right now. I've hated it my whole life, and what's gonna happen to my gums in the next six months?"

"You've got much longer than that."

"You think any dentist is even treating me again? I've got no dentist to yell at me! I'm never going in for another cleaning! I

could eat s'mores for dinner every night and not brush my teeth."
He dropped the dental floss on Yale's lap and grabbed his shoulders. "Ten-year-old me would *love* this." And then he collapsed in frantic laughter that Yale couldn't manage to join.

Yale said, "Do you know when you even got infected? Listen, what if you got it like a month before you took the test? You could have years before you're even symptomatic. And lots more time after that. By which point—didn't you always believe they'd find the cure? You're gonna want to floss, Julian."

"First of all." Julian sat up, serious. He wiped his face; he'd been laughing out tears. "I *do* know when I got infected. Summer of '82. There was this director I'd been following like a puppy for months, and he finally gave in, pity-fucked me. He died maybe a year later of, you know, ear cancer or something. And I went to his funeral and I was like, *Wow, mortality, how sad, you just never know.* And it was already in me. I was in denial so long, Yale. I was in denial till the nurse was looking me in the face, telling me I had the virus. She had to tell me three times.

"So yeah, let's say it takes a few years. That's *now*. I'm at the top of the slide. I'm hoping it starts with herpes and thrush at the same time, so I look like some kind of white-tongued dragon when I open my mouth. What's the thing where you bleed from your gums? I want that too. But then just for you, Yale, when I open my scabbed-up lips to show my bloody gums and the yeast farm I'm growing in my throat, I'm gonna look in the mirror, and just for you I'll floss. Because I wouldn't want any *plaque* in there messing things up."

Yale held the floss container between his thumb and finger. He said, "Did you sleep at all?"

"I can sleep on the plane."

"When you're gone, when it's been a few days, can I tell people where you went?"

363

"You can say you saw me, and I looked like a handsome fucking devil, and I said I'm sorry. Feel free to tell them Puerto Rico, because by the time Teddy could fly his ass down there to find me, I'll be gone."

"What about your family?"

"I'll send a postcard."

Yale found a pen and wrote his office number and the Sharps' number inside the back copy of *Pet Sematary*, the one book in Julian's backpack.

He said, "Let me call you a cab."

That night, Yale tore off a bit of Julian's dental floss and threw it away, and then he tore himself some to use. The next night, he used it again. He only did this before bed; he used his own each morning. It was a way of making Julian's last longer, but it was also a way of reflecting back on his day. One day since Julian had left, two days since Julian had left, and what was different? What had he done?

Not that Julian's absence should be such a great hole, but about an hour after Julian had taken off, as Yale worked the Sharps' elaborate coffee machine, he'd been hit by the fact that this was another friend gone from his life. Nico was gone, Terrence was gone, Charlie was on another planet as far as he was concerned, Teddy judged him, and now Julian had gone off to curl up under a palm tree and die. Asher was left, but he was so busy. Fiona was left. There were people he knew a bit who weren't fully associated with Charlie—Katsu, for instance—but everyone seemed lately to be hunkering down with their oldest, closest friends, not clamoring for new ones. There was Roman. He talked more to Roman than to anyone else, which wasn't saying much. Roman had gone to the Alphaville show, and told Yale about someone stomping on his foot. Roman was wearing a Pisces T-shirt, and they talked about astrology. Yale tried to drop details that modeled self-acceptance into the conversation: "I haven't been to Mexico since '72; that was the year I came out, at least to myself." Once, when they talked about food, he said, "My ex-partner only knew how to cook three things, but one of them was paella." Roman never asked more.

He flossed his teeth the night he found a bright purple bruise on his ankle and freaked out all over again.

He flossed his teeth the night of the day the bruise started to fade, turn yellow at the edges.

The night after Bill Lindsey excitedly told him the Soutine experts were on board, Yale weighed the floss container in his hand and tried to guess how much was left. Surely there was some fairy tale like this: a story of a king whose reign would end when the magic ball of twine ran out. That sounded right. He wasn't going to floss with a two-inch string just to make it last, but he also wasn't going to waste it the way Charlie always did, an arm's length every night.

On Valentine's Day, he looked in the mirror and worked the string between his molars and told himself he'd made it through the week, at least. He'd made it through the test and through the awkwardness with Roman, and he hadn't broken down and called Charlie, and he hadn't jumped off the balcony, and he hadn't gone out and had suicidal sex in some video booth, and he hadn't cried. He'd done his job. He'd kept Roscoe alive. If he could get through another week like this, then another—if he could stand here at the end of the month and congratulate himself again on getting through in one piece, then he could keep doing it forever.

That Monday afternoon, Roman came bounding into the office ahead of schedule. Roman had four weeks left on his internship. Yale had told him he'd be happy to keep him on for the spring quarter, but Roman had shaken his head and said something vague about other plans. Yale couldn't blame him. He said, "I found some Ranko Novak stuff!" and he dug from his backpack a thick library book with the kind of rough canvas cover Yale couldn't stand to touch. "He's a footnote. A literal footnote." Roman came around Yale's desk—the closest he'd gotten since Wisconsin—and opened the book to where he'd stuck a circulation slip. The footnote took up half the page, and Yale had to lean close to see the part Roman had marked with pencil. "It's basically everything she said about the prize," Roman said before Yale could read for himself. "I mean, it's not very complimentary. Like, he really shouldn't have won. Wouldn't that be the worst, knowing no one thought you deserved it?" Yale saw the dates, the names of the winners, the information about three slots being open that year, the fact that the award was delayed. *Despujols and Poughéon eventually traveled to Rome after the war*, the book stated, *while Novak's injuries and eventual death (1920) prevented his ever accepting the prize.*

"Show Bill," Yale said. "Wait, don't tell him it's a footnote, though. Can you Xerox just that part, so it looks like it's the main text?" He cared more and more about Ranko's inclusion. It felt like a matter of principle now—that poor Ranko, locked-in-the-castle-with-no-reward Ranko, should finally get his showing alongside his betters.

Bill was now talking about the show going up *next* fall. Such a cruelly long time to wait. Yale wished they could rush things just so Nora could die knowing it had happened, but according to Bill, fall of '87 was already a rush. It would be his last show—he'd made that clear—and he'd be out of there in time to spend the winter in Madrid.

Roman stayed close to Yale for longer than he needed. Yale found himself indulging in the fantasy that later this spring, when the internship was over, he might call Roman and invite him for a drink. He wouldn't actually do it, but he was allowed to think about it.

The phone rang, and Roman jumped and backed away, headed

toward his desk and then, remembering the book, walked out the door with it.

The voice on the other end was impossibly loud. "Mister Yale Tishman!" A man's voice; it sounded like an accusation. If Terrence were still alive, Yale might have imagined it was him, doing some impersonation, a prank. "Chuck Donovan here. Trustee, Wildcat class of 1952. I'm calling from the office of Miss Pearce, on her phone. Miss Pearce tells me you've been responsible for dealing with the Nora Lerner estate."

Yale stood, looked around. Poor Cecily—the guy had actually commandeered her phone. He imagined her sitting there, eyes closed, fingertips at her temples.

"That's correct," he said. "I've been coordinating a—"

"Because there seems to be a miscommunication. Those paintings actually belong to a friend of mine."

Yale picked up the phone base, tried to stretch the cord into the hall. He could only get about a foot out the door. Bill's office stood ajar. He said, "Could you hold—" but Donovan was still talking.

"Now, Miss Pearce and I had a very specific understanding, and what I want to know, I want to know two things. *First*, who is responsible for this miscommunication, and *second*, how are we going to make things right?"

Yale took off his left shoe and hurled it down the hall at Bill's door. Roman emerged, followed by Bill. They looked at the shoe, the floor, and Yale beckoned them frantically. He said, for their benefit, "Mr. Donovan, are you in Ms. Pearce's office right now? You're on campus?"

Bill hit his forehead with his palm.

Yale said, "I'd like to invite you over to the gallery, and we're going to get our general counsel here too."

"Great," he said. "Great. That's what I like to hear."

*

367

It was 5:30 before they could assemble everyone. Roman had gone home, but Bill, Yale, Cecily, Herbert Snow, and Chuck Donovan—Yale had imagined someone paunchy and red-faced, and was surprised at Donovan's lankiness, his neat white mustache—gathered in Bill's office, where Bill's intern brought them coffee that Yale was too nervous to drink. He had told Bill, in the meantime, about his slipup in Wisconsin. He steered clear of his hangover, his other distractions that morning.

Donovan said, "I'm glad for the chance to address you all."

Before he could begin his speech, Yale said, "The bequest is a done deal. There's no undoing it."

Herbert Snow jumped in with some legal language, and Yale was able, as Snow talked, to make eye contact with Cecily. She looked like a woman about to meet the firing squad. Yale had dropped by her office right after his negative test to give her the news, and she'd hugged him, clapped him warmly on the back. "Now you just need to stay that way," she'd said.

Donovan said, "I've been made a fool. I give money to this university, and I sit on this board, with very little thanks. One of the only rewards I'm promised in exchange for my significant time and work is a bit of leverage. Now I'm not the type to poke my nose into the curriculum. I'm not, for instance, going to complain if you put up some nudes in your gallery. But I ought to be able, as a man of my word, to make a promise to a friend with the understanding that I can follow through on that promise. That my requests won't be ignored. I'm looking foolish now in front of my friend, my business associate, and frankly this makes me question my relationship with the university as a whole."

Yale wondered if Cecily might speak, but she sat deflated. He imagined she'd already said everything she could, back in her own office.

"I speak with Miss Pearce, and I assume it's taken care of. Then

I learn from my friend Frank that a deal has been struck, he's very upset, but he says *You've done enough, it's over, we'll let it go.* And then. Then! This weekend I get a call from Frank, who has learned, via his daughter, that you're valuing the art at *millions of dollars*."

Bill said, "Mr. Donovan, I understand your concern. But that's three million dollars that is now an asset of Northwestern."

Yale coughed, tried to stop coughing, tried, with his eyes, to stop Bill from saying the thing he'd already said. Yale hadn't heard anything about *three* million. It must have had to do with the Soutine expert. Sure enough, Donovan's eyebrows rose to where his hairline would have been.

He whipped his head toward Cecily. "You didn't share that figure with me."

"I did not have that figure," she said.

"That's three million dollars that rightly belongs to my friend Frank Lerner."

Yale said, "Emotions are running high, but listen, we're excited about this collection. We're about to go public in the next week or two, and you're getting the inside scoop."

Donovan ignored him and talked to Cecily. "If these people aren't in a position to do anything, I don't know why you dragged me over here."

Had this really been Cecily's idea? Had she handed Donovan the phone and said to call Yale? Yale said, "This has absolutely nothing to do with her. Nora Lerner contacted *me*, and I was the one who handled the acquisition. To be honest, we did not fill Ms. Pearce in on the proceedings from that point on. She was an advocate for you and your concerns at every step."

Cecily put her hands to her cheeks, looked at him, and he couldn't tell if she was trying to warn him or thank him. Yale hoped Bill would say something now to back him up, but Bill was staring at his own knees. Herbert Snow was taking notes. Yale realized, with a chill, that he was writing down what Yale had just said about circumventing Cecily.

Yale said, "Because you've been so understanding—perhaps we could arrange a private showing of the works, for you and a select group of friends. It could be soon, or it could be after the show is fully curated. Champagne and hors d'oeuvres in the gallery. What do you think?"

Donovan stood. "I'm paying a visit to the president. And I think people are going to be *very* interested in this story. I have a few journalist friends, in fact."

Yale stood, too, a moment before everyone else. He reached into his pocket, extracted a business card. "Please understand that the acquisition was my undertaking, and that we acted against the direction of Ms. Pearce."

Bill said, "That *we* includes me. If you're going to complain about someone, please complain about me personally. Yale was only acting—"

Yale held up a hand to stop him. He said, "This was my project. We did nothing unethical or illegal, but any anger should be directed at me." It would be dishonest, Bill taking the fall. Especially when Yale was the one who'd messed up, the one who'd been too distracted by his own life to do his job properly in Wisconsin.

Cecily adjusted her shoulder pads and followed Donovan most of the way out the door. She stopped and looked at Yale before she left the room, a look you'd throw a drowning man as you took the last life preserver.

Yale sat numbly that night on Asher Glass's floor, along with everyone else who didn't fit into the chairs or along the walls. Half of Asher's living room was his office, with desks and phones and file cabinets, and the other half held a ratty couch, a small TV. Yale's

370

tailbone pressed into the wood, and down here you could see every dust clot, of which there were many.

Asher promised them the pizza was on its way, stood in front of the TV to talk about a community housing fund, slush money for people who couldn't make rent because they were sick. Someone asked if Asher could guarantee the money would stay in the gay community, and Asher said, "Hell no, are you kidding? We don't own this disease," and then there was loud debate. Whenever Asher was exasperated, the parallel creases between his eyes would grow so deep they looked etched.

Yale was free now to lust after Asher, free to fantasize not just a dream scenario but an actual possibility. He could stay late, help clean up, put his hand on Asher's shoulder ... But Yale had never been one to make a first move. Not in his life, not even drunk. And he doubted Asher would ever notice he was interested unless he grabbed him by the actual cock.

Besides which, his life didn't need more drama right now. He needed a nice boring stretch, a few months when someone could ask what was new and he'd be able to say, "Not much, just plugging along." He couldn't sacrifice his job and risk rejection on the same night.

But no, everything would be fine at the gallery in the morning. The transfer of property was airtight, Herbert Snow had reassured him. It had to be okay.

Rafael, Charlie's Editor in Chief, kept scooting closer to Yale on the floor until he was right beside him. He whispered, "Bummer of a party."

Yale had nervously checked the crowd when he'd come in, even though Asher had guaranteed, when he invited Yale, that Charlie wouldn't be there. It wasn't going to be easy to avoid the most ubiquitous gay man in Chicago, but he could manage it till things had cooled, crusted over. Teddy leaned on the windowsill next to his friend Katsu. Yale hadn't talked to Teddy tonight, probably wouldn't. Teddy and Katsu were exactly the same size, and Yale squinted till they were identical silhouettes. Katsu raised his hand, and when Asher shouted over the din to call on him, Katsu said, "For those of us living with it—" and Yale only barely heard the question, something about tenant rights. He could have guessed, but he hadn't known.

Someone asked a question about anonymity, and Rafael whispered, "I heard you're living large! When you gonna have us plebes down for a party?" Rafael wore a Palestinian scarf around his neck, and he hid his chin in it like a turtle.

"I'm just crashing there," Yale said, although it felt more and more like that was where he lived, in a little capsule above the city, while down here everyone else's suffering and drama continued.

A minute later, Rafael whispered again: "Charlie's totally unhinged. Everyone at the office is like, *Oh my God, bring back Yale.* Was he always this nuts? And you were just, like, absorbing it all for us?"

Yale said, "He's going through a lot."

"I mean, he's a *disaster.* Did you used to force-feed him? We started leaving snacks on his desk just so he'll eat."

All the heads in the room turned at once toward the door, and when Yale turned he fully expected to see Charlie standing there. A nightmare, a relief, an avenging angel. But it was Gloria from *Out Loud,* carrying a stack of pizza boxes, telling everyone to calm down and stay put till she'd put out the paper plates, the napkins.

Yale let the sounds around him blend to a dull buzz. He watched Asher talk, gesture, whap his hand against the TV antenna. He watched Katsu and Teddy lean on each other.

Rafael said, "Nobody's even listening. Everyone's so tired of listening."

*

There were flowers on his desk in the morning, a bunch of yellow dahlias from Cecily. A note that said, *I can never repay you.*

But before he'd even sat down, Bill was there. He'd brought Yale a coffee, even though Yale already had one. He said, "It seems our friend is on a power trip." He paused, waiting for Yale to ask what he meant, but Yale didn't feel like playing along, and eventually Bill cleared his throat and continued. "He's been to the president, which—I don't know how everything's going to play out. I don't. He's calling around the board. Not *our* board, the *board.* And meanwhile, Frank, Nora's son, is taking some kind of legal action. I don't know if he's fully suing or what, but you have a message from Snow."

"That's a major waste of his time," Yale said.

"Yes. Yes." Bill looked past Yale and out the window. "But it's not great for the gallery. You were so noble, giving him your card and everything, and I wish you hadn't been. You know I was willing to take the blame."

"I'm the one who messed up," Yale said.

Actually, he'd lain awake last night wondering why the hell he'd done it. For Cecily, of course. But also maybe it was some kind of self-flagellation, a way to punish himself, for—what? Well, everything. Messing around with Roman. Taking the art from Debra and maybe even Fiona. Walking away from Charlie. Evading this disease. It wouldn't take a genius shrink. How easily he'd brushed off Dr. Cheng's offer of counseling, his warnings to be careful out there, and here he was. A different kind of reckless behavior.

Bill said, "I think if there's anything you want to finish up with Nora—I mean, personally, since you were the one—I think maybe the next few weeks might be the time to do it. I'm just thinking of timing, in a general way."

"You think I should wrap up my business with Nora." Yale tried to read his face.

"Well, just that you might want to."

"In the next few weeks."

Bill's thumb worried his chin cleft. "I don't have a crystal ball. One thought is if I could tell Donovan you're off the case on this one, so to speak—that I was handling it personally, right? We take you off Nora and see how the rest plays out. And you were done there anyway! But I'd take you off any grant writing related to the show as well. The publicity and so on."

Yale said, "Bill, if I should be tying up loose ends with other situations, it would be in your best interest to tell me."

"Oh! That's not what I meant! Yale, we can't lose you! I won't let that happen!"

But by the end of the week Bill was meeting privately with Herbert Snow, and when he emerged from his office, his eyes were more rheumy than usual, his face grayer.

Allen Sharp called up. "There are rumors afloat among the board of advisers," he said, and Yale had to explain the whole thing. Allen seemed placated, but he was worried about everyone else. "This is the kind of thing people will want to distance themselves from," he said. "Anything unethical . . . I've seen how these stories can blow up."

Yale could picture it too clearly: the piece in the *Times*' Arts section, the gleeful art world gossip. Which Chuck Donovan would personally see to, if he could. Chuck didn't care about the art; he probably didn't even care about his business relationship with Frank Lerner. He cared about looking like he had clout.

Yale leaned his forehead onto his typewriter's space bar.

At lunchtime he walked down to the lake, stood on one of the mounds of ice right by the water. It had been winter for so long that the air didn't hurt anymore.

374

The frozen lake edge was the surface of another planet, rippled and fractured and gray. Yale couldn't feel his fingers, but he waited till he couldn't feel his head either.

He walked back and into Bill's office. He felt like he needed the bathroom, but it was just nerves. He said, "Call Chuck Donovan and tell him you're going to fire me. Ask if that would make things better, if he can call off Frank then. Make it like you're striking a business deal. He'll like that."

"I'm not firing you!" Bill said.

"I'll quit before you can fire me."

It was like vomiting everything bad out of his body, like somehow this would set not just the gallery right but the universe.

He said, "Even if this lawsuit is ridiculous, you won't get funding while it's dragging on. You can't ask the board—"

Bill said, "Yale." But already he looked brighter.

"Just call him and see if it'll work."

Bill's shoulders dropped. He looked at the ceiling, covered his mouth with his hand. He said, "You know that if it comes down to it, I'll write you a hell of a letter of recommendation."

Even though Yale had asked for this, Bill's acceptance of the idea was a bullet to the gut. "Call right now," he said. "I'll wait in my office."

Yale opened his top drawer. There were at least fifty ballpoint pens, most inherited with the desk. He took one and squiggled a line on his legal pad. It didn't work at first, but then it did. He put it in the empty mug by his left hand, and then he forgot what he was doing and sat there blinking. Then he remembered and grabbed the next pen and tried it, and it was dead, and he dropped it into the trash can, where it landed too loudly. The next two were dry, the next clotted, the next fine. He went through all the pens. Twelve good ones. Two with Northwestern logos, a few plain Bics, a couple of fancy erasable ones, a few cheap ones advertising insurance companies. At least Yale guessed that was the writing on the sides; he couldn't focus his eyes.

When Bill walked in ten minutes later, Yale already knew from his face—the pained, hesitant look that didn't quite cover his relief—that it had worked.

"I think it's going to pan out," he said. "I mean your—your idea. What I said to him. It's all about ego for him."

"I know."

"You're a genius, Yale. You realize that? And now the problem is I've lost my genius. That's a fine kettle of fish, isn't it. He said he felt *listened to*, and then he started going on about something with the music school. We'll see how things play out. Maybe we can—maybe he'll move on to other things, and we can reverse this all."

"No." Yale could hear his own flat voice with remarkable clarity, as if on tape, some message he'd recorded years ago. "If it works, let's not mess with it."

"I want you to finish your projects first. We can't have the office empty. Yale, I want to say that—"

Yale said, "If you can spare me next week, I'll go to Wisconsin."

"Yes! Fantastic! And take Roman!" Bill said it as if Roman were a consolation prize. When he left, he made a great show of closing the door quietly.

Yale considered both his stapler and his Rolodex, and decided on the latter. He picked it up and hurled it, with all his strength, at the wall.

That next Tuesday, Yale rented the most expensive car he could, a red Saab 900, and he charged the snacks he bought to his university credit card as well. He picked up Roman outside his apartment on Hinman—he'd made sure to give Roman an out, but Roman had wanted to go—and they drove down Lake Shore Drive to scoop up Fiona.

Fiona was along to appease Debra. They weren't close, but Fiona was the one who'd called up there, told Debra how Yale had been fired, made her feel as guilty about it as she could. She'd told Debra that Yale wanted to say goodbye to Nora and that she wanted to see Nora, too, and Debra could call her father or even the police for all she cared, but they'd be there. "The last part probably wasn't necessary," Fiona said, "but I'd practiced it, so I said it."

Yale figured Fiona's presence would reassure Roman too; it would be a nice buffer. And Fiona hadn't seen Nora since the wedding where she'd first told her about Yale and the gallery. Yale didn't feel the least bit guilty about charging a third hotel room to Northwestern; he considered it a personal gift from Chuck Donovan.

Yale had spent yesterday calling donors, starting to tie up loose ends. In part he was doing his actual job, but he was also rein-forcing his relationships. If he landed at another museum three months from now, he'd want to be able to call them up again.

That weekend, he'd gone over his CV and put in some tentative calls to old colleagues from the Art Institute. One was at the MCA now. And there were other cities besides Chicago. For the first time in ages, he was free to live wherever a job might take him. New York, Montreal, Paris, Rome. He tried to see it this way, tried to look at the gifts he'd just been handed: his life, his health, the freedom to move across the globe.

During the drive, between bites of Fritos, Roman told Fiona every detail of the Ranko story. It was the main reason they were going, aside from Yale's desire to say goodbye to Nora. If Yale had just quit over some Modigliani drawings, he was an idiot. But if he'd quit to save this collection, and if this collection remained complete, the way Nora wanted it to, then he'd have done a good thing, one great good thing, in his life. And getting Ranko's story nailed down, making sure it was told—wasn't this the whole reason Nora wanted the collection to go to the gallery? Hadn't Nora chosen Yale precisely because she thought he'd understand?

They stopped at a rest area near Kenosha, one of the woodsy ones, and as Fiona and Yale waited outside for Roman, she said, "You should call Asher. This is what he does, wrongful termination stuff."

"I wasn't wrongfully terminated. I messed up and I quit. And Asher has bigger fish to fry." The thought was tempting, though—a reason to spend time with Asher, a tangible reason to cry on someone's shoulder, a substantial shoulder to cry on.

"I don't understand why you did it," she said. "You can't sacrifice your career just to be noble!"

He imitated her voice. "Just like you can't sacrifice your *college education* just to be noble!"

Fiona decided she wanted a soda, and so as Roman came out, she went in. Roman looked comically out of place next to the scattered Wisconsinite families with their puffy coats. He wore a black bomber jacket over his black T-shirt, and of course his jeans and shoes and glasses were black as well. Like a terribly chic undertaker. He came and stood next to Yale, who pretended to read a historical sign about Marquette and Joliet. He was still thinking about Bill, about Asher, and now here was Roman, reading the sign too, close enough that Yale could hear him breathe. Their arms, after a minute, were touching. Their shoulders, their hips. Roman moved his hand behind Yale as if he were going to touch it to his back, but Yale never felt any pressure. He seemed to be just hovering his hand there, daring himself.

Roman said, "I didn't know Marquette was a priest."

"Wasn't everyone a priest back then?"

378

"Well."

The sidewalk exploded under them.

Or rather, it shattered, glass fragments all around, the concrete still in place, their shoes and feet still there.

Yale spun to see a large woman with teased-out hair and a jean jacket—looking back at them, but walking toward the rest-stop doors. Another woman walked quickly ahead of her, laughing. Her friend, maybe, embarrassed by the scene. It was a bottle that had broken at their feet, a root beer bottle, the remnants of the drink foaming up around the glass shards.

"You make me ill!" the large woman shouted, and then she ran to catch up to her friend. "Fucking pedophile perverts!" They disappeared inside.

Roman took a step back, into the mess. He made his mouth into a small *O* and blew out slowly.

Yale said, "I guess she's not a fan of historical signs." He was shaking, but he wanted to make everything okay. He felt responsible, as if by giving Roman that hand job he'd made this all happen, turned Roman noticeably gay. It was ridiculous, he knew.

Roman got off the sidewalk and rubbed his shoes on the hardened snow. "She couldn't even see our faces. All she saw was our backs."

Yale said, "Are you okay? I'm sorry. That—"

"It's not like I haven't heard it before."

"I mean, it's Wisconsin."

"Don't pretend that happened because we crossed the Wisconsin border."

Yale said, "Look, let's not tell Fiona."

And here she came.

They found Nora looking better than last time, her wheelchair pulled up to the dining table, where she had her shoebox letters laid out in stacks. She stood precariously to hug Fiona, to tell Yale he looked tired. Debra had seen them in, pecked Fiona coldly on the cheek, avoided Yale entirely, and then left to go grocery shopping. Yale hoped she was doing more than that, was seeing friends, rolling in the dirt, pawning her jewelry, *something*.

Yale told Nora they were aiming to put the show up next October, but he didn't say he was losing his job. If she'd heard it from Debra, she didn't let on.

"We'll kidnap you and drive you down!" Fiona said. "We'll wheel you around and make everyone get out of your way!"

Nora laughed. "People do make room for a wheelchair."

Yale told her this was a more social visit than the previous ones. "And believe it or not, we aren't here to pin you down on dates. We want to hear about Ranko, for one thing. You kind of left us hanging."

Nora was thrilled to fill them in, but she insisted they make themselves sandwiches first. She'd prepare them herself, if it weren't for the chair. The three of them found Wonder Bread and cheese and sandwich spread. Wilted iceberg lettuce, too, which Yale wanted nothing to do with. Roman put a piece on his sandwich, arranged it so the green showed around the edges.

Yale and Fiona headed back to the living room ahead of him. "He *is* cute," Fiona whispered. "Can you give me one reason you shouldn't seduce him again?"

Yale could think of a couple, but they were already back at Nora's side, and Roman was coming up behind them.

"You're lucky I have my wits," Nora said, "because I do remember what I already told you. We were in 1919, weren't we."

Fiona sat next to Yale at the table, and she took Yale's notepad and pen, wrote in block print: DO IT. He suppressed a laugh, an eleven-year-old-in-synagogue laugh, as she drew a lewd stick-figure coupling.

Roman turned on the tape recorder he'd brought, and Nora began talking about that summer, the way the modeling led to wild parties and long dinners, inclusion in a circle of real artists that hadn't been available to her as a female student.

"It had been five years," she said. "I actually believed he'd survived the fighting, because several friends had seen him right at the end. You never knew about the flu, of course. But in any event I'd written him off for lost. Everyone knew he hadn't claimed his prize."

She told them about Paul Alexandre, a name Roman seemed familiar with, a patron who'd rented a crumbling mansion and let artists use the house for parties that lasted days.

"There was a lot of cocaine," she said, and Fiona burst out laughing. "Well, honey, we'd just survived something horrendous, and we didn't know what to do with ourselves. Modi was the magnetic center, and he brought me there. Now he was no more than five foot three, and he'd lost a lot of teeth. And he'd fly into *rages*, which were a product of the TB. And sometimes he'd just *cry*. He was drawing me one day and he had an absolute temper tantrum about Braque, how Braque was *over the horizon*, and he was lost in a rowboat. I'm making him sound terrible, but he was tremendously sexy. He'd taken me to Alexandre's house, and I was quite drunk, and I looked up—and Ranko was standing in the doorway like a ghost."

Roman gasped aloud, as if the whole story hadn't pointed to this.

"His right hand was shoved in his pocket, and I didn't understand that this was because it was ruined, the nerves gone. He hadn't been shot, so I don't know what caused the damage, but it might have been psychological. He could move the pinky finger, but not the others.

"I can't remember the beginning of our conversation—but it ended with the two of us out on the lawn, Ranko yelling that he knew what it meant that I was a model. Now, he was right. He was absolutely right. I never was able to explain to him that modeling was the only way left for me to be an artist. And look, didn't it work? After all this time, my show is going up!" She laughed and smacked the table.

"But you still could have been an artist," Fiona said. "Couldn't you? Just because you weren't in school anymore?"

"Oh, sweetheart. Name a woman whose work you know from before 1950, besides Mary Cassatt. But it wasn't just that. I was honestly never that good. Now, I *might*'ve been, if I'd kept up the training. I was someone who needed the instruction. Ranko was destroyed by the teaching, but I'd have been helped."

"Berthe Morisot!" Fiona said, but Nora had moved on.

"I was back in love the instant I saw him. It's the strangest thing, isn't it, to find someone again after a great deal of time. Your brain resets itself to the last time you saw them."

She looked at Yale intensely, as if she needed him to agree. He wondered how long he could possibly avoid Charlie, and what might happen if they next met five years on. If Yale moved away, for instance, and came back to town for some funeral. The jolt of seeing Charlie across a crowded room, featherweight and pale. But no—in five years, it would most likely be Charlie's funeral.

"He was angry enough with me that he went off to Nice for a month. I don't know what he'd been expecting; he was lucky I wasn't married with three children. But I've always imagined what really rankled him was my being around those successful artists. He came back and we fought terribly, and then we made up. He moved in with us, to the flat I was sharing with my friend Valentina. But I kept modeling, and he'd fly into jealous fits. He tried getting me to paint for him. It was awful; we went to the studio of a friend of his, and he'd sketch out a scene with his left hand, very rough, and try to direct me like a puppet. He'd mix the colors and he'd point, all with his left hand. It was absolute torture, and in the end it looked painted by a child. I'd have done better if he weren't yelling over my shoulder. The—I shouldn't tell you this, but I'm afraid I've already slipped. The painting—"

"The man in the argyle vest," Yale said. His head was floating away like a balloon. "You said it was from after the war."

"Now, it's *his*! It's not mine! He wanted a self-portrait, and he'd never done one he liked. Of course I was willing to be his hands. And you can see how similar the style is to the painting of me as a young girl!"

Yale wanted to crawl under the table, curl into a little ball. He'd have to get Roman to delete that part of the tape later. If Bill caught wind of this, he'd be off the Novak pieces forever. If anyone else heard about it—good God, it could throw off all the authentications. It was a—not a forged piece, exactly, but close. He couldn't think straight.

Roman said, "That's him? That's what Ranko looked like?"

"Well, no. It didn't turn out too terribly like him. I do think I got the *eyes* right. I pride myself on that. But it's hard to paint when someone's yelling in your ear."

Fiona said, "Why did you put up with it?"

"Guilt, I suppose. He'd been through so much. And I was madly in love, and you're never reasonable when you're in love."

Fiona didn't look satisfied with the answer. But then she hadn't understood, either, why Yale had put up with Charlie so long. She'd figure it out herself, sooner or later—the way a person could change, and yet you couldn't let go of your initial conception. How the man who was once perfect for you could become trapped inside a stranger.

Beside Yale, Roman had taken the top off his sandwich and was disassembling it. He took his square of cheese and folded it in half and put it in his mouth. Neither he nor Fiona seemed disturbed by Nora's admission.

"Now, you know how Modi died. In January, Jeanne got herself to Paris, pregnant. I heard she was in town, so I kept my distance. He lived right around the corner from La Rotonde, and it makes me sick to think I sat there several times while he was dying just a block away. What happened was his neighbor finally checked in, and he and Jeanne were unconscious, half dead of cold. They didn't even have wood to burn. Jeanne recovered, but he didn't. It was the TB he died of, but the cold finished him off."

Yale had read this much at the library.

Nora squinted at the three of them. "Do you have a strong stomach?"

"Sure," Fiona said. Roman looked suddenly uncomfortable.

"Some friends of Modi's wanted to make a death mask. One was Kisling, the painter, who'd become a friend of Ranko's in the war. And Lipchitz the sculptor. They had no idea what they were doing. The third was an *astrologer*. And they invited Ranko to watch. I was jealous, because I'd wanted to say goodbye to Modi, and Ranko, who'd hated him, got to go instead. The trouble was, Lipchitz used the wrong plaster, something too abrasive, so when they took it off"—she glanced at each of them—"it peeled off his cheek, and his eyelids. The men panicked and dropped the cast right on the floor. In the end, they pieced it back together, and Lipchitz ended up essentially carving the face. It's in the museum at Harvard now, and I've no desire to see it."

Fiona seemed fine but Roman looked pale. The imagination that had been allowing him to picture Ranko so vividly was probably not his friend right now. Yale felt woozy himself.

"It drove Ranko over the edge," Nora said. "He'd already been a wreck, but I think seeing someone—someone of great talent, no less—turn into a skeleton before his eyes ... Well, he managed to tell me the story, but it was about the last thing he ever said to me. I'm sure he'd seen worse in the war, but this was different.

"And meanwhile, Jeanne killed herself over Modi. She leapt out the window of her parents' house, unborn baby and all. I wonder about that, too, the effect on Ranko. You know, when they call us the Lost Generation—Was it Hemingway who said that, or Fitzgerald?"

Roman said, "It was—sorry—it was something Gertrude Stein said to Hemingway. But, I mean, he was the one who wrote it down."

"Good. Well. I can't see a better way to put it. We'd been through something our parents hadn't. The war made us older than our parents. And when you're older than your parents, what are you going to do? Who's going to show you how to live?"

Nora ran her finger along the edge of the shoebox. She said, "The funeral was a circus, just the worst sort of irony. He'd died cold and hungry, and here was this opulent affair at Père Lachaise. Now—Yale, you need to tell me when to stop. You've driven so far, and I'm ruining everyone's day. You should know we had so much joy as well! But when you boil a story down, you end up with something macabre. All stories end the same way, don't they."

Yale wasn't actually sure he could take one more mention of death, but he said, "Keep going."

"You know the basic fact, which is that Ranko killed himself. It was the same day as Modi's funeral. A group of us went, afterward, to La Rotonde. We were drinking and carrying on, and I wasn't looking at Ranko. Someone said later they saw him put his hand to his mouth. All we saw was that he started shaking violently, fell off his chair. Everyone thought he was having a seizure. But then he wasn't breathing, and blisters popped up around his lips. I couldn't stop screaming. By the time the medics came, he was dead. What they figured later, from the powder on his hand and in his pocket, was he'd swallowed cyanide crystals. Popped them straight in his mouth. Why he chose that particular moment, I've spent a lifetime wondering."

"*Cyanide!*" Roman said. "So he—he had to have planned it, right? You don't just carry that stuff around."

Yale said, "Why do you think he did it?"

"Good lord. People take their reasons with them, don't they?"

Debra was back with the groceries, and she refused help carrying them, but then she banged through the room four times.

Roman stepped outside to smoke, and when he was gone, Nora said, "I'm sure you think I'm foolish to stay so devoted to someone so difficult." Neither of them protested. "It's not as if it kept me from living my life. If he'd lived, we'd have parted ways soon enough. He'd have had a life out there in the world, outside my mind. But when someone's gone and you're the primary keeper of his memory—letting go would be a kind of murder, wouldn't it? I had so much love for him, even if it was a complicated love, and where is all that love supposed to go? He was gone, so it couldn't change, it couldn't turn to indifference. I was stuck with all that love."

"This is what you're doing with it," Yale said. "The collection, the show."

Fiona, he realized, was quietly crying. He reached over and scratched her back.

Before Roman returned, Yale told them both the story of how Nico, waiting tables at La Gondola, once chased after two customers into the rain when they hadn't paid—pinning a man twice his size against a lamppost until the cook came to provide backup. Yale and Charlie had watched from inside the window. "He was like a kid," Yale said. "The way he ran and the way he tackled him. Like his limbs were wound up with springs." Fiona had heard the story before, but she laughed as if she hadn't.

Yale said, "This might have to be our last trip for a while. But you can call me with anything you think of." He wrote his new number. "And—I want you to know that as the gallery grows over the next year, there could be changes in my role."

Nora opened her mouth, and he was worried she'd ask what he meant. But she put her hand, cold and weightless, on his. "This was meant to be," she said. "Do you believe in reincarnation?"

Yale looked at Fiona for help, but she was only waiting for his answer, bemused. "I'd like to, I guess."

"Well." She patted his hand. "If we get to do it, let's all come back at the same time. You two, me, Nico, Ranko, Modi, everyone fun. It'll be a party, and we won't let any stupid wars break it up."

At the B&B, Yale and Fiona watched the evening news out in the TV nook. Roman disappeared into his room.

Yale said, "What have you heard about Charlie?" He wasn't sure it was healthy to ask. He wanted to know what Teresa was going through, and how the paper was doing, and if Charlie missed him. He wanted to know if Charlie was still skulking around the city. He wanted a full-color diagram of Charlie's heart and all its failures.

"I don't know much. Asher's organizing that thing against Cardinal Bernardin, and I know Charlie's involved. I haven't seen him, except—well, so Teddy had a birthday party."

"Ouch."

"No, I mean—"

Yale laughed at himself, but it really did hurt. A third-grade hurt, a primal hurt. "Who was there?"

"It was small. You didn't miss anything. Everyone just talked about Julian the whole time. Asher was there, and Katsu, and Rafael and his new boyfriend, and Richard. And Teddy's Loyola people, who were honestly dull as hell. And then Charlie brought that big guy he used to date, the one with the beard. Martin."

"Martin!" This particular fact entered Yale's mind more as lurid gossip than as a personal affront. He wondered if it was a new development, or if Charlie had kept things going with Martin the whole time.

"Everyone missed you. I mean, *I* missed you, and your absence was palpable."

"I guess that should make me happy."

"Wait, what are we doing for *your* birthday? May, right? Do you want a party? Or we'll do a dinner! We'll go to Yoshi's!"

Yale found he was incapable of imagining what his life would look like in three months. He smiled and said, "That sounds perfect."

On the way back to his room, Yale stopped and knocked at Roman's door.

Roman's shirt was untucked, his hair a mess.

Yale said, "We should get going early. Is seven okay?"

"Sure. Listen, this trip finishes off my internship hours, right?"

"Oh. Yeah. I think you have more than enough."

"So I'm sort of done at the gallery. I mean, if it's okay, I'm not coming in anymore."

"I'll barely be going in myself."

Roman took his glasses off and rubbed the dents on the bridge of his nose. He said, "You're not my supervisor anymore."

There was no one else in the hall, but Yale felt he should whisper. "Right."

"So maybe you could come in." Roman stepped back, made space for Yale.

The room was dark, and Roman smelled like honey and cigarettes, and Yale walked through the door like he was diving into a sunken ship.

2015

At noon the next day, an email on Serge's laptop. Fiona didn't remember writing her address down for Fernand the art critic, but either she'd done that (dizzy with wine and blood loss) or Fernand had asked Richard for it.

"This is what my speedy friend was able to find," he wrote, "but with minimal searching. He says this is 1911. Ranko Novak is third row, second from left. If it's something more you want, let me know details! Happy to help Richard's friend. My regards to your injured hand."

Fiona clicked the attached scan. A triangular group—ten in front, seven in the next row, and so on—of mustachioed men, gazing at one another rather than at the camera. A skeleton draped across the laps of the front row. On a rug in front of them all, a naked woman, ample backside facing the camera. A spoof photo, the belle epoque version of a goofy group shot.

She moved her finger on the screen to the third row, the second man. Dark curly hair, a long slit of a mouth. Hair slicked and parted down the middle. A skinny, floppy bow tie.

What had been so special about him? Fiona didn't know what she'd expected, but something more than this. Ranko Novak was worth seventy years of devotion. Ranko Novak was irreplaceable, a hole at the center of Nora's universe. And this was it? A face, two eyes, two ears.

Well, try telling that to someone in love.

She zoomed in. He didn't get any clearer, just larger.

Her affair with Dan had started with a conversation after yoga class, a walk to the juice place around the corner, where he'd asked her thoughts on what the teacher had said that day about letting go of attachments. He said, "Money is one thing. If I wanted to be a monk I could give up my car and it would only hurt for a week. But *people*. That's the hard part."

They'd sat a long time, talking. Fiona said, "I always thought geese were so funny." Dan had started laughing, and she said, "No, what I mean is, they mate for life, right? But they all look exactly the same. They *are* exactly the same! How would you ever tell one goose from another? I mean, what, do they all have different taste in music? But a goose could recognize its partner from miles away."

"And we think we're so special," Dan said. He got it, and this was when she started falling for him. "*True love* and all that. You think we're as random as the geese?"

"But the tragedy," she said, "is that knowing it doesn't change a thing."

And here, a hundred and some years on, was Ranko Novak. A face among the faces, a goose like all the other geese. He was gone, and Nora was gone, and what had happened to the passion that had consumed them both? If Fiona could convince herself that it was floating around the world—just disembodied, leftover passion—wouldn't that be a wonderful thing to believe?

At two in the afternoon, Cecily called and said she'd changed her mind; she was about to board her connection at O'Hare and would be there late tonight. She didn't need a hotel. An old college friend lived in the Latin Quarter. "I won't be in your way," she said. "I'll work on Kurt. And then—do you think I should bring presents? For the little girl?"

At five o'clock, Fiona unwrapped her bandage to apply the ointment the doctor had given her. Her hand was hurting less. It was amazing how quickly you could forget physical pain, how soon you couldn't even summon its echo.

At eight, Jake called. Serge had given him the number. He wondered if she'd come out and grab a bite. She was tired, she said, and managed to hang up. She'd have to have a word with Serge.

At nine forty-five, lying in bed, she started hearing sirens. Far too many, for far too long. At nine fifty, her phone started ringing. First Damian and then Jake—frantic, cryptic questions about where she was. Stay inside, they said. Then Richard was knocking on her door. She came out to the living room to watch the news. She stood in her nightgown, her feet cold. Serge paced the floor, swearing. Richard lay on the couch.

Fiona made herself breathe.

The attacks were far enough from here that she tried to imagine she was home, hearing about something on the far side of the world. There was no chance Claire had been out at what sounded like some kind of heavy metal concert; a person's tastes couldn't change that much. She might have been at that restaurant, or walking down that sidewalk, but the odds were small. The soccer stadium was up in Saint-Denis, where Claire lived; that worried her most. But Claire had a young child, and it was so late at night. Claire had *her* number, at least—but why hadn't Fiona tackled her and made her write down her own? She didn't have Kurt's either. Running around the city to search for her was out of the question. She should go get a sweater, but she didn't want to move.

There was nothing to do but keep calm. Cecily was in the air, and hopefully they'd let her plane land. What were the odds that

Claire would show up for work tomorrow morning? What were the odds that the city would be thrown into such chaos that Fiona would never find her again?

She was surprised by her numbness, at least regarding the tel-evised carnage, the bloodied, sobbing people on the streets. Was it because it wasn't her city, or because the rituals of outrage and grief and fear felt so familiar now, so practiced? Or maybe it was the pain pills she'd popped after dinner for her hand.

She was struck by the selfish thought that this was not fair to her. That she'd been in the middle of a different story, one that had nothing to do with this. She was a person who was finding her daughter, making things right with her daughter, and there was no room in that story for the idiocy of extreme religion, the violence of men she'd never met. Just as she'd been in the middle of a story about divorce when the towers fell in New York City, throwing everyone's careful plans to shit. Just as she'd once been in a story about raising her own brother, growing up with her brother in the city on their own, making it in the world, when the virus and the indifference of greedy men had steamrolled through. She thought of Nora, whose art and love were inter-rupted by assassination and war. Stupid men and their stupid violence, tearing apart everything good that was ever built. Why couldn't you ever just go after your life without tripping over some idiot's dick?

Richard's show: No one knew if the preview could happen on Monday as planned. His publicist called, and his manager. "They need to calm down," Richard said. "You'd think they'd have better things to worry about."

Serge said, "We're screwed. The whole world is screwed."

He hadn't stopped moving for the last hour and a half.

"I don't mean to sound callous," Fiona said, "but we've been through this in the States. And it's not—"

"*No*," Serge said, "whatever, a hundred dead people, I don't care. That could have been a bus crash. What I care is, now they elect right wing across Europe. And then, yes: You, me, all of us, we're screwed. Everyone acts from fear, the next year, two years. What happens, you think, to people like us?"

Fiona felt herself sinking. She said, "Things might seem different in the morning."

Serge wheeled on her. "When people are afraid, we get the Christian Taliban. We get it here, you get it there, and we're all in jail. We're all in jail."

Richard had been so quiet for so long that Fiona kept wondering if he'd fallen asleep. He stretched his arms overhead and said, "Serge, that's enough."

"I'm going out there." Serge grabbed his helmet from the counter. "Hollande can fuck his curfew."

Fiona expected Richard to stop him, expected Serge to stop himself, but Serge was out the door. Richard's phone rang again, but he ignored it.

"I didn't mean to offend him," she said. "I'm not naive, you know that."

He said, "It's always a matter, isn't it, of waiting for the world to come unraveled? When things hold together, it's always only temporary."

1986

Roman had a scar on the meat of his left arm from his smallpox vaccine: an indented circle made of a thousand tiny dots. Yale could put his thumb there. He could put his tongue there.

Roman would come over drunk. It seemed to take some alcohol to get him to show up without all the baggage of twenty-seven years of Mormonism. Roman would call at 8 p.m.. on a Saturday and say he'd be over "in a while," but he wouldn't come till after midnight. And during that time, Yale would blast music, start drinking himself. Because he didn't want to go out and miss Roman, but it was pathetic to sit there on the couch watching reruns and waiting.

Roman had silver fillings in his molars, and he always needed to blow his nose after he came.

Roman would show up like rain, once every couple of weeks, and he'd stay till four in the morning, leaving before the city woke up. Every time, as he put his shoes on, he'd say, "I don't know what I'm doing." And Yale would think, but not say, that they were both lost in the woods. Only Roman thought Yale knew the way out.

*

Roman liked to do it spooning on their sides, his chest against Yale's back. He'd drench both of them with sweat. He would groan, shaking, into Yale's hair. The first few times he was too fast, too spastic. Then he relaxed, learned to slow down, started to seem like he actually enjoyed it and it wasn't a thing to race through in shame. Now he'd even stick around and talk afterward.

Roman said, "No offense, and it's—I mean it's a *good* thing, but your dick is like a fucking pepper grinder. I mean, I've never seen—like, I don't really—" and Yale said, "Don't worry. I'm not gonna try to fuck you." Yale asked Roman if he'd thought about going to the Pride parade, which was ten days away. They were starting to sober up; it was three in the morning. "Just being counted matters," Yale said, and heard how he sounded like Charlie. "Last year we had thirty-five thousand."

Roman rolled toward Yale and grinned, his eyes molelike without his glasses. "You're saying size matters to you."

"I'm saying we want to top that."

Roman laughed, ran a finger up Yale's groin.

"It'd be good for you. There's something about seeing some drag queen doing a pole dance in a flatbed right there in the street that makes it easier to go back to work the next day and not worry about being a little faggy." Not that Yale went to work anymore. "And also—" but Roman sank his teeth into the top of Yale's ear, moved his hand up his side. "Also, it's educational."

"*You're* educational."

Yale hadn't heard from Roman since that night, and meanwhile he'd decided he might not even go to the parade himself. He bought a ticket for the Cubs-Mets game, which wouldn't start till 3:30 but at least gave him a fairly solid excuse, one he used when Asher called the day before the parade and asked if Yale could lend a hand on the AIDS Foundation of Chicago float. "Actually," Asher said, "it's not your hands we want. It's your cute face. We're wearing clothes, no Speedos involved. Unless you *want* to, of course. Who am I to stop you?" Yale would have done just about anything else for Asher, but he couldn't be in a *parade*, couldn't roll down the street past everyone he knew, couldn't run into Charlie in the staging area.

Ross—the redhead who'd been flirting with Yale in the Marina City gym for the past month—said if Yale wanted to hang out, some friends would be watching from a fire escape at Wellington and Clark, with mojitos. Yale didn't want to lead Ross on, but the setup was appealing. When he first moved to the city he'd been in love with all the fire escapes, kept feeling Audrey Hepburn might appear there with her guitar, her hair wrapped in a towel, that she might sing him "Moon River" and grab his hand and pull him across town.

He had a mental list of reasons not to go: He wanted to see Sandberg face off against Gooden. He didn't want to stand there getting turned on by beautiful shirtless men just to come home and jerk off sadly in the bathroom. He didn't feel like worrying about how he looked, scanning the crowd constantly for friends and former friends. He did not want to watch the *Out Loud* float go by. Plus, he worried every year that this would be the time someone would set off a bomb, open fire on the crowd. He'd watched on the news last night as a thousand KKK supporters filled a park in a black neighborhood on the southwest side. Yesterday it was racial slurs they were shouting, but they'd announced their plan to rally again in Lincoln Park before the parade, in the free-speech area. It couldn't end well.

Over the past four months he'd contacted every place he could think of, even the aquarium and the planetarium, small places in

Michigan, remote university galleries where he had no contacts. His CV was strong, but no one seemed to be hiring for more than grant writing. He'd been replaced at the Brigg, had gone in for the last time in early April.

Cecily still had her job. The gallery was in good shape. The lawsuit was off and Chuck Donovan had moved on to other ego battles. Yale called Bill once in a while to check in and learned that the restorations on the Modiglianis and the Hébuterne painting were going to take much longer than anyone had thought. Bill was beginning to doubt the show could go up next year. Yale himself had deleted the section of tape where Nora had talked about painting on Ranko's behalf. "One small step," he said to Roman, "in my journey to becoming Richard Nixon."

The Sharps had come to town for a week in April, and Yale had kept out of their way as best he could. He hid Roscoe over at Asher's place, where Roscoe got noticeably fatter. Allen, just because he'd called Yale up that one time, felt personally responsible for Yale quitting, despite everything Yale had told them both. They doubled down on their insistence that he stay there. They'd be in Barcelona for the summer anyway.

The morning of the parade, he tried calling Roman with the excuse of talking him into going. When Roman didn't answer, he found himself unduly disappointed. Out of proportion with how much he actually cared about Roman, which was only somewhat. Roman was fun and maybe Roman was therapy, but Roman certainly wasn't the only man in the world.

Which was another reason to go to the parade himself.

At eleven the phone rang, and Yale answered "Sharp residence" as always, although no one ever seemed to call for the Sharps.

It was his father's low, lazy grumble asking how everything was.

The way an underpaid nurse might, poking her head into your room to make sure you didn't need the bedpan changed.

Yale said, "I'm fine. I'm great."

"I'm sitting here doing the crossword, myself."

"Okay."

"I'll, ah, I'll thank you if you can give me a six-letter word for 'harpy.' I was sitting here the longest time thinking it said 'happy,' but no, it's 'harpy.'"

His father was the slowest talker in the world, a trait that drove Yale crazy in adolescence.

"I got nothing."

"What are you up to these days?"

There was no way to answer. Yale hadn't told him about the breakup, just the move. He'd never even told him he'd left the Art Institute last summer; the AIC was something his father had actually heard of, something he took some mote of pride in, and although surely he'd heard of Northwestern as well, Yale had figured he'd leave well enough alone.

He could have talked about the Cubs game, but instead he said, "I'm on my way to a parade." Because now that his father's voice was wrapping its way around his right ear, now that going to a ball game would have felt tainted by his father's approval, it was true: He was going to the parade.

"What kind of parade?"

"A really gay one, Dad. A big gay parade."

Yale read in his father's silence a kind of sarcasm. *Listen to yourself*, the silence said. *Do you hear how ridiculous that sounds?*

Yale said, "So I kind of need to run."

He thought his father would hang up, glad for the dismissal, but instead he said, "Listen, have you been following the news on this disease?"

Yale found himself stretching the phone cord to the window

just so he could make incredulous eye contact with his own reflection.

"No, Dad, I haven't. What disease would that be?"

"It's—are you being ironic with me? I can never tell."

"You know, the parade is starting. I really have to go."

"Alright then."

By the time he got to Clark, the route was packed and the first few floats had gone by. He wound his way behind people, looking for someone he recognized. At Wellington he looked for Ross and his friends and their fire escape, but not too hard. After two blocks, he spotted Katsu Tatami across the street, and when a few people ran across behind the Anheuser-Busch float, he crossed too. He didn't know the guys Katsu was standing with, but Katsu was always good for a hug, an enthusiastic greeting. He had to shout in Yale's ear: "So far so good! You want my soda?" He thrust a McDonald's cup at Yale, and a thought about germs flashed across Yale's mind, but he willfully ignored it. He took a sip and then wished he hadn't: warm, flat sugar water.

A bunch of Harleys rolled past, followed by a lesbian dojo—women kicking and chopping their way down the street, dressed in white. Miss Gay Wisconsin; earnest middle-aged women with PFLAG signs; a huge brass bed pulled by a convertible and occupied by two men making out with tremendous gusto, their torsos bare above a thin white sheet.

Yale asked Katsu how he was and Katsu said, "I'm becoming a legal expert." He explain-shouted that he'd gotten new insurance two years ago. In January he was feeling terrible and finally got tested—and he had it, did Yale know? Yeah, son of a bitch, he hadn't even told his mom—and his goddamned insurance was trying to claim that the virus was a preexisting condition so they wouldn't have to cover it. "Even though I got the insurance before

399

the fucking test came out! But they're claiming I *should*'ve known because three years ago I was treated for thrush. *One time.* And that's enough for them to turn me down." He needed pentamidine treatments, and he'd need hospital care that wasn't at fucking *County*, where he'd been a couple times, and was Yale aware what it smelled like in there? There was a reason it was free! So Asher was helping him apply for the Social Security he had to have before he could get Medicaid, because apparently that was how things worked in this stupid country. "And do you know what we have to prove? Okay, this is insane. We have to prove I'm disabled. Which I *am* now, because I could work maybe four days a week, but the fifth day I get the runs so bad I'm glued to the bathroom floor." This was tenable for his part-time gig at Howard Brown but not for the administrative assistant work that used to pay the bills and supply the useless insurance. "But the runs aren't a disability category, you know? So Asher's finding me this junior litigator, I guess? And here's what he has to prove at this hearing. He has to show that I can't do any *unskilled sedentary labor* in the national economy. Like, the entire nation. And the fucking *examples* they use! You want to hear the examples?"

Yale was exhausted just listening to Katsu, but sure, he wanted to hear. A drag queen passed on stilts in an elaborate Statue of Liberty costume, all green sparkles and gauze.

"I shit you not. *Nut sorter.* That's not a euphemism, by the way. Bowling ball polisher. Also not a euphemism! Silverware wrapper. Like, sitting there wrapping silverware in napkins. Everyone wants their spoons handled by a guy with the AIDS runs, right? Wafer topper. I don't even know what that means. The last one—for real—is fishhook inspector *in Alaska.* They don't care that I can't get to Alaska and I could never get this job. They care that it's a job *in the national economy.* So yeah, my survival now depends on my proving I can't top wafers."

Here came a bunch of guys in leather, a poster that read "*Bound Up With Pride!*" Some kind of garden club followed.

"But I'm gonna get in on whatever clinical trials I can, meantime."

"And Asher's helping," Yale said.

"Yeah. Asher. He can sort my nuts whenever he wants, am I right?"

Yale felt his face catch fire.

"Oh come on, you'd let him polish your bowling balls!"

Yale attempted a noncommittal laugh.

And here, ridiculously, before he could properly recover, was Asher's AFC float. Here was Asher, waving like a politician. Yale waved, but he didn't catch Asher's eye.

Three guys on unicycles came next, cutoffs and denim vests.

A series of aldermen and state senators in convertibles, most looking pained.

The *Out Loud* float. A red flatbed truck. Yale took a small step back so Katsu couldn't see his face, so he didn't have to worry what his eyes and mouth were doing.

Posterboard signs all over it: "Fight Out Loud for Safer Sex!" and "Out Loud Says / Cover Your Head!"

Six beautiful shirtless men—Yale didn't recognize them, except for Dwight the copy editor—angling cucumbers from their crotches, slowly rolling rubbers onto them. Peeling them off, doing it again. Opening new packets with their teeth, milking the crowd for cheers.

From the side of the truck, Gloria and Rafael threw rubbers from a bucket.

He couldn't see Charlie. And then suddenly he could. He had shaved his beard. He was the one holding the boom box that blasted "You Spin Me Round."

Yale tried to wrap his mind around the irony of the whole thing, but his body was busy reacting with some strange combination of high and low blood pressure.

A Trojan hit Katsu on the chest and he caught it, laughing, and handed it to Yale. He said, "I'm a LifeStyles man. You want?" And although Yale could not see an occasion in which he'd want to use a rubber that had come, indirectly, from Charlie, he stuck it in the pocket of his shorts. He'd need to get used to them. Until he'd redone the test in March, until Dr. Cheng had told him that again the ELISA was negative—though this time he really had made Yale wait two weeks, as he'd vowed—Yale had barely let himself ejaculate in the same *room* as Roman. Lately, since the second negative, he'd been letting Roman suck him off—though what did "lately" really mean, when it was all so sporadic?

Yale wished the *Out Loud* float would disappear, but it was still making its slow way down Clark, Trojans still flying.

Someone scratched him between the shoulder blades, and he turned to see Teddy grinning, bouncing. "Look who came out of hiding!" Teddy said. Yale should have known that Teddy might have been part of Katsu's group—and honestly it was good to see him. Good, especially, that Teddy was talking as if he didn't think Yale was a monster.

Teddy told them about the Klan activity in the park. He said, "They're gone now. They didn't want to actually *see* any of this, you know? They left right before the parade started."

Katsu said, "I bet half are secretly sticking around. Bet they're jacking off under their robes."

"Only one guy had a robe, actually. I found that so disappointing! They had, like, combat gear, with these weird little shields."

Yale said, "What do they even want? Besides attention?"

"Um, according to their giant banner, they want to *quarantine the queers*. Real original. Anyway, we yelled back for a long time, and these dykes made out right in front of them. Then they just packed up. I stuck around to talk to a reporter. Anyone want a hot dog? I'm starving."

There was no point trying to move till the parade was over, and when it finally was, they followed the crowd to the park for the rally. Katsu took off, and Yale found himself alone with Teddy in an endless line for food. Yale said, "I hope we're still friends."

"I was mad at you, but it was temporary. I was judging you for being judgmental. Ironic, right?"

"I'm not sure I was being judgmental. I know that for you the news was Charlie testing positive, but for me the news was him cheating on me. Maybe everyone else already knew, but I didn't. And things hadn't been great between us for a long time. We actually—he accused me of sleeping with you, the night of Nico's memorial."

Teddy whistled between his teeth. "Yeah, I don't remember fucking you." He laughed. "Must not've been that good."

The line lurched, and Yale checked to make sure the guys behind them were strangers. He said, "I feel like we're all caught up in some huge cycle of judgment. We spent our whole lives unlearning it, and here we are."

"The thing is," Teddy said, "the disease *itself* feels like a judgment. We've all got a little Jesse Helms on our shoulder, right? If you got it from sleeping with a thousand guys, then it's a judgment on your promiscuity. If you got it from sleeping with one guy once, that's almost worse, it's like a judgment on all of us, like the act itself is the problem and not the number of times you did it. And if you got it because you thought you couldn't, it's a judgment on your hubris. And if you got it because you knew you could and you didn't care, it's a judgment on how much you hate yourself. Isn't that why the world loves Ryan White so much? How could God have it out for some poor kid with a blood disorder? But then people are *still* being terrible. They're judging him just for *being sick*, not even for the way he got it."

Yale tended to find Teddy mentally draining, but he was right this time.

Way over at the bandstand, Mayor Washington had begun to speak. "As a black man who has suffered discrimination," he was saying, "as part of a race of people who have suffered . . ." and Teddy said, "He's a good one, yeah? We lucked out."

"He'll be up for reelection by the time we get out of this line."

Teddy said, "Check out the cast of *The Addams Family* over there."

Yale looked and couldn't see.

"Three o'clock, behind the guy with the bird."

Yale saw, first, a dark-haired man with a blue and green macaw perched on his shoulder. He was laughing with someone, and for a second it was hard to look at anything other than this beautiful man and his beautiful bird. But then behind him, Yale saw a group of terribly chic young people, all dressed in black. One of them was Roman. Yale started to wave but stopped.

He had never seen Roman's friends, and this wasn't what he'd pictured: two tall, pale, handsome men who may or may not have been gay, but given the surroundings probably were, and a young woman with waist-length blonde hair, a silver ring in her nose. What on earth had he imagined? He hadn't let himself think about it that much, was the thing. In general, the more he thought about Roman, the more confused he became. Roman was best as a shadow that came in the night, an empty screen onto which he could project whatever he wanted. Roman was not the kind of person who showed up to Pride, on his own, with fabulous friends Yale had never heard about. Roman stayed home and worked on his dissertation.

Teddy said, "I know the one with glasses."

"The one with glasses?"

Yale's brain turned slow, arthritic cartwheels. Roman wasn't even supposed to be here. That wasn't Roman. He tried to get a better angle. Roman's glasses, Roman's bony shoulders.

"He's a piece of work," Teddy said.

"Where do you know him from?"

"I mean . . ." Teddy shrugged and laughed.

"No, seriously."

How many nights had Roman come over? How drunk had Yale been? What had happened, exactly, and on what bed and when? He'd been careful about *himself*, protecting Roman. They hadn't been careful the other way. Because Roman was a virgin. Because Roman was a virgin. Yale said, "*Tell me.*"

"He's not *that* hot, chill out. I met him last year at my friend Michael's lecture at the Cultural Center. He's got this whole tortured artist thing going on, like he just suddenly has to leave the room and be alone."

"Oh." Yale relaxed. "I thought you met him at a bathhouse or something."

"God, Yale, I go other places. I mean—" he laughed, leaned close "—I ploughed him like a fresh spring field, but we definitely met at the Cultural Center."

Yale let Teddy step ahead of him in line. The park was more sound than color now, more vibration than reality. If he opened his eyes, he'd be in bed next to Charlie, and it would be last summer. He told Teddy he'd be back and he stepped toward Roman's group, which was still quite far away. He needed to see that it wasn't Roman. The mayor was still talking, and the air still smelled like hot dogs, and yes, it was Roman standing there looking bored, just like his bored and beautiful friends.

Yale might have run home and hidden under his blankets, but instead he made his way past a pack of leatherdykes, past the guy with the bird, and straight to Roman. Roman tried to angle his body away, a teenager who didn't want his friends knowing that this embarrassing person was his dad. Yale said, "May I have a word?"

One of the boys in black hooted; the other said, "Who is *she*?"

Roman opened his mouth as if he wanted to make an excuse not to talk, but then he wiped his brow with the back of his arm and stepped away with Yale. Yale didn't care if Teddy looked over and saw them together. He was far beyond caring.

He said, "We'll make this really quick. Did you misrepresent yourself?"

"I'm sorry?"

"I should have been—I should have asked you more questions. I should have made you take some kind of written exam. Is this what you do? You go around doing the confused Mormon act? Like, role-playing?"

Roman said, "What are you talking about?" His friends were watching, snickering. They were too far away to hear. "I'm a Mormon. That wasn't a lie."

"But you're a Mormon who sleeps with a lot of men. Who's been doing this for a long time."

"Well, no. Not a lot. I mean, I *used* to. I was trying to be monogamous."

For a second Yale thought Roman meant monogamy with *him*, that their hazy midnight assignations were meant to be some kind of steady relationship, but that made no sense. And Roman kept talking.

"Or, like, I *had* been, and then he was—like, he felt kind of suffocated, I guess. He was trying to get rid of me, or I thought he was. He wanted me to be with you, and I didn't even really want it. Not that I'm not attracted to you, just—I don't know. But then after that first time in Wisconsin, he *knew*, and all of a sudden he was so jealous. He wanted me to quit."

Yale tried to understand who this boyfriend was who knew about Yale, who knew about Wisconsin, and then he got it, he got it.

Roman said, "If you're mad because he fired you or whatever, I mean, I'm mad, too, but it's not about *us*. I mean, really you quit, right? He likes you! He was seriously bummed when you left. Look, did he tell you to do it?"

"I'm sorry?"

"Since we're already talking. I've always wondered, and it won't hurt my feelings. Did he tell you to come on to me, that first time? It's so weird, he wanted to push me away, and then ever since it happened, he got possessive as hell. He's still—I don't know. Do you think I should leave him?"

Yale had too much to work out, and the sun was too hot, and his stomach was too empty, and what he needed to do was go home and find his fucking pocket calendar, go through the whole hellish calculus again. And it should be easier this time, he should feel stronger, knowing he'd already dodged a bullet, but it wouldn't be, because this didn't feel like a bullet but a cannonball.

Roman was still looking at him, earnestly waiting for advice. He'd been nothing but honest, it was true. Whatever Yale had projected onto him was his own fault.

Yale said, "Yes, you should leave him. For fuck's sake. He's married to a woman, and he smells like mothballs. I need to know if you've been tested."

"What, like the—oh. That. I don't know, I keep reading all these things about how it's not really accurate. And also, like, I don't do that kind of stuff."

"I'm sorry, what kind of stuff?"

"You know, needles and fisting and alleys."

"Needles and fisting and alleys?"

"You know what I mean."

Yale turned from him without saying goodbye, and he didn't go back to Teddy either. He headed south through the park instead of north, even though he should walk straight to Dr. Cheng's office. Well, no: It was Sunday, and it was Pride, and no one would be there.

He walked along the harbor and then the lagoon, and he wandered back up through the zoo, and he ended up in the conservatory. He hadn't been inside in ages: a glass bubble of tropical plants, the only sound the waterfalls, the only light the filtered sun.

He walked back to the third room, the quietest, the emptiest, and he sat down right in the middle of the floor.

2015

Fiona didn't sleep at all, but she waited till morning. When Richard was in the shower and couldn't stop her, she stepped outside onto the eerily quiet streets. The movie production had halted; the vans remained in place, the blockades stacked against the buildings. On nearly every corner stood paratroopers with red berets and machine guns, as if some child had spilled a tub of army toys all over Paris. She was surprised to find a cab. The driver might have been Somali or Ethiopian. He didn't talk. He took her to the address she gave for Claire's bar, and when she saw the gate pulled over the entrance, the hand-lettered sign, she directed him straight back to where he'd found her.

Cecily's plane had landed just after the attacks began, and she was at baggage claim when the news reached her. She'd managed to get through to Fiona at one in the morning, and by early afternoon she was in Richard's flat, taking her shoes off in the doorway. Fiona hadn't seen her in ten years, didn't know which changes were exhaustion and which were age. Cecily did look like a grandmother. People in their seventies could be grandmothers. Fifty-one-year-olds should still be leading spin classes and staying out too late, in Fiona's opinion.

"What happened to your hand?" Cecily asked, and Fiona said,

"Stigmata." Cecily didn't laugh. Well, she'd never had much of a sense of humor.

Fiona got her some tea, told her about her meeting with Claire, although she didn't quite convey the humiliation.

Cecily sat on Richard's couch, her body angled toward the window. She said, "I've never seen Paris before. What a strange time to get here."

"I hate that we have to live in the middle of history. We make enough mess on our own."

Cecily smiled. "I've missed you."

"Richard says hello. He's gone to his studio. It's funny, I went out myself today, but it scares me that other people are out. I mean, Richard can't *run* if something goes wrong."

Cecily agreed, and Fiona told her she couldn't reach Claire. Cecily said, "It's natural to worry, but I'm *sure* she's fine." It hadn't occurred to Fiona till then to worry about Kurt as well. Kurt was more likely to be out at night. She didn't imagine he liked heavy metal, but still.

Serge came through the front door then, hair sticking up with sweat, eyes ringed. He nodded at them both and ducked into the bedroom.

"I feel I'm imposing," Cecily said, and Fiona assured her she wasn't.

"We're all in crisis mode here," she said, "just for different reasons. Listen: What I think we could do, is go to Kurt's apartment. Maybe he'd let us have Claire's number, given the situation. And now that I've seen her myself."

Cecily examined her unpolished nails. "Better if I go alone, don't you think?"

Maybe—and besides, they'd want privacy. Fiona wouldn't have wanted some third party there when she'd seen Claire the first time.

So after some lunch, after Fiona walked her down and got her a cab, Cecily took off for the Marais. She promised to call the instant she knew anything.

When Fiona came back upstairs, Serge was in the kitchen with his laptop. "I yelled at you last night," he said. She understood this was his apology. "Your daughter is not on Facebook?"

She almost laughed. How much easier that would have made everything. A message to her in-box, rather than flights and detectives. "No," she said. "I'm not either." Damian was, and he'd checked obsessively over the past few years.

"So, two things. One is, people can check in safe, like this." She looked over his shoulder, saw a list of names and faces, friends of Serge who'd marked themselves alive. "But here," he said, and he clicked to something new, "this is a forum to ask after people. I write a message, okay?"

She nodded and he started to type.

"Claire what?"

She grabbed the grocery pad and pen from beside the stove and wrote for him: *Claire Yael Blanchard.* "I guess she could be using Pearce. For a last name." And she wrote that too.

"Okay," he said. "Posted. We wait." Dear God, it was exactly what Arnaud had said to her, what felt like a thousand years ago. *We wait.*

Damian called and she filled him in.

"Do you think she's scared?" Damian asked.

"I hope not. I mean, not more than everyone else. She's not a kid anymore."

"But she's a mother."

"Right," Fiona said. "Right."

"Maybe this is how we get her home."

Fiona doubted it. The chaos of the world had never helped her before. That it might help now seemed ridiculous.

She said, "Let's not get greedy."

411

July 15, 1986

Lake Michigan, impossibly blue, the morning light bouncing toward the city.

Lake Michigan frozen in sheets you could walk on but wouldn't dare.

Lake Michigan, gray out a high-rise window, indistinguishable from the sky.

Bread, hot from the oven. Or even stale in the restaurant basket, rescued by salty butter.

The Cubs winning the pennant someday. The Cubs winning the Series. The Cubs continuing to lose.

His favorite song, not yet written. His favorite movie, not yet made.

The depth of an oil brushstroke. Chagall's blue windows. Picasso's blue man and his guitar.

Dr. Cheng said, "I'm going to write down everything I say to you, so you can read it again later."

The sound of an old door creaking open. The sound of garlic cooking. The sound of typing. The sound of commercials from the next room, when you were in the kitchen getting a drink. The sound of someone else finishing a shower.

All of them growing old together on the Yacht for Old Queers that Asher always joked about. Right off the Belmont Rocks, he said, with binoculars for everyone.

Art Nouveau streetlights. Elevators with gates.

Fiona having kids. Being a surrogate uncle, buying the kids sweaters and gum and books. Taking them to the museum. Saying, "Your Uncle Nico was a good artist, and maybe you will be too." If it was a girl, letting her paint his nails. If it was a boy, taking him to ball games. You could take a girl to ball games too.

Dr. Cheng said, "You're young and you're strong, and you're going to take excellent care of yourself."

Good, thick, Turkish coffee. Sanka with too much cream after a long dinner. Sad, weak office coffee.

The year 2000. The last party of 1999.

Red wine. Beer. Vodka tonics on a summer day.

Christmas, which he'd just really started to love.

Getting to Australia someday. Sweden. Japan.

*

Dr. Cheng said, "I know the last thing you feel like right now is having more blood drawn, but we're going to get your T-cell count today. Since we know this is a brand-new infection, I expect your count to be very strong. So we'll have some good news on top of the bad. We'll do the draw right here."

Arthritis. Gray hair. Bushy eyebrows, like his father's. Dentures, canes, prostate issues.

His twenty-fifth high school reunion. He might really have gone, despite everything.

A dog he could walk by the lake.

Dr. Cheng said, "You might not feel like talking at first, but I'm writing down the info for the Test Positive Aware Network support group. It's on the bottom of the first page here."

The brutal wind on the El platform. Fifty people huddled under the heating lamp. Pigeons crowding at their feet.

Owning a house. Painting the door, so he could tell his friends to look for the purple door.

The foods that hadn't yet made their way to America. The things he hadn't tasted that everyone would be crazy for in ten years.

The way Chicago looked from an airplane window, flying in from the east. The only time you could really see the city's face.

Dr. Cheng said, "We have no idea what advances are down the road. In my opinion it's a waiting game. Because better medicine is out there. Some flower in the Amazon, who knows. It could be tomorrow, it could be next year. There's no reason not to believe that at some point there will be survivors."

The cement beach up by Bryn Mawr, the psychedelic foot someone had painted there.

The next Harvey Milk. The first gay senator, the first gay governor, the first woman president, the last bigoted congressman.

Dancing till the floor was an optional landing place. Dancing elbows out, dancing with arms up, dancing in a pool of sweat.

All the books he hadn't started.

The man at Wax Trax! Records with the beautiful eyelashes. The man who sat every Saturday at Nookies, reading the *Economist* and eating eggs, his ears always strangely red. The ways his own life might have intersected with theirs, given enough time, enough energy, a better universe.

The love of his life. Wasn't there supposed to be a love of his life?

Dr. Cheng said, "Our counselor is here today, and I'm going to have Gretchen walk you down the hall and wait with you till he's available."

His body, his own stupid, slow, hairy body, its ridiculous desires, its aversions, its fears. The way his left knee cracked in the cold.

The sun, the moon, the sky, the stars.

*

The end of every story.

Oak trees.

Music.

Breath.

Dr. Cheng said, "Whoa, there, let's lie down. Let's get you lying down."

2015

Serge said the phone signals were jammed all over the city. Which was *possibly* why Fiona hadn't heard from Claire, and likely why she hadn't heard from Cecily, who'd been gone all afternoon.

Fiona had become, throughout the day, simultaneously more and less panicked. Less, because many names of the dead had been released, and Claire's and Nicolette's were not among them. More, because she still hadn't heard anything. Less, again, when she realized the problem with the phones. More, every time she stopped to think about it.

At six o'clock, Cecily finally buzzed up from the street. "He's with me," she said.

It was hard to tell how much, if at all, Cecily and Kurt had reconciled in that time. The fact that he came with her certainly meant something. But they wore matching looks of concern, and the vibe Fiona got was more of two people assisting each other through crisis than of some touching mother-son reunion. They sat a couple of feet apart on the couch. Fiona knew this must be painful for Cecily— but she couldn't imagine being the one, as a mother, who'd broken off contact, the one who'd given up. Well, no; she mustn't confuse it with what her own parents had done to Nico. Cecily had been protecting herself after Kurt stole from her and lied to her, again and again. She hadn't rejected a helpless teenager. Still.

Kurt said, "I left her three messages." The woman whose apartment shared a kitchen with Claire's, he said, would have found a way to get him word if something bad had happened, if Claire had never come home. "I'm worried, but I don't have a *reason* to be worried. And there's no way she was out that late."

Fiona didn't mean to shout, but it came out too loud: "Can't you just go over there?"

"That's not our—we have an arrangement. Not a legal arrangement, but if I ever showed up when it wasn't my day, she'd split. She's made that crystal clear."

Cecily said, "But in an emergency situation—"

"No," Kurt said.

A siren blasted right outside the window. It was short—police warning someone to move out of an intersection maybe. Nevertheless, all three of them jolted, and Fiona's heart started beating like a hamster's.

"Give me the address," she said. "I'll say someone at the bar gave it to me, and if that doesn't work I'll say I tricked you. I broke into your apartment and got it off an envelope." It wouldn't be far from the truth. "No, wait, I'll say the detective found it."

Cecily put a hand on Kurt's knee. "Wouldn't that be for the best?" she said. "Then you'd know they were safe."

He seemed to relax, rather than bristle, under Cecily's touch.

If nothing good came of this for Fiona, at least maybe she'd have been responsible for the Pearce family reconciliation. Maybe Cecily could send her weekly updates on Nicolette, as she got to watch her grow up, as Fiona sat home alone in Chicago.

Fiona handed him her phone. "Just type it into my GPS," she said. "As far as she knows, I haven't seen you in years."

Kurt sighed and took the phone.

As soon as she had it back, Fiona grabbed her purse. She said,

"If you want to wait here, you can." Kurt squeezed Fiona's shoulder with his giant hand.

Saint-Denis was a zoo of blocked-off streets. The cab driver had asked three times if she was sure she wanted to head up there.

"I wait to make sure you get in," he said. "You here long? I wait to drive you back too."

She told him she'd be three minutes. She hoped she'd be coming out to tell him he could leave, to give him an extra tip.

A young man was heading in the door right ahead of her, so instead of messing with the jumble of buzzers and names, she followed him into the narrow hallway. The place was labyrinthine, but she finally found number eight. A red plastic bucket and green plastic shovel outside the door.

She knocked with her uninjured left hand, which felt wrong, unlucky.

When Claire opened the door, she left the chain in place.

She said, "What the fuck."

"Honey, just—"

"No, this is not okay."

"I had no other way to reach you."

"This is not okay."

Her hair was pulled up sloppily on top of her head. She looked as if she hadn't slept.

"You're safe?"

"Obviously."

"I'm alright, too, in case you were concerned."

"Listen, it's her nap time." Claire's voice softened slightly. "This, just—I can't deal with this right now."

"I understand."

"I'm not sure you do."

"Can you give me your number, at least? So I don't have to stalk you at work?"

419

"I have *your* number."

"Listen, what's the harm?"

"*This* is the harm."

"Okay." Fiona put her hands up in surrender. "You're alive, your daughter's alive, that's all I needed. I'll leave now."

Claire let out a loud, angry sigh that Fiona couldn't begin to decipher.

Fiona wanted to storm off, but the whole point of coming to Paris—she and her shrink, together, had been clear on this point—was to put herself out there. To keep her arms open even when Claire closed hers. To be the parent, not the child. She said, "Call anytime. I love you, sweetie."

Claire shut the door without saying anything, without even waving.

1986

That September, Katsu Tatami fell on the street. Someone took him to the ER at Masonic, where he was sent up to the AIDS unit. Teddy reported that Katsu was wishing aloud to die before he was stable enough to be dumped back into County. But he got stable, and back he went. County discharged him almost immediately, and when he was unable to breathe the next day, they told him they no longer had an available bed. He waited two weeks, not quite bad enough to go back to the Masonic ER, until finally, too late to do much good, County readmitted him.

Yale knew he had to visit eventually. Partly because it was the right thing to do, and partly because in the worst-case scenario, he'd end up at County himself, and he needed to see it, needed to get it over with.

One night, he pulled on Julian's dental floss and the last of the string came out, just long enough to use. He tried not to take it as a bad sign, but it felt like one. He decided to visit Katsu the next morning, before it was too late.

He'd been a finalist for a job at Saint Louis University, and he was still in the running for a regular development job at DePaul, here in the city, but he was still unemployed. Dr. Cheng had told him to take the first job that offered insurance. "The bigger the company the better," Dr. Cheng said, "so you'll get lost in the shuffle." Meanwhile he was on COBRA, which would quickly drain his savings. He could afford it till January, barely, and then he'd have to choose between insurance and food.

In the meantime Dr. Cheng would keep the tests off Yale's record. As far as he was concerned, Yale had only come to see him for a sore throat. When he applied for new insurance, Yale would just be asked about a history of AIDS—not about the virus. "You will not be lying when you say no," Dr. Cheng said. "And then a month after you're approved, you come in for the test again. Officially." But it was risky, and if it was ever discovered—if the government seized test results, anonymous as Dr. Cheng claimed he'd kept them; or if Yale was in an accident, had blood drawn at the hospital, etcetera—he could be denied coverage forever. He'd wind up like Katsu, praying one of the beds at County would be open when he needed it.

Yale called Asher, hoping he'd say something reassuring, but what Asher said was "Get a job fast."

Complicating matters was the fact that he could no longer get a letter of recommendation from Bill Lindsey. And it didn't look great that Yale had worked at Northwestern less than a year.

Right after his own positive test, Yale had sent a note to Roman through campus mail, and then he'd addressed a letter to Bill at the office:

I have specific reason to believe that if you haven't done so already, you might consider getting tested for HTLV-III, the virus known to cause AIDS. I hope you'll advise your wife to take this test as well; please be assured that I have not contacted her and will not do so.

He'd thought for days about Dolly Lindsey, ways to reach out to her. He'd debated it with Asher, with Teddy, with Fiona. They all surprised him by shaking their heads in the same skeptical way, saying, "I don't think you really can." Teddy had thrown some Kant at him, made a particularly compelling argument. In August he heard from Cecily that Dolly had left Bill. "I've seen her around town," Cecily said. "Shopping and stuff. Really, Yale, I don't think they were even sleeping together, do you?" But he'd never heard back from Bill, with the exception of a note written in Bill's spidery script, attached to a stack of semipersonal mail the gallery had forwarded him: *It's grand to hear you've landed on your feet!* Yale had indicated no such thing. He heard from Donna the docent that Bill was no longer talking about retirement.

His visit to County would be short; Katsu was doped up, and Yale wanted to get the hell out of there. The beds were all in one huge room, separated only by hanging sheets, so that the sounds and smells of thirty different stages of death surrounded you. How anyone could sleep in that place, how anyone could harbor a single hope, Yale couldn't fathom.

Katsu said to him—slurred, really—"My armpits hurt. Why do my armpits hurt so bad?"

Yale had brought him a milkshake, and he left it on his tray for when he felt up to it. He knew from Teddy that Katsu kept his Walkman under his pillow so it wouldn't get stolen, but no one would steal a milkshake, would they? Certainly not the nurse who'd avoided even looking at Katsu when she changed his IV bag.

Yale wanted to get Asher in there to raise hell, but what could he possibly accomplish? Yale had signed his own power of attorney over to Asher last month, confident that Asher would at least know how to yell at the right people.

Katsu said, "Can you make them turn the lights off?" But the lights were huge and fluorescent and covered the whole area, and Yale already knew they *never* turned them off, even at night. He folded two Kleenexes together and put them over Katsu's eyes, a makeshift sleeping mask.

When he got home, the strangest thing: a letter addressed to him in Charlie's print. Charlie's odd way of making *E*'s, three floating rungs with no vertical support. Light blue paper, dark blue pen.

He'd heard, it said. It said that Teddy and Asher and Fiona, all three, had assured him he wasn't directly responsible, but that he wanted to hear it from Yale. It was terrible, Charlie wrote, to assign blame to people rather than to the virus itself or to the power structures that let it thrive, but he couldn't help it, and he wanted to know. Even though he was, at the very least, *indirectly* responsible. He wanted absolution, Yale gathered. It wasn't something Yale was ready to grant.

Yale didn't write back, but he didn't throw the letter away either. Six months ago he might have burned it. Now he smoothed it flat and put it under the pewter bowl on the dresser, the one he kept his change in.

He picked up Roscoe and carried him to the window and stood looking down at the river, at the tour boat gliding by, impossibly slow. Soon enough it had passed.

Richard said, "The best one for dancing was Paradise. I'm sure that's long gone as well."

Fiona said, "Brace yourself: It's a Walmart now."

"No." He turned from his studio sink, hands dripping. Serge, from the reclining chair in the corner, listened with amusement. Cecily sat with Fiona at the big wooden table. She wore a beige turtleneck sweater today, one that in its solid plainness made her look protected—from the chaos of the city, the poison darts of family.

"It's like they were *trying* to be symbolic," Fiona said. "At least it's not a GOP headquarters or something. Richard, listen, there's a Starbucks at Belmont and Clark. It's—it's not as sterile as I'm making it sound. But it's not the same. Every winter they have this soup walk. You go from restaurant to restaurant, and you get soup. Everyone's out there: gay guys, straight couples, babies in strollers. And soup. It's beautiful. You wouldn't *want* it to be the same. Because the vibe before, it came from an outsider place, and there was—you know, there was desperation all around. Even before AIDS."

"So it's grown up," Richard said.

"No more Boystown!" Serge laughed. "Man's town!" No one else appreciated it.

Richard said, "Do you ever think it's just a fleeting moment?"

No, she didn't. Not really. It was hard to imagine going back, losing ground.

He said, "Because I do. I'm sure I'd roll my eyes at the gentrification, but listen, honey, I'm old and I've seen a lot of shit, and I'm telling you, let's enjoy it while it lasts. Because this isn't Mother May I. You're not always advancing. I know it feels that way right now, but it's fragile. You might look back in fifty years and say, *That was the last good time.*"

Fiona pulled her sleeves over her hands. It was so tempting to think of the fires of her twenties as being the great historical struggle of her life, all past tense. Even her work at the store, her lobbying and fundraising, always felt like aftermath. People were still dying, just more slowly, with a bit more dignity. Well, in Chicago, at least. She considered it one of her great moral failings that, deep down, she didn't care on quite the same visceral level about the ongoing AIDS crisis in Africa. It didn't stop her from donating money to those charities, but it bothered her that she didn't feel it in her core, didn't cry herself to sleep over it. A million people in the world had died of AIDS in the past year, and she hadn't cried about it once. A million people! She spent a long time asking herself if she was racist, or if it was about the width of the Atlantic Ocean. Or maybe it was because it wasn't happening primarily to the gay community there, wasn't only killing beautiful young men who reminded her of Nico and his friends. Of course all altruism was in some way selfish. And maybe, too, she only had room in her heart, in this lifetime, for one big cause, the arc of one disaster. Claire, it seemed, had certainly grown up feeling it—that her mother's greatest love was always focused on something just over the horizon of the past.

Cecily said, "That's the difference between optimism and naievty. No one in this room is naive. Naive people haven't been

426

through real trials yet, so they think it could never happen to them. Optimists have been through it already, and we keep getting up each day because we believe we can keep it from happening again. Or we trick ourselves into thinking it."

Richard said, "All belief is a trick."

Serge said, "No one in France is an optimist."

Richard's studio was L-shaped, with screens and cameras and lights at one end, desks and computers and mess at the other, and in the middle—where they all were now—a seating area, a kitchenette. The place had been decimated by the move to the museum, and loose power cords and packing peanuts littered the floor. Fiona had not come here to see the videos. She'd made it clear—this wasn't the right time.

It was two o'clock on Sunday. Tomorrow was supposed to be Richard's *vernissage*, but everything was still up in the air. There was a manhunt for one of the terror suspects under way near the Belgian border. As soon as they'd gotten to the studio, they'd locked the door behind them. The radio on the counter played the BBC news too softly to hear, and Serge kept updating them from his Twitter feed, but there wasn't much to report. Richard was waiting on the call from the Pompidou, the decision on whether it would open at all tomorrow, let alone proceed with the festivities. Even if things were a go, the party would be sparsely attended. The Pompidou wasn't far from the Bataclan Music Hall, which was still a "scene of carnage," according to the news, although the only photos Fiona could bear to look at were of flower heaps, teddy bears. Some of the most important guests would have been coming from out of town, and lord knew what would happen to their flights, their trains.

Late last night, Damian had called to say that Claire had emailed him at his university address. Just five sentences to say she was fine and he shouldn't worry. He spelled Claire's email address

427

for her—an address she wasn't supposed to use, of course—and he read her the email twice through. No apology, but no anger, no stiffness either. How different from the two tense conversations she'd had with Fiona.

Well, Claire's issues were largely with *her*, not with Damian. The child psychologist had explained it, years ago: They lash out at the parent they live with, the safe one. And it came out during therapy that Claire understood far more than they'd hoped about Fiona's affair. "She believes," the psychologist had said, "that you were looking for another family, a better family."

Fiona stuck the piece of paper with Claire's email address into her bedside drawer. She had already memorized it.

Richard's phone finally rang, and he retreated down to his desk to pace and talk. When he returned, he shook his head. "Not the Pompidou," he said. "At this point, if they call, I'm going to say no. I want to wait a week. Next Monday, don't you think? They can let the public in whenever the hell they want, but if we're doing the *vernissage* at all, we're doing it right. But listen, good news. Fiona, I told you there was a surprise for you. It was going to happen tomorrow night, but—you know."

Fiona braced herself. Richard sometimes had strange ideas of what other people would enjoy, and if he was about to present her with a video of Nico, she wouldn't be able to handle it.

"That was the call," he said. "Go wait by the door, okay? Two minutes. You'll see."

"Just me?"

"Just you."

She gave him a skeptical look but walked out into the hall and then into the little entryway, where she could see through the glass door and onto the street. Her stomach didn't feel good. Her head didn't feel good.

A dark-haired man in a blue coat passed, looking at his phone, and then backed up and faced the door fully. He grinned at her.

He was around her age, with strange cheekbones, a face that was somehow *wrong*, skewed, scrambled.

Then the features rearranged themselves, and rearranged themselves again, and instead of unlatching the door, letting him in, Fiona took a step backward, because she was looking at a ghost.

This man could not be, but was, Julian Ames.

And because he was still grinning at her—because what else was she supposed to do?—she finally stumbled forward and figured out the lock and tried to push the door before realizing she needed to pull, needed to flatten her body against the wall to make room.

He clasped her arms, brought his face close to hers.

He said, "Well, look at *you*!"

1988, 1989

Charlie had an infected eyelid. This was what Asher told him, and then he said, "I'm not going to update you on every little thing, but I thought I'd tell you, and then I thought I'd ask how often you want a report. Basically, the doctors are saying this definitely counts now as rapid progression."

Asher's Chevette was heading down Lake Shore Drive, and they both had to shout over the engine roar. Yale had grown skittish about public transportation, about the germs on the handrails, the spittle in people's coughs. He'd do it occasionally, but he was tired today and the AZT made his legs weak, and so he didn't feel bad taking Asher up on the ride home from support group. Besides which it was the first spring day when you could drive with the window down, and the lake looked like a glassy cliff, like if you walked to the horizon you could jump off the edge of the world.

Yale said, "Mostly people have been filling me in on the drugs. Like I'm supposed to take some perverse pleasure in this."

Asher turned on the radio, but it was just ads. He said, "I want to throttle him. He could be doing so much good with that money."

About a year ago, thanks to the sudden proliferation of 1-900 numbers and the companies willing to spend a lot of money advertising them, Charlie's paper had become, for the first time, quite lucrative—more lucrative than Yale had ever imagined a gay newspaper could be. On top of this, he'd sold off the travel agency—just cashed out, intending to spend his remaining time in luxury, if not in comfort. And then he had apparently spent all the money on coke. It surprised Yale, at least in the sense that Charlie had been, in the past, a highly selective drug user—and it also didn't surprise him at all. But meanwhile the paper was falling apart, or at least the staff was. Rafael had defected to *Out and Out*, Dwight was dead, and Gloria was still there but wasn't speaking to Charlie. There were new people, but from what Yale had heard, they hated Charlie, and Charlie hated them, and it was, in general, a horror show.

One of the stranger results of Charlie's coke habit was that, following a long pause after that first letter, he'd taken to writing Yale manic eight-page missives about once a month. Yale suspected he wasn't the only one receiving these letters, but he was presumably the only one for whom Charlie made obsessive lists with titles like "Dreams I've Had About You" and "Here Are All the Books You Left." Some of them were darkly funny. "Ways I'll Kill Myself If the Republicans Win This Fall" included an entry on letting leeches suck all his blood and then having someone serve those leeches at the inaugural ball.

Charlie never proposed meeting. After that first, needy letter, he never asked for anything at all. Yale had become a figure in a writing exercise, a static memory for Charlie to bounce feelings off of. He never apologized, either, not in so many words. There were just the lists, and then, in jagged print that carved at the page, meticulous accounts of his days: what he ate, his weight, his digestive issues, the plots of movies he'd seen. He was keeping strictly vegetarian, and Dr. Vincent implored him to eat more protein. Teresa had gotten herself an apartment not far from Charlie's, and Martin seemed a permanent appendage, although Charlie spared

Yale any details about their sex life, including whether they even had one. Sometimes the letters weren't about Charlie at all. Once, for no discernible reason, there were five pages about Wanda Lust, a drag queen who'd died before Yale even moved to the city.

Yale tended to wait a few days before opening a letter. He'd sit, finally, on Saturday morning with coffee, consider the thickness of the envelope, and finally slide a finger under the flap. He'd never written back. Not out of spite or stubbornness so much as the fact that he couldn't imagine where to begin.

The letters had softened him on Charlie, at least a bit. Had made him seem less the villain and more the pathetic sap Yale had always known he really was.

Over the past two years, he'd seen Charlie from a distance a number of times. He imagined Charlie had seen *him* from a distance too, on days when Yale was too distracted to notice. He imagined that Charlie caught his breath, turned, made some excuse to leave the party, the bar, the meeting—the same way Yale always did.

Yale tried to picture an infected eyelid. *Puffy*, he assumed. *Red.* It made his own eyes water.

They turned off the Drive and at least the engine was quieter now.

Asher said, "I think he's scared. I—Okay, I'm just going to say this. He wants to see you."

"I doubt it."

"No, he told me. Several times. I'm supposed to tell you that he wants to see you."

Yale had meant to knock the side of his head into the window, but since the window was down, his head flopped out into the rushing air.

"Think about it. I'm just planting a seed."

"If he wants to apologize, that's one thing. I'll—I'd consider giving him some closure. But I'm not swooping in to hold his hand."

"I know."

Asher had one of those "GAY $" stamps and a pad of red ink in his center ashtray, and Yale wondered if he was still stamping all his money. He picked up the stamp, ran his thumb along the letters. Leave it to Asher to keep this stuff in the car so he could engage in civil protest the instant he got his change at the McDonald's drive-thru.

Yale would at least have things to *talk* about with Charlie, information with which to fill the void. The fact that he'd never written back meant he had endless fuel. Charlie might not know yet about Fiona's college acceptance; she only got the notice last week. People had surely told him Yale was working in fundraising at DePaul, but they might not have conveyed the dreariness of the job, the way everything was about money; no art, no beauty. He'd sweated his way through the insurance interview, said no to the AIDS question. Dr. Cheng had submitted the first claim for AZT five months ago, and it was still under review. The insurance company wanted the names of every doctor who'd treated him in the past ten years, and Yale was worried they'd do to him what they did to Katsu—find some minor illness from years back or the one dermatologist he'd forgotten to list, and then claim misrepresentation. The insurers had a year to review it all, while Yale paid thousands of dollars out of pocket, hoping he'd eventually get reimbursed. But at least he had the job, a desk to cling to.

He could tell Charlie that Bill had delayed Nora's show till the fall of '90 at the earliest, and that although Yale was in great shape, thanks for asking, he was afraid he'd never see it happen. He could tell him Nora had passed away last winter; that he'd hoped so much he could at least send her photos of the show, even if they couldn't roll her into the Brigg as they'd dreamed. Of course Charlie might not even remember who Nora was.

He could say that his lymph nodes had been swollen last summer, but they were fine again, and his T cells were fantastic, and he was drinking vitamin shakes and doing visualizations. He could tell him Roscoe had gone to live with Cecily and her son after Dr. Cheng had told him he could not, under any circumstances, keep the cat and its litter box in his apartment. He could say he'd left the Marina Towers finally, was living in a sublet in Lincoln Park, that the paint was peeling but the place had its own washing machine.

Asher said, "Can I get you to the DAGMAR meeting next weekend?" Yale was never clear on DAGMAR's mission, in part because the *R* kept changing—Dykes and Gay Men Against Reagan, or the Right, or Republicans, or Repression. Every time you asked it was something different.

Yale said, "It's Rutabagas now, right?"

He pressed Asher's stamp onto his left palm; the slightest trace of red ink came off.

"You'll feel better," Asher said. "Everyone I know who isn't political, it's just because they haven't tapped into their anger. And once you do, it'll feel right. Listen, direct action—direct action is the third best feeling in the world."

"What's the second?"

"Peeling off a wet swimsuit."

"Huh."

Yale actually wanted to say yes, but the way he felt around Asher was unsustainable. It wasn't good for the nervous system. Besides which, what he'd seen of direct action protests involved lying down in the street, pepper spray, getting handcuffed and locked in a paddy wagon—where, in summer, they'd close the doors and turn the heat up. He hadn't even been able to fight off other boys in his seventh-grade locker room. How was he supposed to hold his own, in front of Asher Glass, against third-generation Chicago cops? He said he'd think about it. He had a lot going on at work, he said.

The one place he did see Asher regularly was at support group. Asher would consistently show up half an hour late, loosening his tie. If Yale had managed to keep an open seat next to him—usually by leaving his coat on it casually for a while, and then removing the coat as if he'd just suddenly remembered it was there—Asher would take it, squeeze the back of Yale's neck as he sat down. Otherwise he'd stand outside the circle, refusing the therapist's offer to grab him one of the chairs that was still folded against the wall. When Asher talked, it was to make a speech—not to share anything about himself, about his own diagnosis or its aftermath. He'd never acquiesced to the test, but last year his weight had suddenly dropped, his stomach had revolted, and his doctor had insisted on checking his T cells. His count was below one hundred. About once per meeting, he'd go off about the cost of AZT. As if they were the ones responsible, as if they could do anything about it. He'd start yelling that it was the most expensive prescription drug in history. "You think that's a coincidence? You think that isn't pure hatred? Ten thousand dollars a year! Ten thousand fucking dollars!" He was never one to break down in tears, never one to sob over lost friends or mortality or survivor guilt.

After the meetings, Asher would tell Yale he ought to get together with someone in the group. After a brief fling with Ross, the redhead from Marina Towers—they'd mostly had dinners together because Ross, who got tested the first weekday of every third month, was terrified of anything more than kissing—Yale had been completely celibate. "That Jeremy, with the chin," Asher said once, when they went for coffee after. "He's got no baggage,

435

he's your age, he has amazing arms. I'm judging from the forearms, but I'm extrapolating. You're both positive, he lives a block from you, and he's financially independent. I'm not saying you move in together, I'm saying you exchange some bodily fluids and feel good about it."

Bodily fluids were the last things Yale wanted to think about. He said, "What if there are different strains? Some people think you could get—"

"That's the biggest bullshit. They want to police your sexuality, and then even once it's too late, they want to police it some more. There's no reason to stop getting laid. It's just that your dating pool's changed."

Now, in the car, Yale wondered if Asher was inviting him to the DAGMAR meeting just to fix him up with someone there. He wanted to ask, and he wanted to ask if he should be offended or flattered that Asher was always so interested in his sex life, yet had never volunteered to participate in it. Not that Yale had ever propositioned him. Not that he could.

Asher said, "You owe me one favor in exchange for this ride. Either you come to the meeting or you visit Charlie."

He took his eyes off of traffic long enough to look at Yale, and Yale's face did involuntary things. He tried his best to smile casually. "Maybe I'll get in touch with his mom."

Asher said, "Does it really ever go anywhere?"

"Does what?"

"Love. Does it vanish?"

Yale looked at his own hand, resting on the dashboard to keep himself steady whenever Asher braked suddenly. "I mean, we never want it to. But it does, doesn't it?"

Asher said, "I think that's the saddest thing in the world, the failure of love. Not hatred, but the failure of love."

*

He didn't go see Charlie that night, although maybe that was the day he knew he would eventually. He didn't see him for a year and a half, not until October of 1989, when Charlie, although it had nothing to do with that infected eyelid a year and a half earlier, had gone blind.

Teresa met him at the elevator. She'd aged a million years.

Yale had been to Masonic for a few tests, but he hadn't been up to unit 371 since he'd visited Terrence that once, years ago. The acquaintances who'd landed here, like Charlie's copy editor Dwight, hadn't been close enough friends to visit.

The place looked worn in now, in a good way. Broadway posters hung on the walls, and the place was done up for Halloween. A man in a gown leaned on the nurses' station chatting, his feet in fuzzy yellow slippers, his arms covered with lesions. There was a board with Polaroids of all the staff and volunteers, their names markered on the white strips. The biggest difference this time was that Yale knew that unless his insurance fell through and he ended up at County, he was looking at the unit where he himself would die. This would be his final home, and the faces of those two passing nurses would, in time, be the ones he was most familiar with in the world. He would know every detail of this linoleum, every light fixture.

He hugged Teresa and asked how things were. "They've moved him to a single," she said, "and I don't think it's a good sign, do you? I just want to sleep. He's—listen, he's been under a lot of sedation lately, and they had to sedate him again this morning for his bronchoscopy, and he's still quite out of it. I don't know that he'll know you're here, necessarily. I should have called you back and said, but I was hoping he'd be recovered by now. The thing is, he's not—even when he's not sedated, he's not fully here. I should have said."

"It's okay," he said. "It's okay."

Yale followed her, and as he first entered the room he squinched his eyes shut. He opened them, slowly, to a man who wasn't Charlie. He wanted to tell Teresa she'd taken him to the wrong place, that this withered fetus on the bed was no one he knew. But Teresa was stroking this man's scalp, and when the man's mouth hung open, Yale saw Charlie's teeth. He was an alien, an Auschwitz skeleton, a baby bird fallen from its nest. Yale's mind kept reaching for metaphors, because the simple fact of it—that this was Charlie—was too much.

There wasn't much room between the door and the bed, but Yale covered it as slowly as he could. He grasped the bedrail, looked at the cards taped to the walls.

Teresa was tired, and Yale told her he could stay, told her to go home and rest. She hugged him and left.

He didn't know if he should talk. He could explain that he was here, check Charlie's face for a reaction. But with the sedative still in effect, and with Charlie blind, Yale had a cushion of anonymity right now—one it would feel safe to stay in, at least for today.

Later, if Charlie was ever lucid, he could tell him everything he'd been wanting to. The good parts, at least. He could say, at least once, that he forgave him. And even if Charlie never fully woke up—well, he'd still say it. Maybe it would still count.

He sat on the chair by the bed.

The nurse came in, and she showed Yale a small pink sponge on the end of a stick, showed him how he could hold it to Charlie's lips to give him water.

He did it for a while, and he ran his thumb over Charlie's wrist, listening to the thrumming of the walls.

He fed him water, drop by drop.

He could feel it, all around him: how down the corridor, and down other hallways of other hospitals around Chicago and the other godforsaken cities of the globe, a thousand other men did the same.

2015

It made no sense. Or maybe it did. It had to. She was awake, and it was 2015, and here was a man, very much alive, whose eyes and gestures and voice were Julian's.

Fiona sat on the studio's cement floor, the back of her head against a cupboard. Julian was explaining to the rest of them what Fiona had stammered in the hallway. "What's the line about *rumors of my death*? Richard, should I be insulted that you never talk about me?"

Serge found the whole thing hilarious, called Julian a zombie, laughed at the look on Fiona's face. Cecily didn't know Julian; she got Fiona a damp paper towel for her forehead.

Richard said, "Fiona, I only found him myself two years ago. We knew you didn't know where he was. That was the surprise. But if I'd thought for an instant that you'd believed he was— listen, I'd never have sprung that on you."

How much had she even talked to Richard in the past two years? Not at all, really. She'd emailed to ask if she could come. Before that ... well, it *felt* like they'd talked, but that was just a product of seeing his name pop up so often in the world, and of their being such old friends.

Julian stood above her, helpless, running his thumb across his chin. She stared at his face, the ways it had changed. Beyond

439

the normal transformations of age, he had what she recognized as some facial wasting from AZT, and—she was certain—cheek implants to counter the fat loss. Not great ones either. A couple of her volunteers at the store had similar cheeks. And his face had broadened—the steroids, presumably—so that he looked blocky, carved. Still handsome but profoundly different. As if he'd been reconstituted from a police sketch.

He said, "I work in accounting for Universal. We're shooting right on Richard's street. Not that I get to be on set. They only flew me in three days ago and I'm in a sad little office."

She said, "Where—usually—" but she didn't have words for the rest of what should have been an easy question.

"I'm in L.A. I looked for you on Facebook, you know. A bunch of times!"

"Oh."

"Hey. I'm sorry."

She wasn't sure why he'd said it, but she worried he'd read her mind: Why, she was thinking, should it be Julian Ames, of all people, to show up, a ghost at the door? Why not Nico or Terrence or Yale? Why not Teddy Naples, who'd evaded the virus only to die in '99 of a heart attack in front of his class? Why not Charlie Keene, for that matter, who was an asshole, but did so much good? She'd loved Julian. She had. But why him?

She made herself smile, because she hadn't smiled yet.

"I really did try to find you," he said. "I should have asked Richard." His voice was the same. Julian's voice.

"You *did* ask, remember? Last year, in L.A. And I said I'd get you her email. I forgot, of course."

She said, "It's okay."

Richard said, "I feel like a lout."

They decided what everyone needed was sandwiches, and Serge was dispatched to buy them. By the time he came back with five plastic-wrapped baguettes of ham and cheese in a paper bag, they were all sitting around the table, and Richard had adroitly defused the awkwardness with a story about the time Yale Tishman had thrown a birthday party for his roommate at Masonic, a man he'd just met who'd had no one in town to visit him. Yale had told them all to bring little presents, and Fiona, to be funny, had bought a *Playgirl* on the way, only to learn on arrival that the guy was straight. A gruff IV drug user from downstate. "He was not amused," Richard said.

Fiona still felt detached, floaty, confused. She kept looking at her own hands. If these were the same hands she'd had all along, then it wasn't impossible that Julian Ames was sitting here across from her, opening his sandwich, asking if Richard had any napkins.

There were events she'd believed herself, for years, to be the sole custodian of—when all along, those parties, those conversations, those jokes had stayed alive in him as well.

Julian said, "Leaving is one of my great regrets in life, Fiona. I want you to know. I thought I was running off to spare everyone, and really I was abandoning them. I'd never imagined they could go before I did. Not in a million years. And I know, from Richard—I know you took care of Yale in particular. It should have been me. I should have been there for him."

"Cecily was there too." Fiona's voice croaked out as if she hadn't talked in a week. "It was me and Cecily in the hospital. We did shifts."

Cecily said, "It was mostly you."

"But he died alone." It was the cruelest thing Fiona could have said, not just to Julian but to Richard and Cecily too. And to herself. "He died completely alone."

Julian set his sandwich down and looked at her until she looked back. "Richard told me," he said. "I know, and I know it wasn't your fault. Anyone could have died alone. You know, the middle of the night, if—"

"It wasn't the middle of the night."

Cecily put a cool hand to the back of Fiona's neck.

Serge mouthed something to Richard, and Richard mouthed back "New York." Serge must have been asking where Richard was when Yale died. Richard's career had been blowing up.

Fiona, to change the subject, managed to ask Julian to recount his last three decades.

"If you're asking how I'm still alive," Julian said, "I have no idea." But he did, really. He'd gone to Puerto Rico in '86, and he'd stayed a year, mooching off an old friend, selling T-shirts on the beach and getting stoned. "I was so sure I was ready to die," he said. "And then when I heard about AZT, it was like—like if you were trying to drown, but someone threw you a rope, and you couldn't stop yourself from grabbing it." The problem was that Julian had no insurance, and the drug cost more than half of what he'd made a year back in Chicago. So he went home to Valdosta, Georgia, where his mother, who'd thought she'd never see him again, was happy to let him live in his childhood bedroom, happy to spend his father's life insurance and remortgage her house for her youngest child. "She was a saint," he said. "A southern gentlewoman. She was built for church and afternoon tea, but it turns out she was also built for crisis." For a while she made him keep working—he got a job with a local film production company—because she was so certain he'd survive, and that when he was cured, he wouldn't want a gap on his résumé. (Fiona remembered Julian's sweet optimism before his diagnosis, the way he was always sure the disease would be cured, sure he was just about to become famous. He must have gotten it from his mother all along.) He grew sicker and sicker despite her care, developed resistance to the AZT. "I had about half a T cell left," he said. "I weighed a hundred and eight pounds."

Richard said, "And that's when I saw you." Fiona knew Richard had run into Julian in New York sometime in the early nineties, that Julian had come up there with a friend to see one or two good shows before he died. He was in a wheelchair. This was when Richard had taken that last photo of him, the third photo of the triptych. Richard had called her afterward, and then she'd called Teddy to marvel over the fact that Julian had lasted that long.

"Right. And after that I was in the hospital for a solid year. That New York trip was a bad idea, in retrospect."

Serge said, "And then what?" He was the only one who'd finished his sandwich.

"Then it was '96! Suddenly the good drugs came out! There's a few months I don't even remember, I was so out of it, and when the fog lifted, I was home again. I could lift my arms and I could eat food. Next thing you know, I'm *jogging*. I mean, really it took a while, but that's what it felt like.

"For a long time—you'll appreciate this, Fiona. For a long time, I wondered if I was a ghost. A literal ghost. I thought I must've died and this was some kind of purgatory or heaven. Because how was it even possible, you know? But then I thought: If this is heaven, where are all my friends? It couldn't be heaven if Yale and Nico and everyone weren't there. So I guess this is just plain old earth. And I'm still on it."

Serge excused himself to answer the phone. He'd been texting all day, and although all his acquaintances seemed accounted for, not all of *their* acquaintances were, and there were still urgent and worrisome things to be discussed.

Julian said, "My husband had basically the same experience. He calls this his second life. To me that sounds too born-again,

443

but then he didn't grow up in the South. He's right, though; that's what it feels like."

There was a ring, a golden wedding band, on Julian's left hand.

How utterly strange that Julian could have a second life, a whole entire life, when Fiona had been living for the past thirty years in a deafening echo. She'd been tending the graveyard alone, oblivious to the fact that the world had moved on, that one of the graves had been empty this whole time.

"Speaking of mothers," Julian said, "and speaking of Yale Tishman. Richard, did I ever tell you I met Yale's mom? Maybe twelve years ago." Fiona put her hands flat on the table, steadied herself. If Julian was indeed a ghost, he was a tormenting one. He turned to Fiona and Cecily. "I was working on set for this sitcom pilot called *Follywood*. You never heard of it, it didn't get picked up, thank God. And she was playing a doctor. I wouldn't have recognized her face, but I knew her name. Jane Greenspan. Remember?"

Fiona remembered the woman's nose, just like Yale's, and her broad mouth. She'd seen her pixelated a hundred times, and in real life only once, only briefly. That Tylenol commercial ran for a few years, and Fiona had slowly memorized her face, knew it well enough to recognize her when she'd popped up in other ads throughout the years. Why?, she'd lamented to anyone who would listen, except for Yale himself. Why did *that* have to be the parent who'd left? Of all the parents of all the gay men she knew? An actress mother would have understood a gay son, wouldn't she? For Yale to be alienated from her for reasons that had nothing to do with his sexuality just felt excessive, perverse.

Richard asked Julian if he'd talked to her, and Julian said, "Not about Yale. It would've felt cruel. I don't know. I mean, how do you even start that conversation? *I was good friends with the son you abandoned.* And then I thought, What if she didn't know he'd died?"

"She did," Fiona said, and her voice was cracked glass.

She couldn't breathe. Even though she didn't want to be out on the street, she was about to say that she needed fresh air. But Serge had gone to the door and was returning, having let Jake Austen into the studio.

And then she was stuck, because everything had to be explained, the story told over: the misunderstanding, the strange reunion, Richard's chagrin, Julian's whole life.

Jake grinned like it was the coolest thing in the world. "Okay," he said, "I gotta say, I feel a little vindicated. This is why I wanted to ask about the triptych, Fiona. Because I saw the update. I mean, you sounded so sure of yourself, I thought maybe I'd misunderstood."

Fiona didn't follow, and Richard explained how last year, when Julian had passed through Paris, he'd taken his photo again. One of the pieces for the show was an updated group of four photos. "A quadriptych," he said. "Doesn't exactly roll off the tongue."

"Can you believe it?" Julian said. "After all this time, I'm a *model* again!"

And the way he said it was so exactly like Julian Ames, so much the way he'd have said it at age twenty-five, that Fiona walked straight over to where he sat and kissed him on the forehead.

"I'm so glad you're here," she said. "I'm so, so, so, so glad."

1990

Even though they were only going to march, not chain themselves to lampposts or anything, Yale and Fiona had written Gloria's phone number on their arms with a Sharpie, as well as the number for Asher's law office—although Asher was far more likely to get locked up than they were. Gloria had a sprained ankle but had volunteered as a remote bail buddy to at least ten different protestors, and Yale was concerned that if they all got arrested, she'd run out of money, leave him to languish. "She's the most responsible person I ever met," Fiona said. It was true; Charlie used to say she was the one writer in the world who'd never missed a deadline. Gloria had left *Out Loud* behind and was at the *Trib* now, writing features. But just in case, Yale wrote Cecily's number too. They both wore bandannas tied loosely around their necks, though Yale had doubts they'd work against tear gas. He felt like a silly cowboy.

They headed down to the Loop on the El, and Yale tried not to let Fiona see how terrified he was. He'd gone to the candlelight vigil outside Cook County Hospital on Saturday night, staying till two in the morning, eating soup and sharing a blanket with Asher and Fiona and Asher's friend from New York, but that had felt far safer. Candles reminded him of a religious service, and after a while everyone was sitting. Only a few hundred people, some guitars. A silly fashion show at one point. An actual march was different, and the overzealous guy who'd called him late last night from the ACT UP phone tree had reminded him to let friends and family know where he'd be. He'd suggested wearing a second, padded backpack in the front. "Sometimes they get baton-happy," he said. "So just, sweaters in there, whatever." But Yale only owned one backpack. He put a sweatshirt in, a spare bandanna, and a bottle of water. He put his inhaler into one pants pocket and a plastic baggie with three days of pills into the other, in case he was detained. Eighty-five pills, seventy-some dollars' worth, thank God for insurance.

The train was full of Monday-morning commuters, men in suits, women in blazers, a few kids in private-school uniforms. Everything had started at 8 at the Prudential Building, but it was already 8:45, and they'd likely have to meet the crowd on its way up Michigan to the Blue Cross offices. Yale had the Xeroxed route map folded in his pocket. A huge loop that looked like way too much walking. The American Medical Association was the next big stop, followed by another insurance place, and finally back to Daley Plaza, where they'd plant themselves in front of the County Building to protest the closure of half the AIDS beds at Cook County and the fact that the ward wouldn't take women.

Fiona managed to find a seat and insisted Yale take it. He felt fine, really, except that his stomach had been a mess for a few days. A different kind of mess than the drugs made it—this was sharp cramping, sloshing. It might have been the start of everything, or it might have been nerves. Once he was sitting below her, she said, "So I have a problem. I'm in love with my sociology professor."

Yale laughed. "Feef! Like unrequited love, or like you're getting some extra credit?"

"I mean, he calls me. At home. But we haven't—it's not against the law or anything!"

"Tell me he's not sixty," Yale said. "Oh God, is he married?"

"No, and no. He's your age, maybe."

"But you're in his class."

"Right. Well, I was. Exams are this week."

"You should be studying."

"Shut up. So, I take the exam, and then what?"

Fiona was flushed. If she was trying to keep her face neutral, it wasn't working. It was a beautiful thing to see: a happy Fiona, Fiona in love.

He said, "Maybe you wait till grades are filed. For propriety. And then. You know."

"Really? I thought you'd be the one to talk sense into me. You're supposed to be my most sensible friend."

"Feef, you're asking advice from someone who's increasingly aware that life is very short. Wait till you have your grade, then go to his office and unzip his pants."

He'd been talking quietly, but Fiona shrieked. "That is such a gay move, Yale!" No one looked; if anything, they thought she was insulting him generically.

"I'm pretty sure it works on straight guys too. Seriously. How many lives do you have? How many times are you gonna be twenty-five?"

Fiona raised an eyebrow. Her eyebrows were darker than her hair, and Yale loved that it gave her a perpetually sardonic look. She said, "Are you following your own advice?"

"I'm about to take part in some mob action, aren't I? Does that really seem like a thing I'd do?"

"Not at all. But I know why you're doing it. It's not because life is short. It's because you're in love with Asher."

He was going to protest, but the blood had come to his cheeks and ears so fast he could *hear* it, and it would be even more embarrassing now to attempt a denial. She'd seen him at the vigil after all, mooning around, worrying whether Asher was sleeping with his friend from New York, watching the way the candle lit Asher's face from below. Yale said, "Well, he had some good points." He was no more or less in love with Asher than he'd always been, which is to say, he'd always been fairly deeply in love with Asher if he admitted it to himself, which, lately, he was willing to do. It wasn't that he'd been spending more time with him than he always had, but he had more opportunity to sit back and *watch* him—as Asher spoke at benefits, headed up community meetings, got himself on TV when the Quilt came to Navy Pier, got himself on TV when he was arrested—and Yale was finally letting himself, from that distance, look at something he'd always known would burn his eyes.

Asher had spent a full hour at the vigil talking Yale into marching today. "You embarrass someone on the six o'clock news," he'd said, "how much more effective is that than writing a letter? Nothing else you do will make this much difference. And this is the big one. This is it." His full New York accent had come out. He'd jabbed a finger at Yale's chest way too hard, and then apologized.

DAGMAR had rolled into the Chicago branch of ACT UP, and Asher was providing a lot of its legal counsel, plus facing the pepper spray himself. Most protests brought out twenty or thirty stalwarts, but this one was national—people flying in from all over to target AMA headquarters and the AMA's opposition to national insurance. And the county hospital system, too, and the insurance companies, and lord knew what else. The whole thing felt confusing to Yale, but bigger was better, according to Asher. "If we're not fighting for poor black women who need beds at County," Asher said, "we're as bad as the fucking Republicans. You don't just go into this looking out for yourself. And Yale," he'd said, and Yale was slightly surprised that Asher had remembered his presence, remembered he wasn't just giving a speech to the ether, "I think you'd be great at this, long term. Maybe behind the scenes, but we need you. We're gonna need new leaders all the time. The problem with this movement is the leaders keep dying. We gotta have subs."

There'd been a drop of wax rolling down Asher's candle, getting dangerously close to his hand. Yale had reached out and stopped it with his thumbnail. Which is probably when Fiona had realized, if she hadn't already.

The crowd was indeed on the move by the time Yale and Fiona joined it, streaming north over the Michigan Avenue Bridge. Some of the protestors wore doctors' coats, a nice touch, and most carried signs—"*Death by Loophole*," "*Bloody Money*," an elaborate one about George Bush having a drug czar but no AIDS czar— and Yale felt like a bland supernumerary. No one wore double backpacks, not a single person; he was glad he hadn't showed up looking like an overprepared kid.

But Fiona eagerly joined the chanting, and once Yale did, too, he found that the rhythm of his feet on the pavement matched the rhythm of what he was shouting and soon his heart fell into sync, as it used to when he'd go out dancing.

"People with AIDS," a woman with a megaphone would yell, "under attack! What do we do?"

And together they yelled, "*ACT UP! Fight back!*"

Yale watched for people he knew, but he'd have to be patient; there were thousands of protestors, and in fact it was nice that these faces didn't all have the look of someone he'd seen around Boystown for years but just couldn't place. It was good to be part of a horde, a wave of humans.

A chant would die out and then stop, as if it had been cut off by an invisible conductor, and then a new one would travel toward them up the street, fuzzy at first, and then he'd hear it clearly once through before joining in. As they passed the Tribune Tower, with

450

dazed tourists looking on: *Health! Care! Is a right! Health care is a right!* Outside the Blue Cross building, right on the Magnificent Mile: *We're here! We're queer! We're not going shopping!* Walking down State, the crowd tighter now, louder: *Hey, Hey, AMA! How many people died today?*

Three laughing teenagers ran right near Yale and Fiona for a while, doing a limp-wristed mocking dance that no one paid attention to. Someone threw an empty cigarette packet out a car window, and it bounced off Fiona's shoulder.

Yale spotted Rafael from *Out Loud*, walking with a cane, but he was too far away to talk to. There were police all around, blowing whistles, shouting things Yale couldn't understand, but no one seemed to be under arrest yet. No one was getting headlocked.

But before they reached the AMA, Yale felt his stomach liquefy. He told Fiona he needed a bathroom, and she told him he looked pale.

They ducked into a hotel, where thankfully no one stopped them, and Yale made it to a fancy single-occupancy restroom down a hall behind the concierge desk, Fiona standing guard outside the door. He called to her that she could leave, and she told him that was silly. She ran out to find a Walgreens and came back with Imodium and Gatorade, although he was feeling better even before she returned. He took his time, sat there fifteen minutes, twenty minutes, worried there would be a crowd of bemused spectators when he emerged. He came out to see just Fiona sitting cross-legged against the wall, and he shut the door quickly behind him. "This'll be my defense if they arrest me," he said. "I can just shit my pants. I'll be like a skunk, or an octopus."

Fiona said, "Remember Nico's comic about Hot Todd getting the runs on a date?" Yale did. The strip ended with Todd rushing home, the dream date alone on the sidewalk, left wondering what he'd done wrong.

Fiona sat with him on a couch in the lobby. He wanted to rejoin the protest, but not yet. He could use a few minutes to make sure.

Fiona smiled like she was about to present him with a gift. She said, "You know he likes you too."

He said, "Who?" even though he knew, or hoped he knew. He'd felt cold and drained, but now all his blood and breath rushed back into him.

"He told Nico. And Nico told me."

"Oh. So it was ages ago."

"Sure. But people don't let go of that stuff. And I talked to him after you broke up with Charlie. I said he should go for it." She kept talking too loud. She wasn't following his cues to whisper—although the lobby was mostly empty, and the family at the desk seemed preoccupied.

"And he *didn't* go for it."

"The thing is, he's not into monogamy, and he knew that was what you'd want."

"Jesus. I mean, I don't believe in it *anymore*. It's the entire reason I'm sick."

Fiona tilted her head. "That's kind of the opposite of what happened."

"Not really."

He was angry and excited and confused. None of which helped his stomach. He wanted more than ever to head back out there, and he knew less than ever how he would hold it together.

When he was finally ready, when they slowly stood, he was overwhelmed with what he thought at first was déjà vu—but no, it was a real memory: leaving the bathroom at Richard's, walking downstairs to find no one there. What if it happened again? What if they walked back out to a normal day in a normal city, the protestors having marched into the void?

452

Fiona said, "Let's go straight to the County Building and wait for everyone by the Snoopy."

"By the what?"

"The Snoopy in a blender. That statue."

It took him a second. "Oh my God, Fiona, that's a Jean Dubuffet." Abstract and white, with black lines. A sculpture that invited climbing.

"I am *not* the only one who calls it that, and we can't all be art experts."

He liked the idea of crawling inside it, watching the protests, watching Asher from inside a sculptural shell.

They did beat everyone there, aside from some organizers milling around with clipboards, megaphones by their sides. They learned from one that there had been arrests at the AMA, some guys who'd blocked the building's entrance. "They've got Mounties out now," he said.

They sat down, leaned against the Dubuffet.

Yale said, "It's called *Monument with Standing Beast*. Just for future reference."

"Nope, no way. Never. Hey, you'll be my date to Nora's opening, right?"

"Maybe you'll bring your sociology professor!"

"Yale, my *parents* will be there."

"Good point," he said. "Definitely better to show up with a diseased gay man. I know that's your dad's favorite."

In February—nearly ten months away—Nora's collection was finally, finally going up at the Brigg. After infinite delays, endless nonsense. Bill had messed things up badly, promising the Foujitas on loan to the Ohara Museum in Japan before the Brigg even had a chance to display them itself. Yale was still on the mailing list for the gallery, and he'd been alarmed to notice that in the write-up of the show, every artist but Ranko Novak had been listed. Even Sergey Mukhankin was there. He'd called the gallery and pretended to be from *Out Loud*—why not?—and asked the woman who answered if there was an artist named Novak whose work would be featured. "I don't see that," she'd said. And Yale had leaned his head all the way back, left his chin and Adam's apple pointed at the ceiling until his neck ached.

At least Nora had died believing she'd given Ranko his show, but whatever part of Yale believed in an afterlife (he was *trying* to believe, at least, lately) felt he'd let her down enormously. She'd trusted him, had left Ranko's legacy in his hands alone, and he'd failed. And it had been her own work, too, even if she hadn't seen it that way. Yale had wanted, more than anything, to see Nora's portrait of Ranko on the gallery wall, next to Ranko's portrait of her—a secret triumph only a couple of people would ever understand. And now it was all relegated to some storage closet. When he thought about it, his throat constricted. He hadn't told Fiona the news yet; telling her would feel like telling Nora.

Yale and Fiona sat by the Dubuffet another half hour, but then they could hear everyone coming down Clark, and then they were there with their wind-battered signs, sweaty and hoarse. *George Bush, you can't hide! We charge you with genocide!* There were news crews now, running backward in front of the mass. He spotted Asher right near the front, and Teddy too. Teddy was doing a postdoc at UC Davis, but he was back for this, and he'd caught up with Yale at the vigil. He was tan and happy, and he'd gained a few pounds, in a good way.

Yale and Fiona joined the chant: *Health! Care! Is a right! Health care is a right!* Whatever momentum he'd lost from their detour to the hotel, he easily picked back up again.

When was the last time he'd yelled? He'd yelled at Cubs games. He'd yelled at Charlie when they were breaking up. But he hadn't

454

yelled about AIDS. He hadn't yelled at the government. He hadn't yelled at the forces that had denied Katsu Tatami health insurance, at the county hospital system that had made Katsu wait two weeks for a bed when he couldn't breathe and then let him die on a ward that smelled like piss. He hadn't yelled yet at this new mayor and his lip service. He hadn't yelled at the universe.

Fiona took his hand and led him into the fray, and they wove their way toward Asher. Asher was busy yelling into his megaphone, but he winked at them, and when he lowered it he said, "You okay?"

Yale said, "You know what this feels like? It's like coming out all over again. I'm in the middle of downtown, shouting about being gay. I'm shouting about AIDS. And it's amazing."

"Stay with me, okay? You want these?" Asher reached into his pocket, pulled out a roll of Silence = Death stickers. "Put them everywhere. My friend stuck one right on a horse!"

Teddy bounded up, told them that back at the corner—Yale couldn't see that far, but he heard the roar from that direction, the whistles and shouting—women had thrown fifteen mattresses into the street to represent the beds that lay vacant from understaffing. They were lying on them, making an impromptu women's ward.

But then Fiona pointed up, and then everyone started pointing up: Five guys were climbing out a window and onto a ledge of the County Building. They quickly affixed their banner below the state flag: *WE DEMAND EQUAL HEALTH CARE NOW!* Asher started jumping up and down, shouting their names. He said to Yale, "They were in straight drag! They had on button-downs!" Now they wore ACT UP shirts.

It must have been a full minute before the police appeared behind the men and dragged two of them away. The three that remained pumped their fists to the chanting. *The whole world is watching! The whole world is watching!* And although Yale couldn't imagine it was true—would this really earn more than a thirty-second spot on the news?—it felt good to shout it. When the cops came back, those last three clung to the very edge, the flagpole, the banner itself. They looked ready to scale the entire building like Spider-Man. Fiona buried her face in Yale's shirt. Yale wanted to look away too, but he made himself watch as the police dragged them in by the legs. They got the last one in a twisted headlock.

Down here the Mounties paced, pushing everyone back. It was time, apparently, to sit down in the street. Asher said, "You can get out of here. You want to go?" But he didn't. Fiona didn't want to either. Asher said, "You've got a support person?" Yale nodded, didn't mention that Gloria was home in her apartment, not out here ready to follow him to jail.

They say get back! the crowd was shouting. *We say fight back!*

He only hoped his stomach would hold out. He took the Imodium out of his backpack and swigged. Way too much, but he could deal with the consequences later. They sat, part of a Red Rover line of twenty stretching across the street: Asher on one side of Yale, Fiona on the other, and Teddy on the other side of her. Behind them people stood and chanted and filmed and shouted at the cops.

The horses were way too close, and it was hard to tell what was going on, hard to see and hard to hear. A rumor spread down the line that someone had already been kicked in the head by a horse, that one of those sirens a minute ago had been an ambulance. The cops were constantly turning the horses backward, so their hind legs were a foot away from people's faces. They were close enough to smell. When their hooves hit the pavement, Yale felt it shake.

An organizer ran down the row. "If they arrest you, go like this!" he called, crossing his wrists. Yale asked why, but no one answered. "Don't go limp!" the guy said. "They'll drop you on your head!"

"Are you afraid?" Yale shouted in Fiona's ear.

She shook her head, her curls in her face. "I'm too angry to be afraid! I'm too fucking angry! Are you?"

"Yes! But I was dying anyway!"

Someone kept shouting *No violence!*—but it was just one voice, not a chant.

The cops swarmed closer. They picked a woman off the end of the line and carried her, screaming, to a police truck. They came back for the man next to her, and the man next to him. They wore blue plastic gloves. One wore a paper face mask.

There were cameras still, but the news crews had all moved to the side; the people dashing through the front lines with camcorders were protestors recording this for posterity. One stopped in front of Teddy. "Say something!" he called, and Teddy shouted, "Their gloves don't match their shoes!"

The crowd took it up, an old favorite: *Your gloves don't match your shoes! You'll see it on the news!*

The camera moved down to Yale. "Say something!" the guy said. "What are you feeling?"

It was perhaps the least like Yale Tishman he'd ever felt. If he'd had the rest of his life ahead of him, he might have considered it the first moment of something new, the moment when he finally learned who he was supposed to become. But because he didn't have that, he recognized it for what it was: a spike of bravery and adrenaline that might never be equaled in his remaining time on earth. He unlinked his arm from Fiona's and he turned toward Asher, and he grabbed the back of Asher's head and kissed him. Whether Asher was just showing off for the camera, Yale didn't care, but Asher fully returned the kiss, his fingers in Yale's hair, his tongue on Yale's. Yale could taste the salt on his lips, felt Asher's thick stubble against his own smoother chin even as the entire city fell away around them.

When they finally pulled apart, he became aware of Fiona shrieking in delight, of Teddy whooping and applauding. Asher grinned at him, held his gaze, but then the cry went down the line to lie down.

Yale flipped his backpack to the front and linked arms again and lowered his back and head onto the cool asphalt. He closed his eyes and braced himself. He didn't want to get up and walk to the paddy wagon. He wanted to lie still, a passive corpse to be transported, the way people farther down the line had done. Light as a feather, stiff as a board.

The shouting got closer, and the whistles got closer, and the screams got closer.

He heard Fiona scream when Teddy was taken away, and then a minute later he felt her arm torn away from his. He reached for her, and she was gone. He kept his eyes shut.

When they picked him up, it was by his clothes. By his shirt collar, by the backpack, by the waist of his khakis, by the shoes. He tried not to be limp, but he was.

He looked at the darkness behind his own eyelids. He thought about how next weekend, he was supposed to help Teresa clear out the old apartment. He was supposed to take whatever he wanted of Charlie's and anything of his own that had languished there for four years. This weekend he'd do *this*, next weekend he'd do that. This was probably easier.

It was like being a child and falling asleep on the couch, flopping when your mother carried you to bed.

But he landed on the ground, hard, his wind gone, and they flipped him over, his ribcage on the backpack, his cheek against the asphalt, a knee in his back. There were so many voices around him shouting. They yanked his arms behind him and they tightened something around his wrists, and he couldn't move at all, couldn't breathe well, but still they knelt on him.

He heard Asher's voice, but he couldn't tell how far away it was. "Why are you doing that to him? Sir! Sir! Why are you doing that!"

"He resisted."

"He didn't resist! Sir, he did not resist!"

He opened his eyes to a horse hoof and the brown fur above it, close enough that he might have stuck out his tongue and licked it. He closed his eyes again.

He felt a shoe on his head, holding him to the street. He felt the Imodium bottle in the backpack, ramming into his left lower ribs way too hard. He felt something snap there. A searing, liquid pain.

"Sir, this is unnecessary! Sir, he did not resist!"

He wanted them to hurry up. He wanted to be in the wagon with Fiona already. He wanted to be home with an ice pack already. He wanted to know his bowels would hold out. He wanted Asher to keep shouting, wanted to keep hearing his voice.

He went back to the kiss in his mind. He could live there a long time. It was warm there, and good.

2015

From the bedroom, Fiona Skyped her therapist. Elena's image kept freezing but the sound would continue, so it seemed as if entire sentences came from her closed lips, or serious questions came from a mouth open in laughter. Elena said, "Waiting for *anything* is hard. And this is a lot of stressors."

It was three days since she'd knocked on Claire's door, and she'd heard nothing. "I feel so foolish sitting here," she said. "And for making Cecily come, when maybe we never even get to meet our granddaughter."

"Has Cecily seen Kurt again?" Elena was frozen now with her head down, her black curls filling the screen.

"I don't think so. I'm not prying. She took a day trip with her friend, the one she's staying with."

"And you're connecting with old friends too."

"I'm underfoot. And I'm just supposed to hang out six more days now till Richard's opening?" Julian would be back then, at least. He'd had to fly to London but would return on Monday just in time. "If Claire hasn't called by then, I'm leaving right afterward."

"Just like that?"

"Well. I could—I could slip a letter under her door first. That wouldn't be such a violation, would it?"

"I think that's a solid plan."

"I ruined things by going over there. How is that even fair? I fucked up all along by not being there enough for her, and now I fucked up by smothering her."

Elena took a deep breath—Fiona could hear it rather than see it, as Elena was now stuck with her lips pursed—and said, "Here's something I've been thinking. We've talked so much about how there are things you can blame yourself for, but how Claire has to share the blame."

"I—"

"And I know that's been hard for you. To blame Claire. But I wonder if it isn't time to let go of the whole *idea* of blame."

The sentence crashed Fiona back into a hundred conversations she'd had years ago. Asher Glass ranting about "blame and shame," the twin scourges that scampered after the virus.

Fiona said, "I've been down that road. The thing is, if you stop blaming people and everything's still crap, the only thing left is to blame the world. And when you blame the whole world, when it seems like the planet doesn't want you, and if there's a God, he hates you—that's worse than hating yourself. It is."

She expected Elena to tell her that she was wrong, that self-hatred was the worst kind—but Elena's pregnant silence stretched too long to be good.

Fiona said, "Hello?"

Elena's hand was frozen near her cheek. She was gone.

It was still dark on Wednesday morning when Fiona's phone rang, and she thought at first it must be someone calling from the States. It was Claire.

She said, "So, I want to let you know I'm safe. There's stuff going on like five blocks away, I don't know. But we're fine."

"What's happening?" Fiona was on her feet.

"It's a police thing, not another attack. But there's some gunfire."

"Oh! Wait, are you—thank you for calling, sweetie. Thank you. You're inside?"

"Yeah, this officer came around. We're basically on lockdown." Claire sounded preternaturally calm. Fiona almost would have believed her steady voice if she hadn't known that Nicolette must have been sleeping there beside her—and what mother could possibly be calm in a moment like that? She wanted to fly across the city.

"You're not near a window, are you?"

"Well, it's a small place."

"Can you move a shelf in front of the window?"

Claire was quiet and Fiona worried she'd offended her. "Yeah, maybe."

"Are the doors locked?"

"Of course."

"And you have enough food? Are you on Twitter? Richard's boyfriend was getting his news from Twitter." Because she wasn't yet awake enough to stop herself, she said, "This is a sign, Claire. That you should come back to Chicago."

And she was sure, then, that this had done it, that Claire would hang up.

Claire laughed. "Everyone here is terrified of Chicago. They can't believe I made it out alive."

"Or we'll get you a safer place in Paris. In a better neighborhood. Your father and I could chip in."

She was literally trying to buy her daughter's affection. Well, her safety first, and then her affection. At five in the morning, with a shoot-out in the background.

"Mom," Claire said, "just go back to sleep, okay?"

"Will you call again later?"

"Sure. I—just don't panic if you *don't* hear from me, okay?"

"I will panic, sweetie. But you could email your dad again, if you don't want to call, and he could pass the message on. He appreciated hearing from you."

Fiona turned on the TV in the living room—on mute, because she couldn't understand the rapid-fire French anyway—and she logged onto Richard's computer to find CNN.

By noon, she hadn't heard from Claire, but she'd learned from the news that they'd caught and killed the last suspect. No reports of any civilian deaths five blocks away.

It occurred to her to check if her phone had saved Claire's number when she called. "Blocked Caller," it said.

She ate lunch, and then she called Jake and asked if she could see him again. He, too, was staying here at least until Richard's opening; his story wouldn't be complete otherwise, and his friend was (against what Fiona assumed must have been this woman's better judgment) continuing to let him crash. He asked Fiona if she wanted to go for a walk, and she said no, she'd very much like to fuck him again if he could figure out where that might happen.

He called her back with an address, a place that turned out to be a small office building in Saint-Germain, and he led her up to a small, empty office with a window, a desk, a chair, some architectural prints on the walls.

"I'm sorry," he said. "I thought there might be a couch at least." It belonged to his friend's roommate's boyfriend, a guy who'd apparently understood instantly and handed over the key. Maybe everyone in France understood things like that.

"This is perfect," she said. She sat him in the chair and unbuttoned his shirt, straddled his lap. It was, fortunately, an armless chair. They got the chair back wedged between the desk and the wall so they wouldn't roll around. She lifted her dress, slid her panties to the side, lowered herself onto him. He groaned and tugged her bra down, and very soon, alarmingly soon, they were both done. The whole thing had been a shudder, a sneeze, some quick and involuntary trick of the body. He wrapped the used condom in a sheet of printer paper.

"Don't throw that in the trash here," she said. "Walk it down to the street." She was lying on the floor, stretching out her back. Jake put the paper wad on the chair and lay next to her.

He said, "Are you okay?"

"I just have strange ways of dealing with nerves."

"Hey," he said. He ran a finger down her chin, her neck. "Why do you think we met each other?"

"Because you were drunk on the airplane."

"I mean cosmically. People don't come into each other's lives like this for no reason. Why'd the universe throw us together?"

"Did you say *cosmically*?"

"Don't pretend you don't believe in it. Nothing's random, it can't be. The people we meet, the people we're smashed together with, right?"

"I'm not, like, *ending up with you*. This is not destiny."

"I didn't mean that. I'm being philosophical. Don't you ever think about that stuff? Like, where we go when we die?"

"Christ, Jake, it's two in the afternoon."

"I think it's like sleeping," he said, "but you get to help dream up the world. So whatever happens here on earth, all the weird stuff that just *happens*, a volcano erupting or whatever, that's the collective dreams of everyone who's ever lived."

"So these attacks—a lot of dead people dreamed them."

"Right."

"Huh." She started laughing. "Yeah, no. That's very wrong."

"I don't actually believe it. But it's nice to think. And it's just that the world is so weird sometimes, it's the only thing that makes sense."

"You think the dead control us."

"Sure."

"I'm gonna tell you a secret," she said, and he rolled onto his side. She had fresh gauze on her hand, and she picked at the edge. "We're in charge of *them*. I mean, my friend Julian? When I thought he was dead, all the things we'd ever said to each other, all my memories of him, they were mine. One of the weirdest things about seeing him again was that something *left* me. Some kind of energy. Like the air whooshing out of a balloon."

Jake said, "Is it a relief, or are you sad?"

"Not *sad*, that would be ridiculous."

"You lost a loss. That's still a loss."

Fiona sat up. "Thanks, Dr. Seuss."

"What, did I hit a nerve? Hey, come back!"

Out on the street, when she turned her phone on, a message from Claire: Everything was fine. And maybe tomorrow, did Fiona and Cecily, together, want to meet Nicolette and watch her for an hour while Claire was at work and before Kurt could get across the city to pick her up? Her babysitting had fallen through.

1990

The broken rib prevented Yale from doing more in the apartment than he'd have liked. Teresa insisted he sit on the couch while she paraded box after box of stuff in front of him. Charlie's clothes, which he didn't want. Charlie's books, which he didn't want either. The kitchen things that had once been his, but which he'd long since replaced. Nico's stripy orange scarf. Yale couldn't believe it. He ran his fingers through the fringe. He rolled it carefully into a fat cylinder. He'd give it back to Fiona, finally. Here was his own Michigan sweatshirt, smelling like a crypt. He wondered if Charlie had kept it on purpose, or if it had just stayed buried somewhere, unnoticed. Here was the map of Chicago that Nico had drawn on top of, illustrating the places they'd all been together—a tiny Richard with his camera on the Belmont Rocks, a tiny Julian holding a tray of food by the sandwich shop where he used to work, Yale wearing a beret at the Art Institute. This, he would keep.

When he reached for it, Teresa said, "Don't keep moving all over. If you don't take full breaths, you'll wind up with pneumonia."

It felt good to be mothered. And with Charlie gone, he didn't feel guilty taking up what little mothering energy Teresa had left. So he stayed on the couch that still, after all these years, softened itself naturally to the shape of his body, and he let her bring him tea with honey, and he let her fill two big boxes with things he knew he might never unpack.

The apartment was bizarrely the same. Charlie hadn't redecorated even a little, hadn't added anything to the walls. The same refrigerator magnets, same sad plant on the windowsill. Yale was glad. It would have felt bad, in some inexplicable, unjustifiable way, to see physical evidence of the ways Charlie's world had moved on. Or maybe it was just that he wanted to believe in a world where this apartment still existed, where it was forever 1985, where the door might open at any moment and there would be Julian with a party invitation, Terrence with beer, Nico with a new comic for Charlie.

Teresa said, "You're not going back to work, are you? Don't even pop in. You know how people are, you check in and next thing they'll hand you a mountain of papers. Tell me you'll lounge at home and do nothing else."

He assured her he'd take as much time as he needed. One of the great things about DePaul was how little emotional investment he had in his work. They were currently raising funds for a new parking garage.

Yale wouldn't be able to carry these boxes home, even in a cab, so he promised he'd return next week when Teresa was here again from California. She'd been back and forth since Charlie died in December, though Yale wished she'd just go sun herself in the Caribbean for a month and sleep. "The fact that this plant is alive," he said, "means you've been doing too much."

He called Asher, who'd volunteered to pick him up. It would be the first time he'd seen him since the protest, since the kiss. Yale had been the last into that particular paddy wagon, so although Asher had been arrested a minute later, he never saw him—in part because, thanks to Fiona's persistent screaming about lawyers, Yale was sent to the hospital rather than put in the holding cell.

Asher could be there in five minutes. Yale leaned his head back on the sofa, smelled the fabric. Teresa was going around with the Dustbuster. He said, "I have a story about the map." The one Nico had drawn on. She stopped cleaning, sat on the floor in front of the couch, her knees tucked under her chin. "Okay, this little car he drew, way over here?" Yale pointed. "We were in our friend Terrence's car, and we were supposed to head south on the expressway, but we ended up shooting off west on the Eisenhower instead. Terrence had *no* sense of direction. Which is odd for a math teacher, right? So we got off the highway and got totally turned around, and it's this *terrible* neighborhood." Yale remembered all of them slinking low in their seats, as if that would keep them safe. "But we went in a big circle and eventually we found all these streets named after presidents, which we thought was good, because they go in order, and they stretch all the way back downtown, to the lake. Charlie was always complaining he couldn't find his way around downtown because he couldn't remember the presidents. If they were named for the British monarchy, he'd be set. So we're going back down through the president streets, you know, Madison, Monroe, Adams, Jackson—and just in that one part of town, before Van Buren, the next thing was this tiny street called Gladys Avenue. And Charlie goes, '*There was a President Gladys?*' He was serious. Terrence never let him forget that, oh my God. He used to make up facts about the Gladys administration."

Teresa let out a small, shallow laugh.

"I'm not telling it right," he said.

"No, I like that. I like it very much. He had such good friends, didn't he? He had a family here."

And there was the low buzzer, a sound from his distant past. Yale kissed Teresa's cheek and she told him again to walk carefully, to breathe fully.

Asher didn't have his car. "It's too nice out to drive," he said. Yale promised he was okay walking—it really only hurt when he bent or twisted—and Asher suggested they stroll around and wind up at St. Joe's, where he had a two o'clock appointment. "I'll get you a cab from there," he said.

Yale was too nervous to talk normally. He found himself chattering and then falling silent for long stretches. Asher needed to duck over to Halsted to find an ATM. As he pocketed his cash he said, "You heard about County, right?" No, Yale hadn't. "Cook County Hospital is now officially, drumroll please, treating female AIDS patients."

"Seriously? That fast? Like, because of the protest?"

"You didn't think it would work, did you. Listen, Yale, I'm not making it up. This shit *works*. I want you to stay involved."

"I'll think about it."

"I need to tell you something." They turned down Briar again, although there were more efficient routes to St. Joe's. "I've put off telling people, and I've particularly put off telling you. But I'm moving to New York."

"Oh." He felt it as a pain in his rib, even though he hadn't twisted, hadn't bent. They were back in front of the apartment now, in front of the same place he'd gotten his heart broken four years ago, so why not break it again in the same spot? His cheeks stung. Not his eyes, but his cheeks—how odd. Asher stopped and faced him.

"There's stuff I can do nationally with ACT UP from there, stuff that'll make a bigger impact than what I can do from Chicago."

"Yeah, who needs Chicago."

"Yale."

"No, sorry. It's good. That's really good."

"Listen, it's like, I was born to fight. I was born angry. I hated my dad, I hated the world, I pick fights with strangers, right? And

469

I look back and it all makes sense, because maybe I was born for *this*. Maybe I'm getting religious or something, but it feels like I'm here for a reason."

Yale looked at everything that wasn't Asher, nodded. "You know what Charlie said about you once? He said if we didn't have you, we'd have to invent you."

Asher laughed. "Well, you have me. You had me. You still have me, just—"

"It's okay."

They started walking again. He could ask him to stay. He could kiss him again and tell him he'd do anything if he just stayed in Chicago. But it wouldn't work. Asher might kiss him back, but there was no version of the future in which Asher chose love—temporary, fragile, illness-laden love—over the fight. (And who was he kidding? It wasn't love. It was attraction. It was a seed that might have grown, given better soil, more sun.) In every version of the story, Asher was correct. He shouldn't stay here, just to make Yale happy for a year, three years, until they both got too sick to make anyone happy. He should be in New York banging on doors and making news. In a way, Yale had already asked at the protest; he'd already received his answer.

Here was the house, the one Yale had picked out for himself a thousand years ago, the piece of the city he was supposed to own.

Yale said, "Stop a second."

"What?"

He faced the house, closed his eyes, and he put his hand on the rolled-up cuff of Asher's shirt. He wanted to bathe in it for five seconds, the future he might be having if it weren't for everything. He'd have broken up with Charlie, sure, and Charlie would be coked up in some downtown condo by now, and Yale would have this house, and he and Asher would be together. He was sure. Asher would be lighting the grill in the backyard. Fiona and Nico and Terrence were on their way over for dinner. Julian was hanging out on the porch with a drink, fresh from rehearsal.

Asher said, "Are you okay?"

Yale opened his eyes and nodded.

They walked east to right below Belmont Harbor, and then they walked through the park on the path.

They talked about Richard, whose solo show was coming up that summer at a gallery in the Loop. "Who ever thought Richard would get an actual show?" Asher said. "I thought it was all an excuse to meet models."

They talked about where in New York Asher would live (Chelsea) and when he was leaving (two weeks) and how often he'd get back to Chicago (occasionally, mostly for work).

They talked about Yale's rib, about the stupid bottle of Imodium that had broken it, about how he didn't care and he'd do it all again.

Yale told him about Bill leaving the most important artist out of Nico's great-aunt's show, the guy she loved her whole life. "It was the whole point," Yale said. "It was the point of everything."

Asher told him he shouldn't be the one holding power of attorney for Yale anymore. "You need someone who can be at the hospital right away. If I'm in New York, I can't make decisions for you. You should ask Fiona. I'll draw up the papers."

Yale might have protested that it took just as long to drive from Madison as to fly from New York, and he might have said he couldn't bear to do that to her, but Asher was right. And there was no one else left, no one he trusted as much.

"She'll be done with college by the time you get sick. You have a lot more time."

Yale said, "I used to worry about Reagan pressing the button, you know? And asteroids, all that. And then I had this realization.

If you had to choose when, in the timeline of the earth, you got to live—wouldn't you choose the end? You haven't missed anything, then. You die in 1920, you miss rock and roll. You die in 1600, you miss Mozart. Right? I mean, the horrors pile up, too, but no one wants to die before the end of the story.

"And I really used to believe we'd be the last generation. Like, if I thought about it, if I worried about death, it was all of us I was thinking about, the whole planet. And now it's like, no, it's just you, Yale. *You're* the one who's gonna miss out. Not even on the end of the world—like, let's hope the world goes on another billion years, right?—but just the normal stuff."

Asher didn't answer, but he took Yale's right hand in his left hand, wound their fingers together. They walked on like that, Yale's heart pinballing around his battered ribcage.

If Yale weren't physically incapable of sex right now, if Asher hadn't just been talking about the leg pain and nausea he was still experiencing from his pills, Yale might have held out hope that the afternoon would end in someone's bed. A one-time thing. As it was, the hand-holding was an end in itself. An acknowledgment, a dip into that same parallel universe he'd spied on back at the Briar house. And was friendship that different in the end from love? You took the possibility of sex out of it, and it was all about the moment anyway. Being here, right now, in someone's life. Making room for someone in yours.

"Get a load of *these* two!"

A male voice, close behind. Asher tightened his grip on Yale's hand before Yale could even figure it out.

"Hey, *Louise*! Get a load of these two!"

"Don't turn around," Asher whispered.

Yale thought Asher might want to drop his hand, but of course he didn't. Asher didn't even quicken his pace.

A woman's voice, farther back: "Bert, don't be an ass."

"I'm not the one into *asses*! Hey, ladies! Gimme your time, will you? I got some questions!"

"Bert!"

"Listen, ladies. Hold on."

But the voices were farther away now; perhaps Louise had detained Bert.

Distantly: "Get a load of *those* two!"

Asher and Yale didn't say anything else the rest of the way to St. Joe's.

Yale promised he'd get a cab, but then he didn't. He walked to the El. He wanted to be near other riders, packed tight. He wanted to see the city from above, to pass close enough to people's windows that he could see their kitchen tables, their fights.

The world was a terrible, beautiful place, and if he wasn't going to be here much longer he could do whatever he wanted, and the thing he wanted most in the world, besides to run after Asher, was to fix Nora's show, to give Ranko Novak's awkward paintings and sketches their due, such as it was.

He thought about people who could help. There were the Sharps, but after everything they'd done for him, he couldn't ask another favor. He hardly knew anyone at Northwestern anymore. He certainly couldn't drag Cecily back into things. Across from him on the El stood a teenager with a column of silver hoops up her ear. It made Yale think of Gloria. Gloria was at the *Trib*. Gloria would help. He had no idea how, but *she* would know how.

One stop before his own, a man limped onto the train and looked like he was about to lurch into Yale's lap, but then he opened a canvas bag. "Got socks for sale," he slurred to Yale and the woman next to him. "Dollar pair. Two dollar, three pair. One size fit your foot." He pulled out a Ziploc with a pair of clean athletic socks, yellow stripes at the top. They looked improbably thick and comfortable. "You got holes in your sock?" This was to Yale. "These make you feel better. Good socks, you feel all better. One dollar, all better."

Yale found a dollar and gave it to the man, who grinned, toothless, and presented him with the socks. Yale stood for his stop and squeezed the bag.

A gift from the city, it felt like. Something soft to put between himself and the earth.

2015

Fiona and Cecily took a painfully long cab ride up to Montmartre, to the garden square where Claire had told them to wait. Traffic was terrible throughout the city; everyone was back on the road, but the roads weren't back to normal. Fiona wondered if news trucks were still blocking things up, or if everyone was just driving distracted, skittish.

Square Jehan-Rictus wasn't square-shaped but an oblong stretch of sidewalk looping through shrubbery, enclosed by fences and low brick walls. The green benches, if it weren't for the bird shit, would have been lovely places to sit with a book on a summer day.

It was sunny but cold, and Fiona already worried Nicolette would be too chilly even as she feared Claire and Nicolette wouldn't show up at all.

Cecily checked her watch. She said, "This should have been the hospital waiting room. The two of us waiting together for the baby to be born. Better late than never!"

They walked the loop, past the tiny playground. They stopped at the mural next to it, a shiny wall made to look like a chalkboard, with white writing and scraps of red. "It must be all 'I love you,'" Cecily said. *Te amo* in one place, a hand making the sign-language word for *love* in another, most of it incomprehensible to Fiona—Thai and Braille and Greek and what might have been Cherokee.

Above it all, a painting of a woman in a blue ball gown, with words in a bubble: *aimer c'est du désordre ... alors aimons!*

Fiona felt, as she had on the bridge, that Paris or its more mischievous ghosts were directing messages straight at her. But that wasn't it at all; this was simply a city that talked about love, that acknowledged its constant invasions, its messiness. What would happen to Chicago, she wondered, if they covered it with things like this? If they filled up Clark Street Bridge with painted padlocks?

Cecily squeezed her arm, turned her to the walkway: A little blonde girl, swinging her legs out of a small stroller. Above her, Claire, smiling uncertainly. Nicolette hopped out and ran straight past them to the playground, her pink coat open, rain boots trying to fall off her feet.

Fiona and Claire hugged stiffly, and Claire and Cecily shook hands even more stiffly. In the midst of everything else, it hadn't occurred to Fiona till just now that the two of them didn't know each other. Fiona must have carried Claire on her hip a few of those times she'd gone to visit Roscoe the cat, to catch up with Cecily—but those visits had tapered off quickly. Whatever bond had been forced upon Fiona and Cecily in Yale's hospital room didn't have lasting power; trauma wasn't always the best glue.

Fiona turned to watch Nicolette scramble up the steps and cross the little bridge to the slide. She had it all to herself, and it was sized just right for her. She looked less like Nico than she had in the picture and more like Fiona herself, really.

Claire called to her, and she ran back from the bottom of the slide, buried her face in Claire's legs. "Can you say hi? Can you say hi to Fiona and Cecily?"

It sounded so odd, but maybe, if everything went well, the two of them could pick out grandmotherly names for themselves.

Grandy, Nana, Mimi. Mémère, even. She could deal with Fifi, a name she'd rejected her whole life, but one that might sound right coming from a French grandchild. She wanted to squeeze Nicolette, run her hands down those soft cheeks, but she didn't want to scare her, and she didn't want to scare Claire either.

Claire handed them a tote bag with Nicolette's snacks and juice, a change of clothes, a couple of picture books. She told them Kurt would be there in an hour and a half. "And you could come to the bar in an emergency." It was only two blocks away.

"She's toilet trained?" Cecily asked, as if she were suddenly remembering a script from decades ago.

"Of course. She won't need to go, she's a camel."

And she was off, with only a couple more instructions, a quick hug for Nicolette—who stared at her two grandmothers with interest after her mother had left, but didn't seem afraid in the slightest. She must have been used to sitters.

Fiona sat on one of the benches by the playground and unpacked the bag so Nicolette could see the crackers, the sippy cup of juice, the *Pénélope* books—a little mouse playing a color game at school in one, learning about seasons in the other. But Nicolette was content for now to do the slide, run up to the two women and grin while they clapped, circle back and do it all again. There was time yet to call her over, see if she'd sit on someone's lap, if she'd speak to them in either English or French.

Cecily said, "She's just so beautiful."

That Fiona should double over crying at that precise moment made a kind of sense, absurd as it was; this was the first time Cecily had shown any real emotion at all, and so Fiona's tear ducts seemed to have taken it as an invitation. She could feel Cecily staring at her with concern, and when she looked up she saw that Nicolette had stopped her circuit and was standing in front of her, her little eyebrows squinched together.

"Did you fall down?" she said in English so perfect and clear that Fiona could only cry harder.

"She's fine, dear," Cecily said. "She's just a little sad about something."

"What is she sad about?"

What a question. She managed to say, "I'm sad at the world."

Nicolette looked around as if there were something wrong with the garden square.

She said, "My friend has a globe!"

Cecily said, "Don't worry about it, honey. Fiona will be fine." This was convincing enough for Nicolette, who was off again, making cat noises. Cecily put a hand on Fiona's back.

Fiona said, "I sent away his mom."

It was the thing she hadn't let herself blurt out to Julian in Richard's studio the other day, the thing she hadn't let herself think about when she learned that Claire had been through labor without her, the thing that had been buzzing at a low vibration beneath her every thought about Claire since she'd disappeared, and before that as well. The thing she'd mentioned only once to her shrink, even then changing the story enough, downplaying it enough, that Elena had barely noticed the telling.

"I don't understand."

"Yale's mom."

"Okay. Yale? You did what?"

"I sent—at the very end. I was there, and you had to be in California."

"Yes. Fiona, you can't—"

"No, listen. You had to be in California, which wasn't your fault, and I was pregnant with Claire."

"I know."

"You don't know. Okay, so I had power of attorney. And this was when he was—all the lung stuff was going on at the same time."

478

"It was terrible," Cecily said, more like she was affirming Fiona's memory than reliving it herself. "I remember he could barely get two words out. And the indecipherable handwriting. It bothered me; his handwriting had always been so tidy. And he'd write those notes, and I couldn't—"

"There were some better days too." Fiona felt bad interrupting but she needed to get this out while she had momentum. "At the end, and maybe this was when you were gone, it seemed like the treatments were suddenly working for some of the lung stuff, and he could talk, he really could. But then his kidneys went, from all the drugs they were pumping in, and the fluids were building up—I can't even remember, but then it was his heart. He drowned. I said that to the doctors and they said, no, that wasn't quite it, but I know what I saw. He drowned."

Cecily said, "You handled it all so beautifully. I can't imagine what you went through, but it was the right decision, keeping him off the ventilator. It was what he wanted."

Nicolette had quit the slide and was making a careful pile of small dried leaves. Fiona breathed in as deeply as she could, tried to start again. "I count it as two whole years," she said, "that he was really sick." Yale had first gotten pneumonia in the spring of 1990, after that stupid fucking cracked rib at the medical protest. It had cleared up, but not really; he had asthma to begin with, and so the pneumonia weakened him more than it otherwise would have. Another issue followed, and another, until he joked that his body was a nightclub for opportunistic infections, joked that he'd named his last remaining T cells after the Cubs' lineup. "And then at the end—Okay." She put her hands on her knees, arms stiff. "Four days before he died, his mother showed up at the hospital."

Cecily's face went still.

"I knew who she was, because she'd been in this Tylenol commercial, and every time it came on I'd stare at her face and try to figure her out. I guess his father—you remember his father came down a couple times, but he just kind of stood around and it was so awkward."

"I don't remember that."

"Well, he did, and Yale hadn't thought he was really in contact with the mom, but apparently he was, or he figured out how to reach her, and she showed up. She was wearing this yellow sundress, and she looked so nervous. It was at night. He was asleep."

Her expression had been so much like the one Yale made when he was anxious—a look that had always reminded Fiona of a rabbit. It might have made Fiona love this woman, just as she loved Yale, but instead she resented her even more. That one of her favorite things about Yale came from someone who'd abandoned him.

"And you sent her away."

Fiona let out a sob that made Nicolette look up from her leaves. Her hair translucent in the sunlight.

"I wasn't a mother yet, not really. I—all I could think was it might upset him to see her. But I was being possessive, too, I know that now. He was *mine*, and here this woman came, and I didn't think about what she was going through. Or what it had taken for her to walk in there. I thought it would kill him. I thought he'd be so upset, and I imagined her messing up the treatment, trying to take charge the way my parents had with Nico. And I hated my own mother so much. I walked her to the elevator and I pressed the button for her, and I told her he'd specifically said he didn't want to see her."

"Was that true?"

"Yes, actually. Yes. It was one of the things we'd gone over. But I could have told him when he was awake. I could have asked what he wanted to do. And I never did. I was going to tell him. I kept being about to tell him."

She'd gone into labor, is what happened, and then when that went horribly awry, she'd had her C-section, been tethered to the bed with IVs and drugs and pain right upstairs from him but unable to get herself down the hall and to the elevator. When Cecily wasn't back yet, and Asher was in New York, and there was really no one left to stay by his bedside. She'd thought of calling casual acquaintances and asking them to check on him, but he was closer with the nurses than with random old neighbors, and these nurses knew what they were doing; they'd held hands for hours with many men dying alone. Besides which, Fiona just needed to recover and then she could get back down there to the third floor, take care of him again.

But meanwhile Yale fell into deep unconsciousness, and Fiona had to make the medical decisions over the phone, the maternity nurses looking on with concern. She'd send Damian down again and again with messages for Yale, despite the fact that he likely couldn't hear a thing, and when he came back up she'd make him tell her what Yale looked like. "He's got so many tubes coming out of him," he said. "He's the wrong color. Fiona, I don't know. I'm so tired. I'll go back again if you need, but every time I'm in there I think I'll pass out." Yale's old friend Gloria and her girlfriend did some shifts, but only in the afternoons. When Nico had died, there were too many people wanting to be in the room, jockeying for position, vying for the roles of caretaker and hand-holder and chief mourner. And now there was no one. Yale had been there for Nico, and Terrence, and even fucking Charlie, and there was no one left for him, not really, and it killed her.

Claire was thirty-six hours old and nursing wasn't working, and Fiona, who'd been prepared for the tearing of a natural birth, was in disbelief at the howling pain that ran through her entire body when she tried to adjust her torso, tried to sit up on her own just the slightest bit. She'd go light-headed and collapse back, blind. In the five minutes the Lamaze instructor had devoted to C-sections, she'd never mentioned the pain, the crippling. Fiona made it to the bathroom on the arm of the nurse, and nearly fainted. She asked if they could take her down to the AIDS unit in a wheelchair, and the first nurse said she'd have to ask the doctor, but then she never came back. The second nurse said it could be done in the morning. Fiona might have fought harder, but the pain was too much, and the drugs were closing her eyes, and in the morning everything would be easier.

Claire stayed in the nursery all night that night, and Fiona slept late. She woke to Dr. Cheng's face. He'd come all the way upstairs. When his expression came into focus she screamed so primally, so loudly, that if she'd been anywhere other than a maternity ward, everyone would have come running.

It was early this morning, Dr. Cheng said. Debbie the charge nurse had been with him.

But that wasn't enough.

And if Fiona hadn't sent his mother away, he might have heard her voice through the haze. He might have been comforted on the deepest childhood level.

Nicolette had come to the bench and was opening her little bag of crackers. Cecily patted the bench and she climbed up, sat with her legs swinging off the edge.

Fiona touched the blonde curls, unimaginably soft.

She said, "It was the biggest mistake of my life, Cecily. I think I'm being punished for it now. I shut my own mother out and I sent Yale's mother away, and it all boomeranged and hit me in the face."

Nicolette said, "Do you live in America?"

Fiona dried her eyes on her sleeve. "Yes. Did you know that I'm your mama's mama? And Cecily is your daddy's mama."

Nicolette looked back and forth between them as if a great joke

482

were being played, as if they'd told her one was the Easter Bunny and the other was the Tooth Fairy.

"Your mama came out of my tummy, and your daddy came out of Cecily's tummy."

"Show me," Nicolette said, and Fiona lifted up her sweater and pointed at the pale line of scar.

"Right there," she said, and Nicolette nodded.

"But it didn't ouch?" Nicolette asked.

"Not a bit."

Nicolette chewed her cracker, and Cecily said to Fiona, "I don't know if this is helpful, but whenever I felt guilty about something when I was young, my mother would say, "How do you make up for it? What's a thing you could do that would make you feel better?" It sounds like Mr. Rogers, I know, but it's always grounded me when I'm upset."

"I could move to Paris," Fiona said, and she was joking until she heard it and realized she wasn't.

Nicolette wanted her books now. Cecily pulled her onto her lap and read to her about Pénélope, about the game she and her animal friends played with their trunk of colored clothes.

1991

Fiona was waiting for them right inside the Brigg's front door. She said, "Rescue me from my family!"

"Help us first," Cecily said. There was a ramp, but the rubber strip right in the doorway was catching Yale's wheels, and so Cecily had to rock him back while Fiona grabbed the armrests and pulled forward, and Yale held tight and tried to lean back so he wouldn't fall forward when they put him down again.

The landing jarred him, knocked the oxygen tank into his spine. But they were in. Fiona helped him pull his coat off.

Cecily said, "We have exactly one hour."

"I actually have two hours of oxygen," Yale said. "She's being conservative."

"Well she's right!" Fiona said. "What if there's a traffic jam on the way back? I can't believe they let you out."

"For the record," Yale said as they wheeled him down the hall toward the gallery, "if you're ever questioned in a court of law, *they* did not let me out, and Dr. Cheng definitely did not help us steal the oxygen or the chair."

"Of course not."

"He says hi."

The gallery was already full. Yale was vastly underdressed—every other man wore a tie, and he wore an old sweater that used to fit snugly and now hung like a tent—but his clothes weren't what anyone would be looking at, anyway.

There was Warner Bates from *ARTnews*, waving, pointing him out to someone else. Warner had come to interview him last fall right after Gloria's initial *Trib* feature appeared. He'd brought along a photographer who'd shot Yale sitting on his own couch, laughing with Fiona. Yale was embarrassed by the attention, by the focus on his role. Gloria's story had been about the collection itself. *"After Seventy Years,"* the headline read, *"an Artist Claims His Prize."* It included plenty of helpful quotes from an unwitting Bill Lindsey, who didn't realize the focus would be Ranko Novak. *The article wasn't dishonest; it* never stated directly that Novak's pieces would be in the show. But in talking at length about Novak's pieces, as well as his life and death, it implied as much. "She wanted him to have his due," it quoted Yale as saying. "She wanted him hanging next to Modigliani." That article itself might not have been enough to force Bill's hand, but the half-dozen more pieces it spawned in the art press were. And suddenly Ranko's name was all over the gallery's own press for the show.

Yale glimpsed Bill standing a few yards ahead of him in the gallery, and Bill, when he noticed Yale, looked terrified. He spun toward the woman he'd just said goodbye to, asked her something, led her quickly in the other direction. Bill didn't look sick. Cecily had told him as much, updated him every few months almost apologetically, as if Yale would *want* Bill to have it.

One thing about being in the chair: From behind people, Yale couldn't see anything yet. He recognized a corner of the Hébuterne bedroom.

He'd imagined, once upon a time, wheeling Nora in here to see the show. He'd imagined pushing her in front of the crowds.

Here were the Sharps, weaving their way to him. Esmé reached down to envelop him awkwardly in her thin arms. Esmé and Allen had been saints, kept calling to ask if he had everything he needed. For his first long hospital stay, Esmé had brought him a stack of novels. They would never be close friends, would never gossip over brunch, but they'd volunteered themselves to form a safety net below him.

"Shall we take you around?" Esmé said.

So while Fiona was shanghaied by a man who wanted to explain to her in great detail how he'd known Nora's husband, Cecily and the Sharps took him around, asked people to let him through.

The exhibit was set up on a small labyrinth of walls, with the pieces hung artist by artist in rough chronological order, and Cecily proposed starting at the end of the circuit. There was a great deal of written explanation for each grouping. Framed letters and notes surrounded the write-up on Foujita. Here, against the snowy field of the gallery wall, was his ink drawing of Nora in the green dress.

In the years since Yale had seen the pieces, they'd taken on the aura of famous works of art. Important because you'd seen them before, and your brain already had a slot for them. An old friend met years later on the street corner. Your high school history textbook found again and, through its distant familiarity, made holy.

Esmé wheeled him by a group that included Fiona's parents, who didn't glance his way, and Debra, who did. She looked at him with utter blankness, though, and Yale wondered if she recognized him. She looked different herself—rounder, a little brighter. According to Fiona, she was dating an investment banker in Green Bay. Not the life of wild adventure Yale would have wished for her, but it was something.

Warner Bates from *ARTnews* was above him suddenly, blocking his view, introducing him to an elderly couple who looked at Yale

486

with undisguised horror. He didn't hold out his hand to shake; he wouldn't do that to them. Warner said, "This is a triumph, Yale! You should feel very happy!"

"I do. I can't believe it's really up."

"This is all your doing, you know." Warner turned to the couple. "This is the guy who made it happen."

They wound their way to the start of the exhibit. There was Ranko's section, at last: the two paintings, the three cow sketches. Fiona, who had rejoined them, squeezed his hand, and Esmé said, "Well, there it is."

He wished it were more spectacular to look at, but things had been nicely framed and the informational plaques on Ranko distracted nicely from the blandness of the cows. The painting of Nora as a sad little girl had been brightened up by restoration, and her dress was now a much more interesting shade of blue than Yale had remembered.

And finally, there was Ranko in the argyle vest. Yale hadn't seen it in person since he learned it was Ranko, since he learned Nora had held the brush herself. It was labeled *Self-Portrait*; Yale had passed along that much information, at least. It really did look like the same artist's hand, at least to Yale, but maybe, now that he really looked, there was something more hesitant in the lines; it was the work of someone desperate to get something right. This one, too, was crisper after its restoration. He hadn't realized what bad shape the paintings originally must have been in. Yale noticed a spark of silver in Ranko's nest of curly hair. He wheeled himself closer, which didn't work, and so he wheeled himself back instead.

He wasn't crazy: It was a paper clip. Not the first thing you'd notice, but now that he was looking, yes, and there was another, too, closer to his brow. The shapes were distinct, and she'd accomplished something very much like a glint of light off each. Had they been her idea, or Ranko's? Had he worn his crown again that day, as he posed? Had she added them after he died? How odd, how inexplicably devastating: paper clips.

He wanted to laugh, to shout it to the gallery, to explain—but he could only ever tell Fiona. To Esmé he just said, "That one's my favorite."

A man beside Yale's chair said to his wife, "I heard they had to include *everything*, it was part of the lady's will." But here it hung, and it was an artifact of love. Well—of a hopeless, doomed, selfish, ridiculous love, but what other kind had ever existed?

It had been an hour and five minutes, and Cecily ran out to start her car. Esmé wheeled Yale backward to the exit, and he had one last chance to look down the gallery. The people in their beautiful clothes, the edges and corners of paintings and sketches.

Esmé said, "Oh, *tar*, it's snowed!"

There was a good half inch on the ground; Cecily's shoes had made soft prints on their way to her car.

Yale hugged Fiona goodbye, told her to look closely at Ranko's self-portrait. He said to Allen Sharp, "If her parents come near her, pretend you're having a seizure or something."

Allen ran ahead, scraping the snow out of the wheelchair's path with his dress shoes.

Allen and Esmé lifted him together into the passenger seat, got the oxygen tank between his legs. Cecily said, "It's a quarter after. Yale, I hate this."

It was already dark out. Cecily drove up Sheridan Road far too fast, illuminated snowflakes shooting past them. "Slow down," he said. "It's not worth a crash."

"If we crash," she said, "they'll take us where we're going anyway. And faster."

"We'll be fine," Yale said. "It was worth it."

"Was it? Are you happy?" She checked his face. "I liked Ranko's stuff. I really did."

"She loved him," Yale said instead of contradicting her, instead of saying it was okay if she hadn't liked it at all. "Even if she shouldn't have. I think it was one of those things where you can't let go of how you first saw the person."

"We *never* let go of that," Cecily said. "I mean, even for parents—that's never not your baby, you know?"

"I think you're right." As he got sicker, it was more and more often how he thought of people—of Charlie, certainly, and of everyone else here or gone: not as the sum of all the disappointments, but as every beginning they'd ever represented, every promise.

"I think your clock is fast," Yale said as they headed south down Lake Shore. 7:49. Eleven minutes left, but he'd be okay for a few more if the oxygen ran out. Everyone was driving cautiously; there was no way for Cecily to get around them.

"That clock is *slow*," she said. "And you're not even wearing a watch."

He closed his eyes, leaned the seat back a few inches.

It was 7:56, according to the clock, when they pulled up outside Masonic.

Dr. Cheng was standing out on the sidewalk in the snow, freezing in his white coat, with a fresh tank of oxygen.

2015

On Monday, November 23, exactly one week after it was supposed to, Richard's show *Strata* finally had its preview at the Pompidou. It would open to the public on Wednesday, a week late, despite the giant canvas sign hanging outside the museum with the original dates positioned on top of a photo of a rather young Richard holding a Kodak Brownie to his eye. The name "CAMPO" stretched across the whole thing.

Fiona had convinced Claire to attend. She'd have loved to believe Claire's acquiescence was about *her*, about making amends and spending time together, but on the other hand Claire had known Richard since she was little, and she was still an artist, or still wanted to be one. And she had a sitter: Cecily had insisted she'd rather watch Nicolette than put on heels and try to speak French.

Fiona arrived forty nervous minutes early. She'd cleared out of Richard's at lunchtime, wanting to give him space to get ready, and had parked herself at a café; and now she wandered the Pompidou gift shop, where she'd told Claire to meet her, looking at bright silicone spatulas and chunky necklaces and art books. She wanted to find something for Nicolette.

She was inspecting a striped water bottle when she felt a chin on her shoulder. Julian. He hadn't done this to her in thirty years, but that was his stubble, his way of coming up from behind and just nuzzling you.

She turned to hug him. She said, "Well isn't this something."

He said, "You look *radiant*!" Then he whispered: "Serge told me you were getting laid here, but wow."

Fiona swatted him with the bottle. She said, "I'm just radiant with nerves."

She had spent the weekend looking into rental properties in Paris, ones that would let her stay one month, two, three. She could sublet her Chicago place easily.

Yesterday morning at breakfast with Cecily she said, "What if we *both* moved here? As roommates? What if we—I don't know, Grannies in Paris. It sounds like a movie! We could do it, we really could. Why should all that study abroad stuff be wasted on the young?"

"No," Cecily had said, and shook her head definitively. "Are you really considering this?"

"I mean, until she agrees to come home. Or until—I don't even know. But listen, when we were young, we'd just plunge into the future without worrying. Right? At least *I* did. I don't know when that stopped."

"Don't you have a dog?"

"And a job. I mean—I'll figure it out."

"Are you sure you'd even be welcome?"

"No."

She explained then all the things she'd halfway worked out, lying awake. That she could work for Richard—didn't he say he needed an assistant? That she could watch Nicolette, help Claire out financially, get her to a better neighborhood. *Claire* could work for Richard, for that matter!

She didn't explain to Cecily the other things she was thinking: how it would be a fresh start, a hugely overdue one. How she'd never really left Chicago. Madison hardly counted, what with her constant trips back, her tethers to the city. How thirty years after Nico died, it was finally time to let things go. How maybe she could throw her fate out into the world as easily as Jake dropped his wallet onto a bar, knowing it would always come back to him.

Cecily had sighed and laughed and tapped her fork on the edge of her plate. "Well, I'll come visit you," she said.

Last night she'd written Claire a long email laying out the idea. "*Don't write back*," she'd begun. "*We can talk tomorrow.*"

So now on top of the social anxiety inherent in walking into this opening, and on top of the anticipation of seeing Richard's footage of the '80s, she was standing here in the gift shop waiting to be roundly rejected by her only child.

Julian said, "I need this pillow! What is this, Kandinsky?"

Fiona never saw what he was talking about, because here was Claire, in a black cotton dress and black boots, her hair in soft waves. She seemed more relaxed than she had in the bar or the park. Perhaps this felt less like an invasion, or maybe she'd just gotten used to the idea of seeing her mother. In any case, she adjusted her purse, gave Fiona a quick hug, scanned the house-wares section as if she expected something else to happen now.

Fiona said, "I want you to meet Julian Ames."

Claire bobbed her head and shook his hand.

"Julian was a friend of your Uncle Nico," she said.

How strange to call him that when he'd never been anyone's uncle. But she'd tried it throughout Claire's childhood. *This was your Uncle Nico's drawing table. Your Uncle Nico didn't like egg yolks either.* And now, she supposed, Nico was a *great*-uncle. Dear God: Great-Uncle Nico. Who the hell was that? Some old man with bifocals.

Julian said, "Your mama took care of us all."

Fiona saw Claire's shoulders draw back.

"I'm aware," she said. "Saint Fiona of Boystown."

Julian glanced at Fiona. She wondered suddenly if the cult had made Claire judgmental of homosexuality, had taught her that AIDS was the wrath of God or something. She couldn't imagine Claire falling for that, but then who knew anything at all about this stranger?

Claire picked up one of a set of melamine plates with Magritte images on them, this one his pipe-that-wasn't-a-pipe on a spring-green background. She rotated it, stared at it.

Julian said, "I've been telling stories about your mom for years. She thought I was dead, and the whole time I was talking about her like she was Paul Bunyan. And for a long time I didn't even know the half of what she did. I left Chicago, and she kept on going."

Claire smiled up drily at Julian. "Well, I'm what stopped her."

Fiona tried to puzzle out what she meant.

Claire said, "I was born the day her friend died. Did you know that?"

Fiona whispered, although it didn't need to be whispered. "She means Yale." And then aloud she said, "No, that's wrong. You were born the day before. Claire, listen, did you tell Kurt that I said that was the worst day of my life? Because I *never*—"

"It always killed me," Claire said. She was talking only to Julian, as if Fiona weren't there. Julian, to his credit, didn't look panicked at being in the middle of this. Maybe he knew what he was: a void, a sounding board, a necessary presence. "There was always—when I was a kid, there was part of me that thought if only I'd been born *after* he died, she'd believe I was him, reincarnated or something. Then *I* could believe it, even. I wished I'd been born that exact instant."

Although Claire wasn't looking at her, just at Julian and the Magritte plate, Fiona said, "It was never a competition, honey."

"Ha!" It was too loud, but no one else was listening. "That is hilarious."

Maybe this was good. Claire needed to say the meanest things she could, so they'd be out in the room instead of inside her. Still, all Fiona could think to do was cry, which wouldn't help anything, so she managed not to. Julian took a step toward Fiona, put a hand on her back.

Claire put the plate down and picked up another, this one bright sky blue with that bowler hat. *Usage Externe*, the hat's label said.

Julian said, "I know she did her best."

"I'm trying to do my best *now*," Fiona said. "Now that you're a mother, don't you—"

But Claire cut in. "She only wants to move here because there's been a disaster. She wants to swoop in and be near the drama."

Julian looked confused.

Fiona said, "What I'd like to be near is my daughter and my granddaughter. I'd like to make up for maybe being a depressed, shitty mother by being a decent grandmother. I'm not asking anything in return."

Claire flipped the plate over as if she were checking the price. A thoughtful, resigned silence.

"You might not resolve this all in the gift shop," Julian said.

Claire said, "I can't control where you live. If you move here, you move here."

It was as good as Fiona could hope to get from her, for now.

"Can I interject something," Julian said, "as we head for the escalators? Because it's probably time to head for the escalators." Claire blinked and put the plate down, and they walked out across the broad lobby. He said, "Everyone knows how short life is. Fiona and I know it especially. But no one ever talks about how long it is. And it's—does that make sense? Every life is too short, even the

494

long ones, but some people's lives are too long as well. I mean—maybe that won't make sense till you're older."

He stepped onto the escalator first, and he rode backward to face them.

He said, "If we could just be on earth at the same place and same time as everyone we loved, if we could be born together and die together, it would be so simple. And it's not. But listen: You two are on the planet at the same time. You're in the same place now. That's a miracle. I just want to say that."

Claire was behind her, so Fiona couldn't see her face, but she could feel her energy—she'd had so much practice, and it was all coming back—and at the very least, she could feel that Claire wasn't annoyed, wasn't rolling her eyes and wondering who this asshole was with his motivational speech. As for herself, she was grateful. She hadn't remembered Julian being this smart, but she hadn't been smart back then either. Thirty years could do a lot.

They were nearing the top. "Turn around," she said, "before you trip."

1992

For the first time in three weeks, he could breathe. Not well, but well enough that he could get out whole strings of words, whole thoughts and sentences. When he'd been so certain, only yesterday, that this was it, that each breath had only one or two more behind it. Part of him thought he should hoard each breath, save it for tomorrow, but mostly he wanted to talk while he still could, say things he wouldn't be able to say later.

Fiona was in the chair beside the bed. Eight months pregnant, barely, and still so small—if she'd worn a baggy enough shirt, you wouldn't have known. When she got to nine months, she'd promised him, she wouldn't risk the drive from Madison. But it had become increasingly clear in the last week that she might not go back up there at all before he died.

The cannula was tickling his nose and he managed to adjust it without sneezing; sneezing would hurt. It was pizza night—Pat's donated every week—and Fiona was eating a slice of pepperoni. Yale hadn't had solid food in weeks, but this was the first time he felt a bit jealous watching someone else eat—a good sign. Or it would have been a good sign if he didn't know full well that he was only feeling better because they'd changed his meds and were pumping him full of pentamidine and amphotericin again—backing off those was what had let his lungs get so bad—but these treatments would end up doing his kidneys and liver in. Dr. Cheng hadn't pulled any punches on that. One of the volunteers had told him a long time ago that whenever someone had a good breakfast, that was it—the patient only had a few hours left. He wasn't about to have a good breakfast, but these full breaths felt as nourishing, as ominous. The haircut guys had come through today, and he'd even sat up for that, with their help, and they'd shaved the back of his neck, massaged his temples with something that smelled like mint.

Fiona said, "Your eyes look so much better."

"What did they look like?" He didn't want to know, though, because soon they'd look like that again, or worse.

"Your pupils were just so dilated. It was like watching someone trapped in a tank of water. That's probably what it felt like too." She sighed, leaned down awkwardly to massage her swollen ankles. "You want the relaxation channel?"

Rafael came in then, getting his walker stuck on the doorway so Fiona had to get up and unwedge his wheel.

"I'm making a delivery," Rafael said. "I lacquered it for you, so it's shiny." He was talking about the small birdseed mandala he held against the walker handle with his thumb, the one Yale had made a month ago in the art room. There was no space for Rafael's walker between the bed and wall, so he handed it to Fiona to hand to Yale. "The art room isn't the same since you aren't there to play your terrible, sad British bands. That guy Calvin commandeered the stereo and it's all fucking techno now."

Yale held the mandala, although holding anything made his arms ache. He didn't know what he'd do with it. Send it to Teresa, maybe, in California. She still wrote him cards once a week.

Rafael said, "Tonight's the night. I'm cleared, and Blake's picking me up in an hour."

Fiona clapped enthusiastically, and Yale didn't know how she had it in her. "Are you ready?" she said. "Are you set up?"

"Open Hand is already over there stocking the fridge, and I'm doing great off the IV."

Yale appreciated that Rafael didn't say it apologetically. He'd been a perfect roommate. Before Rafael, Yale had shared a room with a tall man named Edward, who kept saying in a sad voice that this was the happiest he'd been in his life, that unit 371 was the first place he'd ever fit in. Prior to Edward there'd been an uncomfortable straight guy, Mark; before Mark was a man named Roger, whose enormous Irish Catholic family surrounded him as PML took his motor control and his speech but left his brain function intact, at least for a while. On an early stay, Yale had roomed with a guy who had ten Dixie cups lined up on the windowsill, each with an acorn planted inside. He was trying to sprout them before he died so he could give oak trees to ten of his friends.

And after all this, Yale had been lying in bed one day recovering from a lumbar puncture when they wheeled someone in on the other side of the curtain, and he heard the normal sounds—nurses explaining things about IVs, call buttons, something about the smoking deck—and then he heard someone say, "*You know* what I want on my Quilt panel? Just a giant pack of Camels!"

Even before he called Rafael's name and the nurse pulled back the curtain, Yale knew it was him. It had to be the most cheerfully anyone had ever checked into unit 371, but Rafael had his routine down, his favorite nurses. He knew which volunteer would read your tarot if you asked. This time he'd packed a bag of VHS tapes for the lounge, a stack of photos for the wall. It was a homecoming for him, or at least he played it like one, and Yale had the sense that if Rafael weren't tethered to IVs, he'd have leapt out of the bed to come bite Yale's face.

498

For the few weeks they were together while Yale could still breathe, they'd talked every night. Old gossip, new gossip, politics, movies. When old staffers from *Out Loud* came to visit Rafael, they'd pretend they were there to visit Yale too. But then one morning Yale had a dream that he was swimming at the bottom of the Hull House pool, looking up but unable to surface—and when he awoke, it was to struggle for breath in a room devoid of air.

"I'll miss you," Yale said.

Rafael shrugged and said, "I mean, it's not like I won't be back."

Yale was tired after he left, but he'd been afraid, for the last couple of days, of falling asleep. He didn't fear dying in his sleep— he'd take it, at this point—but waking up under water again. He wasn't afraid to close his eyes to his last day but to close them to his last *good* day. And so for now he kept them open, kept Fiona talking. He asked her to sing him "Moon River," and she said, "I still don't know the words!" but she managed anyway, laughed her way through it.

She said, "Nico would have loved it here. The art room! Can you imagine? I guess I'm picturing a version of him that would live a little longer. Like, if he got sick *now* and had good meds and everything. I mean, his nurses wouldn't *touch* him. And here you get massages."

"Well, I used to. Before I had tubes everywhere. But yeah. He would have liked it."

She looked so tired. Her hair was limp and greasy, her face swollen. She should have been home taking care of herself, resting up before the baby came—not sleeping on her side on a cot in his room. Most people's own families didn't do that for them. He asked if she was okay.

"My back just hurts," she said.

"You don't have to sleep here."

"I want to."

499

He said, "Fiona, I hate that I'm putting you through this again. I'm worried what this is doing to you."

She rubbed her eyes, made a feeble effort to smile. "I mean, it's bringing back memories. And it's killing me that it's you. You're my favorite person. But I'm pretty tough."

"That's what I mean, though. I keep thinking of Nora's stories about the guys who just shut down after the war. This is a war, it is. It's like you've been in the trenches for seven years. And no one's gonna understand that. No one's gonna give you a Purple Heart."

"You think I'm shell-shocked?"

"Just promise me you'll take care of yourself."

"I'll find a shrink in Madison. I will." Then she said, "Is there anyone—is there anyone you wish would come here that hasn't? I could call your dad, if you want. If you have any relatives, any old friends—even if it were awkward. If I had a magic wand. Is there anyone?"

"I don't feel like making small talk with my cousins."

She looked upset. "If there's *anyone* in the world that you'd want to see, even if you didn't think they wanted to see you. Is there anyone at all?"

"Christ, Fiona, you're making me feel really friendless right now. Unless your magic wand can bring back the dead, *no*. You're as bad as the chaplain."

The chaplain wouldn't stop checking if Yale wanted anything, wanted to chat. "No," Yale said every time, at least when he had air to talk, "and I'm Jewish." Yale had once caught him composing himself before he walked into the room, making his face as sad and pious as he could, pouting down at the Bible in his hands. Not long after that, he saw Dr. Cheng do the exact opposite. Yale was in the hallway waiting to be wheeled down for his bronchoscopy; Dr. Cheng had stood outside a patient's door reading through his notes, looking deflated. It wasn't an expression Yale had ever seen on him before. It occurred to Yale for the first time that Dr. Cheng was only around his own age. And then he lowered the notes, drew himself erect, took a breath Yale could hear from yards away, and transformed himself into the Dr. Cheng Yale knew. Then he knocked on the door.

Fiona gave up on her questions and scooted closer so she could stroke the skin between Yale's eyebrows. He couldn't stand to be touched anywhere else anymore, but that one spot worked. He closed his eyes.

He said, "When I was a kid, I used to shut my eyes in the car when we were ten minutes from home. And then I tried to feel it, feel that last corner that was the driveway. I tried not to count the turns, just sense when we were home. And I usually could."

Fiona said, "I did the exact same thing."

"And when I couldn't breathe, I was doing it too, but with—you know, with the end of things. And I know I'll wind up doing it again. I'll lie here with my eyes closed, and it feels like, *Okay, this is it. This must be it.* Only it's not."

"Sometimes it was like that with the car too," Fiona said. "Didn't you ever have that? It would feel like you were done, and you'd open your eyes, and it was just a red light."

"Yes. Yeah, it's like that."

He was glad she didn't tell him he was being morbid.

"That glow of the red light," she said. "Do you remember how magical the glow of a red light at night was? As a kid? Just being outside after dark."

He remembered.

He thought he might cry then, thought his body might wrack itself with dry tears, but Fiona stopped stroking his forehead and when he opened his eyes he saw that she was already crying herself, and it stopped him. He said, "I'm okay. It's okay."

But she was shaking her head fast and he saw, turning, how

tightly she gripped the bar of his bed. Her face had gone pale even as her cheeks had gone red.

He said, "Fiona. What."

"My back hurts."

"Your back?"

"I think—"

"Hey. Hey, it's okay."

She gasped in air as if she'd been holding her breath, which maybe she had. "The thing is, it keeps spasming like two minutes apart. But it's in the back."

"That sounds like contractions, Feef."

"It's probably just those false ones, those Brixton whatevers. But I keep thinking maybe I should like—no, don't do that!" Yale had pressed his call button. "Why'd you do that?"

"Maybe don't have your baby on the AIDS ward."

"I'm not having—it's not due for four weeks."

"And I wasn't supposed to die till I was eighty."

Debbie was already in the doorway. "Not me this time," Yale said.

Fiona said, "I'm okay."

"You don't *look* okay," Debbie said.

"Is there—there's a maternity ward here, right? Or do I have to go around to the ER?"

"Heavens! Well yes, we do provide that service. One-stop shopping. Let's get you a wheelchair."

"They're not even that bad," Fiona said. "I mean, I'm basing that on the movies, people screaming and whatever, but they're not that strong. It's just, they're coming pretty fast."

Debbie said, "Here's what we're doing. I'm calling up to maternity, I'm getting you an escort up there, no ER for you, and Yale is sitting *very* tight and I'm staying right with him all night. Maybe you come back a lot skinnier, maybe you come back a couple ounces bigger. Okay?"

And Fiona, who appeared to be holding her breath again, squeezed Yale's hand and nodded. "But they'll—can you keep me filled in? If I'm there a while, I want to know what's happening. I still have power of attorney, right? Even if I'm up there?"

"We can call you," Debbie said, "and you would not believe how fast I can make an orderly run." She was already beckoning someone in from the hallway, already picking up Yale's phone to call Labor and Delivery.

When Yale woke from night sweats, Debbie was still there. Fiona was resting, she said, and they were trying to delay the labor. Her husband was on his way from Canada, where he'd been speaking at a conference. She'd let Yale know as soon as she heard anything. Meanwhile, she'd get his sheets changed.

His heart felt bad. He could feel it working so hard, a fist trying to break through a wall. Which was exactly what Dr. Cheng said would happen. "The thing about you having multiple concurrent pathogens," he'd said, "is we're going to treat them all, but the treatments won't necessarily get along. And it's a lot of medicine, a lot of IVs, a lot of fluids. The risk is that we're going to stress your heart out, more than it's already stressed." The almost inevitable result, in short, would be congestive heart failure—the same thing Nora had died of. How had she seemed so serene through all of it?

In the morning, everything was much worse. Debbie was gone and Bernard had taken her place. Bernard changed the catheter bag, and Yale tried to ask about Fiona, but all he got out was her name.

"She's calling the nurse's station every ten minutes, I swear to God," Bernard said. "She wanted to know when you woke up. No baby yet."

Dr. Cheng came by. He said, "You're gaining weight, which is, for once, not a great thing. We've got some fluid collecting in your abdomen now. Which means the kidneys and liver aren't doing too well."

Yale's fingers tingled from low blood-oxygen, and he wasn't sure he could feel his toes. His heart was climbing a mountain with every beat.

In second grade, Mrs. Henry had been hospitalized with pneumonia and the substitute, a man who mostly told them stories about his time in the Peace Corps, had attempted to explain what was wrong with Mrs. Henry. "Take the deepest breath you can," he said, "and don't let it out." They did, and then he said, "Now take another breath on top of that. Don't let that one out either." They tried. Some of the kids gave up and let it all go with a wet raspberry noise, fell off their chairs laughing, but Yale, who always did as he was told, managed to keep going. "Now take another breath on top of that one. That third breath is what pneumonia feels like."

There was something comforting in the midst of all this about knowing he'd been warned so early. That sitting there with his healthy, strong little body, he'd felt, for one second of his seven-year-old life, how things would end.

Dr. Cheng said, "I want you to just nod or shake your head. If I can't understand you, we'll go to Fiona, alright? I want to know if I have your okay to take you off the pentam and the amphoterrible. That means we'd be officially starting hospice. And I want you on morphine."

It was one of the things Yale appreciated about Dr. Cheng, that he just went ahead and called it amphoterrible.

Yale used all the strength he could to make it as clear as possible when he nodded yes.

He woke up after God knew how long to see a very tall young man hovering over the bed. He couldn't quite focus; the face was cloudy. The morphine was a rug, a warm, numbing rug that was on him and in him.

"Hey, it's Kurt," the man said. "Cecily's son."

Yale tried to breathe in to say something, but he coughed out far more air than he'd taken in, and each cough was a morphine-dulled boot against his ribs.

Debbie was here. It must be night again. Now that he thought about it, he'd known Debbie was here. He'd felt her beside him for a while now. She knew about the spot between his eyes.

"Hey, I'm sorry. I don't need you to talk. My mom wanted me to check how you were, and I—" Yale could see, foggily, Kurt glancing to Debbie for permission. He unzipped the duffel bag he carried. "I brought Roscoe."

A blur of gray. Yale had held Roscoe on his lap every time he went to Cecily's for dinner, and each time, Roscoe settled in as if he knew exactly who Yale was.

"Mom's back from California on Friday." Yale had no idea how far away Friday was.

Kurt hovered near the bed, but he didn't put Roscoe on it. He surely hadn't been prepared for the number of tubes, the number of machines. He might have imagined Yale propped up with pillows, reading a book.

"I know he appreciates it, honey," Debbie said. "Here, let me bring him close for a second."

She took Roscoe, who didn't object, and she raised Yale's hand and put it down in the thick fur. Yale was aware, as he moved his fingers as much as he could, that this was the last time he'd ever touch animal fur, the last time, in fact, he'd touch much of anything besides his own bed and people's hands.

Kurt said, "But I'd better get going."

The poor kid. Yale wanted to tell him it was okay, that he wouldn't blame him if he ran for his life.

When he was gone, Yale managed to make an *F* sound with his lips, and Debbie understood.

"She's in labor," she said. "She's going to have a beautiful, healthy baby. I'll let you know as soon as we get the news."

He was aware that he was dreaming, but it felt like a dream that would never end.

Fiona, alone on the street. Only sometimes he *was* Fiona, looking down at the stroller she pushed, a stroller that was empty at first and then held twins and then again was empty. After a while there was no stroller. And sometimes he was looking at Fiona, following behind her, above, reaching out to touch her hair.

Fiona alone on Broadway, walking south. A hot, thick summer night, windows lit around her, but the streets were empty. The windows were empty, the parking lots. Broadway and Roscoe. Broadway and Aldine. Broadway and Melrose. Broadway and Belmont.

Airplanes crossed the sky, and far away there was traffic, but *here* there was no one. Fiona shouldered her way through clots of cold air. She felt the wind on her neck, and she said, "They're *breathing* on me. They're all around." She caught a glimmer of a teenage boy sitting on a bus stop bench, writing in a journal with a blue fountain pen. She turned and he was gone, and she said "*Oh*, he was only—" and Yale—because he was there now, was somehow behind her—tried to say that no, she was wrong, this boy had died all the way back in the '60s, he died in Vietnam, and there were other, older ghosts here too. But Yale could make no noise because he wasn't really there.

Fiona was on School Street now, a street Yale didn't really know, but he'd always liked its name. Streets that carried their histories with them: He was fond of those. Was there still a school on School Street? Well, sure. There it was, abandoned and mossy. It stretched for blocks and blocks and blocks, and Fiona looked down at the stroller, at baby Nico. Because yes, it was Nico, she'd given birth to her brother and he only had to start again. He was swaddled in his orange scarf. He wore a crown of paper clips. She said, "He's not old enough for school yet." She said, "You have to wait until the year 2000."

But wasn't it close? They were back on Broadway now, and the year 2000 was very close. That was why everything was ending. New Year's Eve was the deadline. The dead line. The last gay man would die that day.

What about baby Nico? "We'll smuggle him through," Fiona said to no one, "like Baby Moses. But he'll have to play baseball."

Broadway and Briar. Broadway and Gladys Avenue. Poor Gladys, lost in the wrong part of town. A statue of President Gladys.

Fiona pulled fliers off the telephone poles, loaded them into the empty stroller. It was her job to clean the streets. She stripped posters from windows, signs from stores, menus from restaurant entrances. She walked into an empty bar and sniffed the half-filled pint glasses still on the counter.

And although she was still alone, Yale could talk to her now. He said, "What are they going to do with it all?"

When she looked at him, he saw that the real answer was that she would live here forever, alone, that she would clean the streets forever. But she said, "They're turning it into the zoo," and he knew this was true as well.

She sat down in the middle of the empty road, because no cars would ever come this way. She said, "What animal gets your old apartment? You're allowed to choose."

And because he felt very, very hot now, so hot, like he'd been knitted into a thousand blankets, and because the heat was filling his lungs even as something inside him was cold, was turning, in fact, to ice, Yale chose polar bears.

2015

They were greeted at the entry to the Galerie de Photographies by a man with a tray of champagne glasses. Fiona plucked one like a flower, but Julian passed. He smiled at Fiona. "Twenty-four years and eight months sober." They were early; only two dozen people in there and half were lugging huge cameras and lighting equipment, snapping eager photos of the earliest guests.

Serge had posted himself near the entrance, and Fiona double-kissed him, but she didn't see Richard.

She held her breath and followed Julian, making sure Claire was still behind her, although Claire was going straight to the wall, straight to the giant mouth photo there'd been so much talk of. It was a man's mouth, stubble below the bottom lip. Black and white, the lips just slightly parted. It should have been trite, something from a high school photography show, but it was one of the most arresting and strangely sexual things Fiona had ever seen. A sense of movement, as if the mouth were about to open wider, about to say something. How was it that you could tell the mouth was opening and not closing?

She hadn't thought about it in years, but she remembered, suddenly and in quite a lot of detail, the opening of Nora's collection at the Brigg, the first real opening she'd ever been to. She tended to think more often of the times she took Claire to see its permanent installation in what was by then the enormous and world-class Brigg Museum. She'd tell her about Soutine and Foujita; she'd show her Ranko Novak's work and say, "She loved him her whole life. Such a long time." And she'd think maybe it was only possible to love someone that long if he was gone. Could you love a living, flawed human that many years? She'd tell her about Yale getting the art, making the show happen, keeping Ranko's work in the collection, and she'd say, "That's where you got your middle name! Yale was right downstairs when you were born, helping wish you into the world! And when you came here from heaven, you left the door open so he could go out." It hadn't seemed such a terrible thing to say, but she could see now, yes, how a child would have misunderstood, heard the guilt in Fiona's voice and taken on its mantle. What had she been thinking? Maybe she hadn't been thinking of Claire at all; maybe it was a fairy tale she'd needed to tell herself.

Fiona spotted Corinne and Fernand in the center of the room, holding court. Their picture was being taken.

Claire was still at the mouth; Fiona would give her space. She was increasingly reassured that Claire wouldn't flee the gallery.

This work was much more postmodern, much more multimedia—Fiona wished she had the vocabulary for it—than anything she'd seen from Richard before. A large photo showed a Polaroid sitting on a stack of papers. The Polaroid, in turn, was of a man in a chair, his face in his hands. It looked like the '80s or early '90s—something about his white T-shirt, his Docksiders—but Fiona didn't recognize him. Next to it hung a photo of an apartment building's facade, three of the windows painted over with red X's. According to the sign, Richard had taken the photo in 1982 but added the X's just this year. She supposed that the show's title, *Strata*, was about this layering of old and new.

She found the updated *Julian* series—the 2015 Julian smiling mischievously. But no face in a Richard Campo photo ever showed just a single emotion. He also looked embarrassed, and also triumphant.

She almost collided with Jake Austen. He said, "There's my girl!"

She patted his chest. "I am not your girl, Jake. But it's good to see you."

It was, really. She'd had the feeling for the past ten minutes that she didn't know what the hell year it was—the year of Nora's show, the year Julian vanished, the year she first took Claire to the Brigg, the year Claire was born—and here was a living, breathing reminder that it was 2015.

He said, "Check it out! From the movie." He pointed across the gallery to where that actor stood, the one someone on the street had called Dermott McDermott.

But no one was looking at him; everyone was looking at Richard, who had just entered the room. Slim gray slacks, a coral shirt open at the neck, his cheeks glowing with attention. Her famous friend. How bizarre life was.

By the time Fiona made her way around the sectional wall, Jake was off toasting with some loud young Brits, and Julian had circled back.

He said, "Is everything okay with your daughter?"

"Lord only knows."

"It'll be okay. I can tell it will. I know these things. And my God, she's just like you."

Fiona laughed. "She's nothing like me. That's the problem."

"Are you *kidding*? Don't you remember yourself? You were the most bullheaded little—you were practically feral! Remember when you told your parents you'd climb in the coffin if we couldn't all come to Nico's vigil?"

"There was no coffin. I said I'd stand up and tell everyone."

"Okay. But you see my point."

"That was the only way I could survive."

Julian smiled. "It's not a bad way to be. Hey, are you really moving here?"

"I actually think so, yes. For a while. I can't believe I'm saying that, but I am."

"Well I'm proud of you. Hey, have you seen it yet?"

"Seen what?"

"Well, two things, really. Three things! Did you see *me*? Do I look okay?"

"You looked smashing, Julian."

"Okay, two other things. This one." He took her shoulders and angled her toward a glowing light box mounted on the wall and covered, every inch of it, with black and white contact sheets. As big as a picture window. Some strips of photos hung vertically, some horizontally. Occasionally they crossed each other. The piece was titled *1983*. Magnifying glasses, strong ones, hung at each side— great, because Fiona didn't want to dig her readers out of her purse.

She started arbitrarily on the top left. A strip of some kind of party, too many men in each frame to make anyone out. A strip of a face she thought was Katsu Tatami's. Four in a row of what looked like that year's Pride parade, men waving flags. There was the really tall guy who used to sell loose cigarettes on Halsted. There was Teddy Naples. They kissed and danced and lounged on couches and wore ridiculous clothes and flipped pancakes and sunbathed on the rocks.

She was hoping to see Nico there, but she didn't.

Julian said, "Look."

There she was herself, an arm around Terrence. In a restaurant, it looked like. She never remembered being that pretty, that happy. Claire was just an egg in an ovary, one more thing Fiona hadn't ruined yet. At the left of the shot was Yale, mouth open, talking to someone out of frame. A mirror behind them all, in which you could see a room of tables, diners, and Richard himself, camera flash for a head.

She wanted to climb into the photo, to say, "*Stop where you are.*"

Wasn't that what the camera had done, at least? It had frozen them forever.

Stay there, she thought. *Stay there.*

Julian gave her a minute and then he said, "I was thinking about *Hamlet*. You know I was in it three different times, and I never got to be Hamlet? Actually it's Horatio I was thinking about. I never got to be him either."

Fiona was filled with ridiculous, irrational love for Julian just then, for whatever he was about to say, because she could feel Nico beside her, and Yale and Terrence and all of them, rolling their eyes at Julian's making this about himself, about his acting, which was such a Julian thing to do, and they all loved him anyway, and she still did too.

He said, "The whole play is about Hamlet trying to avenge his father's death, trying to tell the truth, right? And then when he dies, he hands it all to Horatio. *In this harsh world draw thy breath in pain, to tell my story.* See, I'd have made a great Hamlet! But what a burden. To be Horatio. To be the one with the memory. And what's Horatio supposed to do with it? What the hell does Horatio do in act six?"

Fiona leaned her forehead against Julian's. They stood like that for a moment, head to head, nose to nose. The warmth of his skin soaked into her body, all the way down to her feet.

She still had the magnifying glass in her hand, clenched tight. She wanted to call Claire over, show her these photos, tell her what Julian had just said, try to explain, or to try to *start* to explain, what her life had been. How this show might begin to convey it all, the palimpsest that was her heart, the way things could be written over but never erased. She was simply never going to be a blank slate.

But she could do that in a minute. Claire was still here and she wasn't going anywhere, and Julian was drawing her further into the gallery. The magnifying glass fell from her hand, swung on its little chain.

He said, "This is the third thing." The video installations. Two screens at the very back, far apart. He stood her in front of the one on the left. "The other is drag shows. This is the one to watch." It showed a crowd on a sidewalk, standing very still. He said, "The Bistro. Do you remember the Bistro, or were you too young?"

"It was the disco, right? I remember everyone talking about it like it was some lost arcadia."

"Well, yeah. It's just that it was such a happy place. Not that there weren't other places, but I don't know if we were ever that happy again. This was the day they knocked it down."

She took a step closer. There was sound to the film, although you had to be standing right in front of the speaker to hear it.

A man in the crowd saying, "It was the biggest place, it was the best place."

Another man: "It was our Studio 54. No, wait. It was our moon. It was our *moon*!"

Another: "Is someone going to tell him about the Bearded Lady? Someone explain about the Bearded Lady."

And there, dear God, were Yale Tishman and Charlie Keene. Charlie with his open bomber jacket and pins. Yale in an oxford shirt, hopelessly preppy. So incredibly, impossibly young. Had anyone ever been that young? Moving easily, their limbs loose, faces full. And there now, right behind them, was Nico. His hair tousled in the wind. Fiona held her breath.

Yale saying: "I keep waiting to find out it's a joke."

Charlie to the camera: "This is where I brought him when he was new to the city."

Yale: "I couldn't believe it existed."

Charlie: "You want to know the state of this city, you want to know whose pocket city hall is in, look at this. You think this isn't political? You think this is an accident?"

Yale: "They had these glitter cannons, and they'd—one time, the cannons shot foam stars. I don't even know how they did that."

Nico: "I'm still hung over from the closing party, and it was *four days ago*."

His *voice*.

It traveled down her neck and arms.

The building, small and undefended.

A voice off camera: "It's mob bosses tearing this place down."

Another: "Well. I don't know."

Charlie: "They're making a bloody parking lot."

Yale: "Watch."

But nothing happened. A shot of the building, just standing there. Static.

Nico: "Now. Look."

The wrecking ball swinging, colliding. Not the topple you'd expect, not a skyscraper's collapse. Just a cloud of obscuring dust and, when that cleared, a hole.

Then another.

Someone shouting "Whooh!" as if out of obligation.

A slow, awkward minute of wrecking ball, and faces reacting. Yale's face. Charlie's face.

Fiona felt Julian take her hand. She'd forgotten where she was, forgotten the gallery and the museum and all of Paris.

The film cut forward; time had passed.

The building, destroyed. The entire place downed, the dust clearing. People leaving.

The sound of wind.

Charlie's voice: "Better be a hell of a parking lot."

Yale: "Oh my God, look."

Yale on his knees, digging in the gutter.

Yale surrounded by the remaining people, showing them something in his hands.

Yale showing the camera: a handful of dust.

"There's *glitter* in it!" he said.

A man Fiona didn't know peered over Yale's shoulder. "That's not glitter. Where?"

It just looked like dust. Yale turned and smeared it down Charlie's shirt.

Yale and Charlie and Nico laughing hysterically. Charlie rubbing the dust between his fingers, sprinkling it on the sidewalk. Nico rubbing it into Charlie's jacket sleeve.

A man smearing it on his cheeks, a woman saying, "That's asbestos, I'm sure."

Charlie, laughing still, giddy: "We're gonna take it home with us!"

A shot of the gutter filled with dust. True, there were glints of light there, but they could have been tiny shards of fiberglass. Surely they were. Fiona tried hard to believe it was more than that.

Nico's voice one more time, disembodied: "I'm ready for my close-up, Mr. Campo!"

The gutter, and a long silence.

She expected the film to end right there, but instead, as the laughter died down, the camera lingered uncomfortably on a man collecting his long black hair into a ponytail. On a mother walking by through the last gawkers, pulling her young son by the hand. On Yale and Charlie walking off down the sidewalk, so clearly a couple—inches from each other, but not touching. Around them, a silence as big as the city.

Then the whole film looped again. There they all stood, the Bistro whole. Boys with hands in pockets, waiting for everything to begin.

Author's Note and Acknowledgments

While these characters and their lives are fictional, I've stuck as closely as possible to actual places and public events, taking liberties only when necessary. A few of those liberties: In order to avoid writing about real people, I reimagined Chicago's gay press scene; none of the publications mentioned here are real. While the fictional Brigg Gallery shares some characteristics with Northwestern's Block Museum, it is not the same place. The Wilde Rumpus was not an actual theater company, but gay companies such as Lionheart did operate out of other theaters. Some of the events of the 1990 AMA demonstration have been compressed. And while the restaurant Ann Sather has been a constant source of support to Chicago's gay community, and was host to many fundraising events, there was not, as far as I know, a benefit there for Howard Brown in December of 1985.

I'd feel bad if I didn't say that the new penguin enclosure at the Lincoln Park Zoo is spectacular, and the penguins look happy; there is nothing grimy or depressing about it now.

There isn't as much in book or film form about Chicago's AIDS crisis as I'd hoped when I began this project. Fortunately, I can recommend a few excellent sources if you want to learn more. MK Czerwiec has written a beautiful graphic novel, *Taking Turns*, about her time as a nurse on Illinois Masonic's AIDS Care Unit 371. She's been a friend to this book as well, and was an invaluable early reader. The documentary film *Short Fuse*, about the life of Chicago ACT UP founder Daniel Sotomayor, is hard to find but absolutely worth watching. Two writers, Tracy Baim and Owen Keehnen, have done much of the heavy lifting in recording Chicago's gay history. I found their journalism and books incredibly helpful, and am additionally grateful to both of them for giving me their time. Owen was also a brilliant early reader for the novel; if you're in the city, stop in and see him at Unabridged Bookstore.

The online archives and oral histories available through the *Windy City Times*—archives Tracy Baim is largely responsible for—are a treasure. The *Windy City Times* itself began publishing in 1985, and I'm grateful to the Harold Washington Library for keeping those earliest issues available. (Speaking of Harold Washington, a tangential acknowledgment: The words he speaks in this book at the 1986 Pride parade are his own.) The Gerber/Hart Library is a wonderful resource on LGBTQ issues and history and provided me with essential assistance and materials. There is footage currently available on YouTube of the April 1990 march on the AMA, and I recommend it highly. The best written account I've found of the protest is "The Angriest Queer," from the August 16, 1990, issue of the *Chicago Reader*. Photographer Doug Ischar's series *Marginal Waters* beautifully documents gay life on the Belmont Rocks in the '80s; while I imagine Richard Campo's fictional work to be quite different from Ischar's, I'm thankful to him and to the other photographers, both artistic and journalistic, who brought the era to life for me.

This project was undertaken with a great deal of ongoing thought and conversation and concern about the line between allyship and appropriation—a line that might feel different to different readers. It is my great hope that this book will lead the curious to read direct, personal accounts of the AIDS crisis—and that any places where I've gotten the details wrong might inspire people to tell their own stories.

Some book world thanks: Kathryn Court and Victoria Savanh; Nicole Aragi, Duvall Osteen, and Grace Dietshe; Eric Wechter; Francesca Drago. Three intrepid summer interns came to me courtesy of DePaul University: Felipe Cabrera, Megan Sanks, and Natasha Khatami. Gina Frangello, Thea Goodman, Dika Lam, Emily Grey Tedrowe, Zoe Zolbrod, and Jon Freeman were essential early readers. Portions of this novel were researched and written at Yaddo, Ucross, and Ragdale residencies. This book, like so many others, wouldn't have been possible without support from the National Endowment for the Arts.

Huge thanks to Maureen O'Brien, Patty Gerstenblith, Adair McGregor, and Cassie Ritter Hunt on the subjects of art, inheritance, and university galleries; and to Paul Weil, Steve Kleinedler, Todd Summar, J. Andrew Goodman, Michael Anson, Amanda Roach, Amy Norton, Charles Finch, and Edward Hamlin, for conversations and introductions too varied to enumerate.

Lydia and Heidi, thank you for being so good at entertaining yourselves while I was writing and editing.

Most important, my endless thanks for the time, patience, and encouragement of those who lived through all this and sat down to coffee or let me into their homes or emailed with me endlessly, in many cases about personal and traumatic things. In addition to the writers mentioned above, thanks to Peggy Shinner; to TB; to Justin Hayford of the Legal Council for Health Justice (a tireless resource and amazing early reader); to Dr. David Moore, Dr. David Blatt, and Russell Leander, who made Unit 371 a beautiful place; to Bill McMillan, who was out there on that ledge with the banner; to the inimitable and indomitable Lori Cannon; and to the memories of the amazing men you all told me about. I did my best.

FLEET

To buy any of our books and to find out
more about Fleet, our authors and titles, as well
as events and book clubs, visit our website

www.littlebrown.co.uk

and follow us on Twitter

@FleetReads
@LittleBrownUK